THE OTHER DAUGHTER

The Homecoming Series

The Other Daughter—Book one
Finding Jeena—Book two

THE OTHER DAUGHTER

The Homecoming Series

By
Miralee Ferrell

MBI

The Other Daughter
Published by Mountain Brook Ink
White Salmon, WA U.S.A.

The website addresses shown in this book are not intended in any way to be or imply an endorsement on the part of Mountain Brook Ink, nor do we vouch for their content.

This story is a work of fiction. All characters and events are the product of the author's imagination other than those stated in the author notes as based on historical characters. Any other resemblance to any person, living or dead, is coincidental.

Scripture quotations are taken from the King James Version of the Bible. Public domain.

© 2018 Miralee Ferrell
ISBN 9781-943959-64-8

Copyright filed with Library of Congress, The Other Daugher/Miralee Ferrell, domestic fiction

The Team: Miralee Ferrell, Nikki Wright, Cindy Jackson
Cover Design: Photo by Miralee Ferrell

Mountain Brook Ink is an inspirational publisher offering fiction you can believe in.
Printed in the United States of America.

Dedication

To my husband, Allen. Your unending support of my writing and your belief in my ability to complete this book were a constant source of encouragement. Thank you for being my biggest cheerleader on this journey.

And to Pastor George Watkins, whose obedience in speaking God's prophetic word into my life one Sunday night set my feet on this extraordinary writing journey. Had it not been for you, this book may never have been birthed.

Acknowledgments

My greatest thanks and praise go to God, for without His wisdom, guidance, and inspiration, this book wouldn't exist. He truly is my best friend and the one who carries me through all of life's troubles. My highest desire is that this story will touch at least one person's heart in a way that makes a difference for eternity.

I wish I could mention all the people who have helped me along this road to publication; I hope you know how much I appreciate and love you. My heartfelt thanks go to . . .

Elizabeth, my friend and fellow author who mentored me—your encouragement to write fiction and our first brainstorming session got me started on this book.

My husband, Allen; sister, Jenny; brother, Tim; and mother, Sylvia, along with my two children, Marnee and Steven, were so supportive and helpful. So many close friends have come forward to help make this book a success: Michaela, Shannon, Kris, Pastor Ken, Kit, Diana, and more. Each of you played a part in my growth through this book . . . either as cheerleaders, advance readers, prayer warriors, or in some cases, all three. I love you all!

Many thanks to Trish, whose story inspired this one. We're glad God brought you into our lives.

My critique group entered the picture when the book was already under contract but helped tremendously on a rush edit. Their input and suggestions were invaluable. Thank you, Kimberly, Sherri, and Teresa for your support.

A special thanks goes to my high-school English teacher, Larry Frownfelter. His encouragement and belief in me pushed me to excel, and his recommendation for honors English in college took me another step scholastically.

To the folks at Kregel who made my first book such an enjoyable experience . . . you're the best! It's been a joy to get to know Dennis, Steve, Amy, and Leslie. I wish I could have become acquainted with the entire staff, as I appreciate all the behind-the-scenes work that made this book a reality. And to my editors, Becky and Esther, thank you from the bottom of my heart for the things you caught and the changes you suggested. The book is better because of you both.

And so very important, I thank Tamela, my agent whom the Lord sent to me. You have been such a blessing to me.

Thank you all.

Chapter One

A MOTOR ROARED, AND THE SHARP ping of flying gravel sprayed the side of the house. Susanne Carson ran from the laundry room and peered out the front window in time to see a battered old pickup tear down the lane away from her home, sounding like a steam boiler ready to explode. *What in the world? Teenagers out playing a prank?*

They must have turned down the wrong lane, an easy thing to do this far out of town. She headed across the living room and stopped in the kitchen doorway, stifling a groan. The kids had tracked in mud before they'd left for school, and dirty breakfast dishes still littered the kitchen counters. She'd been busy changing beds, vacuuming bedrooms, and catching up on laundry all morning and had forgotten about the kitchen. She leaned against the wall, feeling about as energetic as the loser of a ten-mile race. Her enthusiasm was drained by the recent phone call from her husband, setting back their plans for her birthday.

The doorbell rang. The truck had disappeared down the road, and she hadn't heard anyone else arrive. *Great.* The last thing she needed was company. The house certainly wasn't in its usual neat state. She sighed and smoothed back her rumpled curls.

The insistent doorbell pealed again, pulling her forward.

"I'm coming, I'm coming!" she muttered.

An hour to put up her feet and relax would help put her back in the mood for tonight, if David kept his word and made it in time for their reservation. She'd get rid of whoever was at the door and try to pull herself together. This needed to be a special evening. They'd had so few of those lately.

Susanne swung open the door. "May I help you?"

A bedraggled young girl who appeared to be about twelve stood on the step, clutching a well-worn suitcase. Small boned and not very tall, she might have been pretty but for her greasy dark hair and dirt-streaked face. Staring up at Susanne was a set of strangely familiar eyes that gazed at her shyly before darting away in apparent fear.

A prickle of apprehension ran through her as she looked into those eyes, but she brushed it away. Her imagination must be working overtime.

"Is Mr. David Carson here, ma'am?" The waif shifted her weight from one foot to the other, glancing over her hunched shoulder to the base of the driveway.

What was someone thinking, dumping off a child? If she was selling something or needed directions, the driver could have stayed nearby, not headed down the road.

"I'm afraid he's at work right now. Can I help you?" Susanne pushed open the screen door, both curiosity and sympathy drawing her forward. "Are you selling something?"

The youngster's gaze returned to Susanne's face, a worried pucker showing around the corners of her mouth. "No, ma'am. I've come to live with him." Her barely audible voice hit Susanne like a rumble of thunder. Confusion raced through her mind. Was this someone's idea of a joke?

"I'm sorry . . . live with him?" She pushed the door open a bit wider. Had David offered to take this poor girl in without discussing it with her? They hadn't accepted foster kids for more than a year. Of all the times for him to drop a strange child in her lap.

The girl took a deep breath, pulling her suitcase a little closer to her trembling legs. "My mama's dead. He's my daddy."

David wanted to stay on the job longer. He hated leaving with problems unresolved, but he'd already pushed the time limit–it was more important to get home. He took one last look around the job site, breathing in the crisp air of the late spring evening with satisfaction.

He enjoyed being his own boss. After ten years of owning his construction company in the Pacific Northwest, he still loved the work. Nothing could compare to working with his hands and seeing old homes brought back to life or new ones built from a dream. Lately, work brought more satisfaction than his marriage. It wasn't anything definite, but there'd been little laughter or joy between him and Susanne the past few weeks.

David looked up at one of his employees straddling a rough-sawn beam in the framework above. "Steve, time to knock off. We're into overtime as it is, and I think we're close to having this problem worked out. I'm running late for my wife's birthday, and I'm heading home."

"Right, no problem. Have a nice evening with your wife, and don't do anything I wouldn't do!" Steve chuckled and lifted two fingers in a casual salute before starting to gather up his tools.

Only part of David's crew was present at this site. His partner, Mike, was at another job where construction would start soon on a new house.

They'd recently relocated the business to a small tract of land, as neither wanted to continue working out of one of their homes. A roomy workshop positioned in the center of the property clinched the deal. David loved the thirty-minute drive through the peaceful countryside. It gave him time to pray and think through his day. He'd better hustle, though. A problem on the job had occurred on Susanne's last birthday and had messed up their evening. Disappointing her again wasn't an option.

He strode across the graveled parking area and reached for

the handle of his truck door. The shrill ring of his cell phone jarred his concentration. He climbed into the truck, then swiped his iPhone.

"Hello, David Carson speaking."

"Hello, David."

"Grandfather? How are you?" David's great-grandfather had been full Nez Perce and had urged his son to remain active in issues that affected the tribe. David had a deep gratitude toward the ancestors who'd chosen to walk the narrow path of heartache to bring truth to future generations, and his respect was reflected in the usage of *Grandfather*.

"Not too bad . . . getting along all right, I guess. I found a box with your name on it among your grandmother's things. She saved items from your childhood, you know."

"I didn't know." It sounded like his grandmother though. She'd been gone for four months, and he still had trouble realizing it.

"I thought I'd bring you the box, and maybe we could go fishing like when you were little."

"Sure. Sounds great." David glanced at his watch and struggled to fasten his seat belt.

"I know you and Susanne are busy. I don't want to be a bother, but it'd sure make an old man happy to spend time with your family."

"We love having you. When were you thinking?"

"I've been at my sister's place the past few days, but she's leaving tomorrow. I don't feel like I'm ready to go back to my empty house yet." Grandfather's voice wavered for a moment. "You probably should check with Susanne first."

"She'll be happy to have you, and the kids will be thrilled. The little apartment over the garage isn't rented, so you can have your own space. Just come ahead."

"If you're sure, I'll see you tomorrow afternoon."

David ended the call and started the truck. Should he have checked with Susanne? He couldn't say no, especially after hearing the longing clouding his grandfather's voice. Susanne had always enjoyed spending time with the older man. Surely she wouldn't mind. Besides, Grandfather had almost become a recluse since Grandmother had died, and David doubted he'd be underfoot much.

On his way through town, he pulled off at a small florist shop. Good thing he'd thought to make the phone call to Susanne earlier, but Grandfather's phone call had delayed him even longer than he'd planned. Roses might help soften his late arrival. Susanne could be a bit of a perfectionist when it came to arriving on time, and besides, he wanted this birthday to be memorable.

A thousand questions slammed through Susanne's mind. David's daughter? Not possible. They'd been high school sweethearts and never dated anyone else. She shook her head. Time to deal with that later. Right now, this young girl needed her attention.

"What's your name, hon?" She stepped out on the porch and extended her hand, but the girl shied away. Better not push.

"Brianna." The soft answer barely reached Susanne's ears.

"Would you like to come in?"

The slender shoulders hunched in a small shrug. "If Mr. Carson isn't home, maybe I should wait outside."

Susanne detected a southern accent in Brianna's speech, unlike anything usually heard in their rural area of Washington. "Do you live nearby?"

Her head shook in a negative, casting the dark hair over the brown eyes. Those eyes . . .

Susanne set the thought aside. No way could this girl be

David's child. The dark hair and familiar eyes didn't mean anything.

"Come in and have something to drink. Really. It's okay. He should be home soon." The girl looked like she could use a hug, but Susanne pushed down the desire to reach for her again and instead held open the screen door. Brianna ventured one last look down the driveway to the country road below, then turned and darted through the door like a creature pursued.

Susanne seated the girl at the table and opened the refrigerator to find something cold to offer. How old could she be? Not much older than twelve, with her undeveloped body and small bone structure. Another reason she couldn't be David's. That would place her birthday only a few months before their daughter, Meagan, was conceived.

Meagan. Yikes! She'd better find out what was going on before Meagan and Steven came home from school. The kids were going to their grandmother's for the evening so Susanne and David could go out to celebrate her birthday.

"Do you like soda?" Susanne set two glasses of ice on the table along with three different flavors of pop.

"Sure." Brianna started to reach for one, then withdrew her hand and glanced up at Susanne. A brief flash of something close to fear crossed her face.

"It's okay. Take whichever one you want." Susanne settled in the chair across the table and waited to serve herself a drink until the girl had opened the can and filled her glass.

How much to ask and where to begin? The girl was frightened, and Susanne hated to push, but she needed to understand what was happening.

"Brianna?" She waited for the girl's brown-eyed gaze to meet hers. "You said your mother is dead?"

Brianna's eyes glinted with tears, and her head dropped, then nodded.

"Who brought you here?"

"My uncle."

Susanne leaned forward, her drink forgotten. "Why didn't he come to the door?"

Another silent shrug.

This wasn't going well. "What happened to your mother? I mean, how did she die and how long ago?"

"She had cancer. She died almost two months ago." Her low voice trembled a little, and her hand gripped the glass.

"You've been living with your uncle since then?"

"Yes."

"Why did your uncle bring you here?"

"My mama told him to. Besides, he doesn't like me and got sick of taking care of me."

"What was your mother's name?"

"Victoria Stiles."

Stiles. She didn't know anyone by that name, and Brianna didn't appear too eager to shed more light on the mystery.

"Mom, we're home. Happy birthday!" Meagan's voice broke the silence, followed by the slam of the front door and the slap of hurrying feet against the wood floor.

"Yeah, happy birthday, Mom. I'm starved." Steven's high-pitched voice reached Susanne's ears right before the eight-year-old burst through the kitchen doorway. Steven skidded to a stop and stared at Brianna. "Who're you?"

"Brianna." A hint of a frown creased the girl's face.

"Hi. I'm Steven." He grinned, then turned to Susanne. "Cool. Can I have a pop, too? Do we have any cookies or chips?"

"Yes. You can put cookies on a plate for everyone to share, but run and wash your hands first."

Steven grumbled an indiscernible reply but dashed off to the bathroom.

"Mom?" Meagan stood at Susanne's side, a small frown pulling down the corners of her mouth.

"Meagan, this is Brianna. Her uncle dropped her off a little while ago to visit. She thinks she might be related to us, but we're going to talk about it later. You kids need to get cleaned up, have your snacks, and get ready to go to Grandma's for the evening."

"How about Brianna? What's she going to do?" Meagan could be counted on to be the practical one of the family. "Is she spending the night?"

Susanne stifled a small groan. Her thoughts hadn't extended past the present. What to do with Brianna, indeed?

"I'll see if Grandma would mind having her stay. Your dad and I need time to talk. Get washed up, have a snack and change your clothes, and we'll head over."

The next few minutes were filled with Steven's chatter, an occasional comment from the quieter Meagan, and a rare yes or no from Brianna. Susanne took a minute to slip away and call her mother.

"Mom? I need to ask a favor."

"You're still bringing the kids over?"

"Yes, they're getting ready. But we had an unexpected guest drop in. A girl named Brianna. I'm not sure what's going on, Mom, but she says she's David's daughter and her mother died a couple of months ago."

"David's daughter!" The shocked tone of her mother's voice echoed Susanne's own feelings.

"I know. But there's no way. I forgot to ask how old she is, but she doesn't look much more than twelve, and we would've been married for several months by the time she was born."

"Doesn't sound like something David would do."

"My thoughts exactly. She does have a resemblance to him,

but that doesn't necessarily mean anything. Would you mind letting her stay for the night? I want time to discuss this with David without any of the kids around. I'm sure it's a mistake, but we need to figure this out."

"Certainly. What's her name?"

"Brianna. She said her mother's name was Vicki Stiles, but I don't know any families around here by that name."

"Me, neither. I'm sure you're right. It's a mistake, and you'll get it sorted out. How'd she get here?"

"I heard a truck peel out of the driveway, like someone was in a hurry. Apparently, her uncle dumped her off at her mother's request and didn't have the decency to come to the door. Brianna said he doesn't want her. She seems to be afraid of something. I'm guessing it could be tied to her uncle."

"Pretty raw, if you ask me. Dropping her off at a stranger's door and leaving like that."

"Yeah, I agree. I'll be over in a few minutes. Thanks for understanding."

"No problem. I'll play games with the kids, and we'll make popcorn and watch a movie. Brianna will be fine."

Susanne hung up the phone and stood for a moment. What was the truth here? Who was Brianna, and why would her uncle leave her without an explanation? She stepped to the open doorway leading into the kitchen and watched her two children interact with Brianna. A small smile flashed across the girl's face. A shock nipped at Susanne. The transformation in Brianna was startling. Suddenly, it wasn't only her eyes and dark hair that resembled David—it was the smile and little gestures she made while talking. For the first time, doubt tugged at Susanne's heart. She'd always trusted her husband. Was it possible she'd been wrong all these years?

Chapter Two

DAVID HEADED UP THE CURVING ROAD toward their home. "Lord, please don't let my being late again or Grandfather's arrival cause stress. I want Susanne's birthday to be special." Somehow it felt as though he and Susanne had been growing increasingly distant.

He pulled his truck into their tree-lined driveway and stepped out, letting his eyes linger on the rustic, two-story home they'd built six years ago. It sat tucked back from the road among towering fir trees, only a hundred yards from the pond where his family loved to picnic and swim. He was proud of this place, proud of all they'd accomplished and worked so hard for over the last few years of their marriage.

They'd built a lot of great memories here with their two kids. So much of their life was good. He loved his wife and children deeply and God had blessed his home and his business. If only his wife shared the most important thing in his life—his love for his Savior.

He strode toward the massive wood door that set off the front of the house, determined to show Susanne how much he appreciated her tonight. She was a beautiful woman in many ways, and he wanted to focus on the positive.

He pushed open the front door, slipping off his boots on the porch before he entered. "Susanne! Happy birthday, honey. I brought you something."

"David, is that you?" Susanne's voice called from the family room. Her voice sounded . . . different. "I have something for you too, and it's not a birthday present."

Susanne sat in the family room, trying to quiet her racing heart. This misunderstanding would be cleared up when she and David talked, so why the feelings of stress? Sure, they differed in several areas of their lives. David had chosen to make God the center of his life not long before they married, while she'd chosen to walk her own way. But her desire to keep her distance from Christianity had nothing to do with the issue at hand. In spite of some of David's rather intense feelings about church and God, he'd been a faithful husband and excellent father.

She needed to give him the benefit of the doubt, but tendrils of fear were weaving their way through her mind and no amount of logic had silenced them. The three hours since taking the kids to her mom's had felt like a lifetime. David's late arrival had done little to soften her mood, and she'd squelched all thoughts of going out for her birthday. Celebrating was the furthest thing from her mind.

"Sorry I'm late." David stepped into the room and stopped in front of the couch, holding out a bouquet of roses. "I'll jump in the shower and get ready to go."

Susanne reached for the roses. "Thanks, David. Before you take that shower, we need to talk."

David's eyebrows rose. "Can't it wait? We'll be late for our reservation. I thought you'd be ready."

"I'm not sure we'll be going to dinner. It's not something I want to talk about in public." She pushed herself to her feet. "I'm going to put these in a vase, and I'll be right back. You might as well get comfortable. This could take a while." She glanced over her shoulder on the way to the kitchen.

"Not go to dinner?" His voice followed her to the next room. "What happened since I called you a few hours ago? It's your birthday, and you've been looking forward to going out. The kids are at your mom's, right? What changed?"

She brought the vase into the room and placed it on the mantle before sinking back into her place on the couch. "Something happened. We had a visitor today."

"Okay. That's not terribly unusual." He settled into his leather chair, his brows drawn down in a frown.

"A girl showed up at our door. She asked for you by name. It seems she knows quite a bit about you, or at least she thinks she does."

"What girl? Someone we know?"

"That's what I'd like to know. Is she someone you possibly haven't mentioned to me?"

"I have no idea what you're talking about. Clue me in. What's her name, and why did she ask for me?"

"She's a young teen with striking eyes. When I told her you weren't home and asked if I could help, she told me"—Susanne took a deep breath and willed herself to stay calm—"that her mother recently died and you're her father."

"What!" The word exploded from David's lips, and he bolted forward in the chair. "Her father? No way!"

"Is there anything you need to tell me, David? Something you've been keeping from me?"

David's face paled, and he shook his head. "Absolutely not! Who is this girl, and what's she trying to pull?"

"That's what I thought, or that she'd been dropped at the wrong house. But she didn't look the type to play a practical joke. After I really looked at her, I felt sorry for her. She's kind of thin, poorly dressed, and a bit unkempt. I invited her in to talk."

"What's her name? How old is she? How did she get here?" The questions flew at a rapid pace, and Susanne held up her hand.

"Slow down. One thing at a time. Trust me—it hit me pretty

hard too. The spooky thing is she looks a lot like you. I really noticed when I saw her smile when the kids were talking to her. Her eyes are the same shape and color, her hair is similar to yours, but her smile—I can't explain it." She desperately wanted an answer to why that smile looked so much like David's, but she longed to believe her imagination had kicked into high gear after the girl's revelation.

"Lots of people have dark eyes and hair. It doesn't mean anything. I've seen kids before that look like they could be related to one of our kids, but it doesn't mean I'm their father." His frown deepened, and he sat back in the chair. "What did she say?"

"Her name is Brianna. I assumed she was about twelve, based on her size, but I heard her tell the kids that she's thirteen, almost fourteen. It's hard to believe, but some girls do mature a lot slower than others."

"Yeah. So how'd she get here? We live too many miles out of town for her to have walked, and at her age, she can't drive."

Susanne ran her fingers through her curls and pushed the loose strands out of her eyes. "Her uncle dropped her off."

"Okay. And what did he say?"

"Nothing. I heard his truck head down the driveway before I even realized she'd arrived. The next thing I knew, she was ringing the doorbell, and he'd disappeared. Brianna said that when her mother died of cancer, her uncle took care of her but refused to keep Brianna much longer. Apparently the mother had asked her brother to bring Brianna to you."

"Asked him to bring her to me? Why?"

"Her mother's name was Victoria Stiles. Does that mean anything to you?" Susanne said the words slowly, deliberately, and watched David's face for a hint of recognition. Only confusion showed.

"No. I've never heard of her. Why would she tell her to come here? I don't get it!" He pushed to his feet and walked to the couch, sinking down next to Susanne. "You believe me, don't you?"

"She would have been born about the time we got married. We dated from the time we were sixteen and seventeen, David. You told me I was the only one you'd ever loved or been with. So yes, if you're still telling me that, I believe you."

"You are the only woman I've ever loved, Susanne. I've never broken my marriage vows and never will." He reached for her hand, and she hesitated only a moment before taking his and giving it a small squeeze.

"Okay. But I think you'd better go to Mom's talk to her. I'm not sure what's going on, but I feel sorry for the girl. She seems so lost. And she acts like she's afraid of something or someone. When she came, she asked for you. You might be able to get more information from her than she was willing to give me."

David stood and reached for the keys he'd tossed on the lamp table. "You're right. I doubt either of us will sleep tonight till we know what's going on."

"Wait an hour or so. I'll call Mom and ask her to put our two to bed a little earlier than Brianna. They don't need to be up when you talk. I don't have much of an appetite, but I'll fix you something to eat. Then you can head over."

David shook his head. "Don't worry about it. I'll fix myself a sandwich. I'm not very hungry either."

The next hour passed quietly, with only an occasional question from David. He seemed as confused and upset as she. Surely it was all a mistake. Brianna's uncle had written down the wrong name or address. David would come home with a logical explanation and life would return to normal. Sure, disappointment over the ruined evening lingered in her mind, but maybe they could go out tomorrow, instead. Mom loved having the kids, and probably wouldn't mind one more night, considering the circumstances.

Chapter Three

DAVID JUMPED IN THE TRUCK, HIS heart hammering in his chest as he headed to his mother-in-law's home, a mile down the road. He needed to resolve this situation, and the sooner the better. Susanne said she trusted him, but he saw the shadow of doubt in her eyes. Had someone sent this girl to their home in an effort to scam them? This had to be a hoax, but what could anyone hope to gain?

Susanne said the girl resembled him, but that couldn't be, could it? He shook his head, hoping to push down the memory. No way. It didn't make sense, but after he talked with Brianna, maybe it would fall into place.

His hands gripped the leather cover on the steering wheel as he pulled into Claire's circular driveway and braked to a stop in front of the modest, one-story ranch. Claire's husband had died from heart trouble before David and Susanne began dating. David had never gotten to meet him, but he enjoyed a wonderful relationship with his mother-in-law. Claire had said more than once that she loved David as though he were her own son, and her grandkids were without equal in her eyes.

He raised his hand to tap on the glass of the front door, but Claire opened it with her finger to her lips.

"Are the kids in bed?" He stepped into the foyer and shut the door. He noted her bathrobe and wondered if he'd gotten her up. It always amazed him how much his wife looked like this woman. If Claire hadn't had a touch of gray in her hair and a few fine lines around her eyes and mouth, a person would almost think the women were sisters.

"Your two are asleep, but Brianna is resting in the living room. I think she expected you to come see her tonight. When

Susanne called to say you were coming over, I let Brianna stay up."

"Dinner is off. Did Susanne tell you what's going on?"

"She said Brianna appeared at your door earlier today, claiming to be your daughter. She asked if I'd mind Brianna staying here with Steven and Meagan."

"What do you think?" David asked, half afraid of the answer.

"I'm not sure. I didn't question the girl, so I only know what Susanne told me. I'm not judging, mind you, but there's a resemblance."

Claire led the way through the foyer, where all the pictures of her kids and grandkids hung, and into the softly lit living room. A small fire crackled in the fireplace and cast a soft light onto the wood floor edging the hearth. A log burned through and broke, sending sparks shooting upward. Its mellow light and the soft sounds were comforting in the otherwise quiet room.

David spotted a young girl curled up in the corner of the couch. An oversized brown throw tucked under her chin swallowed her small form. Her heart-shaped face nestled in her hand, partly obscured, and she appeared to be sleeping. He stopped, not wanting to wake her. He'd like a chance to see this girl before having to speak.

When he gazed down at the still form, he took an involuntary step back. A memory from the past slithered to the surface, and he shook his head, unable to believe it could be true. He hadn't bought it then, and he wouldn't now.

Claire came to stand at the end of the room beside David. He spoke softly, hoping the tension in his voice wouldn't waken Brianna.

"I'm not sure what to say to her. I hate to wake her."

"Talk to her and see what she's able to tell you. Maybe there's an explanation. It's worrying Susanne, and it's not doing this girl any good, either. She needs to get to bed, but you should give her a chance to talk. Let her ask questions, or neither one of you will be able to sleep."

Her compassionate voice penetrated the haze clouding David's mind, giving him a sense of purpose.

"You're right. I haven't thought about what this might be doing to her." He shook his head, hoping to clear it of the lingering cobwebs.

He walked across the room, easing himself onto a chair near where Brianna lay. He waited, letting Claire take a moment to gently wake the girl from her light sleep.

Brianna opened her eyes, her body stiffening as she became aware of her surroundings. She clenched the blanket that covered her, staring at David.

He waited a few seconds longer, giving her a chance to adjust. "Brianna, that's your name, right?"

"Yes," came a quiet voice.

"I'm David Carson." He leaned forward in his chair. "Can you tell me how you got here?"

"My uncle dropped me off."

"Why did your uncle bring you here?" David gripped the arms of his chair and worked to keep his face smooth. He didn't want to frighten this girl, but he needed to solve this mystery.

"Because my mama told him where you lived before she died and that you're my daddy."

"But why did she tell him that?"

The girl frowned. Did she imagine the answer was so obvious he was ignorant even to ask?

"When did your mother die, Brianna, and how old are you? When is your birthday?"

"She died a couple of months ago, and I'll be fourteen next month."

"Did your uncle give you any paperwork—a letter, your birth

certificate, anything to bring with you?" He looked from Brianna to Claire.

Brianna shrugged and then covered her mouth as a huge yawn escaped. "I don't know for sure. My mama put some papers in an envelope. I think they're in my suitcase, but I haven't looked at them."

"Is it all right if I look? We can talk more tomorrow. Claire can take you to your bedroom and show you where the bathroom is so you can get washed up. I'll give the envelope back to you tomorrow, if that's okay."

"I guess. I think Mama kept it in case I ever met you." Her voice trembled and almost broke. She released a small sigh then her mouth set in a frown. "She said you didn't want me, and I might need to prove I was your daughter." She pushed her hair out of her face and rubbed her eyes. "I'm kind of tired. I'd like to go to bed now."

Claire's warmth spilled over as she smiled. "Come on, honey. I'll take you to your room. You can sleep in as long as you want, and we'll have a nice breakfast in the morning." She stepped toward the girl with her hand outstretched.

Brianna slipped off the couch, her arms wrapped closely around her waist, shrinking from the outstretched hand. Claire picked up the old suitcase on the hearth, opened it and took out the envelope, then shut it and handed it back to Brianna. The girl clutched it as though it were her only possession in the world.

David watched the slender woman and the petite shadow so like him walk from the room and thanked the Lord for Claire. She didn't consider herself a Christian, but the compassion she bestowed could've taught a few Christians he knew a thing or two, including himself. The thought of Brianna's feelings had barely registered tonight. Even now, all he wanted to do was to rip into the envelope, hoping it held the key to turn his world right side up.

He took a deep breath, released it slowly, and prayed. *Lord, You know I can't do this alone. Please step into this mess and take control. Comfort my wife, and don't let this drive her further away from You.*

The kitchen table stood a few steps away, and David sank onto a chair, dropping the packet on the table and staring at it. If Brianna were almost fourteen like she claimed, he would have been out of high school for about a year when she was conceived. He thought back, his mind combing over the years. High school was almost a blur, although the number of parties he'd attended hadn't helped his grades. David had had a social reputation to maintain, though, and he hadn't planned to attend college. His parents tried to keep track of him, but by the time he was seventeen, he pretty much ran his own life. The friends he chose weren't always the best, but nobody was perfect.

Susanne and he had started dating when he was seventeen, and he'd never had eyes for anyone since . . . except that once when he was nineteen. But that was a one-time thing, and he never saw her again. No. It couldn't be that.

He stared at the packet and drummed his fingers on the table. "Quit stalling, Carson." He slit the top of the manila envelope and removed a paper, not realizing he was holding his breath until he suddenly let it out. What he saw on the document made him suck it back in. He stared at a birth certificate for Brianna Carsen Warren.

His unbelieving eyes searched until he found the mother's name: Victoria Warren. *Oh Lord, help me! Vicki Warren? Please, God, don't let that episode come back to haunt me. Susanne will never forgive me.*

His nerveless hands dropped the document on the kitchen table. He stared at the paper, willing the words to change.

"What am I going to do?" His voice shook, and a soft groan

escaped his lips.

Claire walked into the room in time to hear his words. "What is it, David? What did you find?"

"Her mother is Vicki Warren."

"Does that mean something to you? Did you know her?"

"No. Well, I mean, sort of, I guess." David stammered. "I'm not sure how to explain." He shoved the chair back from the table, reaching once again to grip the offending document.

"There was a girl named Vicki who moved here with her dad and older brother, and she used to hang out with some of the guys. I wasn't especially attracted to her, but she came on to me one night. I'd had a few beers, and I didn't think too much of it."

Claire sat beside David, leaning forward in her chair. She nodded silently.

"She asked for a ride home, and I said okay. She didn't make an effort to hide her feelings. When we stopped in front of her house we... well, you get the picture." His hands clenched into fists, and his voice dropped. Afterward, guilt had set in, and he'd tried to shut it out of his mind, hoping he wouldn't see Vicki again.

"I never saw her again. She quit hanging around, and a few months later, I heard she had moved south to live with her mom."

"Weren't you engaged to Susanne at the time?" Claire leaned back in the chair, her mouth pulled down in a frown.

"Yes. It was in the fall after she left for college. I don't know how I'll tell her if Brianna really is my daughter."

"Have you looked at the rest of the papers? Maybe there's something that'll help you figure it out." Claire rose and stepped away as he reached for the envelope.

"Yeah. Thanks, Claire."

"This isn't going to be easy for Susanne. The two of you had just gotten engaged that summer, and I know she's always trusted you. You need to give her some answers."

"I know. I should have told her."

"I think so too, and I hope it's not too late. I'll bring the kids over about mid-morning so the two of you have time to talk. I'm going to bed so you can have some privacy. Take your time here and lock the door behind you. Good night."

She looked at him with a shadow in her eyes, and David could see from the tense set of her shoulders that she hurt for Susanne. He hated that he'd made her think less of him. She turned to go, leaving David to unravel the rest of the story.

Torn between dread and hope, he dumped the envelope's meager contents onto the table. His distracted mind registered the sounds of the bathroom door shutting down the hall. The night sounds outside the kitchen window faded into silence as he blocked out everything except the letter he held. He could hear Vicki's voice now, dropping her g's at the end of her words with her soft, southern accent.

A few minutes later, David hung his head, his mind reeling. His daughter. Now that he'd read the letter and seen Brianna, he knew it must be true. His mother had told him a girl came to the door, claiming to be pregnant. But he hadn't believed the baby could be his. A lot of the guys had bragged about being with Vicki, and he'd chosen to believe them. Looking back, he realized most of the bragging had started after his episode with her. At nineteen years old, he'd shrugged it off and laid it at someone else's doorstep, never giving it another thought.

This wasn't something he wanted to deal with right now. The timing couldn't have been worse. Some rough times had rocked their marriage in the early years, their finances nearly wrecked by the obstacles his struggling new business had encountered.

His growing faith had opened a widening chasm between him and Susanne in the years following their marriage. However, this past year Susanne had seemed more open. A glimmer of hope had begun to emerge, but that could easily be destroyed by this new revelation.

"Oh God, help me, please." He held his head in his hands and rocked back and forth. What had he done? Why hadn't he told Susanne the truth about Vicki? Why hadn't he followed through in case the child might be his? At the time, he'd thought he'd made the right decision. He hadn't wanted to lose Susanne. He'd convinced himself that if he loved her it had to remain a secret. The pain of being honest wouldn't be fair to Susanne. Now he could see what hiding the truth had caused—pain and probably distrust.

How about Brianna? She'd been told her father didn't want her. How much resentment simmered behind those sad eyes? Sure, he didn't have DNA proof she was his, but it was all too possible. The biggest question of all—if there was no other family who wanted her, what would they do with Brianna? Would Susanne be willing to keep her, or would the girl's presence be a constant reminder that would doom what was left of their marriage?

Chapter Four

SUSANNE SAT AT THE KITCHEN TABLE in her bathrobe and nursed a cup of decaf tea. Coffee would only keep her awake tonight, although she had her doubts she'd get much sleep, regardless. She wished she'd gone to Mom's with David. Why had she sent him alone? Wouldn't it have been better to be there and see the interaction between him and Brianna? Besides, it wasn't fair to put this off on her mom. If only David would come home and tell her Brianna wasn't his.

The truck lights flashed past the window, then dimmed. The truck door slammed, and Susanne heard the crunch of gravel as David crossed to the house. Finally.

She set her teacup on the table and started to rise as he entered. "What did you find out? Did you talk to Brianna?"

David pulled out a chair and tossed his baseball cap on the chair beside him. "Yeah. I talked to her for a few minutes."

"Did you get it straightened out?" She sank down and reached for her cup, running her finger around the rim.

"I'm not sure." David glanced around the room but didn't meet her eyes.

Pain shot through her chest, and she felt herself grow cold. "What do you mean, you're not sure? Of what?"

"Much of anything, right now." His eyes raised to hers, and she saw the pain and fear written there.

Her hand that held the cup stilled. "What is it? What aren't you telling me?"

"I'm so sorry, Susanne." His face contorted, and he turned away again.

"Sorry. You're sorry. Are you trying to tell me you think Brianna could be your daughter?" Her voice sounded flat, almost emotionless, but a deep hurt stirred inside. This couldn't be true. It couldn't be. David wouldn't have lied to her, kept something like this from her.

He raised agonized eyes to hers. "It might be possible."

She felt her body start to shake and tried to control it. "So all these years, you've been living a lie? You let me think you'd always been faithful to me, that you were a virgin when we married, and now you tell me you weren't?" She pushed back her chair and stood. "I feel sick to my stomach. I'm not sure I want to hear this tonight."

"Susanne, let me try to explain. I know it's late, but I don't want you going to bed upset like this."

She shook her head and raised a hand to silence him. "I can't, David. You can talk to me tomorrow, but not tonight. I feel like I'll fall apart if you do. You lied to me, betrayed my trust. I don't want to end up screaming at you or losing it, and right now, I'm feeling close to that. I'm going to bed. All I ask is that you sleep in the guest room tonight. Please."

He stood, then reached out to touch her shoulder, but she stepped back, avoiding his hand. She needed time to think, time to sort through what she felt. She didn't want him getting too close. David's touch always had the ability to soothe her, and she didn't intend to go there tonight.

He dropped his hand, a look of quiet defeat crossing his face. "I understand. We'll talk in the morning. For what it's worth, I'm sorry, and I love you."

She didn't answer... couldn't answer. She felt frozen, like something had died inside. What explanation could there be? David had lied. He had a daughter he hadn't told her about and had had a relationship with another woman and conceived a child with her when he'd sworn he'd never been with anyone but her. How could she trust him to tell the truth now?

David crawled into the guest-room bed with a quiet groan. The pain on Susanne's face had cut through his heart. What had he done? Never in a million years had he thought his actions of one night, so many years ago, would come back to harm his family. But they had.

A girl had been conceived who no longer had a mother, much less a real home. She'd been told her father didn't want her, then been left with an uncle who at best appeared to be careless and irresponsible, and at worst might be a drunk or abusive.

His wife, whom he'd tried to spare nearly fifteen years ago, was lying in their bed alone, probably crying herself to sleep. How would she view his claim of Christianity now, especially when she knew the rest of the story?

And what about Steven and Meagan? How would this affect them? They had a sister they didn't know existed. It would have been a simple matter, asking Vicki to submit to a blood test for paternity results back then. No reliable DNA testing had been available at the time—at least nothing he could have afforded—but they'd have been able to get a good idea if he was Brianna's father. Instead, he'd believed the gossip that she'd been with every guy in school and had disregarded her claims against him. Now he would have to tell Susanne how he had ignored the possibility that he had fathered a child.

He pulled the pillow over his face. He didn't want to think about that right now. Not tonight. He had enough to repent for tonight. All he could do was pray Susanne would forgive him and trust him again.

And pray for Brianna.

Susanne slipped into her white cotton nightgown and crawled under the covers in her darkened room, exhausted yet unable to sleep. *Have I accused David unfairly? Can there be any other explanation for this girl? He seems to think she might be his. That's enough to deal with for now.*

Susanne tossed off the quilt that seemed to suffocate her and stared out the window at the sprinkling of stars. The darkness in the room felt oppressive. Right about now, she'd like something to drink that would help calm her nerves. Why was David so unreasonable about keeping alcohol in the house? Didn't he know it helped her cope with her stress? It wasn't as if she had to have it; it just helped her feel more relaxed and probably made her easier to live with.

David always says we shouldn't judge people when we don't understand their motives but look at him. She could hear his voice. "Don't drink, Susanne. It's a bad influence on the kids. Can't you say no when you're stressed instead of drinking?"

Who is he to talk? Whose life is in a mess now?

She slipped out of bed and stood at the open window, unwilling to turn on a light. No breeze stirred the trees. As the silence pressed in, the quiet no longer enfolded her.

Maybe she should go downstairs and turn on the TV. No. She didn't want David to hear and come in to talk.

David continually made claims about God. God was love. God could do anything. *David's wrong. Let's see You bring anything good out of this, God.*

Right now, she trusted herself more than she trusted God— she probably always had. Wasn't she a capable mother and a faithful wife? She'd never broken David's trust, never hurt him like this.

She slipped her hand over her mouth and stifled a sob. David's silence about his past had created a well of pain that seemed to have no bottom. Somehow, she needed to regain control. Her kids were the most important. She couldn't take a chance of them being hurt or let them see how much this upset her. She'd do her best to act as though everything was normal between David and her, at least when the children were around.

She headed to her bed, determined to rest. Her bare toe slammed into the wooden base of the footboard. "Ouch!" She grabbed her foot and hopped to the edge of the bed. She muffled a small moan and rocked on the bed but couldn't stem the tears. The pain in her foot seemed to release a floodgate in her heart that she'd been damming for too many hours. She covered her eyes, but the tears traced a path down her cheeks.

Knock it off! She shook her head and swiped at her eyes with the heels of her hand. She needed to think, figure out what to do.

What about Brianna? We'll have to call social services. She felt sorry for the girl and hated to see her caught in this mess. She'd be kind until the state agency located her extended family, but she had no strength for anything else right now. There was no proof Brianna was David's biological daughter, and their kids had to come first. They knew nothing about this girl. She could have all sorts of emotional problems harmful to Meagan and Steven.

Having reached a decision, Susanne's mind started to relax. She slid into bed and curled up under the handmade quilt, a gift from her grandmother years ago. The late spring night had turned cool, and the warmth of the quilt brought comfort, lulling her into sleep.

Chapter Five

DAVID GOT UP EARLY THE NEXT morning, thankful it was Saturday. He didn't expect to see Susanne until later. She'd be exhausted from the stress of the night before. He shut the guest-room door and walked quietly downstairs to the kitchen, needing time to think, pray, and have a cup of strong black coffee. As he stepped into the doorway between the dining room and kitchen, his hope for a peaceful morning died. Susanne sat at the table with her latte. Her eyes stared at the steaming mug cupped in her hands.

He never tired of looking at his wife. With her slender build, she looked more like a teenager than a woman in her early thirties. But her normally happy face was solemn this morning, her green eyes rimmed with dark circles, and her curly hair disheveled.

"I didn't hear you get up. I thought you might sleep in." He headed for the coffee pot across the room.

"Sleep in? I don't think I slept much at all." She slumped in her seat, looking as though the weight of the world rested on her shoulders.

"I know I have a lot of explaining to do, and it's not going to be easy for either of us. Your mom will be bringing the kids over soon, and Grandfather will be here later today. We need to talk and have some kind of plan." He filled his mug and set it on the table, then slipped into the chair across from her.

"Grandfather? What are you talking about?" Susanne's incredulous eyes stared at him, and he felt the blood drain from his face.

He slapped his forehead. "Oh man, I'm so sorry. With everything that happened last night, I totally forgot to tell you."

"Somehow, that doesn't surprise me." Her voice was laced

with sarcasm. "So Grandfather's coming today? When was this arranged?"

"Really, I'm sorry. I planned on telling you on the way to dinner last night. Then I came home and got slammed with the news about Brianna, and I forgot."

She sniffed. "*You* got slammed. Right."

He heaved a sigh. One more strike against him. Better to let that last comment go. "Grandfather called while I was leaving the job site last night. He's been visiting Great-Aunt Julia and dreaded the idea of going home to an empty house. He found some childhood things Grandmother saved of mine and thought I'd like to have them, then mentioned going fishing together. I told him we'd love to have him visit. I didn't think you'd mind."

She crossed her arms over her chest. "Normally, I wouldn't mind. I love having him here. He's a sweetie, and the kids adore him. It's just not the best timing. We don't understand all the ins and outs where Brianna is concerned, and it's going to be hard to explain."

"I know. But we can't turn him away. He isn't over Grandmother's death. He needs his family. We'll have to make it work."

"Easy for you to say. I'm the one left at home entertaining your grandfather and a strange girl who could be your daughter, while you go to work."

"I'd like to talk about that."

"So talk. Is she yours or not?"

"I think she could be." David pulled a paper out of his pocket. "You need to read this. It's a letter from Brianna's mother. Maybe it'll help you understand." He placed it in front of her and eased back in his chair.

Her eyes widened, and she pushed the letter away. "I have no desire to read anything written by your girlfriend."

"She wasn't my girlfriend. Please, would you listen?"

"What is there to say? You obviously cheated on me when we were engaged or married."

"We weren't married."

"So that makes it okay?" The words were measured, cool.

David winced. "No, it doesn't. I can't begin to tell you how sorry I am."

"You lied to me. Last night you said again that you'd never broken your marriage vows and had always been faithful."

"This happened before we got married. I didn't lie. I just didn't tell you about Vicki."

Her eyes narrowed. "Vicki. What was her last name?"

David hung his head. "Warren."

"You've got to be kidding! You slept with Vicki Warren? She had a horrible reputation. My gosh, what were you thinking?" She pushed away from the table and stood glaring at him.

"I wasn't."

"We got engaged the beginning of that summer!"

He felt his face redden. "I know."

"And where was I?"

"At college."

"So as soon as I left town, you found yourself a new girl friend?"

"No. I didn't even know Vicki. She started hanging around me and the guys not long after you left, and she made it obvious she was interested in me. I didn't care about her. I was missing you so much."

"Huh. So missing me made you sleep with her?"

"She threw herself at me. I'd had a few too many beers, and she followed me out to my truck and asked for a ride home. I stopped in front of her house and I didn't mean for anything to happen. I've felt guilty about it for years." His voice hoarsened on the words.

"Not guilty enough to tell me."

"I wanted to, but I was afraid. I figured you'd dump me, and I was in love with you. I didn't want to lose you."

"Right. And how about after you went through your huge salvation experience not long after we got married? You made a big deal about how much you'd changed and how your life was going to be so different. And when you asked me to marry you, I said how happy I was that neither of us had ever been with anyone else, and you agreed. You lied to me." Her hand hit the table.

"I know, and I'm so sorry."

"Why? Why didn't you tell me?"

"You remember the pastor from the first church we ever attended together?"

"Yes."

"The experience shook me up. I went to our pastor for advice. I told him what I'd done and asked if I should tell you. He felt no good would come from it, as Vicki was gone and you'd only be hurt. He counseled that I should ask God for forgiveness and put it behind me. I was a new Christian and assumed he knew best. Besides, a part of me was relieved I didn't have to admit what I'd done. As time went on, it got harder to talk about, and eventually I buried it as part of my past before I knew the Lord."

Susanne's face grew red. "And you want me to be a Christian. A pastor tells you to keep a secret like that, and you do it. Sorry, I can't see past the dishonesty and broken trust."

"He was trying to be kind, and he thought it would spare you unnecessary pain. And he said since it happened before I became a Christian, the Lord had forgiven me. He felt I should accept that and move on. The pastor didn't know the full story. I didn't tell him all of it. If I had, I think he would have urged me to be honest and come clean. I guess part of me wanted to forget it too."

She leaned her hip against the kitchen counter, her eyes narrowed. "The full story. What didn't you tell him?"

He hung his head. He'd give anything not to tell her this. But keeping this secret had brought them to the place they were in today and avoiding it longer wouldn't be right. He took a deep breath, then let it out. "Vicki came to the house when I was gone and told Mom she was pregnant."

The anger drained from Susanne's face. Pain took its place. "All these years, you knew you had a child?" she whispered.

He shoved back his chair and pushed to his feet, wanting to hold her, comfort her. "No. I didn't believe it. I didn't try to find out, but I didn't believe the baby was mine when my mother confronted me. I told her Vicki had a bad reputation, and it had to be someone else's." He reached out a hand and tried to pull Susanne toward him.

She shook her head and stepped away, walking to the other side of the table. "Don't. Please. Not now. I don't know what to say. You have a daughter, and you ignored her all these years? I'm not sure I know you. That I ever really knew you."

His heart felt frozen in his chest at the shock on his wife's face. "I didn't want to lose you, and I didn't believe it. I know it's no excuse, but it's the truth."

Her silence made the words sound so foolish. He'd taken the easy way out fourteen years ago, and his family was paying for it now.

"What else have you forgotten? For all I know, you kept seeing Vicki."

"Nothing. I promise you that. I never saw Vicki again after that night."

"Whatever. I don't know what to believe. Some girl claiming to be your daughter shows up, and you tell me you were unfaithful, lied to me when we were engaged, and ignored the child you fathered. Now you ask me to believe in you? Sorry, but it's not going to be that easy."

"I know it's not. But I've never done anything else to break your trust. Please, can you forgive me?"

"Don't expect me to forgive you right now. You betrayed my trust, David, and you can't ask me to act like it didn't happen."

"I can't change the past, but I'd give anything to undo what I've done."

"Well, you can't, and now the result of your past has shown up at our door."

"I know. And we need to make some decisions."

"I've already made mine. Based on what I remember of her mother, Brianna was raised in a dysfunctional home. She could've been abused for all we know and have all sorts of problems, especially if the uncle who dumped her off is any indication. You and I agreed when we took foster kids that they'd be younger than Meagan and Steven so they couldn't influence our kids. I'm not changing that rule, even for a girl you think may be your daughter." Susanne's mouth hardened in a grim line. She looked like a mother cougar ready defend her cubs.

David wanted to lash back, but he couldn't blame her. This was hard for him, and Brianna was his daughter, not Susanne's. "I'm concerned about Meagan and Steven too. I haven't been able to think of much else all night."

"I'm having a hard time believing that."

David stared at his wife. Her stormy eyes glared at him from across the room.

"I know you're upset, and you have every right to be. None of this is your fault—it's mine. But we need to discuss it. We're talking about a child's life, and we can't throw that away." He grabbed his mug, setting it down in front of the coffee pot and jerking the pot from its plate. He snatched up the sponge to clean what splashed over the rim.

She waited till he returned to his seat. "I didn't say anything about throwing her away. I'm calling the Department of Social and Health Services first thing Monday morning." Susanne's voice was firm. "I'm sure DSHS will find her family. Maybe they can track down her uncle and talk to him about other family members."

"I'm not so sure the uncle is the best option."

"Fine. But we have to start somewhere. On top of that, we have the kids and our reputation to consider. How will this look? We have a good name in this community, and people will assume you had an affair, then ignored the mother and baby. I don't understand why God let this happen—why He's punishing me and our kids for something you did." She swiped the back of her hand across her eyes and turned to gaze out the window.

David knew his wife hated to cry. Nothing he said right now would help. He bowed his head, shoulders hunched against the weight pressing down.

"Please believe me when I say I love you." He raised his head, willing her to look at him. "You and the kids are the most important thing in my life, and that'll never change."

She kept her face averted, and a small sniffle escaped. "I can't promise how much I can give right now. I'm confused, I'm hurt, and I don't know what to think. I know it isn't fair for this girl to be caught in the middle. I feel sorry for her that her mother is dead and she's alone. It sounds like her uncle isn't going to be any help, but I don't see what we can do. There's no proof she's yours." She kept her face resolutely turned from him.

David shook his head. "This isn't easy for me, either. I wish none of it had happened, but you said yourself the resemblance is strong. I'm willing to see if any relatives want her, but I won't dump her into foster care if she's mine. I'd want blood tests run to find out for sure. I promise I won't make a decision without your agreement. Can we think about it for a few days before we call DSHS?"

She turned away from the window and walked toward him, her eyes dark with pain. "What are we going to tell her, and what do we tell the kids? Summer vacation doesn't start for another two weeks."

"She doesn't need to be in school. This is a big enough adjustment." David ran his fingers through his hair. "Let's take it a day at a time. We'll tell the kids she's a relative. That isn't a lie, but it's enough information for now. Brianna may have told the kids. She has no reason to keep quiet. And you know Steven. He questions everything."

"Wonderful. I should've kept them apart. Now we'll have to answer questions from our kids."

"We'll deal with that if we have to. I'll talk to Brianna and tell her we're struggling because we didn't know about her until now. She believes I didn't want her. Think about the hurt that must've caused. She deserves the truth. I'll let her know she'll be staying for a few days. Is that okay?"

She picked up the dish towel sitting on the counter and plucked at the fringe. "All right. I guess we don't a choice. We can wait for a few days. But knowing it isn't her fault doesn't change anything. I'll be kind and treat her the same as any other foster child we've had, but I'm not promising I can love her."

"I understand." David got up to top off his coffee and sat again to drink it in silence.

He longed to protect his wife and children from the turmoil sure to ensue. He wanted to believe Brianna was someone else's, but his heart told him that hope was in vain.

Chapter Six

LATER THAT MORNING, THE PHONE RANG. Susanne looked at the caller ID. Mom. She got right to the point. "Do you want me to bring the kids home?"

"I'd appreciate that. David and I have been trying to sort this out, and we need to talk to the kids."

"Not a problem. I'll drop them off and not come in. I'll be there in about thirty minutes."

"Thanks, Mom." Susanne set the phone down and turned to David. "Who's going to talk to them? Do we split them up and talk to Brianna separately or keep them together?"

"It might be better together. It won't seem like a big deal, and we'll probably keep the questions to a minimum. I'll explain, and you can add anything you think I've missed."

She leaned her hip against the kitchen counter. "Fine, but I prefer to stay out of it as much as possible. She isn't my daughter, and I don't want to get involved. Our kids are my priority, and I don't want them hurt."

"I feel the same way, and I'll do my best to protect them."

Susanne knew David had always made the safety and peace of his family a priority, but the next few hours were going to be difficult and emotional. Somehow, she had to keep her mind off David's past and try to focus on the kids.

A few minutes later, the crunch of gravel signaled a car pulling into the drive.

Three car doors slammed, followed by the sound of a motor disappearing down the hill. No noise of chattering children met her ears, only Steven's voice raised in eight-year-old exuberance. The high-pitched tone preceded him through the door like a piping horn, the volume rising and falling haphazardly.

When the kids came into the living room, Susanne eyed them carefully, anxious to see if Meagan and Steven were upset or worried in any way. Meagan was quiet, but that was normal. She'd never been a chatterbox.

Meagan resembled Susanne, small-boned and petite with red gold hair. People often thought the two children were much closer in age, not realizing Meagan was three years Steven's senior. The confusion didn't last long when they got acquainted. Meagan's maturity was far beyond her eleven years, and Steven, well... Steven was Steven—a fun-loving, typical little boy.

Steven looked more like his dad with his dark wavy hair and sturdy bone structure. Someday, he'd hate those waves in his hair, but his mother knew the girls would go crazy over him with those sea green eyes, the only feature he'd inherited from her, and that winning smile. Right now, he was his normal talkative self, his face lit with animation as he explained to Brianna the intricacies of an old transistor radio his dad had allowed him to disassemble not long ago. "I love taking stuff apart. It's cool to see inside. I'll show you sometime if you want."

"Yeah, but you can't put them back together again." Meagan made a face at her little brother.

Steven stuck out his tongue in response. "I don't care. I like to see how things work."

Susanne noticed Brianna was listening attentively, and Steven positively glowed when she asked him a question about his latest adventure. That was all it took for the boy to begin bouncing around, talking at the speed of a racecar in the home stretch. Meagan tried to shush him a time or two, but Brianna shook her head as if already knowing the effort was futile.

"Kids, come in here for a minute." David beckoned from the kitchen doorway.

Three heads turned his direction with varying degrees of curiosity, even dread on their faces.

Susanne hadn't gotten over the feeling of surprise that shot through her every time she looked at Brianna. The more she was around the girl, the more Susanne wondered how she'd missed the strong resemblance the first time she'd seen her. She didn't like it, but she admitted she'd choose that over the girl resembling Vicki. That would be too much to deal with.

"Everyone needs to be quiet." David waited for the chatter to fall silent as the kids pulled out chairs at the table. "As you know, Brianna came to our house because her mama said she's our relative."

Susanne watched closely to see what kind of response this incomplete truth might have on Brianna, but the girl's face remained impassive.

"I asked, and she said she's our sister. Is she going to live with us, Dad?" Steven piped up. He squirmed in his chair, unable to sit still.

Susanne should have expected as much. She'd been foolish to hope they could keep the whole truth from their children.

"Let me finish, Steven," David said. "Brianna is going to stay with us for a few days until we can find information about the rest of her family. There might be other relatives worrying about her. We need to check on that first." He turned an inquiring look in Brianna's direction.

"No, sir. I don't have any relatives except my uncle, and he doesn't want me," Brianna stated in a flat voice.

David's posture stiffened, and Susanne's heart contracted, not wanting to believe that could be true.

"We still need to try. We can't keep you without checking."

It was as if a shutter closed over Brianna's face, as though she expected rejection again. How many times in her nearly fourteen years had she been told her father didn't want her? Now all she saw and heard could only lead her to the conclusion nothing had changed.

But Susanne wouldn't let guilt force her into a corner where Brianna was concerned. With foster kids, they'd had a choice—background information on each one and the option to bail at any time. They knew nothing about this girl, and Susanne wouldn't chance her children's safety or welfare for a stranger.

"How come she looks so much like you, Dad? You never told us you had another daughter," Meagan's eyes narrowed as she stared at her dad.

"Yeah, is she gonna call you Dad too?" Steven asked, rocking back and forth in his chair.

David held up his hand in a gesture the kids knew well—time to stop talking.

"We don't have all the answers yet. We'll know more in a few days, and we'll talk about it then. I don't want you pestering us or Brianna with questions. Is that clear?" David looked from Steven to Meagan and back again.

"Yes," both voices answered at once.

"Brianna, do you have any questions?" David asked.

Brianna shook her head, her eyes downcast. "No, sir." She sat hunched in her chair, her foot scraping noisily on the floor.

"Was that one suitcase all you brought with you?" Susanne asked.

"Yes, ma'am. That's all my uncle let me pack."

How odd. Susanne held back a small smile at the quaint manners the girl showed. What teenager called adults *sir* and *ma'am*? None she'd ever met.

"Why do you call us that?" she asked.

"Call you what, ma'am?"

"That. Why do call me *ma'am* and David *sir*?"

Brianna shrank back at Susanne's question.

Susanne stretched her hand across the table, touching the girl on the shoulder for a moment. "I'm sorry, honey. I'm not criticizing you, but I'd like to know why you call us that. It's unusual for someone your age."

The foot under the table grew still, and Brianna raised her head, seeming to relax at the touch. "Because of Grandma."

"Your grandma?" David asked. "You mean your mother's mom, down in Texas?"

Brianna nodded again, glancing at Susanne. "My grandma's daddy was a Texan. He said children should talk to their elders with respect, that too many kids nowadays are sassy. I loved Grandma, and she told me I should be polite to adults."

"I agree about being respectful. It's rare in children these days. Could you call us by our first names for now, though? It might be easier," David said.

"Yes, sir. I mean, okay . . . David." She pulled back, her words halting.

Did she expect some type of harsh discipline? Susanne had seen that look on the faces of foster kids in the past, when they anticipated a sharp smack or a cruel comment in response to a small mistake.

"You aren't in trouble," Susanne said, keeping her voice gentle. She couldn't help but hurt for this child. "If you forget sometimes, it's all right. It's nice that you're respectful, but it's okay for you to use our names."

Brianna dropped her head, looking down at her hands twisted in her lap.

Pushing her chair away from the table, Susanne stood and motioned to their two children. David might need to talk to Brianna privately. Both Steven and Meagan were a bit too attentive, and she'd better distract them before they decided to ask questions no one was ready to answer.

"Come on, Meagan and Steven. Let's go check the horses' water. I didn't have time to do it this morning."

"Is Brianna coming?" Steven jumped up from his chair.

"You and Meagan can show her around later. Brianna can stay here at the house while we do the chores." She held her hand out to her son.

David watched Susanne urge the kids through the door like a general ushering troops to retreat. Her purpose was clear—give David time to talk to Brianna without the younger ones listening. But what was she thinking? Would she ever forgive him or be open to the idea of Brianna being more than a visitor in their home?

"Mom, why does she talk so funny?" Steven's voice piped from the adjoining room.

"She doesn't talk funny, Steven. It's called an accent. People from different parts of the country often speak a little differently from each other," David heard Susanne reply, right before the front door shut firmly behind them.

He felt so torn. The damage he'd done with his lie seemed irreparable, robbing his wife of her trust. He desperately wanted her forgiveness and to see the joy return to her life. But he had an added responsibility, one he knew God wasn't going to let him skate out of even one day longer. He couldn't abandon Brianna. Although his wife and kids needed protection and care, so did this girl.

"Brianna, can I talk to you?" David asked as she sat unmoving and silent. The dark head was bent down, eyes staring at her hands gripped in her lap.

"I guess so."

"I know you're confused. You're dropped at someone's house,

and you don't even know us. That has to be scary, right?"

She shrugged without looking up.

David could see his direct approach wasn't bringing any results. "Can you tell me a little bit about your mama, Brianna? What she did for a living? What she was like?"

Brianna cautiously raised her eyes to meet David's. "She loved me and took good care of me." Her hands stilled as her attention shifted to a subject she clearly loved.

David leaned forward and smiled. "Go on."

Her hesitation seemed to lessen. "She tried to find work, but it was hard. When I was in grade school, she waitressed at a little diner, but they closed a couple of years ago." Her voice became defensive. "We had to go on welfare or go hungry. It didn't make Mama a bad person." Her body tensed, her shoulders hunching like a child trying to protect herself from another blow.

"Of course it doesn't. I'm sure she was a good person, Brianna, and I know you're proud of her."

Her face cleared.

"I need to talk to you about something else—something your mom might not have understood."

Brianna's back stiffened, and her mouth set, but David saw no way around what he needed to say.

"Your mother told you that your father didn't want you?"

She narrowed her eyes. The shutters hid her emotions again.

How could he explain to this girl that he hadn't loved her mother, hadn't even known her?

"Brianna, if I'm your dad—and I think I might be—I want to explain some things. I didn't know I was your father."

She shoved her chair back and sprang to her feet. "That isn't true! My mama said you didn't want me."

"Your mama told you what she believed. She didn't lie, but I'm not lying, either. Please, Brianna, sit down and listen." *Lord, help me explain and open her heart to listen.*

"When your mama found out you were coming, she went to my mother's house. I wasn't home. She told my mother about you and that she thought I was your father. My mother had heard things about your mama that weren't very nice."

Brianna took a seat, her mouth pulled down in a scowl.

"When I came home, she told me what your mother said and told me she didn't believe it. I'd heard that your mama had a lot of different boyfriends, and I thought one of them was your father. I know now the gossip about your mom probably wasn't true. I guess my mom and I didn't want to believe you could be mine, and neither of us really talked about it again."

The look of scorn remained on her delicate features. "Where's your mom now?"

"A few years ago, she had a car accident on the way home from work. She died a few hours later."

"Oh."

Was she glad the woman who had rejected her had died? David understood the ache Brianna must be feeling over her own mother's death, but he doubted she would be as spiteful as that.

"I can't promise what I would've done if I *had* believed it. I was too immature to have married your mom, and I didn't know her well enough to be in love with her. I was stupid. I wasn't thinking about her or the consequences the night she got pregnant, and I'm sorry I didn't."

He suddenly wondered how she might take that. "Please, don't misunderstand. I'm not sorry you were born. I am sorry I didn't do things right. It's wrong to have sex outside of marriage, and it's even worse when it's with someone you barely know. I have to be accountable to God for that. *If* you are my daughter, then I need to be accountable to you too. I'm not exactly sure how, but I want to do what's right."

She gave a small snort of disbelief, shaking her head and avoiding his eyes. "You don't want me here."

"You've known about me most of your life, but my family and I just found out about you. Susanne is having a hard time dealing with this. You're old enough to understand it's hard for her to accept that I could have a daughter who isn't hers." He felt a bit guilty putting it off on Susanne, but how could he explain to this girl that he'd kept this from his wife, hiding his knowledge all these years, rather than own up to what might have been his responsibility? How did he unwind this web he'd woven? Susanne was already disappointed and hurt. He hated strengthening Brianna's idea that he'd never wanted her.

He saw a slight tilt of her head he took to be a nod and continued. "I want to do what's right. But I also have a wife and two other kids to consider. It might take a few days before I can give you any answers. I'd like for you to be able to stay, but I need Susanne to feel the same way. Also, we'll need to see if any relatives are wondering where you are."

He held up his hand to acknowledge the reply she started to make. "I know you told us your uncle is your only family and he doesn't want you, but we have to make sure. We can't keep you without checking."

She bit her lip, her eyes turned away. "I knew you wouldn't want me to stay. Mama warned me before she died."

"We're not going to kick you out. Would you do what I want Susanne to do? Take it one day at a time and see how it goes?"

"I guess." She shrugged.

He heard Susanne and the kids chattering as they came into the house. Good timing. Maybe Meagan could take Brianna for a ride. He knew little to nothing about this girl who might be his daughter.

"Brianna?" He waited until she turned toward him. "Do you

have enough clothes? Do you have everything you need?"

Her answer was what he expected, a half-hearted shrug. He'd need to get Susanne involved in this or maybe Meagan could help—that might be easier for Brianna.

He tried again, hoping to find something that would interest her. "Have you been around animals much? Did you have any at home?"

"Grandma was allergic. I always wanted a kitten, but they made her sick, so I couldn't," she stated matter-of-factly.

"Did you live in a big town or out in the country?"

"In a town. I guess it was big, at least bigger than the ones I saw around here."

He decided not to push anymore, knowing the questions would be answered as time went on and sensing she'd had enough for one day. He'd let Meagan take charge. Quiet and kind, she might help Brianna feel more at home.

"Dad, Meagan won't let me listen to her iPod," Steven complained as he flopped down in a chair.

"That's because you won't just listen to it, Steven. You'll take it apart. I don't want it ruined!" Meagan shot back, glaring at her little brother.

"That's enough, you guys," Susanne said from behind them. "Meagan doesn't have to let you use her iPod, Steven, so you'll have to find something else to do. You can ride your bike for a while or play video games."

Steven's face fell.

"Meagan, do you want to show Brianna your horses and take her for a walk? I'll bet she'd enjoy going to the barn and seeing Smoke's kittens," David said.

Brianna's eyes lit up.

"Sure. I'll change into my grubbies first. Steven, don't bug Brianna while I'm gone." Meagan gave Steven a stern look before heading upstairs to her bedroom.

Steven chattered to Brianna about his bike and the trails on their place. David took Susanne aside. "Could you slip into Meagan's room and talk to her?"

Susanne raised her eyebrows but remained silent. She seemed in a softer mood since returning with the kids. Her face looked relaxed, and her tone had more of the kindness he always associated with her. The stress showed in the set of her shoulders and the worry in her eyes, but her body was no longer stiff or rigid.

"We don't know what clothes Brianna brought or things she might need. Maybe Meagan can take Brianna to her room. She could help her unpack and check it out. We can't let her go without."

Susanne's eyes narrowed a little. "I don't intend to. If there are things she needs, I'll take her to town."

David took a step toward Susanne. A look of longing flitted across her face, followed by frustration. She drew back and turned her head.

He wouldn't push her. At least she was willing to try. He knew she'd do her best with Brianna whether her heart was in it or not. That was all he could hope for today.

Chapter Seven

SUSANNE STEPPED INTO MEAGAN'S ROOM, CLOSING the door softly behind her, hoping Steven wouldn't notice and question. "Meagan, I need to talk to you."

"Sure, Mom. What's up?" Meagan finished changing into old jeans and pulled her red-gold hair into a ponytail. She made the perfect picture of an All-American young girl.

Meagan's heart was tender, and Susanne didn't want her negatively influenced or hurt. She was mature for her age but could be overly sensitive where injured and hurting animals or children were concerned. Susanne hated to see her get too involved with Brianna when they knew so little about her past.

"Mom? Did you want something?"

"Yes. We need your help."

"Like what?"

"Brianna only brought one suitcase, and we have no idea what she has. Would you take her to the guest room and help her unpack? If we need to get her some under things or more jeans or shirts, we'll run into town later and pick them up."

"Yeah, no problem." Meagan reached for the doorknob.

"Oh, and Meagan? We don't know if she's been around horses, so be careful."

"Gee, Mom, I know that! My riding instructor drummed that into my head since I was little. You always have to be careful around horses, especially with someone you don't know." She rolled her eyes and let out a sigh.

A few minutes later, Meagan clattered down the wood stairs in her riding boots with their hard heels. Her slight figure was clad in her old jeans, worn at the knees, and her favorite T-shirt that proclaimed, "Horse Poor and Loving It!" on the front.

"Hey, Brianna, how about I show you where you're going to sleep and we get your stuff put away, then go see the kittens and horses?"

"Okay. I'll get my suitcase. I left it by the door." Brianna pushed back from the table.

The two girls headed out of the room, making a detour to grab the suitcase before running up the stairs, Meagan leading the way.

"This is yours." Meagan opened the door to the sunny guest room. She looked at it critically, glad her mom had vacuumed and dusted it a couple of days ago. Meagan loved things clean. She was thankful she didn't have to share a room with Steven. It drove her nuts that he turned his bedroom into a little pigpen.

"I'm not sharing with you?"

"Nope. You get your own room. Mine doesn't have another bed. Don't you like it?"

"Yes, a lot. It's huge, and I love the colors. Are you sure I should stay in here? I probably won't be here long and don't have to have my own room. I can sleep on the couch." Brianna stood in the center of the room and slowly turned full circle.

Meagan tried to see its size and colors through the eyes of a stranger. She knew her mom did a great job decorating, and this room was one of the nicest in the house. If she didn't love horses so much, she'd have wanted the theme in this one. It made you feel like you were in the mountains. Meagan knew a lot of girls at her school who only liked girlie stuff and acted stupid around boys. If Brianna was that kind of girl, then Meagan doubted she'd want this room.

"You don't have to sleep on the couch, silly! That's what the guest room is for and you're a guest. Come on. We'll put your clothes in the dresser." Meagan pulled out a drawer in the dresser standing beneath a wood-framed mirror on the wall.

Brianna carefully laid her suitcase on the bear-and-moose quilt. "This is nice, and you have pictures that go with it." She looked over the rustic room.

What kind of place had Brianna lived in while she was growing up? She seemed nice, but she'd been so quiet since she arrived it was hard to figure her out.

"Yeah, I love all the animal stuff. The bed and dressers are pine that came from our land. Steven and I each have a set. Pretty neat, huh?" Meagan flopped onto the bed next to the suitcase. "I have horse pictures and horse stuff all over my room. I'll show it to you later if you want."

"Okay." Brianna continued to stare around the room.

Meagan motioned she was ready for the clothes.

"I don't have much to put away." Brianna's hand hovered over her suitcase without unlatching it.

Meagan reached out to help. "That's okay. You're bigger than me, so I guess you can't borrow my stuff, but if you need something, Mom can get it for you." She'd love to ask Brianna questions about her real mom and why she said that Dad was her dad. But he'd been firm about not asking this new girl too many questions, and while she was dying to know, she'd better not disobey.

"I'm probably not staying here, anyway, and they won't want to spend money on me."

"Mom and Dad won't care. They like to help people. Come on. Let's get your stuff put away so I can show you the animals." She unlatched the old suitcase and opened the lid. She lifted out two pair of jeans, rather well worn. The suitcase emptied rapidly as they put away three slightly shabby T-shirts and a meager supply of underwear. *Boy, she sure must have a mean uncle,* Meagan thought. *He didn't let her bring many clothes.*

When they'd finished, they headed downstairs and out the side door onto a patio. "Hear the baby ducks? Two mamas come to our pond every year to have their babies. It's a fun place to play when the weather gets hot." Meagan pointed toward the pond glinting through the trees.

Brianna's steps slowed and she glanced toward the pond, nodding her head. The girls stepped off the deck and onto the path leading to the pasture.

"Have you ever ridden a horse?" Meagan asked. School was almost over, and the days were growing longer. It was going to be a lot of fun having another girl here this summer if Mom and Dad decided to let her stay.

"No. I've never even been close to a horse."

"You'll love ours. Steven and Dad don't like them very well, but Mom and I love to ride. I'm taking English lessons, but I've ridden Western all my life. Mom and I mostly trail ride, but I'm learning to jump."

Brianna listened, a confused expression on her face.

The girls reached the rails of the wood fence surrounding the ten-acre pasture where the barn stood. The horses saw the girls coming from a distance. They nickered softly and trotted up to hang their heads over the fence.

"It smells funny down here." Brianna wrinkled her nose and looked around her. "But all I see is a barn and the horses."

Meagan giggled. "Oh, that's the smell of the barnyard. It's the horses, hay, and manure. The hay smells kind of sweet, the horses are kind of dusty, and the manure . . ." She waved her hands in the air and laughed. "You'll get used to that. I kind of like the smells. It's part of living in the country."

Brianna didn't look convinced.

"Do you want to pet my mare?" Meagan reached out to rub the soft muzzle of a dark chestnut mare stretching her neck and head over the fence toward her. The mare nudged Meagan's shoulder, sniffing at her shirt and stomping impatiently.

Brianna pulled back sharply. "Is it safe? Will she bite?"

"She won't hurt you. She's looking for treats. I usually bring her a carrot or a piece of apple, but I forgot this time." Meagan reached out to scratch the mare's forehead under her wispy forelock, then ran her hand down the long neck stretching over the fence. "Sorry, girl. I'll bring them next time, I promise." All three horses pressed forward, jockeying for places along the fence.

Meagan stopped scratching her mare and looked at Brianna. "We have two mares, Khaila is an Arabian and she belongs to my mom, and Glory is mine. So is the gray gelding. He's a quarter horse, and his name is Bones 'cause when we got him he was really skinny."

"How come? Didn't he eat?"

"My mom said the animal shelter people saved him when they took him away from people who starved him. He's super quiet and gentle, and almost anybody can ride him. Want to ride with me?"

Brianna shook her head, tentatively reaching out her hand to stroke the velvet muzzle of the gelding. "I'll just pet him. He looks awful big. I'd probably fall off."

"Mom and I can teach you. She won't mind. She taught me when I was little, and she loves working with kids."

Meagan noticed Brianna's skeptical look but kept on talking. "I can show you how to groom your horse, tie it up, and lead it." She wasn't too sure how much Brianna understood and hoped the newcomer would want to learn more.

"Maybe. But I don't think I'll be here long enough to learn. Can we go see the kittens in the barn now?"

Meagan led the way back to the barn, wondering about Brianna's comment. Her parents wouldn't kick her out, would they?

Chapter Eight

"I DON'T THINK WE SHOULD GO to church tomorrow." Susanne surprised David with her statement.

"Why not? We go every Sunday."

"Think about it. Our kids are curious, and we haven't given them any details. Their friends will be asking who Brianna is and why she's here. The pastor will wonder what's going on."

David stared at Susanne from his place at the kitchen table, not sure where she was headed. He remained quiet, waiting for her to continue.

She turned to pluck a dead leaf off her African violet on the windowsill. "People are going to ask questions about Brianna. As it is, I go to church because it's important to you and the kids, not because it's where I really want to be. But I don't care to be under a microscope. It's obvious Brianna's related to you, and it's going to raise eyebrows—even at church." She kept her hands busy wiping imaginary crumbs from the countertop.

"I don't think it's a problem. We can't hide her, and sooner or later we have to tell the truth."

"What if she only stays for a few days? We might find a relative who wants her. Why stir up questions if we don't have to?" She tossed the sponge into the sink and faced him.

David turned to find the two girls standing in the kitchen doorway. How much had they heard of the conversation? Both faces were a study, one with anger written across it, the other with pain and resolute acceptance.

"Come on, Brianna. Let's go to my room and I'll show you my horse pictures and books." Meagan stared at her parents with angry and questioning eyes, then reached out for Brianna's hand

and pulled her toward the stairway.

"I'm sorry they heard that," Susanne said in a low voice.

He waited until the girls' footsteps receded up the stairs. "I'm sorry they did too, but I doubt it's new to Brianna. I think she knows she isn't welcome. I imagine life has thrown a lot of hard knocks her way." He pushed back his chair, stood, and crossed his arms over his chest.

"You're probably right. But the past isn't our fault, and we certainly can't change it. I didn't mean to hurt her, but maybe she needs to know the truth. We aren't sure we're keeping her, and I don't want to be pushed into a decision because the girls feel bad." She threw him a frown and walked from the room, leaving David to wonder if his home would ever be the same.

Susanne stood on the deck, thankful for the sunshine brightening this otherwise dismal day. She drew a deep breath, the fragrance of the fir needles released by the late afternoon sun on their boughs. Late spring normally held such promise for her. New life sprouting around her brought renewal to her soul. The long winter with its short, depressing days was past, and the hope of summer's sun glowed on the horizon. How had her life gone into such a downward spiral? She and David had had their difficulties over the years, but no marriage was perfect. She'd given up hoping for perfection some time ago.

Deep inside, Susanne longed for something better. Although she didn't care for what she considered the expectations imposed by Christians, she admitted a number of the couples at church seemed happier than she and David. Was it possible she'd been wrong most of her life?

Until she was twelve, her grandfather had lived with their family. Susanne was an only child, and the old man doted on her.

Both of her parents worked, and Grandpa became her primary caregiver during the day. While loving and accepting of those around him, he couldn't tolerate the thought of God or the church interfering in his life.

Susanne could remember his words clearly, imbedded in her mind as though seared there: "Don't ever believe God or some preacher knows how to run your life better than you, Susanne. That's a crock. Those church people will cram it down your throat. They act nice enough, but they're weak. They need someone to hold their hand and tell them how to live. You think for yourself, decide for yourself." He pulled his bushy eyebrows low on his forehead, and a scowl marred his normally kind expression. "You're a smart girl, so don't you be forgetting that, you hear?"

"Yes, Grandpa, I hear."

His death when she was twelve years old had left a huge hole in her life, and she determined to remember Grandpa's every word. She'd make him proud and never allow someone else to shape her life.

A year after he had died, she spent a summer with her aunt, her Dad's youngest sister. At first she was reluctant to attend church, but finally she agreed, deciding she wouldn't listen to anything those people said.

Youth meetings were another story as the youth pastor, an energetic young man with a charismatic personality, pulled her into the life of the group. As the summer wore on, her heart softened to the possibility God might love her. She yearned to pray the prayer of salvation near the end of her time there and felt the first stirrings of change in her young heart.

At the end of August, she returned home, and her mother, like her grandfather, didn't have an interest in church attendance. Over the next couple of years, Susanne gradually lost her interest in God. The memories of that summer began to fade, but the words of her grandfather remained.

Grandpa hadn't lied, and what he'd taught her was right. Susanne firmly believed she shouldn't give control of her life to anyone, not even God. Look at their situation now. David had put God in control of his life, and God hadn't prevented this mess. God didn't care about people. He wanted to make their lives miserable.

Most of the people at their church were decent, she couldn't deny that. But they were sheep blindly following the leader and using God as a crutch. How else could she explain their willingness to give up control? They might seem happy, but a deeper look at her own family proved you couldn't always tell. People thought she had it all together but lurking under the surface were secrets she didn't want anyone to know.

Brianna was an innocent victim in this, a tiny voice whispered. She was barely a teenager and certainly not to blame. Susanne closed her mind. She'd made her decision. She would put on a happy face for the sake of the kids but try to find this girl's relatives as soon as she could.

Chapter Nine

THE DOORBELL RANG, PULLING SUSANNE FROM a light doze. David's Grandfather! He couldn't be here already. David and the kids were feeding the trout at the pond. She headed to the door, pushing her hair out of her eyes and putting on a smile before opening the door.

Grandfather had aged in the four months since his wife's funeral. His gray hair had taken on a silver tinge. He'd always prided himself in keeping it neat, but the shaggy ends almost touched his collar, and his rumpled clothing appeared soiled. Shoulders that had been straight and firm slumped forward, and the sorrow in his eyes caused her heart to melt.

"Grandfather, how wonderful to see you!" She took the suitcase out of the frail, wrinkled hand and wrapped her arms around the slight form. *How much weight has he lost?* She could feel the bones under the nearly translucent skin.

A deep sigh escaped his lips. "Susanne, honey, that hug is exactly what this old man needed."

She felt a small shock of surprise at the strength in the arms that gripped her shoulders and gratitude at this small indication of good health. "Then I'll have to give you one every day!" She patted his arm and drew him into the room. "David and the kids are outside. Before I get them, I need to share something with you." She settled him into David's comfortable recliner. "Would you like something to drink?"

"No. I'm fine."

She sat on the couch nearby and curled up in the corner.

"What were you saying?" He leaned forward.

She drew in a deep breath and wet her lips with the tip of her tongue. "We had a bit of a surprise last night. A thirteen-year-old girl named Brianna came to our door, claiming to be David's daughter."

Grandfather's eyebrows rose, but he said nothing. She knew his Native American heritage gave him a great deal of restraint but couldn't help but feel surprised at the lack of response.

She rushed on, feeling anxious to get this behind her. "She said her mother's dead. David and I are going to see if other family might be looking for her. Of course, we don't have any real proof she's David's. He didn't know about her until last night."

He gave a brief nod. "Will you keep her?"

She drew back, nonplussed at the question. "We don't know yet. We're still discussing it, and we need to see what the authorities have to say."

"Hmm." He pushed himself from the chair. No longer did he look like a feeble man. "Let's go meet this girl who claims she's my granddaughter."

Susanne tucked her hand in Grandfather's arm and walked toward the door. Why hadn't she insisted David delay Grandfather's visit? There was no way she'd reveal David's lie to the loving older man, he'd never understand. But without that explanation, would he think her unfair? She'd forgotten his intense love for children and sensed he'd champion the idea of Brianna's remaining in their home. David inherited his stubbornness from him. Grandfather was half Nez Perce, and his pride and determination were 100 percent male.

Susanne led the way down the hard-packed dirt on the far side of the house and onto the grassy area where the three kids played badminton. No, it looked like only Steven and Meagan were taking part. Brianna simply stood with her racquet and watched. Wild cries emanated from the younger two as the birdie hit the net or the ground more often than it sailed over to the other side.

Grandfather slowed his pace and stood off to the side, seeming not to want to intrude on the game . . . or maybe simply observing the newcomer without her being aware.

"Grandfather!" The high-pitched squeal from Steven jerked Meagan's head around and caused Brianna to retreat a step.

"Yippee! You're here!" Meagan dropped the racquet and rushed into the man's open arms, with Steven right on her heels.

"When did you get here? Did you bring us something?" Steven jumped up and down, his eyes gleaming with excitement.

Susanne stepped in and placed her hand on the boy's shoulder. "Steven. That's not polite."

His bottom lip stuck out to the point that Susanne wanted to laugh, but she didn't dare. "You need to be thankful Grandfather is here to visit and not be worried about presents."

His toe scuffed the grass. "All right, I guess." His face brightened, and he grasped his grandfather's hand. "You want to come watch me do jumps on my bike?"

Grandfather chuckled and pulled the boy into a hug. "Not yet, my boy. I'm a bit tired from the drive, and I think I'll rest for a while. Besides, I haven't met your friend."

Steven's tone took on a note of importance. "This is Brianna. She says our dad is her dad too. But I don't see how he can be 'cause our mom isn't her mom and she doesn't live with us."

Susanne covered her face with her hands and sighed. Leave it to Steven to say something blunt.

Meagan stuck her elbow in her little brother's side. "Hush! That's rude."

Grandfather patted the boy's head and tugged on Meagan's ponytail, then turned to Brianna, who stood a few paces back from the group. "Hello, Brianna. I'm Grandfather, and I'm very happy to meet you."

A shy look crept across the girl's face, and she dipped her head. "Hi."

The older man dropped down to one knee and held out his hand. "Do you like stories, Brianna?"

She drew a step closer and nodded. "Yes."

"Grandfather tells great stories!" piped up Steven.

"Shush, Steven. Don't interrupt," Susanne said.

Grandfather smiled at the boy, then turned his attention back to the quiet girl. "My ancestors were the Nimi'ipuu, or Nez Perce Indians as many people choose to call them. My tribe came from eastern Oregon in the Wallowa Mountains. My father was half Nez Perce, and his father before him was full. The stories of our people are passed down through the generations, and we keep our ancestors and their history alive by the telling. Would you like to hear some of my stories?"

Brianna's face brightened, and her voice grew stronger. "Yes, I would."

He reached a hand out and clasped her smaller one. "Good." He beckoned to the two younger children and drew them both close. "Why don't we go sit under that big tree over there, and I'll tell you a story? Your father will be home soon, but I'll bet I can think of a couple before he gets here."

Steven took off like he'd been released from a catapult and bounded over to the tree, then ran partway back. "Come on, you guys. Hurry up. We don't have all day."

Susanne laughed and shook her head. "I'll get glasses of lemonade and join you in a bit." She glanced over her shoulder on the way to the house. Brianna's hand remained in Grandfather's brown one all the way to the tree.

Later that night, the stars peeked out, miniature crystals hung in the black reaches of the sky. A gentle breeze sprang up, swaying the tops of the firs and whispering over the surface of the pond, bringing peace to David's troubled spirit. The evening called to him, drawing him outside, reminding him the universe was so much more than his small corner of life.

He was tired, bone-creakingly tired. He knew emotions were not supposed to govern a man, but he felt like he'd been dragged behind a truck until he was raw. He leaned against the rough bark of a pine, thinking over the events of the past few hours. Raising his eyes to the heavens, he silently asked for wisdom. If only God would turn back the hands of time and let him start over.

He shook his head, stifling a sigh and shoving away from the tree. Time to get back to the house and try to make sense of this mess.

He found Susanne scrubbing the kitchen countertops like a woman on a mission to destroy every germ that existed.

"I agree with you, Susanne."

Her head shot up, and her hand ceased its motion.

Her hopeful look made him realize he'd better rephrase that before she got the wrong idea. "We should stay home from church tomorrow. It might be too difficult for the kids. Brianna has a lot to deal with, and I don't want to put any of them in the position of answering difficult questions—at least not until we've answered those questions ourselves."

"I don't see where we'll get the answers." She returned to rubbing invisible spots with renewed vigor.

He leaned a shoulder against the doorjamb. "I don't know about you, but I'm tired, and I don't want to fight."

"Fine. Whatever."

David sighed. "One more thing?" He waited until she turned to look at him. "Brianna is in the guest room tonight, and I don't think it's a good idea for me to sleep on the couch with the kids home and Grandfather here. Is it okay with you if I come back to our room?"

Her body stilled, and she turned away. "I guess. But don't think because you're back again that everything is all right."

"I understand." He dragged his heavy feet from the kitchen, feeling as though a boulder lodged in his chest. How long would it be before his wife would start forgiving him?

Chapter Ten

"MOM, WHY DIDN'T YOU WAKE US up in time for Sunday school?" Steven's voice held a note of surprise when he came down for breakfast the next morning.

Susanne understood his confusion, since they rarely missed a service. Although she was never excited about church, David and the kids loved it.

"Yeah, Mom. Carrie was bringing a picture of her new horse today. Why aren't we going?" Meagan asked, running her fingers through her flyaway hair.

They were both changing so fast, and before long, neither would care to hang out with their parents. Susanne's heart contracted at the thought of her babies growing up. It seemed like only yesterday Steven was dragging his teddy to breakfast with him and Meagan was losing her first tooth. The years had flown so quickly.

"We're going to town to get a few things for Brianna. We'll go out to breakfast, then do some shopping and make a fun day of it."

"Yippee! Breakfast!" Steven whooped, his disappointment about missing Sunday school apparently forgotten. He left the box of cereal on the table and rushed to his room to dress.

"Well, okay, I guess," Meagan said. "Brianna's jeans are worn out, and she only has three T-shirts. Was her family poor?" Her voice dropped to barely above a whisper as she glanced toward the stairs. "Where are Dad and Brianna? And how about Grandfather?"

"Your dad is taking a shower, and Brianna isn't up yet. Grandfather asked that we let him sleep in this morning. He's tired and wants to take it easy today. To answer your question, honey, I don't know. I think her family might've been poor." Susanne reached out to tuck Meagan's hair behind her ear. "Let's not make her feel bad about what she doesn't have. Instead, we'll try to make it a fun day for all of us, okay?"

Meagan turned and pulled open the refrigerator, pouring a glass of juice and taking a swallow before answering. "Yeah. I'm glad you and Dad have decided to be nice. I like her."

Susanne's eyebrows shot up, and she planted her hands on her hips. "Meagan, we haven't been mean."

"Maybe not mean, but I think she can tell you don't want her. We heard what you said to Dad yesterday. She's a nice girl, and she's sad right now. Her mom died not long ago. She told me about it when I showed her my stuff. You guys don't care about Brianna's feelings at all."

Susanne recognized that angry and stubborn voice well, having sounded the same way more than once in the past twenty-four hours. "I'm sorry, and we'll both try to be nicer. You're right. We need to think about Brianna's feelings. I guess it's been hard for your dad and me to have someone we don't know in our home. We're not sure what to do right now." Susanne hoped her halfhearted explanation would satisfy her irritated daughter.

"Ah gee, Mom, that's dumb. We've had foster kids before, and you said Brianna is a relative. Why can you be nice to foster kids and let them live with us, but not her? You and Dad said you'd tell us more sometime. What are you going to tell us?" A slight frown pulled at the corners of Meagan's normally smiling mouth.

"That's something I can't discuss with you right now. Adults have to deal with things that kids don't always understand."

"We're not little kids, and we know she's a relative, even if you don't want to say she's my sister. Why can't she live here?"

"We only have Brianna's word that she's your sister. Your dad and I need to check it out."

Susanne knew Meagan was right. She wasn't being fair to Brianna. "We have to make sure no other relatives are looking for her, so please don't get your hopes up, Meagan. We'll be kind to her for as long as she's here."

Meagan set her glass in the sink and rinsed it before turning to face her mother. "Does that mean you won't kick her out?"

"We're not kicking her out, but I'm not promising anything except that your dad and I will do what we think is best."

"Okay. I won't tell her that she might get to stay," Meagan assured her with the confidence of an eleven-year-old. "I'll see if she's up. I'll tell her we're going shopping and she gets to buy new stuff," she called over her shoulder as she disappeared up the stairs.

Susanne felt it'd been a successful day, although it had its difficult moments. By early afternoon, purchased several outfits for Brianna, and stopped for pizza. She modeled the last outfit, a slim green skirt and matching blouse, smiling a little and pivoting when Meagan clapped and squealed.

"Are you sure you want to buy me so much?" Her smile faded as she glanced from one adult to the other.

"It's fine, Brianna. We've only gotten a couple pair of jeans and shorts and a few shirts. This outfit will be a little nicer for church," David assured her.

"Go ahead and get changed while I check out, and we'll head home," Susanne said.

"Oh, doesn't she look cute? And she looks just like her dad!" the young sales clerk's voice echoed through the small shop, causing several customers to stare. "You guys each have kids that look like you and not a bit like the other. You see that a lot in second marriages, I guess."

Susanne frowned at the clerk before turning to Brianna. "You need to get changed."

Brianna froze, then spun around and dashed to the dressing room, a stricken look on her face.

"Uh, thanks, miss. I think we're ready," David broke in.

"I'm sorry. Did I say something wrong?" the clerk tittered, glancing in Susanne's direction. "I'll go check on your daughter, okay?" She hurried to the dressing room and tapped on the door.

"I'm almost done." Brianna's muffled voice came out of the little cubical.

Susanne shot an irritated look at the clerk. "Meagan, Steven, let's head to the car. Dad can wait for Brianna and pay for her things." She shoved the outer door open a little harder than necessary and frowned at David when he looked her way. "We'll be outside."

Once in the car and on the way home, Steven was his normal irrepressible self. "That lady was funny, huh? Did she think you and Dad just got married or something?"

"Hush, Steven. She didn't think before she spoke and made a mistake," Susanne said.

The sound of traffic on the road seemed to increase in volume as the absolute quiet in the car intensified. Susanne stared with unseeing eyes at the scenery flashing by. Her irritation increased at the added annoyance of David's Christian music. Her hand shot out, and she snapped the dial to the left, avoiding his glance.

"Dad, can we stop for an ice-cream cone?" Steven broke the silence, zeroing in on the parent most likely to say yes.

"We had pizza an hour ago. How can you possibly be hungry?" Relief laced David's voice.

"'Cause I'm a growing boy, and growing boys are always hungry. Don't you know that?" Steven giggled, causing the rest of the family to smile. "You guys want an ice-cream cone, don't you?"

"Yeah, ice cream sounds good," Meagan said. "Do you want

one, Brianna?"

"I guess so." Brianna's quiet, hesitant answer told Susanne that Brianna hadn't yet recovered.

"I guess it's up to your mother." David kept his eyes straight ahead, his grip on the wheel tightening.

Susanne didn't reply. If only Brianna didn't look so much like David, this type of thing wouldn't happen. They could've gone to church today, passing her off as a distant relative or a friend of the kids. But no one would believe that. The clerk in the store proved that. It wasn't fair. She shouldn't be forced to raise another woman's child, especially when the other half of the equation was her husband.

A softening had begun with Meagan's comments about not being mean, but Susanne felt her hurt stirring all over again. The ache in her heart intensified and she wished someone could understand her struggle. No one knew the pain and betrayal she wrestled with when lying awake at night, thinking about her husband's past. They'd been so young when they'd married. She'd always believed herself the first woman in his life. All these years of trust, to find out it was broken years ago. He said the brief affair held no meaning, but could she be sure? Could she ever put the image of her husband with another woman out of her mind?

It isn't Brianna's fault, a gentle voice whispered. The young girl already had a lot dumped on her shoulders, with her mother's death and all of this turmoil. She shook her head, longing to silence the voice and needing to nurture her pain.

"Mom! Can we have ice cream or not?" Steven's voice pulled her back.

"It's fine with me," Susanne said. "Let's stop and get the kids a treat. They've all been great today. I think they deserve something special before we head home." No sense in upsetting Meagan further, and this was a small place where she could bend.

Three pairs of eyes in the backseat brightened, but the relief in one set was apparent as Susanne glanced in the visor mirror. She quickly averted her gaze, resisting the tug she felt in her heart for this girl who had gone through so much already.

"Dad? Can I talk to you?" Meagan's voice pulled David's attention away from the evening paper, and he set it aside. "I asked Mom to keep Steven busy, and Brianna's up in her room putting away her new clothes. I wanted to ask you something without anyone hearing." She sank onto the couch near his easy chair, and David noticed her normally sparkling eyes seemed dim.

"Sure, honey. What's up?"

She clasped her hands in her lap and stared down at them.

"Meagan? What is it? Are you okay?" He pushed the handle to snap his footrest down and rose from his chair. He slipped onto the couch beside her. "Come here, sweetie."

Meagan snuggled against him and buried her head against his chest. A muffled sob issued from her somewhere in the region of his heart and caused a pang to shoot straight into that startled organ.

"I'm worried." The quiet voice of his daughter barely registered in David's ears.

"About what?" He pulled back a little and looked into her damp eyes.

"That you don't love me as much anymore."

David frowned, then realized how she might read that and tried to smile. "Of course I love you, and I always will. Why would you think that?"

"I'm not your oldest daughter anymore. Brianna is. Maybe she'll be your favorite girl now."

"Oh, honey. I'll always love you more than you can ever

know. And you'll always be your mother's and my oldest daughter. Nothing can ever change that."

She sniffed and rubbed her eyes. "How about Mom? Did you tell her you're sorry?"

He brushed the hair off her forehead. "What do you mean?"

She blushed and ducked her head again. "I know about sex, Dad. I know what it means that Brianna is your daughter. Did you love her mother?"

David sat for a moment without moving, unsure how much to tell her. "No, Meagan. I didn't love her mother. I barely knew her, and yes, I've asked your mom to forgive me."

She sat back against the couch and met his gaze. "Were you a Christian when it happened?"

He shook his head. "No. I became a Christian a few months later, right after your Mom and I got married."

"Have you asked Jesus to forgive you too?"

"Yes, honey, I have. I knew at the time that what I did was wrong, and I've been sorry for it ever since."

She slowly nodded and pushed herself to her feet. "Okay. I guess if you weren't a Christian and you asked Mom and God to forgive you, then it's okay. But you're sure you still love me as much?"

He stood and gave her a hug, then kissed the tip of her nose. "Yes. Always. I love you, Meagan."

"Okay, Dad, I love you, too. I think I'll see how Brianna's doing." She smiled and waved, leaving David to sink back onto the couch, all thought of returning to his paper forgotten.

Chapter Eleven

"IF YOU FIND OUT ANYTHING ABOUT her extended family, let me know. Yeah . . . thanks." David hung up the phone at work the following day, his brows knit together in concentration. The sound of his partner's footsteps on the concrete outside the door alerted him to Mike's presence right before he stepped into the room. David had been preoccupied and busy most of the day, and this was their first chance to speak privately.

"Is there something I need to know about?" Mike asked.

David glanced up. Mike must have heard the loud sigh he'd released seconds before. He tapped his carpenter's pencil on the desktop. "Nothing to do with the business."

"I don't want to shove my nose in, but if you need help . . ." Mike let the question hang.

"I'd love some input, but I'm not sure if it'd be fair to Susanne if I talk to you." He swiveled around in the rickety office chair.

"No problem. I'm here if you change your mind. Either way, I'll be praying."

"Thanks. The guys are heading home for the day. After they're gone, maybe I could bounce a few things off you."

"Any time." Mike raised a hand on his way back outside.

David sat for a few minutes, listening to the indistinct voices of the guys outside. The familiar smell of stain and paint thinner drifted in from the cabinet shop where Mike was finishing an order. He closed his eyes, clasping his hands behind his head and propping his feet on the desk.

How much should he tell Mike? The man would keep anything he told him confidential. That wasn't the problem. He needed someone to talk to, especially after his call to the caseworker at DSHS. His life had spun out of control the past three days. It felt like it would take a miracle to put it back where it belonged.

The next hour passed quickly as the men swept the floors in the cabinetry room and put equipment away. David and Mike secured the tool room, accounting for everything.

After Neal and Gary headed for their cars, David approached Mike. "You still have a few minutes, or you need to get home?"

"I'm not in a rush. Amy has a women's function at the church. She's leaving dinner in the oven for me. I'm worthless in the kitchen, and she always takes pity on me when she's gone." He chuckled and patted the slight paunch above his belt. "How can I help, Dave?"

He knew he could trust his partner. Mike was older than David and a committed Christian with a solid marriage and two grown kids. He'd moved to the area a couple of years ago and stopped by a job site to introduce himself. It didn't take long before they both knew the Lord had brought them together. Mike had a strong background in interior finish work, an easygoing personality, and was well liked by the building supply owners in the area. With David's knowledge in construction and design, they made the perfect team.

He was grateful when Mike pulled out a new filter and coffee for a fresh pot. Right now, a steaming cup would hit the spot. "I don't know where to start. I got off the phone with DSHS when you came in the office earlier." He sank down on a metal chair.

"DSHS? Are you thinking about taking another foster child?" Mike slid the pot onto its base and flipped the switch, then tipped his chair back and propped his feet on the battered surface of their desk.

"Not exactly. It's a little confusing. Friday evening a girl showed up before I got home from work. She told Susanne she's my daughter and her uncle dropped her off to live with us."

Mike lunged forward, the legs of his chair slamming against the floor. "Your daughter! How old is this girl and what do you know about her? Wait a minute, you said Friday? Wasn't that Susanne's birthday? You had plans for dinner that night."

David had figured this announcement would get a reaction from his normally unflappable partner, and he wasn't disappointed, but the reaction didn't bring any pleasure. "Yeah, and that didn't happen. I got home to an upset wife. All three kids were at her mother's for the night."

"Three. So this girl stayed the night? Was there an adult with her?"

"She stayed the night, and no, there wasn't anyone with her. We don't know a lot yet, except her mom died a couple of months ago and she's been living with a deadbeat uncle since. He's the one who dropped her at our house without a word."

"Nice guy," Mike scowled.

David noticed the full coffee pot and got up to grab two cups. "No kidding. I'd like to tell the guy what I think, but I doubt it'd do much good." He took a gulp of coffee.

"Do you think this girl is trying to put one over on you?"

"I wish that was the case because it would make things a lot simpler. No. There's little doubt in my mind she's my daughter. Even a clerk at a store yesterday saw the resemblance."

Mike leaned forward, whistling softly. "Whew."

"Trust me, I was surprised too."

"Yeah. How's Susanne dealing with it?"

David picked up his mug and took another couple of swallows. The smell of the sawdust in the nearby shop mingled with the strong aroma of coffee. He topped off Mike's cup and set the pot on its base.

"I haven't told you the worst. I was engaged to Susanne at the time I met Vicki, Brianna's mother. Susanne was at college, and Vicki started hitting on me pretty hard. I'm not especially proud of where it led."

Mike gave a low whistle. "Susanne just found out about all this?"

"Yeah. I didn't tell her at the time. I was afraid of losing her. And after I got saved, I went to my pastor. He counseled me to accept God's forgiveness and move forward, as he didn't see any point in hurting Susanne."

Mike frowned. "I can see how he might say that, although coming clean may have been the better choice."

"Yeah. I know that now. I guess I kind of knew it then, too, but it's what I wanted to hear, so I didn't question it. And to be fair, I didn't tell him the entire story."

Mike's eyebrows rose, but he kept quiet.

David shuffled the papers on his desk, then cleared his throat. "Brianna's mom came to our house while I was gone and talked to my mother. Vicki had a pretty bad rep among the guys in our area for sleeping around. Mom thought she picked me because we had a nice house and I had a job, and she turned her away. I'm afraid I didn't help any when I denied the baby might be mine. I didn't believe for a minute that a one-time deal would produce a baby, not when rumor had it Vicki had been around the block with other guys."

"Uh-oh. So you knew the baby might be yours and never mentioned it to Susanne? Does she know?"

David gave a curt nod. "I'm afraid it hasn't helped her image of Christians much. She's blaming me and wasn't too happy with the pastor, even though I assured her he didn't know. Brianna's appearance broadsided her."

"I can see why. It might take time for her to trust you again."

"I know. Right now she's hurt and angry."

Mike rocked back in his chair, his eyebrows scrunched together. "Susanne's a great mother, and she loves kids. Do you think she'll accept this girl?"

"I wish I knew. She's been kind to Brianna, but I can tell she wants to keep her distance emotionally. I don't blame her."

"Susanne goes to church, but how's her relationship with the Lord?"

"Almost nonexistent. I was a new Christian when we married, and I wasn't too concerned about Susanne's spiritual condition. Before long, I discovered she wasn't interested in a life centered around God. In her early teens, she came close to accepting the Lord. The youth pastor had a huge influence on her at the time, but she never took it any further than that."

Mike raised brown-stained fingers, taking off his baseball cap and scratching his head. "That's tough. And now she feels Christians betrayed her. You've got your work cut out for you."

David stretched out his legs, knowing Mike's words were true. Susanne did feel betrayed, and he'd been the cause. The cawing of a crow came through the open window beside him. It sounded like his nerves felt right now—grating, harsh, and under attack. He dropped his hands to his knees and leaned forward.

"I'm praying she'll forgive me, and we can make some sense of this mess. When I called DSHS, they weren't much help. They told me they can't force the uncle to take her and there are no reports of any other family trying to locate her."

"Uh-huh."

"They have a heavy case load and kids with no place to go. They said if she's my daughter, then it's our problem and we need to figure it out."

"Is foster care the place for her?"

"That's the problem—I know it isn't. But I can't see Susanne ever taking Brianna into her heart, either." He shuddered, the image of some foster parents he'd met over the years stark in his mind. Most were kind, generous people, but the system had its small group of "takers," who only cared about the money they'd gain.

"Are you feeling Susanne is the biggest problem, or is part of it that you aren't wanting Brianna?"

"I guess you've nailed it. Susanne is struggling, but frankly, so am I. It's my responsibility, but taking in a teenager right now... I don't know. I believe she's my daughter, but I have no feelings for her." He drummed his fingers on the desktop, his frown deepening the lines between his brows. "I'm no more sure how to deal with this than Susanne is."

Mike cocked his head to one side, his glance direct. "What do you think the Lord wants you to do?"

"I know exactly what He wants, but it's clashing with what Susanne wants, and I'm not that thrilled, either. But I want to do what's right, even if my heart isn't in it."

"I wish I could give you answers, man. You need to pray about it and leave Susanne and yourself in God's hands. If you're willing to let Him guide you, that's a start. Do you think Brianna wants to live with you?"

David was thankful for his partner's support, but he grimaced at the rather pointed questions hitting too close to home. "I have no idea. Meagan's been spending a lot of time with her, but I haven't. Brianna's been kind of quiet, but I guess that's expected. She'd been told for years her dad didn't want her, so that must hurt. I feel sorry for her, but that's about all. Know what I mean?" David set his cup on the table with more force than he realized. This was getting to him. He found himself relating more deeply to what Susanne was feeling.

"I imagine that's normal. I'll pray for you. I wish I could do more, but this needs to be between you and God."

"I appreciate that."

"No problem." Mike stood and stretched, then glanced at the clock on the wall covered with work orders held in place by colorful pins. "Hey, we better head out. Your wife is going to be wondering what's taking so long. You don't want to give her more reason to be upset."

"Right! See you tomorrow." David pushed himself out of the chair, then moved to the sink to wash their cups before leaving the office.

David headed across the gravel parking area toward his truck. He was grateful their business was booming as the influx of windsurfers and Californians moving to the Columbia River Gorge on the eastern edge of the Cascade Mountains increased the need for new homes. Their close proximity to Portland and the international airport had made the area even more attractive, and local contractors were scrambling to keep up.

The sun was staying up a little longer each day, and the air was losing the nippy feeling from earlier in the spring. The sun warmed the trees, coaxing them to release the heady odor that made him long for a hike in the woods.

David drove rapidly on the way home, heeding Mike's warning about not giving his wife more reason to be upset. *God, all I can say right now is help. You're the only One who can bring healing to our family.*

Chapter Twelve

LATER THAT EVENING, THE FAMILY GATHERED in the living room to spend time with Grandfather. He had rested during the day and seemed stronger to Susanne than when he'd arrived. She hadn't allowed the children to disturb him earlier, but his spirits seemed high this evening as he sat on the couch with Steven on one side and Meagan on the other. Brianna kept her distance and lay curled in the corner of the nearby love seat.

"Grandfather, would you tell us a story? Please?" Steven tugged on his great-grandfather's sleeve.

"Tell us one about the little Indian boy who was your grandfather." Meagan tucked her hand through his arm and smiled up into his face.

He chuckled and ruffled Steven's hair, then turned and kissed Meagan's forehead. "I'd love to tell you a story about Little Raven. Let me think of which one you might enjoy."

The room grew hushed while Grandfather sat still, seemingly immersed in the memories of the past. A few moments later, his voice deepened as he began. "Many years ago, there was a boy who lived with his people in the Oregon Territory. One night, when the morning stars were beginning to dim, he made his way to his grandfather's teepee." Rapt faces turned toward him as his story unfolded.

"'Grandfather?' His quiet voice spoke from outside the closed flaps of the teepee, rousing the old man from his sleep.

"'Yes, Little Raven, I'm here.'

"'May I come in and speak to you, Grandfather?'

"The old man smiled. His daughter had done well with this one. He had the markings of a chief... polite but inquisitive, gentle but brave. Yes, he would do well, of that he was certain.

"'Come in.' He spoke quietly, not wanting to awaken the old woman beside him. 'You are up early, Grandson.' He slipped from beneath the buffalo robe and scooted away from the bed. Motioning to the ground on the other side of the smoldering fire, he directed the young boy to sit, then reached for a few small sticks of wood nearby. The nights were no longer as cold. Spring stole softly over this valley, and soon the dogwoods and oak trees would be unfurling their banners and waving them to the sky.

"'I couldn't sleep. I dreamt about the white children and didn't understand. I knew I needed to ask you about it because you are old and wise. Mother says you know more than ten men have known and you have counseled the wisest chiefs.'

"He kept from smiling but decided he would speak to his daughter about the tales she told her son. *But maybe it wasn't such a bad thing, a grandson thinking his grandfather was wise, not such a bad thing at all.*

"'What were you needing help understanding, Little Raven?' He poked the fire with a stick, sending sparks shooting from the pine needles that still clung to the small branches.

"'At the mission school yesterday, I asked the missionary what he does when he isn't teaching us. He said he works at a ... what did he call it?' His small face twisted in a frown and he scratched his head. 'An orphanage. He said it's a place where white children go to live when they don't have a family.'

"Grandfather waited for the young boy to continue.

"'Why do they throw them away?' His voice sounded confused.

"'Explain what you mean, Little Raven.' The man leaned forward toward the fire, pulling his blanket around his shoulders. *My old bones don't stay warm as easily these past few years.*

"'The white children. Why do their families not take care of them as we do? Why do they send them away to a big house and pay a missionary to raise them?'

"Grandfather frowned, but his spirit smiled within him. He would need to think about this for a moment, but not too long or the boy would question his wisdom. 'Hmm. That is a good question. What do you think the answer is?' He'd give the boy a chance to answer first.

"Little Raven shrugged. 'Because they don't want them anymore?'

"'I do not think so, my grandson. The children who live there do not have parents. The parents have died or are lost and have not returned to claim their children. They have no other place to live.'

"'But we take care of our children whose parents have died. Why don't they? The missionary is always telling us that the white man knows more than we do. He says we must learn from them and become like them. Do we have to throw our children away? If Mother and Father died, would you throw me away to an orphanage?' His brows drew together in worry, but Grandfather saw a spark of anger there also.

"*Good*, Grandfather thought.

"'Do not believe everything you are told at the school, Little Raven. Children are precious gifts, and we do not throw them away. If your parents died, I would take you in. If I died, someone else in the tribe would take you into their teepee. No, we do *not* throw our children away. The missionary must be a sad man. He preaches that his God is a God of love, but he must work in a place that proves love has been forgotten by the men around him.'

"Little Raven nodded and rose to go. 'Thank you, Grandfather. I think I'll go back to bed now. I'm glad you won't throw me away.'

"'Sleep well, my grandson.' The old man lay back down, pulling his blanket up over his shoulders. His wife stirred, then asked if all was well.

"'Yes, all is well. Our grandson needed to know he is loved, that is all. Go back to sleep.' He lay close beside her. Though he tried, Grandfather could not return to sleep. A question tugged at his thoughts, keeping him from the peaceful slumber he sought. Was it possible? Would there come a time when his people would throw away their children?"

Silence lay over the room as Grandfather finished the solemn tale. Susanne watched each face, struggling to keep her tumultuous thoughts from showing. Grandfather smiled at Brianna, then turned his gaze toward David and raised his eyebrows, a question shining in the warm brown eyes.

Guilt flickered across David's face. "Kids, you need to thank Grandfather and give him a hug, then get ready for bed." He averted his eyes from the old man.

"Gee, Dad, we wanna hear another story. That one was cool. I'm glad you and Mom don't want to throw us away." Steven's voice snapped Susanne from her thoughts.

"You heard your father. It's time for bed."

"All right." Steven slid to his feet, then reached back for a hug.

Grandfather wrapped his slender arms around the boy and held him for a moment. "We'd never want to throw a child away, my boy. Not you or any other child." He kissed Meagan on the cheek and patted her shoulder as she slipped off the couch, then beckoned to Brianna. "Come give an old man a hug before you go to bed?"

Breathless, Susanne waited, wondering at the girl's reaction. There'd been no real sign of openness since her arrival.

Brianna hesitated only a moment, then uncurled her legs and scooted off the love seat and crossed the short distance to where Grandfather sat. His wrinkled hand grasped her trembling one, then pulled her down beside him and gave her a gentle hug, leaning to whisper something in her ear. The young girl's face transformed as a sweet smile shyly lit her face.

What had Grandfather said? Susanne couldn't help but rejoice that someone had reached Brianna's heart, but a battle stirred in her mind. Of all the stories Grandfather could choose to tell, why that one? A niggling of suspicion arose. Would he interfere in their family if he believed a child's welfare was at stake?

"I'm going to let you two men visit for a while. I'm heading to bed after I get the kids settled." She braced her hands on the arms of the rocker and heaved herself to her feet, feeling much older than her thirty-three years. Right when she thought she had David's agreement in finding an alternative for Brianna, Grandfather showed up. Why hadn't David thought to delay the visit until they had time to decide where Brianna really belonged?

Chapter Thirteen

SUSANNE HAD SPENT THE LAST HOUR at the table, paying bills and balancing the checkbook, while Brianna played in the barn with Smoke's kittens. The phone jarred her and she jumped.

She crossed the living room, sank into the easy chair by the large picture window, and picked up the cordless phone. "Hello?"

"Susanne, honey, where *have* you been? I thought we were having lunch yesterday, but I didn't hear from you." Her friend Jeena's voice sounded over the phone.

With all that had happened in the past few days, Susanne had forgotten the lunch date they'd tentatively scheduled.

"It's been crazy the past few days. I'm sorry I didn't call."

"That's okay, sweetie. What's going on?" she said in the honeyed tone Susanne knew so well.

She might as well share, as her friend would eventually wring it out of her. "Family stuff." Susanne got up and walked across the room to the kitchen, stopping at the window overlooking the pasture and the barn. Thankfully, Brianna wasn't on the way back from playing with the kittens.

"Like what? You and David having problems? The kids aren't old enough to be giving you too much trouble, so it has to be your marriage. Am I right?" The voice on the other end sharpened with interest.

Susanne sighed. Jeena cared about her, but their outlook on life occasionally caused stress. Jeena's dislike of David colored her attitude to the point where Susanne couldn't always trust her friend's judgment.

"It's really nothing I can talk about now."

"All-righty then. Why don't you head down the hill, and we'll go get something to drink and catch up on girl talk, huh? Your mom probably wouldn't mind being at your house when the kids get home, and you can get back in plenty of time before your honey gets there. What d'ya say?"

This might be an opportunity to get her mind off her problems. Susanne looked at the clock. It would be an hour before the bus dropped off the kids and more than three hours before David got home. Maybe Mom wouldn't mind spending time with her grandkids until David got home. Grandfather was taking an afternoon nap, or she'd ask him.

"Okay. Let's do it! I haven't had an afternoon out for too long."

"That's my girl!" Her brisk voice moved into take-charge mode. "I'll meet you in forty-five minutes at Henry's Bar and Grill in Hood River, and it's my treat."

"I'll have to call Mom and make sure she doesn't mind." She hesitated, not sure how much to share. "I have so much to tell you. You have no idea what you're in for."

Jeena's voice sobered. "Now you've *really* got me guessing. Hurry up and call your mom!"

Fifteen minutes later, Claire tapped on the door, then poked her head around the corner and hallooed before coming in the rest of the way. Susanne hadn't heard her car drive up, but the day was sunny and warm, and Mom loved to walk. It was a short distance between houses, and the kids would enjoy it if she decided to walk them home.

"Hi, Mom. I'll be out in a minute," Susanne called from the bathroom.

Makeup might be a good idea, even though she usually saved it for church and going out in the evening. But her ego needed a bit of a boost. Jeena was meticulous about her appearance even if a bit flamboyant in her clothing choices. Susanne didn't want to look like a country mouse sitting across the table from her friend and decided to wear a soft cream blouse and a flowing, calf-length skirt. She applied rose-colored lipstick, blush, mascara, and a touch of perfume, then sailed out of the bathroom and into her mother's waiting gaze.

"My, don't you look pretty." Claire's eyebrows rose. "Not that I don't like it, mind you. I'm just a bit more used to seeing you in work clothes, your hair pulled back, and not much makeup. You really should wear your hair down that way more often, dear. It's very becoming."

"Thanks, Mom."

With a short wave, Susanne headed to her car, climbed in, and pulled on her seatbelt before turning the key. She drove down toward town without any of her normal appreciation for the beauty of the countryside.

Susanne took a deep breath and scolded herself for feeling anxious about seeing Jeena. She'd met her friend three years ago while visiting Doris, an elderly woman at a private nursing home where Jeena's grandmother Emma lived. The two younger women met in the dining room when Emma introduced Jeena to Doris and Susanne. The friendship had grown and blossomed as their love for the two older women continued to draw them together.

Susanne wanted someone to talk to but dreaded being caught in the middle between her husband and her friend. Jeena was warm and caring and had gone out of her way more than once when Susanne was sick or needed help with a special project, but she didn't agree with David's philosophy of life, especially the religious part. Sure, Susanne felt hurt and confused and a part of her wanted to vent. But the other part wanted to be loyal and not hear anything against David.

He'd never been controlling, Susanne had to give him that. He didn't care for the friendship between the two women, but wouldn't try to force her to stop seeing Jeena, although it had been an area of contention over the last couple of years.

She remembered one time in particular when they'd agreed to meet for an evening. Susanne didn't intend to drink, but Jeena loved her wine and kept urging Susanne to have one more glass. She and David were experiencing a short spurt of stress in their finances, and it didn't take much for Susanne to give in. Two drinks led to three, and before she knew it, she'd had a few too many.

David was waiting up when she got home. At first, he'd admitted to being frightened nearly out of his wits. He'd called the police and every hospital within miles for accident reports. When she'd stumbled in the door, his fear turned to anger. How dare she worry him and the kids? Why hadn't she called?

It took more energy to explain than she felt capable of, so she'd waved him off and wobbled her way to bed, barely getting undressed before falling asleep. The next day, they scarcely spoke, and both avoided the subject. David was too proud to bring it up again, and she was too angry to apologize.

Besides, why should she? She was a grown woman and should be able to take a drink if she wanted to. It was rare that she went over the edge. The last time it had happened, Susanne knew she should've called David so he wouldn't worry. She wouldn't make that mistake again.

Susanne hoped Mom wouldn't tell David who she was seeing. Not that she'd hide it from him if he asked—she wouldn't be dishonest—but there was no need to wave a red flag in front of a bull. She'd make sure she arrived home first, and all would be well. If she *did* stay a bit late for some reason, what right did David have to talk after recent events? He was late on her birthday and had kept secrets that were now impacting their lives, not to mention inviting Grandfather to stay for an indefinite amount of time in the middle of this turmoil.

By the time Susanne turned into the parking lot of Henry's Bar and Grill, she felt better about meeting Jeena and not a little irritated at David. She might make it home to fix dinner, or she might not. She'd have to see how the afternoon shaped up.

Jeena stepped out of her BMW when Susanne pulled in. Susanne looked with longing at the car, then patted the steering wheel of her trusty Subaru Outback and sighed, envisioning cramming their family and a full load of groceries into her friend's sporty car. Single and a successful interior designer, Jeena was currently under contract to design and decorate a multi-million-dollar complex of townhouses and would receive a hefty commission from the job.

"Susie!" Jeena grabbed her around the waist and hugged her.

Susanne wasn't overly fond of the nickname but had quit trying to fight her friend over it.

"Hey, you're looking great! What's it been, two weeks?" Susanne hugged her friend again. They had a lot of catching up to do.

"At least. Let's find a good booth before the place fills up." Jeena grabbed Susanne's hand and tugged her across the parking lot, giggling as she went.

"Hey, slow down. What's the rush?" Susanne laughed.

"I want to hear all your juicy gossip, that's what. So get a move on, girl!" Jeena said with a grin.

As they entered the restaurant/bar, Susanne studied her friend. Nothing about Jeena was conventional. She looked as colorful as a prize-winning peacock and certainly stood out in a crowd. She could pull off any outfit she chose to wear, and her perfect figure, dark hair that cascaded over her shoulders, and almond eyes would be the envy of any model. Susanne always felt a bit small and insignificant beside her, but Jeena's vibrant personality normally snapped her out of that.

The hostess seated them quickly when she recognized Jeena as one of their regulars. Henry's was a hot spot in this area, pulling in locals and tourists alike.

A minute or two after the hostess seated them, the waitress appeared at their side. "I'll have a glass of white wine, Lacey," Jeena instructed the brunette.

"Just a soda, thanks." Susanne smiled at the girl.

Jeena shook her head, but Susanne was determined not to repeat her past performance.

"Spill it, girl. What's going on? Are you and David splitting up?" Jeena leaned forward, her hair framing her face.

"Jeena! Of course not! I love David, and I'm not planning on leaving him."

"How about you start from the beginning, hon?" Jeena leaned across the table and lowered her voice. "I think you need a real drink. In fact, I stumbled across a new martini that you *have* to try."

Susanne started to shake her head, but Jeena reached out a hand to stop her. "Now, Susie, David isn't going to come running in to stop you."

"I may be upset with him, but I'm not worried about what David thinks. I don't want a drink, that's all."

"Then one drink isn't going to hurt, right?"

Susanne glanced around the room, her eyes searching for Lacey. "Maybe I'll have one glass of wine. I guess I didn't realize till now that I could use one."

After her drink arrived, Susanne took a sip and closed her eyes for a moment. "It's been such a mixed-up week, and I'm so confused."

Jeena leaned forward. "I'm listening, honey."

Susanne smiled her appreciation, then took a deep breath.

"My birthday was on Friday, and we had an unexpected 'present' show up at our door."

"Someone dump a stray dog or cat?" Jeena smiled and cocked an eyebrow.

Susanne set down her glass, running her fingertip around the rim for a minute. "Worse. A teenager."

Jeena's casual look disappeared, and she sat straight up, shock chasing across her face. "What? Someone left a kid at your house? Did you call the cops?"

"No, not after we heard her story. She's a teenager and resembles David." She heard Jeena suck in her breath and knew she'd shocked her friend.

Compassion warred with humor in Jeena's eyes. "Holier-than-thou David? He has a child you didn't know about? That's too much!" Her voice rose, attracting curious eyes. "Oops, sorry about that," she whispered. "I'll shut up. Go ahead and tell your story." She lifted her glass of wine, and the light glinted off the large amethyst ring on her manicured hand.

Susanne picked up her glass, drained it quickly, and set it down with a thump. "Her name is Brianna, and her good-for-nothing uncle dumped her at our door without even coming to the door. He tore out of there, leaving her to explain. She brought a letter from her mother stating David is her dad."

At the small shake of Susanne's head, Jeena's eyes widened. "You didn't keep her, did you? It's got to be a scam. I can't believe this!" She clapped her hand over her mouth as Susanne signaled that her voice was rising again.

"If you saw how much she looks like David, you wouldn't think it was a scam. Besides, David admitted he slept with her mother while we were engaged."

"While you were *engaged*?" Jeena reached across and patted Susanne's clenched hand lying on the table. "That's rough. Kind of makes his Christianity sound phony, doesn't it, hon?"

Susanne winced. It hadn't been long since she'd had the same thought, but it sounded bleaker somehow coming from Jeena.

Jeena leaned back and crossed her arms, eyes narrowed. "You aren't going to believe her without proof, are you? I'll bet her mother's lurking in the background waiting to ask for money."

"It never occurred to me someone might be trying to get money. She said her mother is dead. We didn't question that. She's a kid, you know? And she hasn't been a bit of trouble." Susanne knew she was trying to convince herself as doubt seeped into her mind.

"You poor thing. Of course I realize it might not be her fault. But her mother might not be dead at all!" Sympathy laced Jeena's voice. "What I don't get is why your husband"—she drew out the word—"would put you and the kids through this. Can't he see through this charade?"

"David would never intentionally do anything to hurt us."

Jeena toyed with the large ring on her hand, then raised her eyes to Susanne. "He slept with her mother behind your back. That sure sounds intentional to me." A shadow of the past from an old sorrow seemed to trickle through Jeena's tight words.

"I know. I'm having a hard time getting past it. He said he's sorry and wishes he hadn't lied. If he'd just told me the truth. But he thought I'd dump him, and he didn't want to lose me."

"It's too little, too late, if you ask me." Jeena softened her tone as Susanne shifted in her seat. "I'm sorry, Susie, but I'm having a hard time understanding why he's letting that girl stay in your home. She has family, whether her mother is alive or not. Who knows. Maybe 'Mom' wanted to get rid of the kid. It happens every day, as you well know."

Susanne knew Jeena was right. Parents threw their kids away all the time, and sometimes they left with the kids having no idea where they'd gone. Was that the case this time? Were Brianna's mother and uncle trying to get rid of their responsibility? No demands for money had come, but not many days had passed. They could be waiting, hoping the family would learn to care for the girl and not want to give her up. The possibilities were endless and left Susanne feeling sick to her stomach. Maybe one martini *would* help steady her nerves and help her to think.

This time Susanne signaled the waitress. "Lacey, do you suppose you could bring me a martini? Jeena had a new one the other night she wants me to try."

Jeena supplied the name, and the young woman hurried off to fill her request.

"I'm worried about you. You're too nice of a person, and I don't want to see you taken advantage of. It doesn't sound like David is thinking clearly." Jeena tapped a long finger on her glass and raised world-worn eyes to Susanne's. "You seem pretty forgiving toward him."

"I haven't forgiven David at all. We're speaking, but out of politeness and for the kids' sake."

Jeena simply raised her brows and waited.

"I was furious the night Brianna came. David betrayed my trust when he slept with some girl while we were engaged. I was terrified he might've continued seeing her after we married. I keep wondering what else he hasn't told me. That was bad enough, but to have an old girlfriend's daughter dumped on our doorstep"— she shook her head—"was too much. It didn't help that she looks so much like him. I know it isn't Brianna's fault, but it's hard looking at her. I suppose I need to get over it and move on."

"Get over it?" Jeena's voice held a hard edge. "You don't know a thing about this girl. A lot of kids that end up in foster care have behavior problems you'd rather not deal with. You need to let a professional take care of this. Besides, how do you know she doesn't use drugs and won't try to hook Steven or Meagan?"

Susanne's face paled, and her trembling fingers covered her lips.

"I see that shocks you." Jeena's tone deepened. "You of all people know what kind of life some of these kids live. You told me that's why you never took in older girls. Your two need to come first. How old is she, anyway?"

"She'll be fourteen next month," Susanne all but whispered. Her shaking hand reached for her martini, and she took another sip, willing herself to calm down.

Jeena cocked her head to one side, drumming her fingers on the table. "Okay. That makes her three years older than Meagan and six years older than Steven. She could teach them all sorts of things. I'm not telling you what to do, but maybe you need to consider David taking his 'daughter' and moving out for a while . . . at least until this gets sorted out."

"I don't know. That seems a little extreme. He lied to me about his past, but I think he's being honest now, and he's told me how sorry he is that it happened."

"Or so he says," Jeena shot back before she signaled Lacey to bring another round of martinis.

"I probably should get home. It's getting kind of late," Susanne remarked a couple of hours later. "I know what you're thinking—why should I care? Right now, I agree. But I don't want my kids to worry. Maybe I should call and let Mom know I'm okay. Then they won't worry if we stay and talk a while longer."

"All I ask is you don't let David push you around. For heaven's sake, you're a grown woman. If you want to sit and visit with a friend, why shouldn't you?" Jeena tapped her long fingernail on the rim of her glass and frowned across the table.

Susanne shook her head sharply. "Don't worry, I won't. I have a lot of thinking to do, and I'm not ready to go home."

At Jeena's nod of acceptance, Susanne slid from the booth, wanting some privacy.

"I'll be right back." She headed across the room with a determined step. Jeena was right. David had no business telling her how to live her life. She wasn't ready to leave him, but her emotions were too jumbled to set Jeena straight. She'd been pushing pretty hard tonight, but Susanne didn't want to argue about it. The coming confrontation with David would be enough.

The phone only rang once. "David, it's me."

"I've been trying to call you for the last hour. Why haven't you answered your phone?"

"I had it in my purse and didn't hear it ring. It's a little noisy here. The kids are okay, aren't they? Nothing's wrong?"

His voice rose a notch. "Do you realize what time it is? Where are you? I've been worried sick. Your mom told me you were running into town, but you planned on being home in time to fix dinner."

Susanne tried to focus on her watch, but the hour hand wouldn't hold still. She shook her head in an effort to clear it and looked again. Still no good. "No, what time is it? You'd better lower your voice because if it's as late as you're acting, the kids are probably sleeping and you'll wake them up, yelling like that."

"You've been drinking, haven't you?" His voice dropped to a growl.

She leaned against the wall, feeling the need of support. "What if I have?"

"Are you with Jeena?"

"It's none of your business, David. You have your life, including the part of it living in our home right now, and I have mine. If I choose to spend an evening with a friend, deal with it, okay? I'll be home later. I didn't want the kids to worry, but if I'd realized they were in bed, I wouldn't have bothered."

He started to reply, but she clicked off her phone.

She didn't have the emotional energy to do battle with him tonight. She'd have one more glass of wine and then go home. Maybe she'd get lucky, and he'd be asleep. Better yet, she'd sleep on the couch and make sure she got up before the kids.

She made her way through the noisy room to their table. The two women continued to talk, and Susanne lost track of the time. Her thoughts couldn't focus, and her emotions were turbulent. She'd begun to accept the possibility of Brianna staying for a few days. Now serious doubts about the wisdom of that decision swirled in her mind. Jeena's questions seemed valid, and somehow, Susanne needed to find the answers.

A couple of hours later, the two women headed to their cars. "I'm driving you home." Jeena opened the door of Susanne's car and held out her hand for the keys.

Susanne shook her head, but uncertainty tinged her voice. "I think I'm okay. Besides, it's almost ten miles, and you're tired too."

"Nope. Nothing doin'. Get in the other side, darlin'. Little Jeena is driving you home. You've had more to drink tonight than I have. No way do I want you getting in a wreck." Jeena waved Susanne away, keeping her hip firmly planted against the driver's door till Susanne slid into the passenger seat.

"What about your car? How are you getting home?"

Jeena held up her cell phone with a grin. "That's what Uber is for. Just a sec, and I'll see if someone can can follow us to your house and bring me back."

Susanne groaned. "But that's expensive!"

"Hey, what're friends for?" Jeena grinned.

"I'm sorry for the hassle. I know better than to drink so much when I'm not used to it. But you're right. Things are spinning a bit, and I don't think I'd be safe driving."

A few minutes later, an Uber driver pulled up and they hit the road, with only the sound of Jeena's soft alto voice singing along with the classic rock tune on the radio.

Susanne slipped into a light doze on the way home and woke up to Jeena gently shaking her shoulder. "Come on, Susie, wake up. You're home. Do you want me to go in with you?"

Susanne leaned against the door, feeling drained. "No. I'll be fine." She wanted to go in, crawl in her bed, and sleep for twenty-four hours. If she didn't wake up for a week, so much the better. Maybe this predicament would straighten itself out by then, and she wouldn't have to deal with it.

"Are you sure? You might need me to sneak you in the house." Jeena softened the words with a chuckle.

The question snapped Susanne out of her lethargy. The alcohol had lost some of its grip, and things were starting to come into focus. She needed time to herself, time to think. "No. David will probably be awake, and he's not going to be happy. You don't need to get caught in the middle of a fight."

"You mean have the fight aimed at me, don't you, sugar? I'm aware he doesn't like me." Her mouth pulled down into a frown. "You think about some of the things I said, you hear? If you decide you've had enough, I have a spare room, and you're welcome anytime."

"Thanks. I appreciate the offer, but I won't leave. I can't do that to my kids." She gave Jeena a quick hug before slipping out the door. She waved and headed toward the house, waiting to go in until Jeena had turned around and driven down the driveway.

Susanne didn't feel strong enough to find the answers to all the questions right now, and she didn't trust David to find them, either. Why was she being punished? Couldn't she have a normal life like Jeena and not have to go through all this stress?

Nothing seemed to make sense. Jeena's urging her to get some space didn't feel right, either. Gratitude flooded through Susanne that she hadn't mentioned anything to Jeena about David knowing about the baby. She'd never explain that to her suspicious friend. It was hard enough swallowing it herself. Moving to a desert island sounded mighty attractive, but the couch would have to do.

Chapter Fourteen

THE FOLLOWING MORNING, SUSANNE WOKE UP in her own room to a quiet house. She wanted to snuggle under the covers and go back to sleep, but a glance at the clock told her it was already mid-morning. David had thrown back the covers on his side of the bed, and the sheets were cold. She struggled to sit up in bed, running her fingers through her tousled hair, commanding her mind to recall what had happened when she'd walked into the house last night.

Her head hammered like a maniac dentist with a runaway drill, and she flopped back on her pillow, groaning in pain. She'd have to make her way to the bathroom and take a couple of aspirin, but something nagged at her mind that needed attention, and it was important she focus.

She remembered being surprised David wasn't up, feeling a sense of relief that she could creep to the bathroom, then fall into bed without facing angry accusations. She'd found the note he left in the bathroom and read it through twice, willing her addled brain to take in what it said.

What was it about the kids? Oh yes, he'd let Meagan and Steven stay at Mom's for the night. They didn't know anything about Susanne staying out late, and he didn't want them to worry. Her mom would see that they got ready for school and caught the bus on time.

Why didn't Brianna stay the night at Mom's? Something about wanting to be here in the morning to play with the kittens. David had told Brianna it was all right, but she would need to get her own breakfast, visit with Grandfather, and let Susanne sleep in. He closed the note by telling her he would be home early today and wanted to talk.

Great. Just what I don't need—another fight with David. Can't he leave it alone? He'd better not try judging me after what he's done. Her head screamed, her stomach was upset, and she did not look forward to this day.

When she'd realized he wasn't waiting up, she'd tiptoed to their door and peeked in. The room was silent. Susanne didn't know if he was asleep or if anger caused him to pretend. Either way, she decided to use the hall bathroom, then crawl into their bed and take her chances. The couch didn't look all that tempting, now that she was home.

Guilt about last night sifted in, but this time there was more. Confusion joined forces with the guilt. She had so many questions, things she needed to sort out. The night out with Jeena hadn't helped at all. She was no further along than the day Brianna had come to their door.

She swung her legs over the bed and winced, then headed to the bathroom, intent on clearing her brain. Her steps slowed, and she came to a halt, freezing in the middle of the room. A memory from last night surfaced. She'd been tiptoeing to the hall bathroom, not wanting to wake David. Brianna had come out of the bathroom and turned to go down the hall to her room.

A picture of the dimly lit hallway sprang into Susanne's mind. She'd tried to be quiet but hadn't been doing a good job of it. She'd stubbed her bare toe and yelped.

Brianna had jumped at the noise, then frozen. "Susanne, is that you? I didn't hear you come in." Her frightened voice had penetrated the haze covering Susanne's mind.

"I didn't mean to startle you." She'd moved in close to the girl, breathing a bit heavier as she stumbled on the bare floor. Why weren't her feet working properly? She was exhausted and needed to get to bed.

Brianna's eyes widened, and she'd stared at Susanne's face in the light of the open bathroom door. "Have you been drinking?"

"Just a little, but it's no big deal." Susanne leaned against the wall for support.

Brianna pulled back a couple of steps. "I... I... I need to get to bed." She'd rushed into her room and closed the door with a sharp click.

What was wrong with the girl? She'd looked terrified. They'd only spoken a few words, so there was no reason for that behavior. Susanne had finished up in the bathroom, slipped into her side of the bed, and forgotten her questions, drifting off to sleep a few minutes later.

Now she stood in front of the mirror, downing three aspirin. What had frightened Brianna? Surely she'd seen her share of drinking, especially the past year she and her mother lived with her uncle. Didn't the letter mention his drinking? A niggling thought dawned. Maybe his drinking had caused her reaction. It was one more question she'd like to have answered.

She showered, dressed, and felt almost ready to tackle the day. Susanne checked the house, then headed to Grandfather's apartment, looking for Brianna.

She rapped lightly on the door at the top of the steps, worried she might wake him.

Grandfather flung open the door and waved her in. "Susanne, you don't have to knock."

Susanne stepped through the door and gave him a quick hug. "It's your house while you're here, and I thought you might be sleeping."

"No, I've been up for a while now—didn't sleep too well last night." The brown eyes peered at her from under bushy brows.

Susanne's heart sank. Of course he'd heard the car pull into the garage last night. "I'm sorry. I didn't mean to wake you."

"Oh, you didn't wake me. I'm afraid I didn't fall asleep till after you returned."

She stifled a small groan and shook her head, trying to hide her embarrassment. "I wasn't thinking."

To his credit, he didn't comment. Instead he placed his hand around her shoulder, drawing her close. "Is there anything I can do to help?"

She shook her head and tried to smile. "No. Really. I'm fine, I went out with a girlfriend last night and stayed out too late. I'm sorry I worried you."

"That's not what I meant. I don't want to pry, and your marriage and personal life are not my business. But I love you and David and would hate to see anything come between the two of you."

"We're fine." She bit her lip, sure he could see through the flippant remark, but he didn't pursue it. "Thank you for caring. I came up to see if Brianna was visiting you. She's not in the house."

"She was here for earlier but said something about visiting the kittens in the barn. I'm sure you'll find her there." He gave her a quick hug, then stepped back. "I'm praying for you. Not just for you, but for your entire family and for that lost little girl who's found her way to your home."

"Thank you." Susanne couldn't think of anything more to say and reached for the door knob. "I'd better go check on Brianna. Would you like to join us for lunch?"

"Sure, I'll do that."

She hurried down the stairs and trotted across the yard, intent on escaping and getting to the barn. Grandfather's wise old eyes saw more than she cared to have seen.

She reached the barn and slowed her pace. "Brianna?" She didn't want to startle the girl. "Are you in here?" The hinges on the barn door squeaked. One of the kittens bolted out of the stall. Susanne leaned over and snagged him as he dashed by. She snuggled his soft body under her chin, glad for the warmth and comfort of this small creature.

She slid open the door of the stall, thankful the track moved easily. The fragrant smell brought back memories of working with David to bring in the hay. She shook off the image, then stopped a moment and allowed her eyes to adjust in the dim light. A movement in the corner caught her attention. Brianna sat curled on a bale of hay shoved against the wall, staring at Susanne.

"Brianna, why didn't you answer me? I was worried."

The girl shrunk closer to the wall.

"What's wrong?"

Brianna shook her head and showed no inclination to get up from her place in the corner.

"You can tell me. I'm not going to hurt you."

"You scared me last night." The whisper was barely loud enough to reach Susanne's ears. Brianna clutched one of the kittens like a man struggling to hold on to a lifeline.

Susanne searched her memory for anything else that had happened last night that she hadn't recalled. "How did I scare you? I spoke to you for less than a minute, and you went back to bed."

"My uncle used to drink, and when he drank, he got mean." Brianna shifted her weight on the hay, causing small flakes to drift around her feet.

Susanne set the kitten she'd been holding on the floor and it scampered around the corner of a nearby stall. "He got mean? What did he do?"

"I don't want to talk about it." Her face set in stubborn lines, shutting down in a way becoming familiar to Susanne.

"I'm sorry I startled you when I came in, but I don't see why you'd be frightened. I wish you'd tell me more about your uncle." Susanne took a step closer to the girl.

Brianna shook her head, her gaze dropping as she swiveled

around.

"Do you want to stay here for a while and play with the kittens?" At Brianna's slight nod, Susanne turned with a sigh. "Come up to the house when you're ready. I'll be fixing lunch in an hour or so."

On the walk back to the house, Susanne barely registered the sights and sounds around her. Normally reveling in the song of the birds visiting their feeders and the sight of her horses grazing in the pasture, she trudged ahead, her mind seeking an answer to this newest problem.

Brianna's fear seemed out of proportion to the incident that caused it. Why wouldn't she discuss it? She mentioned her uncle being a mean drunk. Could the man have abused the girl after her mother died? Worse yet, did the mother know and not do anything to stop it?

After Jeena's suggestions, it was hard to know how much of Brianna's story she could believe. Somehow, she doubted that at one in the morning the girl could stage such a convincing act. How much of Brianna's story was true, Susanne wasn't sure, but one thing was certain—her fear last night had been real, and it made Susanne sick to her stomach. She'd never frightened a child before, and it shamed her to think of it. A few of the doubts Jeena had stirred were losing their strength. What secrets did the girl harbor, and would she ever trust Susanne and David enough to reveal them?

Chapter Fifteen

DAVID HAD NO IDEA WHAT TO say to Susanne when he got home. He would try to arrive before the kids got off the bus. Grandfather always took a nap in the afternoon, then watched TV till dinnertime. Their discussion needed to be private.

He hadn't felt so discouraged in a long time. The recent addition to their family combined with Susanne's hurt over his hiding the truth had added strain to their already struggling marriage. Susanne's choice to drink last night hadn't helped either, although he was grateful she'd called.

He'd faked being asleep when she got home. No way did he want to discuss her behavior at one o'clock in the morning or wake Brianna with an argument.

When he'd gotten home yesterday, David had planned to talk to Susanne about his phone call to DSHS, but that hadn't happened. Now he wasn't sure he wanted to bring it up. And to make life more complicated, his latest construction project was becoming a nightmare.

When he and Susanne had first met, she'd talked about almost accepting Jesus in junior high. Could he help her return to that relationship? He'd been praying for his wife for years, but now his behavior had sent any forward progress reeling backward. Besides, Susanne wanted to live life her way. True, she'd had more motivation for her actions last night than usual, and he knew some of the blame rested with him. But could he help her see that drinking would only succeed in driving them further apart?

At two o'clock, David stopped work for the day. He couldn't concentrate on the intricacies of the plans anyway, so better to quit than make a mistake. "Hey, Mike, I'm heading home," he called up to his partner working on the second-floor joists.

Mike quit hammering and leaned over, keeping a grip on the beam where he perched. "Everything okay?"

"Just things I need to sort out at home. I'll make mistakes if I stay." David tossed his saw in the box at the foot of the ladder and hung his tool belt on a nail.

"No problem. We've got it covered. Remember, man, it belongs to God. Your wife, your kids, all of it."

"Thanks. I appreciate handling things the rest of the day." He strode to his car, his mind already working on the problems at home.

The drive home was a blur. He kept envisioning Susanne hurting over his betrayal and downing glasses of wine. His grief over his wife turned to anger at her friend. Why couldn't Susanne take his advice and stay away from that woman? Jeena instigated this behavior, and Susanne needed to realize it.

He'd never trusted Jeena. He suspected the evening of "girl talk" was a ploy to drive a wedge between him and Susanne. Jeena thought he was too religious and considered himself better than people like her. David didn't think he tried to control his wife's behavior, but Jeena disagreed. She'd rejoice if something destroyed their marriage.

Before he realized it, he'd pulled into their driveway. He dashed off a prayer, fumbling with the door handle of the pickup. He pushed the door open and slammed it behind him, then strode toward the house and the wife who waited inside.

Susanne watched David's truck pull to a stop—she dreaded the coming confrontation. It was too beautiful a day to deal with this mess. The kids weren't home from school yet, and the last thing she needed was David coming home and ruining her day.

Grandfather had taken Brianna for a walk a few minutes ago, and Susanne had looked forward to an hour alone.

"Susanne, you home?"

She could hear the tight control in David's voice. He walked into the family room, where she sat on the couch.

"I'm here. Did you think I'd be gone again?" She knew she shouldn't taunt him, but his stormy look set her nerves on edge.

"I have no idea what to think," he said, stopping in front of her.

"Well, it's nice to see you too." She pulled her legs under her and gathered a couch pillow into her arms.

"I'm sorry. I didn't mean to snap. Guess I'm kind of worried after the last few days."

"Yeah, well that makes two of us."

"I'm glad you called last night. I'm sorry you felt you had to go out drinking with Jeena to deal with the pressure."

She wished he'd sit down, not stand there towering above her. "Just once I wish you wouldn't judge me. Try to accept and love me for who I am, not for what you want me to be," she shot back, her head high.

"You don't think I accept you or love you for who you are?" Shock edged his voice.

"No, I don't. You're always trying to change me, wanting me to meet your standards. Well, I can't. I'm not perfect, and I never will be."

"I don't want you to be perfect. I just wish you wouldn't drink."

The pleading tone in his voice didn't move her. "No, that isn't all you wish, and you know it. You want me to stop seeing Jeena and become a model church wife." She smacked her fist into the pillow. "Oh yes, and to take in your illegitimate daughter and be happy about it."

"Is that really the way you see me?" David dropped his hands to his side and took a step back.

Her eyebrows rose, and she cocked her head to the side, meeting his look. "Pretty much."

"But I'm not trying to change you, and I don't expect perfection."

At her snort of disbelief, he held up his hand. "You're right. I don't particularly like Jeena, and I wish you wouldn't spend so much time with her. I think she's a huge factor in your decision to drink."

She scowled. "I'm a big girl and perfectly capable of choosing my own friends. No one forces me to drink. It's my choice, so don't blame her."

She watched his expression of doubt increase and shook her head. "I'm an adult, David, and you're not treating me like one. I want to live my own life and not be told what to do."

"Even if it drives us apart?" He sank to a seat at the far end of the couch.

"You're one to talk. If anything will drive us apart, it's the truth you've hidden from me all these years. Don't start preaching about drinking. You lost that right when you hid your past. Besides, the drinking isn't the main problem. It's the Christian expectations you impose. They aren't me."

"You're right. We have deeper issues to deal with than what happened last night, and most of those are my fault."

She sighed, putting a hand over her eyes and dropping her head. "Yes, they are. I'm not perfect, but neither are you. You make me feel like I can't do anything right."

David shifted his weight and cleared his throat. "I haven't meant to, and I'm sorry. Any changes you make should be because it's what you want, not to please me. My biggest worry is the kids. When you drink, you're sullen and argumentative. I realize they've been in bed or at your Mom's the last few times you've been drinking. But what if they were up and saw you? You could easily scare them without realizing it."

Her lips parted, and she shook her head. "Like I'd ever do anything to hurt them."

Images of Brianna's face in the hallway last night and the girl cowering in the barn today hit her again. Would she scare her own kids? Surely not.

"Not intentionally, no," David said.

"That's not the issue right now. At least not the most important one. We need to make some decisions about Brianna. She says her mother is dead and her uncle doesn't want her, but how do we know that's true? They could be working a con to get money." Part of her felt foolish. Jeena's argument didn't seem as strong today.

His expression turned from apologetic to disbelieving. "You're kidding."

"Don't decide until you hear me out. People pull scams all the time. You can't trust everybody and certainly not strangers. How do we know her mom didn't put her up to this?"

The howl of a dog from a neighboring property floated through the window, a haunting sound that echoed through the room. Susanne shivered.

David shoved up from his seat, giving a snort of disgust. "I'm sorry, but I don't buy it. You heard Brianna talk about her mother dying. She's spoken to Meagan about it, too. It's possible the uncle might be hoping to gain something. But I don't believe Brianna's mom is still alive."

"Maybe not. But you didn't check anything out. You took in a total stranger with no regard to your family, and I don't appreciate it."

"I called DSHS yesterday and planned on telling you about it last night, but you weren't home." He stood a few feet away, legs spread like a boxer protecting his corner.

Susanne didn't know what to say. Shame flooded her. She'd gone out with Jeena, dealing with her stress by having too much to drink. Was the solution to this mess drowning it in alcohol? She knew it wasn't, but she couldn't admit that to David.

"When did you call them?"

"Before I left work yesterday."

"Do you mind telling me what they said?"

He seemed to relax, the crossed arms dropped to his side. "I asked if any relatives have contacted them about Brianna, then asked what they suggest."

"And?"

"No one's called them about her, and they didn't offer much help after discovering I'm her father. They pretty much told me it's my problem and to deal with it."

"You didn't ask them to check out her uncle or verify her mother's death?"

"I didn't suspect her mother's death, and I still don't. As for the uncle, we know he exists. He hasn't contacted us, and until he does, I don't see what the authorities can do. I suppose we could try to force him to take her back." He stepped to the end of the couch and perched on the armrest farthest from her.

Susanne shook her head. "She's afraid of him. She mentioned it today. I don't think she'd want to go back to him, and I'm not sure it's the best idea." She knew Brianna's fear of the man was real.

"So what do you suggest?"

Her shoulders slumped, and her head fell against the couch. "I don't know. There isn't much we *can* do right now. Call a truce between us and wait to see what happens? I still think we'll hear from her uncle, if not her mother, and we'd better be prepared. I have a feeling that man is no good. He won't hesitate to do whatever he thinks will gain him the most."

"Are you suggesting we keep Brianna for a while? How long are you thinking? And can you deal with that?"

Susanne met his eyes. "We don't have a lot of choices at the moment if DSHS won't get involved. We need to keep our options open, though. I'm not ready to make a permanent commitment, even though I do feel sorry for her. I'll be kind to her if that's what you're worried about. She seems like a good kid, and I know she's the innocent victim here." Susanne sighed and stood, tossing the pillow on the couch.

David drew back with a frown. "I appreciate the truce—I hate being at odds with you. I know you care about kids and you'll be kind to Brianna. I've never tried to push you for a long-term commitment, but we need to give her a chance."

"I'll treat her as I would any child. One other thing. I won't be going to church this Sunday, and I'll keep Brianna with me. I'm not up to the disapproval or the questions people will ask. I don't think Brianna is, either. You can take Steven and Meagan and Grandfather. I'm staying home."

"I don't think people at our church are like that."

"I have no intention of finding out. I'm staying home."

Her chin lifted, and she spun on her heel, walking past him toward the kitchen. "The kids' bus will be here any minute," she shot over her shoulder. "Grandfather and Brianna should be back from their walk soon, and I need to think about dinner."

The argument with David hurt. She knew her attitude hadn't been the best, but she longed for David's support and understanding. Her heart felt raw from the emotions that had pulled it in so many directions the past few days. The feeling of betrayal that struck her when she looked in the girl's eyes seemed to have erected a wall she couldn't remove, even if she tried. And somehow, she wanted to try. She shook herself. It wasn't her problem. This wasn't her daughter. Her two children were the ones that mattered, and they had to come first.

Chapter Sixteen

EARLY THE NEXT MORNING, SUSANNE RINSED her coffee cup and put on her old tennis shoes, intent on getting a bit of work done before Brianna woke. So many problems and not enough in the way of solutions. She'd almost slept in but had forced herself to climb out of bed.

Why couldn't Grandfather watch the TV in his apartment at night instead of in the house? Due to his diminished hearing, the volume got cranked up as soon as he sat down to watch. No wonder he liked to sleep so late. Staying up to watch the late-night shows until one in the morning every night would probably flatten a younger man. David hated to talk to him about it, and she had to agree. He'd be embarrassed that he'd kept them awake. However, something would have to be done if it continued many more nights.

She shook off her irritation and headed for the aspirin again. In spite of Grandfather's nocturnal habits, she loved the man who'd embraced her as his own. This morning, he was the least of her problems.

David felt the responsibility of talking to Brianna was his, but Susanne couldn't shake the sense of shame she'd experienced over the scare she'd given the girl. Brianna had avoided Susanne yesterday and spent most of the day with Meagan. Did the encounter in the hallway still bother her? Maybe she needed to address that first.

Last night, another incident had occurred. Nearly asleep, Susanne heard a noise coming from Brianna's room. She slipped out of bed, not wanting to wake David. Muffled sobs drifted into the hall. Susanne pushed open the door, going to stand at the foot of Brianna's bed.

"Brianna, are you okay?"

A full moon cast its soft light through the window, giving the form on the bed an ethereal look. The sobbing stopped, and the movement on the bed stilled. "I'm fine."

"I heard you crying. Are you sure you're okay?"

"I just miss Mama." A hiccup accompanied the words, giving lie to her earlier assertion and reminding Susanne of the sobs.

Susanne had been at a loss. She'd doubted Brianna's honesty a day or so earlier, but would a girl her age cry in the night to convince someone of her mother's death? Susanne felt ashamed for doubting Brianna's grief and helpless to console her in it. She didn't remember what weak platitude she'd offered before telling Brianna good night, although she'd stepped to the bed and patted the girl's shoulder. Somehow she knew Brianna wouldn't accept more. She'd climbed back in her own bed, trying to block the waves of remorse that washed over her.

The weather was warming, the days were getting longer, and May was ending. She surveyed the yard with satisfaction. The lilacs were fading but had been glorious a couple of weeks ago. Her pansies and peonies were a riot of color, and her favorites, the roses, were setting buds. Soon, the oriental lilies would be casting their fragrance and crowning the yard with their glory.

David had mowed the lawn yesterday evening, and the aroma of fresh cut grass lifted her spirits. She loved spring and loved summer even more. Riding her horse with her daughter, playing kickball on the lawn with her son, and taking walks with her husband brought her a deep sense of peace and contentment.

Why did David feel she needed more? She had her family, her home, and her health. This new problem was causing stress, but somehow she and David would deal with that without God's help. She believed in God and believed Jesus was His Son. She'd never had a problem with that, but she didn't like the idea of turning over her life, and all that that entailed, to God. What if His choices didn't line up with hers? No, He wanted too much from people. Making Him the Lord of her life didn't make sense, and she knew enough about Christianity to know that this complete submission was the ultimate goal. She didn't believe in making half-hearted commitments and letting anyone direct her life didn't appeal to her.

She heard a sound and turned to see Brianna standing in the doorway, wearing her new green pajamas. The girl looked cute with her tousled hair and sleepy-eyed look. Susanne put down the spade and pushed the wheelbarrow over to the side of the path. A more pressing need existed that couldn't wait for another time.

"I'll be right in to fix breakfast," she called to the girl. "Why don't you get dressed, then come to the kitchen?"

Brianna was still a mystery, and Susanne knew that this was partly her own fault. She was determined to set things right. She couldn't abide the thought of anyone being afraid of her. First, however, she needed to get the garden dirt cleaned off her hands.

Susanne headed to the kitchen, concentrating on what to say. Would Brianna listen, or would she demonstrate the same studied indifference she showed whenever Susanne was around?

She moved around her kitchen, scrubbing her hands in the sink, and then setting two plates at the table. She loved this sunny room with its bay window looking out over her flower beds. A crystal prism, a gift from the kids, reflected the morning sun streaming in the window and cast colorful beams on the nearby cupboard.

"Brianna, breakfast is about ready. Are you dressed yet?" Susanne called from the bottom of the stairs.

"Yes. I'll be right down."

Susanne went back to the kitchen and poured pancake batter

on the griddle, then added a liberal sprinkling of huckleberries.

Brianna came in, glancing at Susanne before taking her seat at the table. "Is Meagan's grandfather coming in?"

"No. He stays up late watching TV and likes to sleep late. You'll see him at lunch."

She nodded.

"Brianna, are you still afraid of me?"

"I guess not." The low voice was barely audible.

Susanne set the plates on the table, working to keep her body relaxed. "I didn't do anything to you the other night when I came home. I don't understand why you were so upset."

"When people drink . . . it scares me. That's all." Her tone was sullen.

This line of conversation wasn't working, so Susanne tried a different tack. "Did your uncle hurt you when he drank?"

The girl bit her lip, shaking her head.

Susanne paused, putting her hands on the table and leaning over to look into Brianna's face. "If your uncle hurt you, I need to know."

Brianna wrapped her arms around herself, retreating farther into the chair. "I don't want to talk about it."

"Okay. We won't talk about it now, but sometime we need to. If an adult hurts you, you have to tell someone so they can't hurt you—or anyone else—in the future. Do you understand?" Susanne straightened and stepped back from the table.

Brianna shrugged, not raising her head.

"I'm sorry I scared you. I didn't mean to, but I'd never hurt you."

"You shouldn't drink. It makes people do mean things," the girl whispered.

"You're probably right. I promise I'll think about that in the future, okay?" She stepped over to the stove and turned the pancakes.

Susanne heard the girl's foot kicking the chair leg.

"I really do mean it. I won't scare you again, and I promise no one in this house will ever hurt you."

Brianna raised her head, eyes narrowed. "Does David drink?"

Susanne started, surprised at the question. "No. He feels like you do. He thinks it's wrong."

"That's good, because I think men get a lot meaner than women. I wasn't so much afraid of you. I was remembering *him*."

The quiet stretched out. Brianna's foot grew still, and her hands uncurled and relaxed. Susanne slipped into her chair and glanced at Brianna, deciding not to push. She looked nice in her new jeans and T-shirt. The emerald green color brought out the rich brown of her eyes. Brianna's hair looked like someone had tackled her with a pair of scissors wielded by a shaky hand. Susanne made a mental note to convince her to get a haircut, but first things first.

"Do you like huckleberry pancakes?" Susanne set one on the plate in front of Brianna.

"I don't know. We didn't have those where I lived."

"Have you eaten blueberries?"

Brianna sat up in her chair, looking at the plate with mild interest. "I haven't had many blueberries, either. Mostly, I ate boxed cereal for breakfast. My mom was gone to work when I got up, and Grandma always slept in."

This was one of the first personal glimpses into her life that Brianna had offered.

A few minutes later, Brianna finished her last pancake. "That was good!" She hadn't used so much enthusiasm since arriving.

"If you like these, I can make a huckleberry pie for your birthday."

Brianna's head jerked up. "But my birthday is over a month

from now. I won't be here."

"That's one of the things I want to talk to you about. Let's sit in the living room for a minute."

Susanne led the way and waited for Brianna to choose her seat. The girl curled up in David's recliner, her hands clenched in her lap.

"Brianna?" When she didn't reply, Susanne tried again. "I need to talk to you. I'm not mad at you, and you aren't in trouble."

Brianna stared at the wall.

Susanne took a deep breath, settling into the nearby couch. "David and I talked, and you're going to stay with us for a while."

The hands loosened their grip, and she turned to face Susanne. Questions shone in her eyes, hope and fear warring in her expression. "Stay with you?" she whispered. "What do you mean by stay with you? Until you find a foster home for me? I don't understand."

Brianna's fear felt like a slap. David was right—this girl had probably lived a rough life. The past few days in their home hadn't done anything to change that. Susanne had enough experience with foster kids to know the terror coursing through a kid's mind when faced with the unknown.

"I'm sorry. Let me explain?"

Brianna's shoulder raised in a half-hearted shrug. "Sure."

"David called DSHS on Monday, and no family members are looking for you. David believes he is your father based on the letter your mom wrote and your resemblance to him. It wouldn't be a good idea to send you back to your uncle—" Her explanation was interrupted by a huge sigh from Brianna. "He isn't a good choice as a guardian based on his actions in dropping you off here without even coming to the door."

Brianna bit her bottom lip, her gaze locked on Susanne's face.

"We can't make any long-term promises right now. We're still checking things out, but you won't be going to a foster home. I wish I could tell you more, but you'll be with us for a little while. We just don't know how long. Things are still kind of mixed up, and we're trying to sort them out."

"Oh." Brianna's mouth turned down in a small frown.

She was making a mess of this. "We're trying to do the right thing."

The hope starting to grow in the girl's eyes disappeared.

Great. She'd stuck her foot in it again. She'd raised Brianna's hopes, then slammed them to the ground. Maybe David should have handled it. Brianna was *his* daughter, after all.

Chapter Seventeen

"MOM, CAN I STAY HOME FROM school today to keep Brianna company?" Meagan begged.

Susanne saw the longing in her daughter's eyes and knew it encompassed more than Meagan's dislike of school. She had a tender heart and probably hated to see Brianna left alone all day, sensing the tension in their home since Brianna's arrival.

"No, honey. You only have another few days of school before summer break. Brianna will be fine with Grandfather and me, and before you know it, you'll be home to stay. Have a good time with Carrie. You know she'd be disappointed if you didn't show up." Susanne put the finishing touch to Meagan's French braid, giving it a loving tug after wrapping the ends in the decorative scrunchie she'd chosen.

"I guess you're right. I do want to see Carrie, especially since she's bringing pictures of her new horse. I reminded her at school yesterday. Besides, I want to tell her that Brianna is going to live with us. She is, right, Mom?"

"We don't know for sure how long Brianna is staying, so maybe you shouldn't say too much yet."

Her daughter's shoulders slumped, and she kicked her toe against the base of the sink.

"We don't need to talk about it now, Meagan. I don't want you or your friends making any permanent plans with Brianna, okay?"

"I'll tell Carrie that she's visiting us, but not that she's my new sister like that lady at the store said on Sunday."

Susanne didn't reply. It might be best not to correct the kids too often.

"Steven, Meagan, you'd better get going. The bus will be at the bottom of the driveway in a few minutes," Susanne said. Steven frequently forgot to take one of his books or a homework assignment, so Susanne kept a close eye on him, making sure he stuffed everything he needed into his bag.

Meagan popped her head into the living room to say good-bye to Brianna, assuring her she'd hurry home and they'd play with the kittens at the barn. Brianna brightened a bit whenever Meagan was around, and the mention of the kittens seemed to pull her out of her shell.

"Brianna, what would you like to do today?"

Susanne walked over to the girl in the window seat, who stared down the driveway at Steven and Meagan boarding the bus, a brooding expression clouding her otherwise pretty face. Cleaned up and wearing nicer clothes, Brianna was an attractive girl. The combination of big brown eyes, dark hair, and clear complexion would be stunning when the girl matured in a few years.

Brianna shrugged, continuing to stare out the window.

"We don't allow the kids to watch a lot of TV, but we do have a number of books they enjoy reading. Do you like to read?"

Silence followed by a shrug.

"It's going to be boring for you sitting by the window all day, waiting for Meagan. How about you help me with housework then we'll find something to do together this afternoon?"

"Whatever."

Was she still frightened, or was she holding a grudge? She'd seemed more receptive yesterday, but with so little stability in the girl's life, Susanne knew she shouldn't be surprised at the sudden changes in her mood. It might be a while before they began to see the true personality of this young stranger emerge.

"You can start by folding the laundry for me while I clean the kitchen."

Brianna stood, a slight scowl on her face.

What was going through her mind? Susanne doubted Brianna would ever fit into this family, even for the brief time she might be with them. She didn't know if she even wanted her to fit in.

"Come on. We'll bring the laundry into the living room, and you can fold it on the couch. When you're done, I'll show you where to put everything." She ushered the quiet girl down the hall to the laundry room and handed her a full basket, then led the way to the living room. "If you need any help, let me know." She stepped out of the room, leaving Brianna to herself.

An hour later, Susanne inspected the rooms downstairs with a sense of satisfaction. Brianna had finished her job but had taken her time with the clothes, making it clear she wasn't happy being stuck with chores.

"I really appreciate you helping me today. Should we see what Grandfather's doing?"

A quiet joy replaced the sullen look. "I'd like that."

A few minutes later, the young girl headed down the driveway with Grandfather. The sound of laughter floated up on the breeze as they started on their afternoon walk. Brianna glanced up and replied to something he said, then placed her hand in his. How had Grandfather managed to earn her trust and create this bond? A sense of sorrow crept over Susanne. Somehow, Grandfather had reached Brianna's heart and achieved a level of understanding where she and David had failed.

Susanne tried to imagine Meagan cast out on her own. She pictured herself dead and her child thrown into the home of someone she didn't know. Her heart contracted at the thought. She'd want her daughter treated well. She hadn't really considered Brianna's feelings since she'd been dumped at their door— abandoned, frightened, and probably very confused. Why was it so hard to accept this new addition to their home when Grandfather seemed to find it so simple?

The past few days, life had settled back into a routine. However, Susanne had been cutting herself off from everyone, even her mother. Mom had her own life and kept busy with her numerous friends and her gardening, but Susanne knew she should give her a call. The last week with all its turmoil had flown by with little contact. They hadn't spoken at length since the evening Susanne went out with Jeena.

She was so deep in thought, she almost missed the persistent ring of the phone. More than likely, her mother had read her thoughts.

"Hello?"

"Hello to you too, Susie. I've been wondering how you've been doing and finally decided to call since I haven't heard from you."

Susanne sank down in the recliner, thankful Brianna was out with Grandfather and wouldn't hear their conversation. "I'm sorry, Jeena. Life's been so hectic I forgot to call."

"Well, I like that! I've been waiting on pins and needles for the phone to ring, worried David threw you out, and you forget to call." The normally sultry voice sounded petulant.

"I'm fine, and David didn't throw me out. He's not like that."

"Oh really? So, did you two kiss and make up? Or did you put any thought into what we talked about?"

"Of course. I haven't been able to think about much else lately."

"Good. What did you decide? Have you called children's services about finding her family? I wouldn't wait much longer."

"David called DSHS, and they aren't interested in getting involved. They said if David is her dad and the mother is dead, it's our responsibility. They have enough needy families and don't have the resources for cases like ours."

"Don't tell me David is considering keeping her?"

Susanne took a deep breath, trying to remind herself that Jeena cared. "We've pretty much called a truce and are trying to work things out. We haven't made any long-term commitments, but Brianna isn't going to a foster home."

A harsher edge crept into Jeena's voice. "Open your eyes, Susanne. David obviously doesn't care about you or your kids. You're being naive."

Susanne gripped the receiver, willing herself not to overreact, but irritation pushed her to speak openly. "What's with the anger, Jeena?"

A slight tremor shook Jeena's voice. "I know what it means to have a man betray you, and I don't want to see you go through the same hurt I've experienced, that's all."

"What happened? Are you okay?" Susanne sat forward in her chair, her attention focused on this new twist in the -conversation.

"It doesn't matter; it's over." Her voice turned brisk. "What matters is you. Please don't let David take advantage of you. Get out before it's too late."

Susanne leaned her head against the back of the chair. This was her fault. She'd opened the door for this conversation the other night when she'd been angry at David and gotten too tipsy to set Jeena straight. "I'm not kicking him out or leaving. We've agreed Brianna will stay for now. It's not my top choice, but she is his daughter. We can't throw her out on the street or shove her in foster care, even if they'd take her. What kind of people would that make us?"

"Smart people, that's what." Jeena's words were hollow.

Susanne got up, no longer able to sit. She crossed to the kitchen and turned to come back. "David has a responsibility, and he's trying to deal with it."

"Right. But where does that leave you? Raising another

woman's daughter and wondering if you can trust your husband? Before you know it, you won't have a life at all. You're not thinking clearly. We need to get together and talk."

Susanne stopped by the window and leaned against the wall. This conversation had gotten out of hand, and she needed to take control before Jeena mapped out her entire life. "No thanks. I'm busy for the next few days. Besides, Brianna is not the issue. In fact, she's surprisingly well-behaved and easy to have around."

"I'm telling you, Susie." Jeena paused and her voice dropped. "David isn't the only guy out there. There are a lot of decent men who won't be bent out of shape if you have a few drinks."

Susanne sank into David's recliner, taking another deep breath before continuing. "Jeena, I'll say it one more time. I am not leaving David. I'm still sorting through my feelings, but I love my husband and have no intention of finding someone else. So please drop the hints."

"Fine." Jeena's voice trembled, and Susanne couldn't tell if it was from anger or a past memory. "But I can see the time coming when David's guilt forces him to choose between you and the girl, and you might end up losing more than you realize. I hope you won't be sorry, my friend."

"I need to go. I've got a lot to get done."

"Yeah. I hope things work out for you, Susie." The phone clicked in Susanne's ear, the wounded voice silenced.

Susanne sighed, happy the conversation had ended. She had enough to deal with right now without trying to tackle Jeena's issues too.

What did she see in Jeena? She could be fun to be around and acted like she cared, but Susanne wondered. How much was genuine caring and how much a driving desire to control? She'd let a lot slide during their conversation at Henry's and hadn't examined her friend's motives too closely. She could only surmise that Jeena had held herself in check that night... subtly suggesting and doing her best not to drive Susanne away. That pattern may have worked in the past, but Susanne wouldn't fall prey to it again.

Jeena's suggestion that Susanne should leave David shook her. Susanne hated to admit she'd thought about it the evening she'd spent with Jeena and wondered now if the thoughts were planted because of Jeena's urging.

She leaned back in the chair, thinking over the past jumbled week. Sure, she was unhappy about a strange girl being dumped in their lap. Who wouldn't be? But was it Brianna's fault? No. David had made the mistake fourteen years ago when he'd lost control with Brianna's mother and again when he had failed to tell the truth.

Betrayal, distrust, confusion, anger, hurt—all had surfaced in this past hectic week. But confusion and hurt were the only ones she could claim with any honesty now. David had expressed his sorrow, and in her heart, she knew it to be true. David didn't appear too happy about any of this himself. He'd barely been near Brianna and almost avoided the girl. Susanne wasn't ready to completely forgive or trust David, but maybe it was time to join forces and see what they could do for the girl who'd been thrown into their lives.

Meagan seemed to be the only one in the family who'd truly seen Brianna's heart. Caught up in her own anger and grief, Susanne had neglected to notice the needs of those around her, including her own family. She pushed herself forward, the footrest of the recliner snapping as it dropped into the chair. It was time to get moving and see what she could salvage of this day.

Chapter Eighteen

TWO DAYS LATER, SUSANNE STOOD AT the entrance of the living room, feeling content. With Brianna's help she had the laundry caught up again. Her kitchen glowed. She'd vacuumed the carpets and polished the wood floors.

The kids always made their own beds before they left for school, although she often had to remind Steven. He was unable to focus on more than one task at a time. Meagan, on the other hand, would be horrified to leave her room a mess or her bed unmade. The eleven-year-old had always loved things neat and clean.

Susanne had been doing a lot of thinking while spending time with Brianna the past couple of days. She'd begun to see the girl for what she was—not a threat to her children, but a lost, confused young teen unsure of where she belonged.

She still had reservations about Brianna's background and wasn't sold on the idea of her living with them forever, but she no longer wanted to rush the girl out the door. She and David needed to talk.

The kids had gotten off the bus an hour before, and she'd decided to ask Grandfather to keep them occupied for a while, so she and David could have quiet time to catch up. Grandfather was puttering in the garden, so she called the kids and herded them that direction.

"Grandfather?" She stopped a few feet from the edge of the vegetable garden he'd helped her plant a few days earlier. "Would you mind a little company down here?"

"Yeah, can you tell us another story?" Steven hopped across the grass on one foot.

"I was thinking you could use help weeding," Susanne

suggested.

"I hate weeding," Steven protested. "Can't we have a story?"

Meagan crossed the dirt patch toward the bemused older man who'd yet attempted to speak. "I'll help you weed. But I'd love to hear a story, too." Her hopeful voice increased Steven's pleading.

Grandfather rocked back on his heels from where he'd been perched on his knees along the raised corn bed. "How about you, Brianna? Would you like to hear a story?"

"Sure." Brianna stepped forward and looked over at Steven. "But I'll help you weed if you need me to."

Grandfather patted the ground beside him, along the edge of the garden. "Tell you what. A story first, then you can help me weed for a while. That'll give me time to think, and maybe we'll have another one. Does that sound fair?"

His twinkling eyes went from one child to the next, but Steven was the first to respond. "Yep. Story first, then weeding, then another story. I like that idea!" He plunked down on the grassy edge and crossed his arms. "What are you going to tell us about this time? Little Raven?"

Grandfather nodded his head. "Yes, I'll tell you a little more about my grandfather, who became known only as Raven when he grew up."

Brianna gave a small gasp. "The story you told the other night was true? Little Raven was your grandfather?"

"Yes. And when he grew to be a man, he fell in love with a young lady who was white. He'd been attending a missionary school in a town near where his tribe lived, and when he finished, he went to work on a nearby farm."

"Who was the girl he fell in love with?" Meagan asked.

"Her name was Meagan. You were named after her. Her family migrated from Ireland to the area where Raven lived."

"Was she our great-great-grandmother?" Steven wiggled

closer to Grandfather and peered up into his face.

"Yes. Her parents died from small pox, and the people in the town were afraid she'd give them the disease and shunned her. Raven befriended her and fixed up a small, abandoned cabin on the edge of town so she'd have a place to live."

Susanne decided this might be a good time to slip away and caught Grandfather's eye for a moment before leaving. He gave a slight nod and continued with his story, three rapt faces hanging on every word.

She walked up the slight incline to the house and headed for the living room in time to hear David's truck come up the driveway. She stepped over to the bay window and sank down onto the seat, watching him step out of the truck. He took off his cap and ran his fingers through his dark brown hair, then stood for a moment, seeming to hesitate. What a handsome man. She'd always loved the rugged and slightly exotic look that came from his Native American ancestors. The family liked to tease him that he could've been a chief in his great-grandfather's tribe, especially when he put his foot down about something important to him.

She straightened in her seat as David pushed himself away from the side of his truck and headed for the house. The smell of fresh cookies wafted from the kitchen. Maybe her little offering would help soften the mood.

The front door opened, and David stepped in. Susanne's heart quickened; she'd missed this man the past few days. She stood and stepped forward, meeting him at the door to the room. "Welcome home." She made a conscious effort to smile.

She wasn't sure how he felt about her. Areas of doubt and hurt still simmered, but for now, she wanted peace.

He stopped and lifted his head, a look of happy recognition lighting his eyes. "Do I smell cookies?"

Susanne chuckled at the voice that sounded so much like her

son's when he begged for another cookie. "Yes, you do, and yes, you may!"

David turned amazed eyes toward her. He strode across the room, stopping in front of her. "Susanne, honey? What's happened to you?"

"Come in and sit down. Grandfather's telling the kids stories, then they'll help him weed. We have a few minutes alone." She led him back into the living room and patted the place beside her on the couch.

David dropped onto the cushion next to her. She took a deep breath before going on, loving the woodsy smell that always clung to David after a day on a job. "First, I'm sorry for the way I acted the other night."

David opened his mouth, but she held up her hand to quiet him.

"I'm not saying I didn't have reason to be upset, but I let Jeena put ideas into my mind that shouldn't have been there. You were right, I've allowed her to influence me to some extent."

"Susanne—"

Once again, she motioned him to wait. "I need to get this off my chest. Give me a minute or two, then you can say whatever you'd like. I don't have any doubt that Brianna is your daughter, and I'm not proud of the way I've acted toward her. I've come to some conclusions if you want to hear them."

"I'd love to." He took her hand.

This time, she didn't pull back. She squeezed his hand in return. "The kids need to hear the truth from us, that Brianna is their sister." She flinched a little at the word, still uncomfortable and hurt by the thoughts surrounding it.

"More than that, Brianna needs to be told we know you're her dad." She pressed forward with determination. "What do you think about telling her she's staying with us, at least for the summer? I don't want to make promises we might not be able to keep as we still don't know her entire family situation, but we can give her that much for now."

Susanne watched David, waiting for some reaction besides stunned silence. The seconds stretched into minutes while David sat unmoving. Where was the man who'd tried to interrupt a few minutes ago? Why didn't he say something? Anything, for heaven's sake!

"David?"

"I'm sorry. I wasn't expecting to hear that. But I'm the one who needs to ask your forgiveness." He shook his head. "No, now you need to let *me* finish. I've been battling this for days. I don't expect to gain your trust back immediately after breaking it the way I have. I appreciate that you're willing to discuss Brianna and I love you for trying. I believe I'm Brianna's biological father, but I don't feel much for her."

"I guessed that much."

"I've been trying to figure some way to find her another home and still live with my conscience." He shifted his weight on the couch, lapsing into silence for a moment.

"I had no idea."

"I knew you didn't want her to stay, and I wanted to make you happy, but I also have a duty to make this right. I know what God wants me to do, and I've been fighting it."

She nodded.

"I'm not proud of it. I bring her into this world, you're the one getting her dumped in your lap, and you're taking it better than I am." He passed his hand over his eyes.

"I don't know how this is going to turn out, but I appreciate that you care. Brianna is still a mystery to us both, and we'll need to work on that. Come on. Let's eat our cookies before the kids come in and clean them out." She stood and pulled him to his feet, gave him a quick hug, and steered him toward the tempting aroma coming from the kitchen.

The issue of David's past still hung between them, but maybe peace could reign for a while in this family, barring any more unexpected drop-ins or "helpful" friends. The future wasn't clear, and Brianna's fears still needed to be addressed, but they would face things one day at a time. After all, things happened in threes, right? And they'd certainly met their quota, so it had to be time for a change.

David was at work, the kids had already left for school, and Brianna was in bed the next morning when the phone rang. Susanne was looking forward to a few minutes of peace with her morning latte before starting her busy day. She reached for the phone, in case it was the school or David.

"Hello."

"Well, you're sounding chipper," Claire said.

"Hi, Mom. I meant to call you yesterday, but the time flew by. You've probably been wondering what's going on."

"Well, yes, I have. I hesitated to call as I didn't know what I might be interrupting."

"I should've called. David and I had a good talk yesterday. To be honest, this whole thing has had me rattled from the minute I opened the door and saw Brianna standing there with her suitcase."

Susanne pulled out a chair and released a small sigh as she sat. "I knew when she claimed to be David's daughter that it might be true. I was already in a bad mood because David was going to be late that night when we had plans for my birthday."

"Oh, honey, I'm sorry. You and I went out to lunch to celebrate before your birthday, but you deserved more of a celebration than that."

"It's okay now. I was disappointed at the way the day was going, then Brianna came, and that topped it off. It didn't help to find out about David's past, but we're working through that. David promised he'll take me somewhere special soon. That is, if you're up to taking all the kids again? David's grandfather is a little too old to stand the strain of an entire evening with the three of them."

"All the kids? Does that mean you're going to have Brianna living with you for a while?"

"Yeah, that's what I wanted to tell you. At first I was so hurt. I automatically went to the worst possible scenario—that he might still be seeing the woman or had kept seeing her after he married me. It was hard enough knowing Brianna had been conceived when we were engaged, but the other possibilities were terrifying." *No sense in telling Mom I haven't been able to forgive David's deception.*

"Don't blame yourself too much. It was a shock the first time I saw Brianna and I'm not David's wife." Genuine sympathy laced Claire's voice. "I was angry myself. I knew you were hurt, but I didn't want to interfere in your marriage by saying too much."

"Thanks."

"So you've made your decision?"

"We have, but it's still tough. I doubt I'll ever have any deep feelings for Brianna. We're keeping her because it's the right thing to do, and we're making a commitment for the summer. We still feel a need to check into her past a little more. Does that make sense?"

Claire was quiet a moment. "It does, although I can see why it's difficult. You're basically taking a stranger into your home because her mother died, and that can't be easy. I'm proud of you."

Talking about it stirred up feelings of hurt all over again. "Thanks, Mom. I'd better go before she gets up. I want to work in my flower beds if I have time. We'll get together sometime later this week."

Thankfully, her late night out hadn't been mentioned. It was something she didn't care to discuss with anyone right now, even her mother.

Chapter Nineteen

SUSANNE HAD PROMISED TO TELL BRIANNA of any changes, and she intended to keep her word. Later that morning they sat in the living room, taking a break after doing the breakfast dishes.

The morning sun filtered through the windows, giving Susanne a sense of warmth and ease. Brianna spent each morning playing with the kittens and taking a walk with Grandfather, and Susanne knew she was anxious to head to the barn.

"Before you go, I want to tell you something. David and I talked about it again, and we've decided you should stay with us through the summer."

"Through the summer?"

"We're still working things out, but you won't be leaving soon." She had to offer some type of reassurance to this girl who seemed so lost.

"Also, I know you haven't felt very welcomed by David and me since you came, and I want to apologize for that."

Brianna hesitated. "Okay."

"I'm sorry for the way I've treated you, and I'd like to explain. I haven't been mad at you, even though it probably seemed like I was. I was mad at David, and well, I was mad at God too."

Brianna's lips parted, and she tipped her head to one side and stared at Susanne. "Mad at God?"

"We'll leave God out of it for now, and I'll explain to you about David. He and I got engaged a few months before you were born. He was the only guy I ever loved. It upset me to think he had a child with someone besides me, but I was wrong to make you feel like it was your fault. I'd like to start over if it's okay with you." She waited for Brianna's response.

Brianna shyly offered a smile. The eyes so like David's lit up. "It's okay with me."

Susanne hadn't been able to say *your dad* to Brianna and hoped the girl wouldn't notice the omission.

"One more thing, Brianna."

The girl cocked her head to the side but remained silent.

"We'll be telling the kids you're staying for the summer, so you might prepare yourself for questions. We'll tell them not to pester you, but I can't promise they won't, especially Steven. He's full of questions, and sometimes it's hard to make him stop."

Brianna smiled. "Yeah, I know."

Susanne didn't know what kind of challenges might lie ahead with this girl, and she still had reservations about Brianna's influence on the kids. Her attitude was quiet and sometimes sullen, making it difficult to know her true personality. They'd need to move slowly and nip any destructive behavior that might occur.

Susanne still wasn't comfortable with the turn her life had taken these past few days, but she wasn't going to let an innocent kid suffer for the choices she believed God had imposed in their lives. After all, David said God was in control, right? If so, He hadn't done a great job so far. She'd have to take charge and somehow make it all work.

David and Susanne decided to attend church on Sunday. Grandfather wanted to stay home and rest, but the kids would certainly question another absence. Besides, the church had a potluck scheduled after services, and it would give Steven and Meagan time with their friends.

Susanne looked forward to seeing Kim, Carrie's mom. The two women had begun to form a friendship over the past few months. Carrie and Meagan spent the night at each other's home occasionally and took riding lessons from the same instructor.

Sunday morning was rushed, with three kids to prod rather than two. Meagan and Brianna were spending longer getting ready than Meagan usually took. Could Brianna be uncomfortable going to a strange church? From small comments Brianna had made about her past, it was doubtful she'd ever attended.

"Come on, kids. We need to get going," David called up the stairs. "We're going to be late if we don't hurry."

Two pairs of feet came racing down the stairs. Brianna's moved a little slower.

They pulled into the parking area in front of the church, and Susanne sat for a moment, trying to see it through the eyes of a stranger. It wasn't a large building. Sitting on the edge of town on a two-acre lot, the one-story church would need a new coat of paint in the next couple of years but remained an attractive building. They'd raised the money to pave the parking area last year, and the grounds were dotted with flower beds and shrubbery.

Susanne didn't think Meagan noticed Brianna's discomfort. When they stepped out of their car, Meagan proved her wrong.

"Mom," she whispered, "would it be okay for Brianna to go with me even though she's older? I think she's kind of scared."

"I'll mention it to your teacher. I'm sure she won't care."

"Thanks, Mom." Meagan skipped ahead to catch up with the other two.

Susanne stepped through the open doors into the foyer and spotted Kim standing off to the side. Kim slipped over and gave her a quick hug.

"Meagan told Carrie about the new addition to your family. Are you doing okay?" the petite blond asked.

"I'm doing better now that some of the shock has passed. It was pretty hard at first."

"I've been praying for your family since I heard. I didn't want to call and impose, but if you want to get together and talk, let me know."

Susanne relaxed, seeing no censorship in Kim's eyes. "Thanks. I'd enjoy that. I'd better make sure Meagan and Brianna are settled in their class."

"I'll talk to you at the potluck, and we can introduce Ashley to Brianna. They're close to the same age, and it might be good for her to have a friend." Kim gave a quick wave before she hurried off to her class.

Ashley was thirteen and would be in the same grade as Brianna, assuming the girl was at the proper grade level for her age. That was one more thing Susanne didn't know and needed to deal with, but no need to worry before the next school year approached.

When the song service ended, Susanne had a hard time concentrating on the pastor's sermon. Had they made the right choice, bringing a stranger into their home with no background knowledge? At least with foster kids, a caseworker brought them up to speed on the child's problems and ran interference with any troubling situations. They also had the option of removing the foster child from their home if necessary.

Brianna hadn't acted out since coming to their home, but she was still settling into the new environment. From past experience, Susanne guessed Brianna's behavior could change as she became more comfortable.

Susanne's thoughts came back to the present, hearing the words that made her rejoice each Sunday morning. "As I conclude this message, let me remind you of one thing." Her mind started to wander again but then jerked back to attention.

"You may have been hurt by the circumstances of life or by someone you loved and trusted. But Jesus commands us to forgive. If we don't forgive, He says He won't be able to forgive us our trespasses." The pastor leaned over the pulpit toward the congregation.

He was dressed casually, never the least bit pretentious in the years she'd known him. Pastor Grant didn't believe in putting on airs or trying to act better than the people in his congregation. He believed in living what he preached and expected others to do the same. Susanne knew he believed every word he spoke.

"When we hold anger against another person and refuse to forgive, we don't hurt that person nearly as much as we hurt ourselves. Often they don't even know we're angry or bitter, and their life continues on unaffected. But unforgiveness in our heart grows, often developing into bitterness. It might start out as a little seed planted because of a slight offense, or it might have deep roots due to a traumatic event. Regardless of how it starts, if it isn't dealt with, it will eventually consume the person nurturing it." He stepped away from the pulpit, coming off the platform and stopping in front of the section where Susanne's family sat. She glanced at David to see him sitting forward.

"The person we're angry with might not deserve to be forgiven. You might think that by forgiving them you're condoning the action that caused the pain in your life.

"You might also feel you can't forgive if the pain is too great. But forgiveness isn't based on feelings. It's based on obedience. You aren't condoning the action, but rather, you're forgiving the person. You don't have to feel like forgiving them, but you have to choose to walk in obedience to God and act on His instructions. When you do, He'll give you a supernatural peace that only comes from Him."

He glanced slowly over the congregation. "Will you still remember what happened? Yes. Forgiveness doesn't wipe out the memory of the hurt, but it does take away the sting. Do you have to become close friends with the person or even pick up a relationship with them again? You might, but then again, it may not be appropriate or necessary. God may call you simply to forgive and release them, then move on."

Susanne fought to stay in her seat and not head out the back door. She knew David would be upset and her kids would question her if she did, so she sat and endured what followed.

The pastor stepped behind the pulpit and leaned across it, scanning the crowd of attentive faces again. "If you're having a hard time, ask God to help you become willing. Do you want to please Him? Do you need forgiveness yourself? Then take this admonition to heart, and don't continue to let hurt or anger fester." He paused for a moment, then dropped his voice. "I'd like to ask everyone to bow your head and take a moment to examine your own heart before we pray."

Emotions and thoughts collided in Susanne's mind, blocking out the rest of the pastor's words. Why would God require that she be the one to forgive? She'd told David she was willing to give Brianna a home, at least for the summer. Wasn't that enough? She didn't particularly care to forgive the uncle who had dropped Brianna at their home, shirking his responsibility. Nor did she want to forgive the woman she felt had pursued her husband and ultimately produced a child.

Other people were to blame for the struggles her family had endured, and it certainly wasn't her responsibility to forgive all of them. Even though David admitted his guilt, a part of her heart wouldn't let go of the pain. She'd accepted his apology, but that was as far as she felt able to go in forgiving David. They'd fallen into a more peaceful relationship, and that should be enough, even for God.

And what was this about God not forgiving her if she didn't forgive first? That was ridiculous. As though she'd done anything God needed to forgive. She was the one cleaning up after everyone else, taking this girl into her home. She should be praised, not told she needed to forgive.

She wished David wasn't so insistent about going to church every week. Had he talked to the pastor? Was the sermon pointed at her? Pastor Grant was nice enough, but she didn't care to trust another pastor after hearing David's revelation about their old one. He'd butted into their lives and given advice that ended up hurting, not helping. He probably meant well, but no way was she letting another pastor tell her what to do.

"Mom, come on. Why are you still sitting here?" Steven pulled at her sleeve. "Everyone is going to the potluck, and I'm hungry."

Most of the congregation had gone to the fellowship hall with only small groups of people still standing and chatting. David, Brianna, and Meagan were leaving the sanctuary. David looked back at her, cocking his head and raising his brows.

Susanne jumped to her feet and grabbed Steven's hand. "Come on, buddy. Let's get some of that great food." She hoped her response would deter him from asking more questions. "I'm hungry too." She shook off her sour mood and grinned at her son, letting him lead her to the fellowship hall.

Everything from wedding receptions to women's Bible studies were held in this room. The well-equipped kitchen stood off to one side. Anything a person might need to make the job easier seemed to have been provided. She moved through the line, marveling at the abundance of food the women in this church always provided.

"Steven, you have to take more than bread and a piece of chicken. Try the fruit salad. You'll love it."

"Ah, gee, Mom, can't I have dessert now? It'll be gone by the time I get done eating all this food."

"No, it won't. There's plenty. Go on, sit with your friends and come back for dessert later." She gave him a gentle push, but he continued to drag his feet. He stared at the dessert table all the way to where his friends waited.

Meagan had introduced Brianna to Ashley and Carrie. The four girls sat in the center of the room. It looked like Ashley was putting out an effort to get acquainted with Brianna, while Meagan and Carrie chattered like little magpies.

Kim waved at Susanne from across the room. David sat at a table with several of the guys, visiting with Kim's husband, Phil. Phil Slater owned Slater's Lumber Yard, and David bought most of his supplies there. She knew David and Phil would probably talk shop until she came take David home.

Weaving her way among the colorfully decorated tables, she was alert for any curious looks cast her way. No one could miss the resemblance between David and Brianna.

"Susanne, how are you?" asked a petite, gray-haired lady with a gentle smile as Susanne passed behind her chair.

"Fine, Mrs. Kendrick. You're looking well today." She braced herself for the questions that were sure to come.

"Thank you, dear, and so are you." She returned to her animated conversation with Mrs. Gould.

A friendly clamor filled the room as friends and neighbors caught up on one another's lives. Small children ran screaming and laughing, weaving in and out among the empty chairs off to the side. Kim's table sat half full with no one close by. Susanne grasped the back of a chair and slipped into it. The other occupants at the end of the table, engrossed in their own conversations, simply smiled and nodded a greeting.

Kim looked up, a conspiratorial smile lighting her eyes. "I'm glad you made it. I was getting worried there wouldn't be any food left by the time you and Steven got here."

Susanne grinned. "Ha! Not much chance of that happening. The ladies in this church think they're cooking for an army. We're all more apt to go home with a stomachache from eating too much."

"Yeah. It's even better not cleaning a dirty kitchen when we're done." Both women chuckled.

They concentrated on their meals for a few moments, and a comfortable silence settled between them. Suddenly, David's hearty laugh rang out and both women smiled as they glanced at their respective husbands.

"Phil is always interested in whatever project David is working on," Kim said.

"David's the same way. Building supply stores are his favorite, and Phil's ranks right up there at the top."

Kim nodded. "Phil enjoys David's company as well as his business."

Susanne narrowed her eyes and cocked her head. "You know, it's funny. I never realized how completely opposite they are in appearance."

"I know what you mean. David at least looks like he's in his thirties. It really bugs Phil when people don't take him seriously because he looks so young. I think it's probably his slender build. His blond hair and cute baby face don't help a lot, either."

Susanne grinned. "You don't have much room to talk. You don't look over twenty-five yourself. And certainly not old enough to have a teenager."

Kim was a nice complement to her husband with her shoulder length, dark blonde hair, sparkling hazel eyes, and turned-up nose, giving her a bit of a mischievous look.

"Yeah, but we married pretty young, and Ashley was born right after I turned twenty-two. It's kind of funny when we introduce the kids to strangers. We always get comments or shocked looks."

Susanne wiped her mouth before speaking. "Yeah, I'll bet, but you'll be thankful when you hit fifty because you won't look it. It never ceases to amaze me that those guys are such good friends considering they don't have much in common besides the construction field."

"Actually"—Kim rested her chin in her hand, glancing across at the two men—"they do. They both are completely sold out to the Lord, and that's enough."

Susanne worked to keep a pleasant expression. "I'm sure you're right."

The women ate for a few minutes interspersed with occasional small talk, then by unspoken agreement went back to choose a dessert before picking up the conversation again.

"I'm sure you're wondering about Brianna." Susanne laid down her fork and picked up her cup of coffee.

"A little. Meagan told Carrie she's her half-sister. Brianna looks so much like David, it isn't hard to figure out which of you is her parent."

"Yeah, you and everyone else in the church."

"I don't think people are talking. You know this church isn't gossipy or malicious."

Susanne leaned back in her chair. "Maybe not, but I'm sure they're wondering where she came from and what's going on."

"Well, that's natural."

"I know. In all fairness, if it wasn't my family, I probably would be too. But it's difficult knowing we're the focus of attention. I wish this had never happened and we could go back to the way things were."

Kim lowered her voice. "I'm not trying to pry, Susanne, but what exactly did happen?"

A few minutes passed while Kim listened to Susanne's explanation. "I can't believe that horrible man would dump off a young girl like that. He didn't so much as come to the door or try to explain?"

Susanne shook her head and frowned. "No. He was nearly out of sight by the time I answered the door. When I saw Brianna standing there, claiming to be David's daughter, I didn't want to believe it. Then when David admitted she probably was, I felt so betrayed."

Kim reached across the table and squeezed Susanne's hand.

For the next few minutes, Susanne poured out the events of the past few days. She avoided the subject of Jeena, thankful Kim wasn't aware of her late night out.

When she finished, she looked around at the empty table. Much of the congregation had already headed home.

"I admire you," Kim said.

"Me? Why?"

"It's got to be tough taking in another woman's child and seeing your husband in her face every time you look at her."

"I think that's been the hardest of all—knowing she's David's and not mine. But Brianna is a sweet girl, and she hasn't been hard to have around."

Kim's eyes reflected the caring in her words. "A lot of women wouldn't have done it, you know." At Susanne's curious look, Kim went on. "Some women would've kicked their husbands out or refused to take on the responsibility of his daughter."

"I admit I considered it. I wanted to stay angry with him and take it out on Brianna. But that wasn't fair, either. The circumstances surrounding her birth weren't her fault, but it took my daughter's disappointment in me to make me see that my actions didn't measure up."

Kim smiled. "Our kids can be good at that. Sometimes my girls say things that stop me in my tracks and make me take a good, hard look at my attitude."

"Don't give me too much credit. I'm still struggling with my emotions."

Kim started to reply but was interrupted by their four girls. Meagan's arm was linked through Carrie's, and her eyes shone. Brianna had lost the worried look from earlier in the day. Ashley nudged her and whispered, causing both girls to look across the room and giggle.

"Hey, Mom, can Carrie and Ashley spend the night? We can watch a movie and maybe take a hike tomorrow or something. Since school is over, would it be okay? Pleeaassse?" Meagan stretched the word out, making the two women grin.

"It's up to Kim. It's okay with me, but we'd need to stop by their house and pick up their things."

Meagan and Carrie let out a squeal of delight, but Susanne held up a hand. "You need to ask Kim."

Meagan, Carrie, and Ashley all started to beg, while Brianna stood silent, a hopeful look on her face.

Kim put her hands over her ears, laughing and waving at them to stop. "I don't care. . ."

The girls whooped and turned to run across the room. Several older people sitting at a nearby table stopped talking long enough to look their way and smile in sympathy.

"Are you sure you don't mind, Susanne? I didn't want to say anything in front of the girls, but will this be too much for you right now?"

Susanne shook her head. "On the contrary, it's perfect. Brianna could use a friend her own age. I think it'll be nice for both girls to have a change of pace."

"It looked like Ashley was as excited as the two younger girls. It'll be nice for her to have a friend when Meagan and Carrie get together."

"Keep in mind we don't know much about Brianna's background."

"Yes, I thought of that, but I'm not worried. From all you've told me, she seems like a decent girl." She propped her chin on her hands and smiled. "Back to our conversation, I guess you did what Pastor Grant talked about this morning."

"What was that?"

"You forgave the people involved and dealt with your anger."

Susanne felt irritation begin to simmer, but Kim had been kind. She didn't want to repay her with rudeness.

"Well, I accepted David's apology," she hedged. "And I told Brianna I'd been wrong in the way I treated her. So, yes, I took care of it, and it's over."

"That's good. And like I said earlier, I'll be praying for you."

This was a subject Susanne didn't want to pursue. "It looks like David's ready to go, so I'd better round up the kids. I appreciate you listening. We'll swing by to get the girls' things." She stood and bent to give Kim a quick hug.

Susanne turned to walk away, leaving Kim with a mystified look.

Chapter Twenty

LATER THAT EVENING, SUSANNE HEARD GIGGLING coming from the family room. All four girls had headed there earlier, popcorn and juice in hand, to watch a movie before going to bed.

David was watching TV in the living room with Grandfather while Susanne finished the dinner dishes. She'd watched as much TV as she could tolerate for one evening. She'd much rather settle down with a good book.

She scrubbed her countertops and thought over the day. She'd been concerned about Brianna fitting in with the three other girls, but her worries hadn't materialized. Meagan, Carrie, and Ashley made sure Brianna felt included.

Ashley wasn't much of a horse person, so the girls contented themselves with taking a long walk and playing with the kittens in the barn. Dinner was the first time they'd been inside for any length of time since arriving. After the meal, they'd brought out a board game and spent a couple of hours laughing and carrying on, with little time spent playing the game.

Brianna and Ashley seemed to have developed a rapport with one another and were talking and giggling along with the other two. Brianna was acting more like a young teenager than a recluse. Susanne hung up her dish towel and headed to her bookcase.

"Susanne?" David's voice called from the living room.

"Yes?"

"If you're done in the kitchen, do you want to watch TV? Grandfather and I found a movie you'd like."

"No, thanks. I started a good book a couple of days ago. Steven went to bed early, and the girls seem occupied, so I'm going to make use of the quiet time."

"Okay. Enjoy your book."

"Thanks."

It had gotten quiet in the family room. It might be a good idea to remind the girls to head to bed when the movie was over, before she got too engrossed in her book. Susanne knew her weakness in that area. Once she started reading, the rest of the world ceased to exist.

Susanne stopped to listen outside the family-room door, not wanting to interrupt if the girls were near the end of the movie. She was ready to step around the corner when Ashley's voice made her pause.

"Brianna, I love your accent. Meagan said you grew up in Texas. Did you like it there?"

"I loved it, but mostly because of Grandma. I didn't have many friends at school, and my Grandma was my best friend. I miss her and Mama so much."

"Why didn't you have any friends?" Carrie asked.

"I think because we were poor. Mama married Tom Stiles when I was a baby, but he died when I was three, so I never had a dad. And since Mama didn't finish high school, we never had much money. I mostly stayed home and helped out around our trailer. We didn't have a yard or anything, but Grandma liked to keep everything clean while Mama worked, even if it wasn't worth much."

"We'll be your friends," Meagan said. "Dad says Jesus especially loves kids, and it doesn't matter to Him if you have much or not. It's really cool. He's my best friend, and I can tell Him anything. You can talk to Him, and He'll help you not be so sad about your grandma and your mom."

"Grandma told me a little about Jesus, but we never went to church much. She believed in Him and said He loved me, but it didn't seem like He cared about our family. Mama never talked about Him, not like Grandma did," Brianna said.

Ashley's quiet voice barely reached Susanne's hearing. "Jesus does love you, Brianna. You need to believe in Him and ask Him into your heart. That way, when you miss your mom and grandma, you can talk to Him about it, and He understands."

"I'll think about it."

Susanne heard Meagan's voice pipe up. "You don't have to be lonely here. Mom and Dad do lots of neat stuff for us. Dad built this house, and Mom goes riding with me. I have the best parents in the whole world. Now they're your parents too." She sounded as though she were conveying a gift to the other girl.

"They're not my parents. Besides, your dad never wanted me, and he didn't like my mom. Why would I want him for a dad?"

"My dad isn't like that!"

"Yes, he is." Brianna's voice grew louder. "Mama told me he didn't want anything to do with me. He told me he didn't know about me, but I don't believe him. Your mom is okay, I guess, but she doesn't really like me. She's just trying to be nice until they find somewhere to put me. And your dad never talks to me. I think he wishes I were dead."

Silence met this statement. Susanne decided she'd better intervene. She tip-toed back a few steps, then let her feet fall on the hardwood floor, calling out before getting to the door. "Girls, is your movie over?"

"Yes, Mom," Meagan said.

"Then it's time you head to bed. It's getting late. How about two of you taking one bathroom and the other two can use ours." She ushered the silent group out the door. "I'll come tell you good night after you're in bed."

Susanne retreated to her room, her book forgotten. Brianna had pegged them pretty closely. David didn't seem to have much interest in getting to know this newly acquired daughter, and

Susanne hadn't pushed him. She had to admit that a part of her didn't want him to love Brianna.

Susanne was tired. Time enough to deal with this over the next few days. David didn't need to know about the girls' conversation. She'd keep it to herself and see how things went. She felt a sting of conscience at her selfishness but pushed it aside. *No reason to set the girl up for disappointment by letting her bond too much with their family.* The effort Susanne had made to be kind was all she could offer for now.

David's time with Grandfather had been limited, but he'd finally made time for a short fishing trip the next day on the Little White Salmon River. The two men pulled out the small dinghy that had been stored in the barn, hooked it to the truck, collected the fishing gear, then headed for the mouth of the small river a few miles away.

When they arrived at the boat ramp, Grandfather slipped out of the cab and directed David back toward the water, signaling when the boat was in far enough. They unhooked and parked the pickup nearby, then walked to the boat and pushed off from the shore.

David felt like a kid again on his first fishing trip with his grandfather. The memories flooded back, bringing a grin to his face.

Grandfather glanced his way and smiled. "I'm glad to see you happy, David. I've been worried about you."

"Me? Why's that?"

"You've been preoccupied most of the time I've been here, and I don't think it's only been about business."

David scrambled to come up with an easy answer that might satisfy but decided the truth might be best. "You're right. This business with Brianna has caused stress between Susanne and me."

Grandfather whipped his fly line back and forth over the water a few minutes, finally landing the fly a good distance from the boat. "Is that all?"

"What do you mean?" David laid down the hook he was baiting and turned his full attention to his grandfather

The fly jumped off the water and flew to another spot on the glassy surface of the river. "How're you dealing with Brianna's arrival?"

"Not great. I want to do the right thing, but I can't seem to spend time with her. Part of me feels that I'm betraying Susanne when I do. I know that's stupid, and Susanne's adult enough to know I'm not thinking about Brianna's mother, but I'm struggling with thinking of Brianna as my daughter."

Grandfather nodded and reset his fly again. "You'd better fish, David, it's good for the soul."

David picked up his line, slipped a worm on the hook, and sank the leaded hook into the still water, leaving the bobber showing on the surface.

A few minutes passed with the sound of the breeze whispering in the trees along the edge of the bank, before Grandfather finally spoke. "Your grandmother and I rarely disagreed about anything. She was a wonderful woman, but occasionally she'd exhibit a stubborn streak, and it took real work on my part to get her past it."

David smiled. "Yeah. I remember a time or two when that happened."

Grandfather grinned in return. "I'm only telling you that to say this. Marriage isn't easy. You both have to work at it, and I'm sure you know that. Love is a choice, not a feeling. We choose to love our mate even when the feelings aren't there, because it's what we promised to do. The feelings follow the commitment."

David nodded.

"Being a parent is much the same. There are times we almost wish we could run away and not have to deal with the problems our children bring us. But God placed them in our lives for a reason. Sometimes it's for their growth, sometimes for ours. God brought Brianna for a reason, and you need to pray about it."

"You're right. I've been so focused on Susanne's reaction that I've forgotten about Brianna's feelings. I've also been concerned about our two. Meagan told me that she was afraid I wouldn't love her as much anymore with Brianna here. I've been trying not to spend too much time with Brianna so Meagan wouldn't be hurt."

Grandfather snorted. "Balderdash. Your kids love that girl, and a little sibling rivalry is expected."

David's bobber started to jump, then dove under the water. Grandfather let out a whoop and reeled in his line. "You've got a big one, David! Don't let it go, play with it now. . . that's right, let some line out. . ."

David hid a smile and continued to work the fish, once more feeling like the ten-year-old boy who went fishing with his grandfather so many years ago.

Susanne got up early on Saturday morning to beat the heat, as she wanted to bake and hated the thought of using her oven late in the day. The kids rolled out of bed about halfway through her second batch of cookies and made a beeline to the pond, hoping to catch sight of the baby ducks making their home in the reeds.

"Yum. My favorite." David's brown eyes sparkled, and his voice took on a pleading note. "Just one more, okay hon?"

Susanne playfully slapped his hand and grinned. "You've had three already. What's going to happen to that slim figure you're so proud of if you keep this up? Hmm?"

"Guess I'll have to chase you around the yard a few more times. That should do it." He reached out and snitched another snickerdoodle before she could stop him and then jumped out of her reach.

Susanne grinned, the relaxed atmosphere a welcome change from the emotional ups and downs of the past few weeks.

"Could I get a glass of water?" Brianna's soft voice halted Susanne and David's banter.

Susanne turned to see the girl standing inside the door. "Of course. And you can take cookies back with you to share. I'll give you a sandwich bag of snickerdoodles and chocolate chip." Susanne wiped the hair from her eyes with the back of her flour-coated hand and smiled at the quiet girl.

Brianna's eyes brightened, and she took a step closer. "I love chocolate chip. But my mom made them with oatmeal and nuts. You should try them that way. She made the best cookies ever, and I'll bet you'd like them better."

Susanne's smile died, and she glanced at David. He stood frozen, glancing from Brianna to Susanne and looking as though he'd like to slide through a crack in the floor.

Brianna finished her glass of water and took the bag of cookies Susanne placed in her hand. "Thank you." She gave a small smile and headed to the door, apparently oblivious to the heavy silence that had settled over the room.

Grandfather had been hinting for several days that he needed to leave, so Susanne wasn't surprised when he announced his decision to return home. The next morning, he stood at the door with his two bags beside him. "You've made an old man happy these past couple of weeks. Now it's your turn to come see me."

"Do you have to go?" Steven wrapped his arms around the

older man's waist and looked up into the gentle face.

"I'm afraid I do. My poor old cat probably thinks I'm never coming back to see her. My neighbor takes care of Tia, but it's not the same as having a lap to sit on every day."

"Are you sure, Grandfather? We haven't seen that much of you. You've kept to yourself quite a bit." David laid his hand on the man's shoulder.

"Yes, I'm sure. I needed time alone to think, pray, and sort through my feelings about missing my Grace. The time I spent with the kids has brought healing, I think. I'm doing better now, and it's time to go home. I'm sorry I dropped in on you so unexpectedly, Susanne."

She took his hand and patted it, then gave him a hug. "Don't be sorry. You're welcome here any time, for as long as you'd like to stay."

"I don't want you to leave." Meagan's mouth turned down and she gave her mother a pleading look. "Can't he move into the apartment and not leave?"

Grandfather chuckled and ruffled her hair. "I have my own house, and it's time I got back to it. Don't worry. I'll come see you again."

"But we'll miss you!" Meagan protested.

"I'll miss you too, Meagan. You take care of your new sister now, you hear?" He leaned over to give her a hug, then tickled her sides before kissing her cheek.

She giggled, then kissed him back. "Yes, sir."

"Come here, Steven, and give me a hug." Grandfather reached out to the little boy who rushed into his arms. "I'll see you again, and I'll come sooner next time, okay?"

Steven nodded against Grandfather's shoulder, his voice muffled in the rough fabric. "Okay, I guess." He released his grasp and stepped back. "Your cat is lucky."

Grandfather chuckled then knelt down in front of Brianna and lowered his voice. "You remember what I told you?"

"Yes."

"And you're my granddaughter, too. You remember that." He gathered her in his arms and held her for a moment.

She wrapped her arms around his neck, then whispered in a low voice, "I will."

Susanne watched the two and wondered again what Grand-father had told Brianna that affected her so.

Chapter Twenty-One

A COUPLE OF DAYS LATER, SUSANNE stood at the base of the stairs. "Meagan."

"Yes, Mom?"

"Can you come down for a minute?"

"Sure."

Meagan appeared at the door of the kitchen. "Did you want me?"

"Yes. I thought you might give a riding lesson to Brianna. I know I promised to help with lessons, but I have things I need to get done."

"Gee, Mom, I was counting on it." Meagan slumped down into a nearby chair.

"I know. But you haven't ridden much since Brianna got here. Maybe it would be fun for you to ride, and she can learn by watching."

Meagan sat up straighter in her chair. "I suppose I could. She asked me about jumping one time. Can you believe it? She's never seen anyone jump a horse before."

"Let's keep it to riding today, okay?"

"You don't want me to do anything! Why can't I go over a couple of low jumps? My instructor said I'm doing good." Meagan's lower lip protruded a bit.

Susanne looked at the ceiling, shaking her head. "All right, since Brianna asked. But you have to promise you'll only do the two small ones."

"I promise. I'll get Brianna." Meagan jumped up, her eyes sparkling.

"I'll come down after a bit and check on you."

"Okay." Meagan raced from the room, her feet thumping as she flew up the stairs.

Thirty minutes later, Susanne went outside. More than enough time had passed for Meagan to saddle Glory and warm her up. She wanted to make sure Meagan had only set up the two small jumps. She felt confident her daughter would keep her word, but if Brianna suggested going higher, Meagan might decide to fudge a little. David was cutting firewood on the far side of their property and had taken Steven with him. It was up to her to check on the girls.

Susanne started down the path. *What a glorious day!* The air always smelled so fresh after a light rain. No clouds today, and the sun was out warming the air.

She could see the girls in the small pasture. *Good.* It looked as though Meagan was using the two small jumps she'd mastered. The mare had started jumping at the same time as Meagan, another reason Susanne didn't want her daughter going higher without her instructor. Neither horse nor rider knew enough yet.

Brianna was off to the side, out of the way of the cantering horse. She must have been getting warm, too, since she was struggling to take off her coat. Her arm pulled out of the sleeve, and she turned, pulling out her other arm and swinging it back. Time seemed to freeze. Susanne started to run, yelling as she went.

"Brianna, don't throw your coat! You'll spook Glory."

Too late. The jacket went sailing through the air and hooked over the top rail of the nearby fence. Susanne watched in horror as the mare came out of the jump, landed, and bolted sideways. She could hear the loud snort the Arabian made when afraid and saw her body coil as though ready to buck.

"Hold on, Meagan!" Susanne was running for all she was worth now, fear choking her. She could barely breathe.

Glory jerked her head down, pulling the reins through

Meagan's fingers, then lashed out hard with her hind feet. The combination of the sideways jump with the jolting kick and loss of her reins sent Meagan flying. Susanne reached the fence in time to hear the hard crack of Meagan's helmet hitting the nearby jump. She heard a shriek, then sobbing off to her right but couldn't take time to deal with Brianna now.

"Meagan, honey, can you hear me?" She leaned over the quiet form, not wanting to move her, fearful of what she might find.

Silence. No movement. *God, why don't You do something?*

"Brianna. Brianna!" She spoke sharply to the sobbing girl. "Go across the field and into the woods. You can hear David's chainsaw. Tell him what happened and bring him back. Hurry!"

"I made the horse buck her off. It's my fault," the girl wailed.

"Hush. We don't have time for that now. Go get David. Run!"

Brianna took off across the field as hard as she could go, and Susanne turned her attention to Meagan. Still no sound. She lay on her back, eyes closed, face pale, dirt covering her face and neck. Had she landed on her face, then rolled over? Susanne couldn't remember. It had all happened so fast.

Oh, God, if You care, You have to do something! Meagan hasn't done anything to deserve this. Don't punish her.

She heard a soft moan, but Meagan's eyes remained closed. Her breathing seemed shallow. *Where is David? Why is it taking so long?* Did she dare move Meagan? No. She could have a neck injury. Better to wait for David. He'd worked two summers as a firefighter and had basic EMT training. He'd know what to do. Maybe she should go to the house and call an ambulance. But she didn't want to leave Meagan alone. *David, please hurry!*

She heard a shout and saw David running across the field, Steven and Brianna trailing behind.

Tears were streaking her cheeks, and Susanne angrily brushed them away. This was no time for tears. She had to remain calm for her daughter. *Meagan has to be okay. I can't survive if she isn't.*

"Susanne, what happened? Is she okay?" David panted, and his chest heaved as he knelt at her side.

"I don't know. She was taking a jump, and Brianna threw her coat over the fence. It spooked Glory. I think Meagan would have stayed on, but Glory bucked after she jumped sideways, and that sent Meagan flying. She hit her head against the base of the jump. Oh, David, she hit hard! I heard the impact."

"She's wearing her helmet. I'm sure it protected her head."

"Then why isn't she awake yet? She's been out for almost ten minutes. I'm going to call an ambulance."

"Wait a minute. Let me check her first." He took her pulse, his experienced hands gently probing the side of Meagan's neck.

"Has she opened her eyes?"

"No. She moaned one time, but that's all."

"Did she land flat on her back?"

"I don't remember. No, I don't think so. She landed on her face, then rolled over. Yes, she kind of tumbled and ended up lying flat."

"I think it's all right to move her. I'm going to carry her to the car. You run to the house and put the backseat down in the Subaru. Lay some blankets and pillows along the side so she won't roll. I'll keep her as straight as I can."

"Wouldn't it be better to call the ambulance?"

"It'll take them close to a half hour to get here. We can get her to the hospital sooner than that, if we hurry. No sense in delaying."

"You think it's serious, don't you?"

"I want to be safe. Let's get her to the car quickly."

Steven and Brianna came sliding to a stop, panting and tear streaked. Neither one spoke. They looked at the still form on the ground, their fear giving way to sobs.

"It's all right, kids. Meagan is going to be okay. Steven, quit crying and help Mom get pillows and blankets. Brianna, you walk beside me and tell me what you saw."

"Come on, Steven." Susanne grabbed his hand, and they sprinted for the house.

Susanne had the back of the car ready and the engine running when David arrived.

"Is she awake yet? I called the hospital to let them know we're coming. They'll have a doctor waiting in the emergency room."

"Good. No, she's not awake. Steven, you and Brianna squeeze in the front seat together, and Mom can ride in the back with Meagan. Hurry." He shut the back of the car and jumped in the front seat.

The ride to the hospital was silent, each one busy with their own thoughts. Susanne knew David would be praying, but she couldn't. This was God's fault. God's and Brianna's. Right when she thought she could accept Brianna staying, this happened.

Meagan had obeyed and only set up small jumps. It should've been fine. Nothing should have gone wrong. Meagan had taken those jumps dozens of times, and Glory had never spooked. The mare was green, but not like Susanne's Arab mare, spooking at everything that moved.

Brianna shouldn't have thrown that coat. Sure, maybe she didn't know better. But if she hadn't been dumped at our house, my daughter wouldn't be hurt.

A soft moan brought Susanne back to her patient. How could she have taken her attention away from her daughter?

"Meagan? Are you awake?"

"Is she waking up?" David asked.

"I don't think so. She seems to be in pain, but she hasn't opened her eyes. Do you think that's a bad sign?"

"She'll be okay, Susanne. I've been praying for her, and I know God is taking care of her."

"If He was taking care of her, she wouldn't have fallen in the first place." She bit her lip and tried to will her voice to stay calm.

"This wasn't God's fault. We can't blame anyone. Meagan will be fine. We have to believe that."

"It was my fault." A tear-filled voice spoke from the front seat. "I scared her horse and made her jump. If Meagan dies, it's my fault. I killed her."

"She isn't going to die, Brianna, and it isn't your fault," David said.

"Is Jesus going to make her well, Dad?"

"I think so, Steven. You pray too, okay?"

"Okay."

How could David promise something like that? God doesn't heal everybody. Why would he tell Steven that? What if something does happen to Meagan? For all we know, God doesn't care at all. What a stupid thing for him to say.

Susanne didn't care what David said—she knew the truth. It was Brianna's fault. If anything happened to Meagan, she would never forgive the girl.

A gurney whisked Meagan into the emergency room as soon as they pulled up to the entrance of the hospital. Dr. Mayhew finished his exam and joined the family in the waiting room. Meagan was still unconscious. Susanne was terrified.

"We're taking a CAT scan right now, and I've ordered an MRI," he said without preamble. "It may be a serious concussion, but I want to be sure there's nothing more going on. Head injuries can be tricky."

"Why isn't she awake yet? That isn't normal, is it?" David stopped pacing and stared at the doctor.

"It could be."

"But the accident was forty-five minutes ago. Shouldn't she be awake?"

"It's not normal to be out that long, but not unheard of, either."

"What else could be wrong if it isn't just a concussion?"

The doctor cleared his throat. "With a more serious concussion, there's always the possibility of the brain swelling or internal bleeding. I'm not finding any fractures to the skull, which means no pressure is being applied, so that's hopeful. Let's wait to see what the test say before we go into possibilities."

"Could she die?" Brianna whispered.

"I don't believe she will." He averted his eyes and seemed to hesitate. "We need to wait for the results to come back before we start worrying. She's young and healthy. Right now, her vital signs are strong, and she's stable. I'll let you know as soon as I know anything more. We'll move her to ICU if she doesn't wake up soon."

Susanne gasped, her shaking hand going to her mouth. "ICU! But that's for people in critical condition. Why are you moving her there if it's only a concussion?"

"The care is constant. We want to monitor her condition around the clock until we know what we're dealing with. It won't do any good to tell you not to worry but try. We'll know more in a few hours." He nodded at each in turn, then walked away, his posture bent.

Susanne turned to David. "The nurse said he's been dealing with emergencies for the past seven hours. They've had quite a run of injuries today. I hope they call another doctor in if he's too tired. I don't want someone who isn't at his best caring for Meagan."

David gazed after the retreating form of the doctor. "I'm sure he knows what his limits are, honey. The admitting nurse said he's the top ER doctor in the area."

"He'd better be."

"Should you call your mom?"

She jumped to her feet. "Oh, my gosh! I should've called her from the house and let her know we were headed here."

"You had other things on your mind. It was more important to get Meagan here. I left my cell in the car if you don't have yours."

"Thanks, I didn't think to grab mind." Susanne hurried out to the parking lot, yanked open the car door, and searched for the phone.

She needed to calm down, or she'd scare her mother. The look on the doctor's face when he'd talked about the possibilities would've scared anyone. He wasn't telling them everything. He hadn't looked them in the eye and had hesitated before answering their questions.

What if Meagan died? Or she woke up with brain damage? Susanne shuddered. What a horrible thing that would be for her active, horse-loving daughter. Would she ever ride again?

She shook herself. She had to stop thinking this way. Maybe it was only a concussion, nothing more. Susanne needed her mom. Claire was a strong person. Susanne had thought she was strong, but right now, she felt as weak as a new-born puppy.

Her eyes closed, and she prayed her mother would answer. "Mom? It's me. You need to come to the hospital. Meagan's been hurt."

"Meagan? How?"

"She got thrown from Glory after taking a jump. She's unconscious, and we're waiting for the results of a CAT scan and an MRI. It may only be a severe concussion, but the doctor doesn't know for sure. I'm scared, Mom." She tried to still the shaking hand that gripped the phone.

"I'll be there as fast as I can. I'm leaving right now. Don't worry, honey. Meagan will be okay." The phone clicked off.

Gratitude flooded her heart that her mother was coming, but none of this seemed real. It felt as though she were wandering in a strange room, pitch black and silent. She had no concept of where the light switch might be or even if one existed. After groping for what seemed an endless time, she was losing her sense of direction and beginning to question her sanity. Would anyone ever turn on the light or open the door?

David wasn't sure what to think. His daughter's condition worried him. He'd been praying but couldn't shake the feeling of dread that hammered him. Susanne must be going through incredible stress. He was struggling, but deep in his spirit, he knew God was in charge. Susanne didn't have that hope. From the comments she'd made, she was blaming God.

A terrified Steven and Brianna huddled together in the waiting area. He had to shake his own fear and take care of them.

"Steven, scoot over, buddy, and let me sit beside you."

The little boy slid over on the seat, his eyes huge as he stared up at David. "When will Meagan wake up?"

He draped his arm around Steven's shoulders. "We don't know, Son. We hope it'll be soon, but the doctor isn't sure."

"What's wrong with her?"

"She hit her head really hard when she fell off her horse. She was wearing her helmet, or she could've been hurt even worse."

"That's why you make me wear a helmet when I ride my bike, huh, Dad?"

"Yes, it is." David pulled him closer in a hug. "Brianna, how're you doing?"

She shrugged and swiped her face with the back of her hand.

"It's not your fault. You shouldn't keep blaming yourself."

Red, swollen eyes met his. "You weren't there. You didn't see. I took my coat off and threw it over the fence. It scared Glory, and she jumped sideways. Then she bucked, and Meagan fell off. It *was* my fault."

He drew a deep breath and leaned toward her. "It was an accident. You don't know anything about horses, and no one told you not to do that. It could've happened to anyone."

She sniffed and rubbed her nose. "Susanne would never have done it, and neither would Meagan. They've told me to be calm around the horses and not spook them. I didn't think about my coat. I didn't know it would scare her."

He pulled out a hankie and pushed it into her hand. "I know you didn't. We don't blame you."

"Susanne does. She'll hate me now." A sniffle interrupted the words. "She was starting to like me. Now she'll want me to leave." Her chin quivered, and the tears started to roll.

"Susanne does not hate you. We need to pray for Meagan and let God take care of the rest."

"I don't care about anything except Meagan. If you want me to leave, I don't care. Just so Meagan gets well." Brianna began to sob.

David looked on helplessly. He reached over Steven and tried to hug her, but she pulled out of his embrace. Steven reached for her hand, and she clung to the little boy. David sat back in his chair, wishing there was more he could do.

The front door opened, and he heard Claire's voice. Susanne must have called her and waited outside. He'd almost forgotten she'd gone to the car.

"Is there any change?" Susanne rushed across the lobby, Claire right behind her.

"Not that we've heard. It feels like it's been hours since the doctor came out last time, but it's only been about thirty minutes.

I'm going to call our pastor and ask him to pray. Did you bring the phone in?"

"Yes. But do you think that's necessary?"

David leveled a serious look at Susanne. "I don't think it hurts to have people praying."

"But I doubt it'll help, either." She flung herself into the chair across from the kids.

"It's the best hope we have right now, Susanne." He waited for her to take the phone from her pocket, then strode across the waiting room and headed outside.

Looking at her watch, Susanne saw it was mid-afternoon. Steven and Brianna were tired, and she knew they must be hungry.

"David, do you think we should try to find the doctor? We need to know what's going on."

"I was thinking the same thing." David heaved himself up from the chair and headed to the nurses' station.

"Susanne?" Claire touched her daughter's hand.

"Yes?" Susanne dragged her eyes away from David's form leaning over the desk.

"Maybe I should take the kids to my house. They need to eat, and I don't think this waiting is doing them any good."

"Let's wait a little longer and see what the nurse tells David."

David hurried back, a frown marring his features. He sank into the chair next to Susanne. "They said the doctor is viewing the test results. The nurse doesn't know how much longer it'll take. Meagan is still unconscious. One of us can stay with her once they get her settled."

"Thank God." Claire breathed a sigh. "At least you'll get to stay with her. I'll wait until we talk to the doctor before I take the kids home."

"Good idea," Susanne said.

The silence was depressing, and the minutes passed slowly. Why was it taking so long? Susanne wanted to sit with Meagan. If she could only see her, be with her, she would know. A mother could sense these things.

"Mr. and Mrs. Carson?" Dr. Mayhew's tired voice reached them from across the empty waiting room. "Your daughter is awake."

"Thank God!" David jumped from his chair, reaching to hug Susanne.

"Can we see her?" Susanne asked.

"In a few minutes. I want to go over the results with you." He sat on one of the chairs and indicated the others should do the same.

"Is it a concussion?" David asked.

"We believe so. It's not normal to remain unconscious for over two hours with a concussion, so we want to monitor her for a day or so. However, the scans both look good. There was light swelling of her brain but no internal bleeding. The helmet saved her from a serious skull fracture."

Susanne leaned forward in her seat. "But her brain is swollen? What does that mean?"

"It means we'll need to put her on steroids to reduce the swelling and watch her closely for the next few hours. We're pleased she's awake, and the prognosis looks good."

"Do you have any idea how long she'll need to stay?"

"I can give you a much better idea tomorrow. We're keeping her awake for now. She's nauseated and dizzy, and she vomited as soon as she came to. We'll keep her still and see what kind of progress she makes through the night. One of you may stay with her if you'd like."

"Definitely. I can't thank you enough." David shook the

doctor's hand. "Would it be possible for both of us to stay?"

He glanced from David to the children, who sat a few yards away trying to listen. "I don't see a reason why not if you don't need to go home with your other children. A nurse will get you as soon as Meagan is settled."

David motioned toward Claire. "Susanne's mom is taking them home. We both want to stay if you think it won't be too much for Meagan."

"That'll be fine. You can talk to her for a bit and help keep her awake. We've decided to put her in a regular room since we've seen the test results. She's past the worst danger, but we'll be checking her every quarter-hour for a few hours before letting her go back to sleep." He stood to his feet and looked at his watch. "I'll talk to you soon. I need to see other patients, but a nurse will call me if you need anything."

"Thank you, Dr. Mayhew. We're grateful for your care," Susanne said.

The doctor walked across the waiting room, stopping for a moment at the nurses' station before he disappeared down the hall.

David held out a hand to each of the drooping kids still sitting on the hard-plastic chairs against the wall. Steven reacted first and pushed to his feet.

"What did the doctor say, Dad? Is Meagan going to die?"

"No, Son, she's not." David stepped over to the boy and kneeled in front of him, then pulled the silent Brianna over to his side. "The doctor said she's out of danger and awake. Grandma will take you home so you can eat, sleep in your own beds, and get some rest."

"But I want to see Meagan." Steven pulled out of David's encircling arm and headed toward the door where the doctor had disappeared.

Susanne intercepted the boy before he could escape. "I'm

sorry, you can't see her tonight. They'll only let adults in her room now. She's still sick and needs lots of rest. But maybe you can see her tomorrow, okay?"

He hunched his shoulders. "I guess. Is Brianna going home with us too?"

David wrapped his arm around Brianna's shoulders. This time she didn't resist. "Yes, and either your mom or I will see you both in the morning."

Claire beamed. She hugged each of the family in turn before she turned to Susanne. "I'm so thankful Meagan is all right. I'll get these kids home. They look exhausted. Do you want me to stop and get you something to eat before I go?"

"There's a cafeteria here, and we can take turns when we get hungry. Right now, all I want is to see Meagan."

Susanne hugged Steven, then turned to speak to David, hoping no one noticed her neglect of Brianna. Susanne knew Brianna blamed herself for the accident. She struggled to be fair, knowing she should comfort the girl, but she wasn't in the mood to deal with it now. A small voice niggled at the edges of her mind, whispering she shouldn't have let Meagan jump without being with her, but she was too tired to listen right now.

Chapter Twenty-Two

THE NIGHT WAS LONG AND STRESSFUL. Meagan's room had two beds, but thankfully, the second stood empty. David and Susanne took shifts, rotating between the bed and the chair. They'd spoken to Meagan when they first entered the room, asking how she felt.

"Like a man with a sledge hammer is trying to get out." She tried to smile but winced instead, and her eyes closed in pain.

The doctor relaxed his quarter-hour vigil after the first two hours and allowed her to sleep but instructed a nurse to check on her every hour.

"Do you have to keep waking her?" Susanne asked the nurse. David had slipped out for coffee and the nurse had entered the room for the third time.

"It's important we talk to her. We're watching for any sign of neurological damage. She needs to know who she is, who you are, that she's in a hospital, those types of things. As long as she's able to answer coherently, we can let her go back to sleep."

"At least she isn't still throwing up."

"Her stomach is empty, and her body is insisting on sleep. I doubt she'll be able to keep anything down for the next twenty-four hours."

Susanne stepped closer to the bed and leaned over to watch as her daughter's eyes drifted shut. "Do you have any idea how long she'll need to be here?"

"No. That's up to the doctor. I've seen head injuries leave the hospital in a matter of hours when someone's at home to care for them. I've also seen a doctor keep them several days. But that's usually only if it's something more serious than a concussion."

Susanne brushed the hair away from Meagan's face and

tucked the sheet in around her still form. "Do you know for sure that's all it is? He's ruled out everything else?"

The nurse glanced at Susanne. "I can't speak for him. Didn't he tell you?"

Susanne stepped away from the bed and slipped into the chair a few feet away. "Not really. He said he wants to keep an eye on her, but that the test results came back okay. I'd like to know if there's anything more that could go wrong at this point."

The nurse turned down the light over the bed. "I'm sorry. I wish I could tell you. She seems good to me, but there are a few things that can develop that he might be watching for."

"What kind of things?" Susanne's voice rose.

"I'm sure it's nothing to worry about. I shouldn't have said anything. Please forgive me." The nurse looked embarrassed and hurried from the room.

Susanne sat next to Meagan's bed, fear gripping her again. What were they watching for? She thought the doctor had told her that Meagan would be okay, but maybe he was hinting at something worse when he said they needed to watch her.

Why was this happening to her daughter? Meagan went out of her way to make Brianna feel welcome and look where it got her—in a hospital bed with who knows what kind of lasting damage.

She cradled her head in her hands. The tears trickled through her fingers. Quiet sobs shook her body.

"Susanne? What's wrong? Is she worse?" David's voice as he came through the doorway penetrated her fear.

"No." She looked up and wiped her tears. "There hasn't been any change. The nurse woke her a few minutes ago, and Meagan answered her questions and went back to sleep."

"Then why are you crying?" He stepped next to her, placing his hand on her shoulder.

She reached for the tissue box on the table near the bed. "The nurse talked like the doctor is watching for something that could go wrong, but she won't tell me what. She apologized for saying anything and rushed from the room. Then I remembered the doctor saying he wants to keep an eye on Meagan. What if she ends up with permanent brain damage?"

He patted her shoulder and smiled. "I'm sure she won't, honey. You have to quit worrying. Meagan's been awake, recognized both of us, and knows where she is. Those are all good signs. We need to trust the doctors and trust that God is taking care of her."

"I'm trying not to be bitter, but I can't deal with you asking me to trust God right now." She kept her voice down. She didn't want to take a chance of Meagan waking up and hearing.

"It was an accident, Susanne. We can't blame anyone for it."

"I can. I saw it happen. And if you hadn't allowed Brianna to stay, Meagan wouldn't be in this hospital." She pulled back from the hand that rested on her shoulder. Her reaction smacked of overwrought emotions and lack of rest, but right now she didn't care. "So I guess it's really as much your fault as Brianna's."

The low hum of the machinery poised above Meagan's head seemed to fill the room.

"We *both* agreed to keep Brianna through the summer. The doctor said Meagan will be okay, and it doesn't help to worry. You'll feel better about it, if you can rest."

"I'm not sleeping. I couldn't sleep if I wanted to."

He held out his hand. "You're tired. Why don't you lie down? I can keep an eye on Meagan."

She took Meagan's hand. "I'm not going anywhere. You sleep if you want to. I need to be sure she's okay."

He shook his head and walked to the other side of the room. "I'll lie down for an hour. If you want to rest, let me know."

"I don't."

She heard the casters under the bed shift as David lowered himself onto the narrow surface. Within minutes, his snores filled the room.

How could he sleep with their daughter still in danger? He'd denied it was Brianna's fault and had asked her to trust God. *What a joke.* After this accident, she'd never trust God with anything.

She wanted her old life back. She wanted her daughter safe and her family of four back, and right now, the chance of that happening seemed about as slim as one of her roses blooming in January.

David woke in the middle of the night. Something didn't feel right. Susanne wasn't lying next to him, and the bed felt too narrow. He jolted awake. He wasn't at home. He was sleeping in a hospital bed.

He swung his legs over the side, trying to get his bearings in the dimly lit room. Susanne slumped in the chair next to Meagan's bed. He stepped over beside her and stooped to look into her face.

He needed to get her onto the bed without waking her up. She was exhausted. She'd wake in the morning with a sore back and stiff neck if she remained in this chair. The least he could do was try to make her comfortable.

He put one arm around her shoulders and the other under her knees, pulling her against him and standing slowly, easing her toward the nearby bed. She remained asleep, stirring only slightly, whispering Meagan's name.

"Shh, it's okay. Meagan's sleeping." He laid her head on the pillow and pulled a sheet over her quiet form. A strand of wavy hair draped over her face. He gently brushed it to the side, then kissed her forehead before straightening.

"Sleep well, honey. I pray you'll let go of your anger and see God's love for our family. I'm having a tough time too, but we're going to be okay." He leaned over, placing another soft kiss on her forehead.

"Um, excuse me..." The nurse from earlier in the evening stepped into view.

"It's okay. My wife's sleeping."

"I need to check Meagan," the nurse whispered.

He stepped away from the bed. "Are you going to wake her again?"

"No. The doctor said we only needed to do that four times. If she had good responses, we could let her sleep the rest of the night." She leaned over Meagan, making notes on the chart and checking her vitals, then hung up the chart and walked toward the door.

"Nurse?" David held out his hand, touching her arm.

She swiveled to face him. "Yes?"

"My wife said you mentioned something earlier about the doctor being concerned. Could you tell me what you meant?"

Her voice lowered, and she glanced at Susanne. "I shouldn't have said anything. I'm new, and I got a little flustered at her questions. I apologize."

"Do you think there's reason to be concerned, or do you know what the doctor might be watching for?"

"It's just routine. With a head injury, they make sure the patient is aware of their surroundings. We don't want to see an ongoing occurrence of nausea or any indication of a seizure or disorientation. So far, it's looking good. It wasn't my place to discuss it, and I'm sorry for causing your wife concern."

"I appreciate that. Susanne was worried, and I'd like to reassure her when she wakes up."

Footsteps walked past the door, and the nurse glanced in that direction before turning to David. "Dr. Bradley will be in at seven in the morning to check on Meagan."

"Not Dr. Mayhew?"

"No. He's the ER doctor. One of the other doctors does follow-up care if we admit the patient. Don't worry. Dr. Bradley is an excellent physician. He'll take good care of your daughter."

David nodded at the young woman, who smiled and left the room. "Thank You, Lord," he whispered, "for taking care of Meagan. Please heal her. And, Lord, please straighten out this mess. Susanne was starting to accept Brianna, but now she's blaming her, and I haven't been much of a dad to Brianna. I'm giving it all to You."

The pastor had promised to pray and offered to call the church prayer chain. It helped knowing others were praying. This was too heavy to carry alone.

He settled down next to Meagan's bed, trying to block out the sharp smells and unfamiliar sounds, holding her hand and continuing to pray. All he could do at this point was trust that tomorrow would be a better day.

Chapter Twenty-Three

LIGHT STREAMED THROUGH THE WINDOW AND reflected off the shiny rails of Meagan's bed directly onto David's sleeping face. Susanne stood next to him and struggled to remember how she'd gotten from the chair into the bed. David must have moved her, taking her place at Meagan's side. He slouched down in the chair, chin touching his chest and soft whiffling noises coming from his slightly open mouth. She should be grateful for the rest, but right now, worry dominated her thoughts.

A rustling came from a few feet away. "Mom?"

Susanne's head whipped around. Meagan was awake.

She leaned over the bed to look into the droopy eyes of her daughter. "Meagan, how are you feeling, honey? We've been so worried about you."

"I have a bad headache. Why am I here?" Meagan's gaze roved around the room, coming back to rest on her mother's face.

"Hi, sugar." David woke up, leaned forward, and touched Meagan's hand.

Her eyes narrowed, and her nose wrinkled. "You both slept here all night?"

"Yes. You're here because Glory dumped you after you came out of the jump. Do you remember?" Susanne asked.

"I remember saddling her and setting up the jumps, but that's all. She dumped me? Why?"

Susanne looked at David, her eyebrows raised.

He shrugged, shaking his head almost imperceptibly. "Glory crow-hopped when she landed. You lost your balance and fell, and your head hit the jump. If you hadn't worn your helmet, you'd have been hurt a lot worse."

She closed her eyes, and the corners of her mouth turned down. "Why don't I remember? My head hurts, and I tried to sit up while you guys were sleeping, but I got dizzy. What's wrong with me?"

"You have a concussion, sweetie. The doctor should be coming in to see you anytime," Susanne said.

A few minutes later, they heard a whistel, right before a person rounded the door. A small man with wire-rimmed glasses exchanged the whistle for an oversized grin.

"Good morning. The Carson family, I assume. I'm Dr. Bradley." He extended his hand to both adults, then stepped over to the bed where Meagan lay.

He picked up her wrist with fingers that seemed too long for his hand. "Well, young lady, you gave us quite a scare. I'm glad to see you're awake now. How're you feeling?"

"Not very good. My head hurts, and I'm dizzy if I try to sit up."

He leaned over the bed, dangling his stethoscope from his hand. "I'm going to listen to your heart, and then I need to look at your eyes. Is that okay?"

"I guess."

His brow furrowed in concentration as he moved his stethoscope from her lungs to her heart. He took several minutes to check her pupils and test her responses before he turned to David and Susanne. "I've read the report from Dr. Mayhew as well as the nurse's reports taken through the night. I'm happy with her progress. She's a lucky young lady, and you're wise parents, making her wear a helmet."

Susanne sank onto the chair by Meagan's bed, trying to still her shaking hands. "Is she going to be all right? The other doctor seemed to be watching for something. We didn't know what, and we've been worried."

His compassionate eyes lingered on her face. "I'm sorry. While ER doctors are very thorough, sometimes they don't give the most thorough explanations. I'm fairly confident she's out of danger. It looks like a concussion and nothing more. I'll be keeping her one more day for observation, but I think we can send her home tomorrow if she continues to progress."

"So soon? That's wonderful news!" David drew Susanne into a hug.

The doctor smiled at Meagan and winked. "You'll need to take it easy for a few days, young lady. No horseback riding or running any races." His smile faded, and his voice resumed its serious note. "We'll want to see her twenty-four hours after you take her home and have another checkup a week later, but I believe she'll be fine. There shouldn't be any lasting effects beyond the dizziness and headache the first few days, and those should fade fairly quickly."

Susanne couldn't seem to stop her tears. "I'm sorry. I shouldn't be such a baby. But I've been so worried."

The doctor patted her hand. "Not a problem. If it'd been my daughter, I'm sure I'd feel the same. I suggest you go home and rest. Take turns staying with Meagan until we release her tomorrow. I'll be in again this afternoon to check on her progress." He hurried from the room, his whistle starting up again when he reached the hall.

"God is good, Susanne. Meagan's going to be all right." David gave Susanne a wide grin, then leaned over to give Meagan a gentle hug.

"I'm thankful, David." Susanne couldn't get anything else out past her tears. She had to admit—maybe God had intervened this time.

The next twenty-four hours seemed to drag, but the time finally arrived for Susanne and David to bring Meagan home.

They'd taken turns at the hospital and at home with the kids.

Meagan's favorite nurse wheeled her down the long hallway, stopping at the nurses' station for a moment. An older woman sitting behind the desk leaned over to give her a card. "We all signed it, dear. You've been a wonderful patient, and we hope you never have to come back again."

"Thank you." Meagan waved and smiled until she rounded the corner.

"You be careful riding those horses." The nurse pushing her chair positioned it next to the car. She kept her arms around Meagan, making sure she didn't move too quickly, and helped her into the front seat.

"I will." Meagan gave her a lopsided smile. "I'm doing better. I can sit up."

"The doctor said you need to take it easy the next couple of days." She reclined the seat all the way back and snapped the seatbelt in place. "I know you're feeling better, but we don't want the dizziness to return."

"Okay. I'm just sick of lying down. I can't wait to get home and see Steven and Brianna." She eased onto the pillow and winced as her head touched down.

Susanne climbed into the backseat and reached forward to wedge a cushion between Meagan's shoulder and the door. "Tell us if it's bouncing too much or you need Dad to slow down." She thanked the nurse before closing the door and snapping her own seatbelt in place.

Meagan didn't complain, but David took it easy on the drive back, not wanting to jar his precious cargo. They pulled into the driveway to find Claire, Brianna, and Steven waiting in front of the house, looking like children waiting for Santa to emerge from the chimney.

"Welcome home!" they shouted.

Susanne jumped out of the car and opened Meagan's door. Meagan scooted out and walked carefully into the house on David's arm, dropping onto the couch in the living room with a sigh.

"Head hurting, honey?" David asked.

"A little, but not too bad. I want Brianna and Steven to stay and keep me company. I don't want to take a nap, just rest for a few minutes."

"That's fine." David gave her a quick kiss and ruffled Steven's hair on his way out of the room.

"I don't want you trying to get up, Meagan. If you need anything, you let one of the kids get it for you or call me. And only a few minutes of talking. Then I want you to rest." Susanne went to the next room to give the kids time alone but kept an ear tuned to the living room. She didn't want Meagan overwhelmed by too much chatter.

"Is your helmet all broke up, Meagan?" Steven asked.

"I don't know. I haven't seen it. The doctors might've thrown it away."

"Are you mad at Glory? Are you going to sell her?"

"No. She's a good horse, and I love her. I'd never get rid of her because she crow-hopped and I couldn't stay on."

"Are you mad at Brianna?"

"That's silly. Why should I be mad at Brianna? It wasn't her fault."

"Yes, it was. I heard Mom tell Dad. She threw her coat over the fence in front of Glory's face, and it scared her and made her jump." His young voice rose.

"That's stupid, Steven. Brianna didn't do that."

"Yes, I did." Brianna spoke softly, making Susanne strain to hear. "If you'd died, it would've been my fault. Don't you remember?"

"No. I don't remember anything. The doctor said I might never remember. But it doesn't matter. It was an accident, and it's dumb if anyone says different."

"Your mom doesn't think so."

"I don't care. You're my friend and my sister, and I'm not mad at you. And, Steven, you be quiet. It's mean to say stuff like that."

"You're not my boss, Meagan."

Susanne had heard enough. She stepped around the corner, her hands on her hips. "Come here, Steven. You've pestered Meagan enough." She took his hand and trotted him out of the room.

Susanne patted Steven's back and shooed him toward the stairs. "You need to find something to do. Run on up to your room for a while."

"Aw, Mom, not fair!" He began to whine but stopped at the sharp look from Susanne. "All right." His steps dragged, and his feet shuffled, making painful progress toward the stairs.

The voices continued to drift out of the living room as Susanne headed toward the kitchen.

"Was your mom listening?" Brianna's voice floated into the nearby kitchen, reaching Susanne's ears.

"I don't think so. But if she was, I hope she heard me say I'm not mad at you and she shouldn't be, either."

"You really don't blame me?"

"No. And I'm going to talk to Mom about it."

"No! I don't want her to get madder because you talked to her. Promise?"

"All right, I guess, but I don't like it. Hey, do you want to go get your ipod? We can listen, and I can rest for a while. Maybe later we can play a game or something," Meagan said.

"Sure. I'll be right back." Brianna's footsteps sounded across the hardwood floor.

Susanne heard the quick steps leaving the room, thankful Brianna went upstairs and not her direction. She needed to watch her attitude, or at least what she showed. She didn't want Meagan upset. She was grateful enough to have her daughter home that she was willing to put her resentment aside.

They had agreed to let Brianna stay, and she wouldn't go back on that decision, but her reservations were stronger than ever.

Chapter Twenty-Four

THE NEXT TWO WEEKS PASSED QUICKLY as the family settled into a routine for the summer. David worked longer hours, trying to please the critical owners of the new house being constructed. Susanne increased her work in the flower beds and spent time helping the kids with their projects.

Meagan tried to convince Brianna no one was mad at her, although Brianna's discomfort around Susanne seemed obvious. The headaches passed, and Meagan wanted to ride again, but Susanne insisted she take it easy. She limited Meagan to riding on their own property, and jumping wasn't allowed, so Meagan concentrated on helping Brianna get over her fear of the horses.

Claire came over a couple of times a week, and the kids had a sleepover at their grandmother's one night, giving David and Susanne a chance to have Susanne's delayed birthday dinner.

"I'm glad we could come tonight. I've wanted to make it up to you, ever since your birthday." David seated Susanne at their table.

"So am I. You picked a nice restaurant." She leaned toward the deep red roses David had purchased and inhaled their fragrance. It couldn't have been a more perfect setting. Candlelight cast its soft glow over the beautifully appointed table, and low music played in the background, creating a romantic atmosphere.

"I've heard great things about this place. It's pretty popular. I worried about getting a reservation on a Friday night, in the middle of tourist season. This time I called ahead more than a week."

"This time?"

"I had a reservation here on your birthday too."

"Oh." The memories of that night resurfaced, and Susanne worked to keep them from showing.

"I'm sorry, honey. I shouldn't have brought that up."

She shrugged and picked up her menu. "It's okay. I guess we need to order."

David tried—she couldn't deny that—but the evening felt a bit flat from that point on. Their lives had been running in parallel lines, flowing downhill and headed in the same direction, but separate and rarely touching. Brianna's arrival and Meagan's accident had cast a cloud over their relationship. Even though they'd talked, it seemed like nothing had been resolved. The episode with Jeena and their disparate views on God kept the tension simmering in the background, and it felt as though it could spill over into their lives again with the smallest encouragement.

A few nights after the belated birthday dinner, they sat in the living room after the kids were in bed. David had been unusually preoccupied all evening and answered in short, distracted sentences when anyone spoke to him. The continuous rustle of his newspaper and tapping of his foot pulled Susanne's eyes away from her book. Maybe she'd slip off to their room and read for a while. The thought of getting into another disagreement held no appeal. She snapped her book shut and shoved to her feet.

David put down his paper and cleared his throat. "I have a question for you."

Susanne paused. "Yes?"

David hesitated. "It's something I've been thinking about for a few days. Were you going to the kitchen? It's not a big deal."

She sank back into the cushions and offered a smile. "I'm fine. What's up?"

He drew in a deep breath and let it out slowly. "I've been thinking about hosting a home group. The pastor mentioned they're needing more leaders and host homes."

"Here? At our house?"

"We wouldn't lead it. Phil and Kim want to start a group, but they'd like to have it at someone else's home."

Susanne frowned. "I'm not comfortable with that."

"Why not? You know most of the people at church."

"That's not the point. I don't want a bunch of people in our home expecting me to tell all my personal feelings so they can pray for me. I don't have anything against them, but I don't want anyone prying into my life."

"I understand, but it's not like you'd have to say anything." He leaned toward her, locking his hands around one knee.

"Why don't you get involved in something else? You start going to another home group or teach one for all I care. Just don't involve me."

"But that doesn't feel right. I'd hate to teach a class or lead a home group without you start to drift apart."

"That's a lot of guilt to lay on me."

David shook his head. "I'm sorry. I didn't mean it that way, and I won't bug you about it. We can find other things to do together that aren't church related. Maybe we should start taking walks in the evening again."

"But it's something you want, and you're giving it up for me."

"It's okay. I love you, and it's not important. We can visit one of the home groups if you're willing, or get together with Kim and Phil occasionally."

"I like Kim and Phil, but I have no desire to get involved in a group."

They'd let it drop, but Susanne could feel the gap widening once again. It was subtle, nothing an outsider would notice, but the closeness they'd felt in the past no longer existed. The combined stresses of Brianna's appearance, Meagan's accident, and their disagreement over spiritual matters had taken their toll. David had chosen to work longer hours this summer and time spent together alone was rare. The issue of what to do about Brianna still hung between them. They'd made up, but Meagan's accident had rekindled the tension, and neither one seemed to know how to deal with it.

Meagan and Steven were enjoying the new addition to the family. After Meagan's accident, Brianna gave all of her time and attention to the two younger children, remaining distant toward Susanne and David. The girl appeared distrustful of the adults and seemed to sense the underlying currents in the family.

"Do you want me to leave?" Brianna's question startled Susanne.

They were sitting alone on the lawn under a large shade tree. David had gone to the kitchen to get cold drinks for the family, and Steven and Meagan chased after a lizard they'd seen scampering under some rocks. They were enjoying a rare couple of hours with the kids after finishing a picnic lunch on the edge of the pond.

"Why do you think that?" Susanne plucked a blade of grass and chewed on the end, not wanting to commit either way.

Brianna sat up and brushed the hair from her eyes. "Not long after I came, David said you did."

Susanne frowned, and her hands stilled, trying to follow the girl's statement. "What did he say? I'm not sure what you're talking about."

"When he talked to me the day after I came, he said you were the one having a hard time with it. I think he kind of wanted me to stay, but he said you didn't want another woman's child."

"He did?" Her mind scurried to take this in. David had put it all on her shoulders? Interesting.

"Maybe you misunderstood. We promised you'd stay at least through the summer. We're not changing that."

The girl nodded and jumped to her feet, apparently satisfied for the time.

David had some explaining to do. Susanne kept a carefully neutral face. She wasn't ready to confront him with this now, but Brianna's revelation did little to deepen her trust in David. Maybe he'd done it to protect himself in Brianna's eyes, in hope of not hurting her further. She shook her head. Better to leave it for now.

The agreement to start over and try to be friends that Susanne offered Brianna a few weeks earlier hadn't materialized. Susanne knew she'd put little effort into trying to correct the situation. She didn't want this atmosphere to exist, but she felt powerless to do anything about it. No solution was apparent, which only increased her tension, making her feel caught in a whirlpool. Never being sucked down through the ever-tightening hole, but always on the edge, pulled and thrown without any control. She had no idea what it was going to take to step out of this vortex, but whatever it was, she hoped it happened soon.

A few days later, the early evening sounds drifted through the open window in the living room. Susanne set aside her book as the bullfrogs bellowed their deep-throated call down at the pond. She leaned her head against the couch as the kids sat on the floor, playing a game. David dozed in his favorite easy chair but started awake when the phone broke the peace of the evening. Steven jumped to answer it, still young enough to find excitement in discovering who it might be.

"Mom, there's a man on the phone who's talking weird. I don't know what he wants," Steven whispered, placing his hand over the mouthpiece.

"Give it to me, please." Susanne reached for the phone.

The rest of the family stopped to listen.

"Hello? May I help you?"

"Yeah, I wanna talk to Brianna." The words slurred together, making Susanne strain to understand.

Her eyebrows rose, and she sat straightened in her seat. "Who is this?"

"Let me talk to Brianna."

"Who are you, and why do you want to talk to her?"

"I'm her uncle. I miss her and want to talk to her."

Susanne lowered her voice. "You gave up that right when you dropped her off without showing your face at our door. Brianna has no desire to speak with you."

"She's my niece. I can talk to her if I want to."

"She's living in our home now. You have no rights here." She stood, walked across the room, and turned her back on the staring children.

"You can't keep me away from my niece." His voice dropped to a threatening growl.

Susanne glanced at David, who had gotten out of his chair and was mouthing questions and gesturing.

Putting her finger to her lips, she waved him off and transferred her attention to the phone. "You've been drinking. Brianna does not want to speak to you, and neither do I. Good-bye."

She hung up and turned to her glowering husband. "That was Brianna's uncle."

David stopped in front of Susanne, his arms crossed over his chest. "I could tell. You should've let me talk to him, especially if he's been drinking."

"There was no point. He wasn't going to listen to you, either, and I wanted to get him off the phone." She glanced at Brianna's white face and noted the gaping mouths of Meagan and Steven.

"Kids, I'm sorry you heard that," David said.

Susanne leaned over and touched Brianna's shoulder. "I

didn't think you wanted to talk to him, and he didn't sound like he was in any shape to talk to you."

"I don't want to talk to him." Brianna shuddered.

"Don't worry," David said. "Why don't you kids find a movie and make popcorn? We'll have a movie night."

"Yippee!" Steven shouted, racing for the rack of DVD's beside the TV.

"I'll make the popcorn, and Brianna can help me," Meagan said, taking the reluctant girl's hand and heading to the kitchen. "Come on, Steven. You get napkins and bowls out, then we'll pick a movie," she called.

David waited until the children were out of earshot before turning to Susanne. "What did he want?" He settled onto the arm of the couch and frowned, his dark eyebrows scrunched over his eyes.

"I'm not sure. He kept saying he wanted to talk to Brianna. When I told him no, he said I can't keep him away from her. I think he's harmless. I'm sure it was the alcohol talking."

The kids could be heard starting the popcorn and setting out bowls, but David kept his eyes turned in that direction and lowered his voice. "Maybe. I doubt he'd do anything, but we can't be too careful."

Susanne shifted in her seat and glanced toward the kitchen. "I agree. I don't think he'd have the nerve to come here, but I'll tell the kids if he calls they aren't to talk to him, but hang up and let us know."

"If he does show up, I'm calling the police." He pushed to his feet. "We'd better find a movie. I imagine the popcorn's about done."

Susanne shook off her sense of foreboding. "Sounds good. Let's make it a good evening for the kids' sake. We don't need them worrying about something that isn't apt to happen."

Chapter Twenty-Five

SUSANNE DETERMINED TO SET ASIDE HER feelings of discontent and enjoy the remaining summer. June had come and gone, and the heat of July had descended. Susanne finished laundry mid-morning while the kids cleaned their rooms. They'd all gotten lax the past couple of weeks, even the normally meticulous Meagan.

Susanne hummed a popular country song, letting her mind drift to nothing in particular. She wasn't a great singer, but she enjoyed music just the same. None of their family was gifted with musical ability, but all of them had their favorite radio stations, except Steven. He thought it a waste of time. Hopefully when he got older and started developing his own tastes, he wouldn't turn into a head-banging rocker. Susanne shook her head and smiled at the ludicrous thought. She couldn't tolerate thinking of her little Steven as a teenager. He was already growing up fast enough. She shoved that thought away and groped for another.

What's today's date? It was hard to keep track when the kids weren't in school. She knew the county fair would be coming in a week and a half, so it must be, let's see ... *Oh, my gosh! It's Brianna's birthday this month.* Not used to another birthday in the family, the date had totally escaped her. She struggled to figure out how soon it would be and realized it would take place the same week as the fair.

Was that something Brianna might enjoy for her birthday? They could invite Carrie and Ashley to go along and maybe even take one of Steven's friends, although that would be more bodies than would fit into their car.

As the plan took shape, Susanne felt a sense of relief. It would be an easy way to celebrate Brianna's birthday without being quite so personal. She would approach David this evening but wondered if he'd use work as an excuse to skip out.

Thankfully, he wasn't late coming home and didn't seem too preoccupied.

"David, we need to talk," Susanne said before he reached for the TV remote after dinner. A game occupied the kids in the kitchen, and this might be the only time to talk privately.

"Sure. What's up?" He looked more relaxed tonight than she'd seen him in the past two weeks.

"First, how is the house going you've been working on? Is it getting any better?" She settled down on the couch.

He leaned forward, a smile lighting his face. "Yes. We've gotten over a couple of big hurdles with the engineer and county building department. We're making progress on the structure and should have it framed and the roof going on soon."

"That's great. You must be happy to have that hornet's nest behind you."

"We are. The homeowners' frustration added to the stress." He quirked his brow at her. "What's up? I'm guessing there's more on your mind than how my project is going."

"You're right. I do want to ask you something."

"Go ahead." He leaned back in his recliner.

"I realized that Brianna's birthday is in less than two weeks. We should put out an effort to do something special, the same as we do for our kids."

"Like what? She doesn't have a lot of friends."

"No, and she might not be comfortable as the center of attention. I don't think she's completely at ease here yet. It might be fun to invite Kim's family and go to the fair for the day. We could hit the pizza place afterward and have a birthday cake. We'll invite Mom too."

"Were you thinking just a party or gifts?"

"Definitely gifts. It'll seem strange to our kids, otherwise. It's probably not what Brianna is used to, but we need to be fair. I can take Steven and Meagan shopping. Brianna might enjoy visiting Ashley for an afternoon, and we can keep the gifts a surprise."

"Sounds good."

"I hate to go on a Saturday or Sunday because of the huge crowds. Her birthday is on a Friday. If we don't leave until after lunch—say about two—can you come?"

"Sure. Mike can take care of the project for the afternoon. I enjoy taking our kids to the fair, and I imagine Brianna would love it."

"Thanks. Now I have to figure out whether or not to keep it a surprise from Brianna."

She mulled over David's comment about the girl being thrilled but seriously doubted anything David or she planned would excite Brianna. However, the anticipation her kids felt would surely be contagious. "I'll tell all three of the kids about the fair. It'll be a lot easier than expecting Steven to keep it a secret."

Steven and Meagan were ecstatic when Susanne had told them about the fair, but as Susanne expected, Brianna showed only mild interest. Her level of excitement grew a little over the next couple of days as Meagan and Steven regaled her with tales of past adventures at the fair.

A few days later, Susanne dropped Brianna off at Ashley's house. Ashley had called to invite Brianna, and Susanne explained her kids needed shoes, deflecting any questions about why Meagan wasn't staying with Carrie.

Ashley's diversion went off without a hitch, and the three conspirators made their way to town, intent on finding the perfect gifts.

"Mom, can I buy her a bike? Then she can go out and do jumps with me in the field. All she ever does is hang out with

Meagan," Steven pleaded from the backseat.

"That's a little more than you have to spend. Maybe if she's really interested in a bike, we can think about it later. You keep thinking, and we'll get her something nice."

"Okay, Mom."

She glanced in the mirror in time to see his nose wrinkle and lips turn down.

"Meagan, where would you like to shop?"

"I want to buy her a T-shirt that says something about horses. She likes mine that says 'Horse Poor and Loving It,' but she doesn't own a horse, so that won't work. Could we go to the Side Saddle Shop and see what they have?"

Susanne smiled. *No surprises from Meagan.*

She turned down the busy street and headed a few blocks away from the business center. It still amazed her how traffic clogged this town. The past ten years had transformed it with the huge influx of windsurfers and tourists coming to the awesome Columbia River Gorge. She liked it the way it used to be, quiet and more rural, but those days were gone. The locals tolerated the tourism since its growth kept the area alive. And the tourists who chose to live here permanently gave her husband's business a huge boost. Thankfully, mostly locals frequented the tack shop, and parking was rarely a problem.

"We always have to go to this dumb horse place," Steven grumbled.

"Remember your manners, Steven. You'll have your turn next."

A glower met her words, but at her sharp look, the drooping corners of his mouth straightened out. "Okay."

"Thanks. I appreciate that." She rewarded his reply with a smile.

They spent the next thirty minutes combing through the racks of colorful clothing, trying to decide what Brianna might like. Meagan picked out two that she loved, and Susanne let her buy both. The girl squealed in delight, giving her mother a quick hug. She held the first up in front of her, a T-shirt with the head of a gray horse on the front. It looked amazingly like Bones.

"Brianna will be tickled with both of them, Meagan. I'm thinking about getting her a riding helmet, since you've been working with her. She seems more comfortable around the horses now, and if she ever does ride, she'll need one."

"Great idea, Mom! Her head is only a little bigger than mine, so I'll try them on."

They finished up, then spent more than an hour wandering the aisles of a department store. How little they knew about the teenager living under their roof. Other than clothing or horse-related items, Susanne didn't have a clue what might make Brianna happy.

"Brianna loves my Christian music, but she doesn't have an iPod or CD player for her room. Could Steven get one for her and you get her a couple of CDs?" Meagan asked.

"Cool, Mom! Could I get her an iPod?" Steven begged. "Maybe she'll let me use it sometime." His face brightened at the thought.

"Don't count on taking it apart. You need to learn to respect other people's property. Ask for one for Christmas, and if you choose to take it apart, fine. But then you wouldn't have one of your own to play. Does that make sense?" She snagged the back of the boy's shirt as he started to dart away, pulling him back.

"I guess."

They stowed the final purchases in the car, pulling the cargo shade across the top to keep Brianna from noticing. At the last minute, Susanne realized they hadn't purchased shoes. They rushed back to the shoe section and finished in fifteen minutes.

"Good job, kids. I don't think we've ever picked out shoes this fast before."

"I'm hungry, and I'm tired of shopping," Steven said.

"I don't care about shoes. I want to get back and pick up Brianna." Meagan flopped down on the car seat with a sigh.

Susanne surprised herself with the contentment she felt at the end of the day. A breath of change in how she looked at Brianna whispered through her heart. She hated to probe too deeply, leery of destroying the tiny seed starting to germinate. A part of her wanted to hold onto the resentment fostered by Meagan's accident, but the thought that she should have been more vigilant surfaced again. Plus, something about buying a gift for a lonely girl and seeing the joy of giving reflected on her children's faces helped push it all aside.

No, she wouldn't examine her feelings too closely. After all, who knew what tomorrow might bring?

The day of the fair dawned sunny and warm with the expectation the temperature would reach the mid-nineties before the day ended. Susanne loved hot weather. Her mother couldn't tolerate hours in the sun, so she opted to meet them later at the air-conditioned pizza parlor. She waited at home for David to arrive with three impatient kids.

"My mom baked me a cake, and I always got a gift from her and Grandma, but I've never had a party before." Brianna's eyes sparkled as she looked from Meagan to Steven and quickly flitted to Susanne and away.

"You'll love what I got—" Steven's sentence came to a halt. "Meagan, stop it!" He slapped at the hand covering his mouth.

"Shh!"

"Oh, I forgot." Steven plunked down on the bottom step

outside their house. "Mom, is Dad ever going to get here?"

"He'll be here soon. Why don't you grab a couple of bags of chips and pop to bring with us?" She patted his back and nudged him toward the kitchen door. Hopefully, the activity of the day would wear out the irrepressible Steven, whose battery kept going and going.

David pulled in minutes later, and the kids piled in the car. His silence betrayed his preoccupation as he let the kids do most of the talking on the forty-minute drive to the fairgrounds. When the kids weren't around, she'd have to ask him what was on his mind.

The bright summer sun glinted off the calm waters of the Columbia River, and Susanne slipped her sunglasses on against the glare. The car began to climb a long hill up toward Goldendale, heading away from the river, and she settled back in her seat. Not long now. They drove through the county seat and on to the outskirts of town. It was a perfect pastoral setting, with rolling hills surrounding rich hay land and the Cascade Mountains peeking up above the hills in the distance. Kim's family had agreed to meet them in the parking lot. A decent number of cars filled the grassy area, but Susanne didn't see any sign of the Slaters' car. She pushed open her door and swung her legs out, and the kids tumbled out the back door.

"Where are they? Aren't they here yet?" Steven climbed up on the hood, shielding his eyes from the sun with his hand.

David gripped him under the arms and swung him back down. "That's enough, young man. You need to calm down." His stern voice quickly sobered the little boy.

"I'm sorry, Dad. I forgot. But how come the Slaters aren't here?"

"I know you're excited, but we'll find them soon enough."

"I sure hope so. I want to go on a bunch of rides! The girls said I could ride with them." Steven's high-pitched voice hit a higher note in his excitement.

They could see the Ferris wheel and hammerhead towering above the tall fence surrounding the fairgrounds.

"Oh, I smell food!" Steven squeaked.

"Listen. There's a band playing, and I heard a horse whinny. We're missing everything, Mom!" Meagan's face contorted, her eyes wide.

Cars were coming into the parking area in a nonstop stream, and most of them held families anxious to get to the fair. A man's voice booming over a loudspeaker pulled the kids' attention away from the search for their friends, but only for a moment.

"They're here. We beat them, but they're here!" The normally reserved Meagan jumped up and down, closely mimicking the earlier antics of her younger brother.

Excitement lit Meagan's face, and Susanne chuckled, sharing her joy. Her gaze swung to Brianna's serious face, clouded with something that seemed like a mixture of anticipation and apprehension. Susanne hadn't thought to ask Brianna if she'd been to a fair before, since she'd assumed all children had enjoyed at least one in their life. A number of their foster children were underprivileged. Why did she keep forgetting that Brianna had probably experienced much the same type of life?

Carrie and Ashley jumped out of their parents' minivan first, their sandaled feet hitting the gravel and scattering little pebbles. The four girls met halfway, three of their voices raised in excitement, and Brianna's face softened into a smile.

Susanne grinned and turned her attention toward Kim, who brought up the rear. "Hey there, I'm glad you guys made it! Our kids were beginning to think you'd never arrive."

Kim pulled off her sunglasses and slid them onto her head, wrinkling her nose. "Oh, dear, have you been waiting long?"

"All of five minutes." Susanne laughed. "But you know kids—

they thought it was an eternity."

Phil came up beside Kim, putting his arm around his wife and giving her a quick hug. "We'd have been here sooner, but Kim forgot the camera. We were only a mile or so from home, so it wasn't a big deal. She can't go anywhere without it. She has to have pictures of every event for her scrapbook."

Kim elbowed him in the side. "Hush, you!"

Susanne glanced at David, who moved up beside her. She caught a look of longing on his face as he glanced at the other couple. He noticed her looking at him, and the look disappeared. He swiveled on his heel and reached for the kids' backpacks.

What in the world is bothering David? It seemed he'd been looking more at Kim than at Phil. She glanced at Kim, wondering if she was watching David. Kim's full attention was focused on Phil. Susanne shook her head in irritation. Jumping to conclusions and assuming things had sent her spiraling into Jeena's clutches a few short weeks ago. She wouldn't go there again.

"Come on, gang, let's hit the rides," David called out to the kids, who ran screaming to his side, Phil close behind.

Susanne waved them on when he looked her way.

"My kids are carbon copies of their dad when it comes to carnival rides," Susanne confided to Kim. "Me, I hate 'em. Make me sick to my stomach, and I think I'm going to die before they're over. I know it sounds ridiculous, but they really scare me. I went on a kiddy coaster with my sister when I was young, and I was so terrified, they had to stop it halfway through."

"I know what you mean. Phil and the girls tried for years to coax me onto some of the rides, but I won't do it. They understand I'm a lot happier on the ground taking pictures of them having fun."

"That's one of the reasons I was thrilled you agreed to come. I wanted company while my family races from ride to ride without me."

They paid their entrance fee, bought tickets for the rides, and wandered into the noise and color of the fair. A small percussion band grouped in a gazebo struck up a tune. The lively music drew a smattering of people, who stood nearby, tapping their feet and clapping their hands. A dark gray horse nickered as he trotted by, led by a teenage girl dressed in English riding garb. Hawkers stood at their booths, trying to cajole passersby into sampling their wares.

A dozen yards ahead, David, Phil, and the children raced for the hammerhead, apparently intent on beating everyone else to the first ride they'd chosen. Kim shook her head and smiled, then lifted her camera and snapped a picture. "Where do you want to head first?"

Susanne stopped and glanced around, then nodded toward the rides. "Let's watch the first couple of rides, and you can get pictures, if you want. We can keep an eye on them and decide what to do afterward. That's one nice thing about these smaller county fairs—it's not as easy to get lost or separated."

Steven was finally tall enough to go on the wildest rides, but David had promised Susanne he would sit beside him, keeping an eye on him this first year. The little boy wiggled and bounced, clinging to his dad's hand in the line. When it was their turn to board, Susanne watched David recheck the safety harness that secured his son. He spoke to the girls before they started and glanced back at Phil, who sat behind the girls.

They had no sooner finished the first ride than they ran for the next. Susanne wondered how the men found the energy to keep up with the kids on their mad dashes. It was making her tired watching them.

After following the group and taking a number of pictures, Susanne and Kim decided to call it quits and visit. They took cold drinks to a covered pavilion with a table and a good view of the rides and gratefully sank onto the seats.

"I'm glad to see Meagan back to normal. Do you mind my asking how you and David are doing, as well as Brianna? Are you adjusting to the changes in your family?" Kim leaned forward slightly.

Susanne gratefully contrasted the compassion Kim expressed to the anticipation she knew she'd have seen on Jeena's face.

"We're thankful Meagan recovered so well. And no, I don't mind you asking about Brianna, but there isn't a lot to tell. I haven't wanted to talk to anyone about this, but I trust you more than I do most people. A few weeks ago, I went out for the evening with a friend. I was stressed, and she was sympathetic, and I ended up having too much to drink. It caused trouble between David and me," Susanne blurted out.

Kim's brows puckered.

Susanne realized it was possible Kim didn't know that she drank. "I guess we've never talked about drinking before. I'm sure you don't approve of it, but I don't think there's anything wrong with having a couple of drinks. It helps me to relax when I'm under stress." Susanne leaned back in her seat, crossing her arms.

"I'm not here to judge you, Susanne. I don't choose to drink, but I certainly have no room to criticize, either." Kim held Susanne's gaze and smiled, her head tipped to one side. "Did it help?"

"What? I don't follow."

"I assume you drink hoping it will change something. Did it solve the problem?" Kim took a sip of her Pepsi.

Susanne felt uncomfortable, not certain she could explain, and not wanting to get trapped in a discussion she wasn't ready for. "I simply meant it helps me deal with the stress because I'm able to relax for a while and not think about it. I'd been really upset prior to that night, and I guess I thought it might help ..." Her voice drifted off.

Kim's question caused her to think. Using alcohol occasionally had been a way to get through tough situations. Was she so weak she couldn't deal with things on her own? Why had she chosen to drink that night when a voice inside her had urged her not to?

Kim reached across the table and touched Susanne's hand. "Please don't misunderstand. I honestly *do* know where you're coming from. When I was in high school and during my first two years of college, I was a huge party girl. More than once, I drank until I passed out."

Susanne felt her mouth hanging open and made a conscious effort to close it. "No way. You're so religious!" She took a pinch of the cotton candy they shared.

Kim shook her head, and a hint of a smile crossed her lips. "Trust me, I haven't always been. I grew up in a home where Jesus was a swear word. All I heard was my parents screaming at each other every night when one or both of them had had too much to drink."

"Then what happened?"

"Nothing for a long time. I not only saw nothing wrong with drinking occasionally; I saw nothing wrong with it regularly. I was following my parents' example, on my way to becoming an alcoholic. But my junior year of college, I moved to the junior-senior dorm and got a new roommate, a girl named Michaela."

"What an interesting name!"

"I know, kind of unusual, huh? Everyone who sees it in writing assumes it's Mi-kay-la, but she always reminded me it's -Mi-shay-la." Her voice grew tender, and her mouth tipped up in a warm smile. "Was I ever shocked when I discovered I had a Jesus freak for a roomie. She fooled me at first because she didn't look the type. Know what I mean?"

"Yeah, I think so." Susanne had to raise her voice over the blare of a horn in the hands of a colorful clown giving balloons to children and entertaining them with jokes and antics.

"I had a twisted view of Christians. When I was that age, I assumed they'd wear out-of-date clothing, use no makeup, and not care about their appearance. Michaela was a cute, tall blond, always up on the latest styles. But I didn't care. The last thing I wanted was some Christian looking down her nose at me."

"I can relate. I hate it when people try to push their beliefs on me."

"Exactly. Unfortunately, I had to study if to graduate. Due to my party habits, I was behind in Applied Science. I had to turn it around because I needed that class to graduate. Wouldn't you know Michaela was a science major and offered to help? At first, I didn't want to accept. It didn't take me long to realize I didn't have a choice."

"Was she pushy like you expected?"

"Not at all, and that's what threw me. She never said a word about what she believed or anything about all the nights I came in late and woke her. I thought she'd blast me for it. Instead, she talked about the class and a little about herself."

"So what happened?" Susanne waved at the kids and the men coming over the top of the Ferris wheel and laughed at Steven raising his arms in the air and squealing.

Kim glanced where Susanne pointed and chuckled. "Looks like they're having a good time. I'm going to get another Pepsi. Want to walk over with me?"

"Sure. It's a bit distracting with all the noise, but I'm really interested."

They wove their way around the booths of games and items for sale. The hawkers shouted at them, hoping to entice them to try their hand at their games, but the women shook their heads and kept moving. Thankfully, the line was short at the concession stand. After buying their drinks, they found a seat on the edge of a grassy area near the rodeo grounds.

They settled on the grass, and Kim took off her sandals to rub her feet. "Ah, that feels good."

Susanne rolled over on her side and slid her sunglasses down onto her nose, peering up at Kim. "So what happened?"

Kim leaned forward and wrapped her arms around her knees. "One night I came home at midnight, completely bombed. We had a lot later curfew in our dorm, and the dorm parents were lax. When I say I was bombed, I mean I threw up, and it wasn't pretty. I didn't even make it to the bathroom; instead, I made a horrible mess all over the floor. I figured Michaela would come flying out of bed, screaming at me, but she didn't." Kim's voice got quiet, and she shook her head.

"Did she sleep through it?"

"No. She got up without a word, put her arm around me, took me in the bathroom, and cleaned me up. She helped me undress and tucked me in bed. The next morning, I remembered what happened. I expected to find a stinking mess on the floor that I'd need to clean, but it was spotless."

"Was Michaela waiting for you?"

"No. She'd already gone to class. She'd left a note and a couple of aspirin on the nightstand beside my bed. She said she hoped I felt better, and she'd stop in between classes to check on me." Kim smiled, then took a sip of her drink.

"Wow."

"Yeah, that's what I thought. When Michaela came back, I slammed her with questions. Why did she do that? Why wasn't she mad? I'd made her life miserable with my behavior. I asked if she was some kind of saint or something."

"What did she say?" Susanne raised her voice over the sound of whistles shrieking in a nearby booth, signaling that someone had won a prize.

Kim paused, and her gaze softened. "She said she was a sinner that Jesus had died for. He hadn't judged her but loved her instead, so it was her job to love people too. Her actions shouted so loudly they almost deafened me. I was ready to listen. My lifestyle hadn't gotten me anywhere, and I was headed for a major train wreck if something didn't change. Michaela showed me how to turn it around by turning to Jesus, and I've never been sorry."

"Did the two of you keep in touch?"

"Yes. She was my roommate the rest of that year and the following one. We ended up best friends and still talk today. I believe she saved my life. I could've ended up a hopeless alcoholic and possibly worse."

Susanne sat up, tucking her legs beneath her. "I can see why you're grateful. I've never had a drinking problem. In fact, I only have a few glasses of wine or a cold beer a couple of times a month. I can't say I've never gone over the edge, but it doesn't affect my life, and I can take it or leave it."

Kim frowned, and Susanne wondered what she'd said wrong. Did Kim think she didn't take her story seriously? Kim had pulled her life together—it sounded like she'd been a real mess. But Susanne was nowhere near that condition and didn't see how it applied to her.

"Seriously, I'm happy for you. To find a friend who cared so much is unusual."

"It was so much more than that. She showed me an entirely new life and introduced me to Jesus. I wouldn't have the family I do now if it weren't for Him."

"I understand what you're saying, but I don't feel the same. My life is good, overall. Besides, I believe in God, but I don't see what I need His help for right now. I've made a few mistakes, but we all have."

"You're right. No one is perfect except God. But being a Christian extends so much further than the initial experience of asking Jesus into your heart."

"I'm as much of a Christian as anyone. I go to church with David and the kids. I just don't think I need help. And with everything going on, frankly, God doesn't seem to do a great job in the decision-making department. I don't plan on giving Him control of my life." Susanne stood and gathered the empty cups.

"I'm sorry you feel that way. I won't say anything more about it after this one comment. You'll never know true fulfillment or peace until you've relinquished control of your life to the Lord."

"If that's the case, I guess I'll never have peace or fulfillment because I do not intend to make that decision." Susanne walked a couple of steps to a garbage container and tossed in the empty cups, perhaps using a bit more force than necessary.

"I apologize if you feel I've been preaching. You did ask me to finish the story. I'm sorry if I offended you by getting personal. I won't bring the subject up again unless you come to me. Is that fair?"

Susanne paused, realizing how abrupt she must have seemed. She didn't want to ruin their day or put a damper on the time that lay ahead.

"I'm not offended, and I do appreciate that you're trying to help. Also, to answer your earlier question, things are much better at home. Brianna seems to be fitting in well with Steven and Meagan, which is about the best I can hope for. David and I made up, or at least we're working on it. Our marriage isn't perfect, but whose is?" She laughed lightly. The last thing she needed was someone trying to fix *that* area of her life.

Kim sat without speaking. Small lines appeared around her

mouth and eyes.

"Really, Kim, thank you for sharing your experience. It was interesting getting to know more about your background." In all fairness, she knew Kim rarely brought God into a conversation other than offering to pray about something.

They wandered through a few of the household exhibits, keeping an occasional eye on the small group of thrill seekers. Hunger would eventually drive the kids back down to earth, along with a desire to see the rest of the fair.

CHAPTER TWENTY-SIX

"MOM, LET'S GO. DAD SAYS WE should head out if we're going to be on time to meet Grandma at the pizza place," Steven called down the aisle of stalls they'd been viewing, an hour later.

Normally, Meagan would have scowled and hushed her little brother, but she headed for the door of the long exhibit hall that housed the horses. Susanne wondered if the rest of the crew were as hungry as she. Pizza sounded great, and she hated to make her mother wait.

A couple of hours later, the pizza and cake were finished, and Meagan heaped a small pile of presents in front of Brianna.

"Are these all for me?"

Brianna had opened up throughout the day, laughing and screaming on the wild rides. She became more subdued when they reached the pizza parlor, and Susanne could only assume it was due to the presence of herself and David.

"Yep, they sure are!" Meagan crowed. "Hurry up and open them."

"Open mine first!" Steven demanded, shoving his package across the table toward the older girl. "You're going to like it best."

"No, she won't. She's going to like all of them," Meagan said.

"All right, kids, let's don't start arguing on Brianna's birthday. Let her open her gifts in peace, okay?" David smiled.

Brianna reached for Steven's present first, carefully opening one end of the box.

"Just rip it open! That's what I always do. We don't save the paper anyway." The little boy bounced in his seat.

Brianna looked a bit startled at this information, and Susanne again wondered at the girl who'd landed in their midst. These tiny incidents gave them glimpses into her previous life.

Her thoughts were interrupted by Brianna's squeal when she saw the picture of the CD player on the outside of the box.

"Yeah, and Mom got you—" Steven's words were cut short as Meagan clapped her hand over Steven's mouth, hissing at him to be quiet. "Sorry," he mumbled.

"That's okay, Steven. I love this. Thanks! I can't believe you got me my own CD player." She carefully turned the box around, looking at it from all angles.

"It's okay if you want to take it out," Susanne said.

The girl shook her head and set the box to one side. "I'll wait till I get back to my room."

Susanne noted the use of *my room* over the word *home* and wondered if it had been intentional. She doubted Brianna thought of their house as home.

Brianna showed equal excitement at the T-shirts Meagan gave her and the CDs from David and Susanne. When she opened the box with the helmet, a stunned look crossed her face.

Her troubled eyes sought Susanne's, and she dropped her hands from the box. "This is too expensive. I can't take this."

Susanne was shocked. It never occurred to her that Brianna would think about the cost. "It's fine. It's what David and I wanted to get. Besides, you really need a helmet if you're going to start riding with Meagan."

She hesitated, then nodded. "Okay. Thank you."

Ashley handed a gift across the table, breaking the awkward silence. "I got one for you too."

Brianna's eyes got big, staring at her new friend. She moved quickly this time, removing the paper on this last, unexpected gift. She lifted the lid of the little box and gasped as her fingers touched the delicate form of the cross nestled below. Gently, she raised the necklace from the box, her face shining.

"It's beautiful," Meagan breathed, reaching out to touch the delicate piece.

"Thank you, everybody." Brianna struggled with the words, looking around the table at the faces smiling back at her.

"Uh, we aren't quite finished," David spoke up.

"But you already gave me the helmet and the CDs."

"No, this one is just from me. I hope you like it." David placed a package in front of her.

The paper was twisted, and the ribbon around it clumsily tied in a bow. Susanne hadn't realized David had purchased a gift on his own and tried to imagine what he had picked for a girl they hardly knew.

"Go ahead and open it," David said as Brianna sat looking at the gift.

She picked up the rectangular box, removing the ribbon and popping open the small pieces of tape. The paper fell apart, revealing the soft glow of a deep blue leather Bible. *Brianna* glowed in the bottom corner, and a satin ribbon peeked out over the edge.

"My own Bible." She looked at David in awe. "And it's engraved. Thank you," she whispered.

David cleared his throat. "I thought you needed one of your own."

Susanne noticed two silent tears slip down the girl's face before Brianna turned her head and wiped them away.

As she lay in bed that evening, Susanne remembered David's distraction on the way to the fair. She had forgotten to ask if he was okay. She didn't feel comfortable questioning if he'd been watching Kim. The tension between her and David the past few weeks was enough without adding more friction. Besides, Kim was obviously smitten with her own husband and wasn't interested in David.

A light doubt nagged at her mind, and a thought whispered in her ear. He had a baby with another woman from a past she'd never been aware of, and he'd let Brianna believe the decision to not keep her permanently rested entirely with Susanne. Was it possible something else was happening now? She pushed the thought aside like a child trying to dodge a parent's reprimand.

"David?" She rolled over in bed and touched his back.

"Hmm?"

"I'm sorry. I didn't realize you were asleep."

He scooted around under the sheet and faced Susanne. "I'm not."

"Brianna said something to me the other day." She hesitated, then plunged on. Better get it out in the open. At least one thing would be off her mind. "You told her the day after she came that I was the one who didn't want to keep her. You let her think it was my decision?"

"Oh, man." David rubbed a hand across his face and groaned. "I knew it was the wrong thing to say. She'd been so hurt already, thinking I'd known about her from the start and didn't want her. I hated the thought of telling her we both were struggling with having her show up. I should have gone back and set it right. I'm so sorry I blew it again."

She took a moment to digest what he'd said. Had she been much better? She'd allowed Brianna to think Meagan's accident was her fault. At least David had acted out of kindness, not out of spite.

"It made me mad at first that you used me. But I honestly understand. I've hurt her too, and I'm not proud of it. I'm glad we made the effort to do something for her birthday."

He reached out and squeezed her hand. "Thank you. I don't deserve that."

They lay in silence. Susanne had so many other questions but hated to shatter the sense of peace she sensed in the room.

"I was thinking about today." David's voice roused her from her thoughts. "I've been thinking a lot about Brianna. I need to be doing more."

"Like what?" She turned the lamp on low and faced him again, not sure what to expect.

"I don't know her at all. I haven't spent any time with her. I've been feeling guilty and trying to figure out how I can change. And I worried about buying her the Bible. I wasn't sure how you'd feel."

"You think I'd be mad you got her a Bible? I'm not that bad, am I?"

"I'm sorry, I didn't mean it that way. I knew you wouldn't be mad, but I knew about the helmet and CDs. I didn't ask if you wanted your name on my gift. I'm sorry."

"So that's why you were so quiet today?"

"Well, yeah. I'll spend more time with her and Steven and Meagan. I won't single her out. I don't want our kids feeling ignored."

"I'm glad you told me, and don't worry about the Bible. I'm kind of tired, and you have to get up early. We'd better get to sleep." She gave him a quick kiss on the cheek, then shifted over onto her side, glad the temperature had cooled off.

"Good night, honey, and thanks for understanding."

She wished she could say she did understand. The Bible wasn't a problem. It might not have been her first choice as a gift, but she understood David's need to give it. What she didn't understand was the confusion she still felt thinking about the look David had shot Kim's way.

But she was determined not to go there. She and David had achieved a measure of peace in their marriage, and she didn't want to lose it.

CHAPTER TWENTY-SEVEN

OVER THE NEXT FEW DAYS, DAVID came home earlier each night. The kids were thrilled and pestered him to help with projects and play games in the evenings.

He put out more effort with Brianna and their own kids, leaving Susanne unsure of her feelings. She was happy for the kids' sake but couldn't help feeling a little jealous now that Brianna was thawing out around David. Did she want him to start loving this girl? That would set them apart even more unless she could find a way to let Brianna into her own heart.

Meagan would be heartbroken if her new big sister lived anywhere but here. Brianna still hadn't completely come out of her shell, but the two girls were forming a bond of friendship based on more than just horses. They seemed to understand one another in a way Susanne didn't quite grasp.

"Mom, can I ask you something?" Meagan asked after Susanne popped her head in Meagan's bedroom that Saturday morning.

"Sure. What's up?"

Meagan finished making her bed, then spun around. "I wish you'd help Brianna with the horses."

"With the horses? But you've been doing fine with her."

The girl reached for her old teddy bear and fiddled with the bow on his neck, then looked up. "Brianna is still afraid of them. I know you don't blame her for my accident, but she thinks you do. Would you give her a lesson? It might make her feel better."

Susanne grimaced. A part of her still blamed Brianna. Not much—it wasn't logical—but she couldn't completely shake it. Meagan's expressive eyes begged her to agree, and Susanne's heart couldn't withstand the plea.

"Okay. Do you want to come too?"

"I do, but maybe it'd be better if you did it alone."

Susanne looked helplessly at her daughter. "It wouldn't hurt to have you there."

"But she'll think it's my idea and that I'm making you. Could you do it alone? Please?"

"Okay. I'll stop by her room and ask."

"Thanks, Mom." Meagan bounced off the bed. "I'll stay in here."

Susanne walked through the doorway, rolling her eyes and shaking her head. Where had the wisdom so often evident in Meagan's life come from?

What had she gotten herself into? Susanne had been happy with the routine they'd established the past couple of weeks. The kids pretty much took care of entertaining Brianna, and her own involvement was minimal.

She stopped by Brianna's room, tapping on her door and pushing it open a crack. "Brianna?"

The girl lay on her bed, a horse book in front of her. "Yes?"

"Would you like to come down to the barn so I can help you for a few minutes? I know you've had a hard time around the horses since Meagan's accident."

"I guess. If you want to." She uncurled, then set her book aside before pushing herself to her feet.

They stopped at the barn to pick up a halter and walked down the path to the pasture. Susanne noticed Brianna's tennis shoes. They'd need to get her a pair of riding boots if she conquered her fear of riding.

When they arrived at the fence, the horses were waiting. Susanne drew a small bag of carrots out of her pocket. "Hold your hand out flat, and don't curl your fingers when they take the carrot. They mostly use their lips to pick it up, but remember, they're animals. They could mistake a finger for a treat."

Brianna laid the carrot on her flattened, outstretched palm, her eyes wide and her expression intent. Susanne's mare, Khaila, stretched her neck, reaching for the treat. Brianna held still and allowed her to take it without flinching.

"Good job! That's the way to do it. Give one to the others."

Brianna's face glowed from the unexpected praise. She eagerly fed Bones and Glory, who nudged each other out of the way.

"They're pushy." She giggled, pulling back her empty hand.

Glory whirled to nip Bones when he pushed his way in.

"Yes, they can be pigs. It helps to bring something down. That way, we never have to chase them around the field."

"What else do they like to eat?"

"The main thing is grass, but in the winter we feed them hay." Susanne decided to start with the basics. "We mostly buy orchard grass hay and grain with vitamins. You can't just throw them out in a pasture and let them take care of themselves."

Brianna listened carefully, her face open. What a huge change. *Is she so hungry for approval and attention? What's happened in her short life that she reacts this way?*

"Let's take Bones out, and you can help groom him." Susanne swung open the gate and clucked to the gelding.

Brianna backed up a step. "He's so big. Will kick me or anything?"

Bones stood patiently, head down and eyes half shut.

Susanne smiled and slipped on the halter. "No. He'd rather take a nap. We'll tie him and brush him for a few minutes. That'll help you get used to being around him."

As they brought him through the gate, Glory and Khaila paced the fence line, screaming their displeasure for taking their pasture mate away. It didn't matter that he was in sight; it only mattered that he'd abandoned them.

"Oh, hush, girls. It's not like the two of you are nice to him when he's with you," Susanne said.

The mares nipped and kicked at each other as they trotted back and forth, lending truth to her statement.

The next few minutes went well, and Brianna gradually relaxed. She wouldn't be ready to climb on Bones anytime soon, but when they finished grooming, she'd learned to brush him. Susanne encouraged her to lead the horse back the short distance to the gate.

"You did fine. Next time Meagan brushes the horses, she can tie Bones up and you can groom him." She closed the gate after the horse, who promptly went and rolled.

"He's getting dirty! We just brushed him, and he's rolling in the dirt," Brianna's voice was tinged with disgust.

Susanne chuckled. "Yep. We get them all pretty, and they want to be dirty. Kind of like Steven!" They both laughed and headed up to the house.

It was a hard balancing act for Susanne to make Brianna feel at home while not encouraging her to plant her roots too deep. She almost wished something would happen one way or the other to release her from the feeling of limbo she floundered in.

The thought had been simmering all day, and Susanne needed to put it into action before she got sidetracked again. She reached for the phone and punched in Jeena's cell number.

"Hello." Jeena's voice answered, sounding slightly out of breath.

"It's Susanne. Did I catch you at a bad time?"

"No, I'm sitting here alone in the Jacuzzi at the club and couldn't reach the phone for a sec. I was just thinking about you.

Want to go to a movie or something?"

Susanne winced, wishing yet again to put off the unpleasant task. "Uh . . . no, I'm afraid I can't tonight, and I only have a second to chat."

Jeena was quiet for a moment. "Is something wrong?"

"I don't want to disappear from your life and never call again. I . . . I didn't think that would be fair." Susanne stumbled a bit.

"Disappear from my life? What *are* you talking about?"

Susanne sank into the easy chair before answering. "I've been thinking, and. . . it might be a good idea if I don't see you for a while. David and I are still trying to sort through some things, and my last evening with you caused stress. I'm not saying it was your fault, but I need time to work things out, if you know what I mean."

"No. I don't. Or maybe I do. I know your husband has you under his thumb and you obviously can't think for yourself. If that's the way you want it, so be it."

"Jeena . . . " The line went dead. Susanne closed her eyes. Couldn't anything go right anymore? What she'd give for one peaceful day without any tension.

Chapter Twenty-Eight

THE KIDS WERE OVER AT CLAIRE'S for the afternoon as they spent at least one afternoon per week at their grandma's home. It was good for them all. Brianna was developing a relationship with her, and Claire seemed to enjoy the girl.

Susanne was settled with a book in David's recliner when the doorbell rang. She wasn't expecting anyone and hadn't heard a car drive up.

"All I ask is a couple of hours of quiet." She sighed and headed for the door, padding across the floor in her bare feet. Since the weather had been too hot for shoes lately, she lived in shorts and flip-flops. She hadn't glanced in a mirror for hours—she must look a mess.

"Hello, may I help you?" The words slowed to a halt.

A man in his mid-forties stood on her porch. He looked like he'd just stepped out of the 1950s. His hair was slicked back and plastered against his head with what must have been handfuls of gel while sporting a jovial smile that didn't quite reach his cool blue eyes. A dark shadow on his jaw line gave him a slightly scruffy appearance, and his thin frame towered above her by several inches. His pants appeared a little worn, and his shirt sleeves a bit too long, but his clothes were neat and clean.

Susanne hesitated a moment, waiting for him to speak. When he continued to stare and didn't respond, she stepped back and started to shut the door.

He took a step forward, and the ingratiating smile grew larger. "Excuse me, ma'am, but I'm here to collect my niece."

She gripped the edge of the door and stared. "Excuse me?"

His eyes narrowed, and the smile faded. "My niece. Would

you call her for me?"

"I think you have the wrong house." She again attempted to close the door.

His wiry hand shot out, stopping the door. "No, ma'am, I don't have the wrong house. I've come to get my niece Brianna."

Shock momentarily froze Susanne, and she stared at the stranger.

"Is she here?" The man sidled over to a nearby window and tried to peer in. "I'm her uncle, and I don't have a lot of time. My wife is waiting in the truck, and we're on our way to an appointment."

Susanne shook herself, unable to believe she'd heard correctly. "Her uncle? What's your name?"

"My name is Warren, Arthur Warren, and I called a few nights ago. I want to apologize for that, ma'am. I'd had a bit to drink, and my manners slipped." His smile dimmed. "Vicki, Brianna's mama, was my sister. Vicki died a while back, and I had to leave her girl with you till I got my affairs in order. I just got married, and I've come to take Brianna home."

Susanne stepped into the house and drew the screen door shut, thankful for the barricade between them. "You might be her uncle, but you dumped her here almost two months ago without a word. Now you think you can take her? No way." The man's brazenness caused her voice to shake. What a blessing the kids were at her mom's.

He stepped in close. "I'm here to get her, lady, and I have no intention of leaving without her." The smell of alcohol wafted toward her.

Susanne placed her hands on her hips and stood her ground. "You need to leave, or I'll call the police."

His smile faded, replaced by a threatening look. "Oh really? I can get the police too, you know. She's my family, and you've got no right to keep her."

"My husband is her father, so we have *every* right, and she prefers living with us."

He leaned closer to the screen, and the strong odor made her take a step back. "You'd better watch your step, ma'am." As he backed away from the house, a strand of his heavily gelled hair hung over his forehead and swung with each jerky step. "I'll get the girl, one way or another." He spun on his heel, then strode down the driveway to an old pickup waiting at the bottom.

"Did you get her?" a loud female voice called from the passenger window of the truck.

"Not yet," Arthur snapped.

A plump woman with heavy makeup poked her head out the window. "You told me we'd get that girl back to work around our place. And we need the money from the state." The angry voice floated up to where Susanne stood in the doorway, listening as this nightmare played out.

"Be quiet. No call for all the neighbors to know our business." He climbed in the truck and slammed the door.

They disappeared from sight, and Susanne ran to call her mother. She couldn't allow the kids to come home. The couple might return and try to take Brianna. After hearing that thinly veiled threat, she'd have to ask David to come home early. She wouldn't put it past the man to try again.

The phone at her mother's continued to ring. *Why isn't Mom answering?* Better jump in the car and head over there—the call to David would have to wait. Susanne was grateful none of the children had been home when Brianna's uncle appeared. He'd tried to hide behind a pretense of civility at first, but it was obvious that money was all he cared about.

Her car gave a false start, then died, adding to her frustration. She tried again, heaving a relieved sigh as it turned over and caught. "Oh, please, God, don't let that man come back before David gets home."

Her mind continued to replay the scene. Susanne couldn't believe Arthur Warren had any legal rights to Brianna.

She pulled into her mother's driveway. No one came to the door, and there was no sign of life in the front yard. The car stood in the open garage, so they hadn't gone anywhere. Thank God for that.

"Mom, you here?" Susanne poked her head in the front door. Silence greeted her. She hurried around to the back of the house, still calling her mother.

"I'm in the garden. The kids are helping me pick green beans." Claire waved from the fenced area below the house. "What's going on? I thought you'd be home with a book." Claire gave a small groan as she pushed herself out of her crouched position over the row of beans, running her fingers through her disheveled hair.

"Could you let the kids keep picking for a few minutes and come to the house so we can talk?"

Claire briefly spoke to her three helpers working down the row, then exited through the gate in the fence. She walked briskly up the path, belying her fifty-six years.

"What's the problem? You look like someone walked over your grave."

"That's exactly how I feel. I don't want the kids to know about this yet, but we just had an unpleasant visitor. I was so thankful they were here with you."

Claire looked at Susanne sharply. "Would you like to come in the house and have a glass of wine? You seem rattled. Maybe it'll help you calm down. The kids can stay outside."

"No thanks, Mom. After smelling that man, wine doesn't sound appealing. Besides, I need to let you know what's going on, then call David."

"Then come and sit. We can keep an eye on the kids, and you can tell me what's upset you." Claire led the way to the low stone wall edging a terraced flower bed. Susanne dropped onto a rock with a sigh.

"He says he's Brianna's uncle. His name is Arthur Warren. He's sneaky, Mother, and that doesn't begin to describe him. He gave me the creeps, and I think he'd been drinking heavily."

"Start at the beginning and tell me what happened."

"An older pickup stopped at the bottom of our driveway, and a man walked up to our door. He was neat and clean, but he stank like stale beer. He was polite at first, but I don't believe that man has a kind bone in his body. He said he'd gotten married recently and had come to take Brianna home."

"Did he offer any proof of who he is?"

"I didn't think about asking for proof, but he had the same last name as Brianna, and he knew about her mother being dead." She pulled a piece of cheat grass off the bank and idly began stripping the heads off the weed.

"Why would he want her back? According to Brianna, he dumped her at your house because he didn't want to be responsible for her."

Susanne pictured the woman who'd poked her head out of the truck. "There was a woman in the truck who yelled at him when he was heading down the driveway. She demanded to know if he had Brianna, and he said not yet. She grumbled about not being able to get the money from the state if they didn't get her. He told her to be quiet, that he'd take care of it, and they drove off. What possible money could they get from the state? There's no way those two would ever be granted a foster-care license."

"Ah, but they could get welfare. Another member of the family will add a considerable amount to their pot."

"Why didn't I think of that?" Susanne rolled her eyes. "The woman also said he'd promised Brianna would take care of their place, so I'm assuming they want to put her to work."

"This could be your way out if you want it, you know." Claire looked at Susanne with a question in her eyes.

"A way out of what?"

"You told me recently you hadn't decided if you wanted to keep Brianna and were waiting to see if anything else turned up. Well, something has turned up."

"Mother! I can't believe you'd say that. If you'd seen that man, you'd know how impossible that is. You, of all people, who are always so careful not to hurt anyone."

"That's exactly the reaction I was hoping you'd have—shock at just thinking about that man taking Brianna. I'd fight him myself before I'd let him have her. But you needed to know that for yourself. If you fight this man, it'll have to be on the basis of David being her parent. That means you have to establish legal guardianship, so this can never happen again. But that also entails making a commitment. You can't save her, then throw her away later if it's not convenient. Do you see what I'm getting at?"

Susanne's shoulders slumped at the impact of her mother's words. Her natural instinct had been to fight and under no circumstances let that man take Brianna. But she hadn't followed the thought through to its logical conclusion.

"I can't believe I even need to think about this," she dropped her voice so the kids couldn't hear. "I don't for a minute want those people to have Brianna. But it didn't occur to me that if we win we'd be keeping her for good."

"Would that be so bad? Has she been that much trouble since she arrived? It seems to me you've had a lot worse foster kids. Steven and Meagan both love her. She is their half-sister whether you want to acknowledge that or not."

Claire's reasonable voice cut through the fog of confusion. "You're right. She's a bit standoffish and has never really warmed up to David and me. But other than Meagan's accident, she hasn't been any trouble."

"Meagan's accident was just that—an accident. And if you haven't accepted that yet, you need to. Do you think it's Brianna's fault how she acts with you and David?"

"You're saying what?"

"That neither of you have given her much of a welcome. Sure, you gave her a birthday party, but you've pretty much left her to the care of the kids. David has had very little involvement with her until recently, from what I've been able to see. Have you noticed she's started to blossom because of his efforts? Brianna adores Meagan and would do anything for her because Meagan accepts her for who she is and loves her back. Those two girls know they're sisters, and they like it. If you don't keep her, you're going to break your daughter's heart and likely turn her against you."

"Man, you don't pull any punches, do you?"

"I've felt this needed to be said for a long time now. I'm sorry for what you've been through, but it's time to grow up and deal with it. None of it's Brianna's fault, and you've been acting like it is. I know," she said, when Susanne started to interrupt. "You've been nice enough to her on the surface, but you haven't even begun to take her into your heart, much less your home. You need to face it, and you need to do it soon."

Susanne bowed her head. Rather than being angry at the accusations, she accepted them for what they were—the truth. The words were hard but not harsh. Mom had kept silent for as long as she could.

"You think I've been selfish?"

"Not selfish so much as blind. When this all started, you had every right to be hurt. But it's no longer about you. It's about

Brianna. Can you imagine what she's been through, living for months with that man when her mother was sick? She's never had a normal life, and you and David have it in your power to give her one before it's too late. If you don't, you *would* be selfish."

Susanne was quiet, letting several moments pass. "I guess I have been blind and maybe selfish too. I was worried about the kids and what kind of influence Brianna might have, but that hasn't been an issue. Then I was irritated I was being saddled with someone else's child and how unfair it was."

Susanne caught the look of understanding that shone from Claire's eyes.

"Then the accident happened, and I quit trying to analyze the reasons and decided I didn't want to keep her. But you're right. It's time to start thinking of Brianna, as well as David and the kids. I'm not the important one here—they are."

"I'm glad. I wasn't saying all of that to be mean. I simply hoped to open your eyes."

"You weren't mean, you were honest. And I'm glad you had the courage to be. I'm just sorry it took something like that man to wake me up."

"Are you going to tell the kids?"

"No. I don't want to worry them, especially if nothing comes of this. I warned him I'd call the police if he continued to bother us, and we may never hear from him again. But I think it's safer to be prepared."

"I agree. Now you'd better run in the house and call David. I'll get back to the kids. It looks like they've lost interest in bean picking."

Susanne glanced down at the garden. The three kids were sitting at the end of a row, laughing and talking.

"Thanks, Mom. I really do mean that." She reached out to give her mother a quick hug before the older woman headed back down the path. "I think I'll head home and call David from there. I'll call you later and let you know when I'm coming over to get them."

"Let them spend the night tonight, dear. I have some old T-shirts they can sleep in and extra toothbrushes they can use. They'll be fine."

"Okay, thanks. I'd better get going," Susanne called as she walked briskly around the house and back to her car. She needed to talk to David so they could be prepared for whatever might come next.

Chapter Twenty-Nine

SUSANNE HAD A HARD TIME GETTING anything accomplished until David arrived. She was thankful he left work shortly after her call and headed straight home. The kids remained at Claire's, so the two adults had a quiet dinner together. Susanne relayed what she'd discussed with her mother, knowing it was important to be honest about her decision.

"Would you like a refill?" David asked, standing next to the counter, filling his own oversized mug with coffee.

"I'm good, thanks."

"I'm proud of you. I know it's been difficult for you to accept Brianna being here." David squeezed her shoulder before taking his seat at the table again.

"Honestly, it hasn't been hard. She's a good kid. With foster kids, we chose to take them. With Brianna, I felt someone else made my choices for me. I never really disliked her. I disliked being forced into a situation without being consulted. I should've snapped out of it a lot sooner, and I'm sorry it took something like this to make me see it."

"It hasn't been easy for me, either. Now we have to figure out what we're going to do about her uncle. Did you get the feeling he'd come back?"

"He was angry when he left, almost threatening. I don't know if he'd bring the police into it because the idea of me calling them seemed to spook him. Who knows? He might have a criminal past he doesn't want brought to the surface."

"Good thinking. I'll have someone check."

Susanne fiddled with her cup, turning it in circles, then raised her eyes to David. "Do we need to tell the kids? I'd rather not, but what if he shows up sometime and finds them alone and tries to force Brianna to go with him?"

David pushed his chair back and crossed his arms. "He'd better not. Don't let the kids take any walks off the property. If they want to go to your mother's, drive them instead."

"We might be worrying over nothing. How about we wait a few days, then talk to the kids if it looks like we need to?"

David drummed his fingers on the table, his forehead furrowed. "Okay, but call me at work if anything else happens. I want to deal with this guy next time."

"Good. I've had enough of him to last a lifetime."

The next few days passed peacefully with no contact from Arthur Warren or any state agency. The summer heat strengthened, and the kids spent a lot of time outdoors in the pond.

Susanne had finished the kitchen cleanup after lunch when Claire called. "Hi, honey. Have you heard anything more from Brianna's uncle?"

"Oh hi, Mom. No, we haven't. He seemed determined to take Brianna with him, so I wouldn't be surprised if he comes back."

"I think the man is all bluff."

Susanne heard a noise in the family room and stopped to listen. She hadn't heard a door open and didn't expect the kids back so soon. Steven was at a friend's house for the day, and the girls were out with the horses in the large pasture behind the house. She hesitated. She didn't want one of the girls to overhear.

"Susanne, are you still there?" her mother's voice prompted.

"I thought someone came in, but I must've been wrong. I don't want Brianna to know about her uncle coming to get her. It would worry her and wouldn't be fair. She's had enough to deal with the past two months without putting her through more."

"I still don't believe there's anything to worry about. He

obviously thinks he can get something for nothing. Now that you've threatened him with the police, I'm sure that'll end it."

"I hope so, but you didn't see how angry he was. The woman seemed as determined, and they were both set on getting more money."

This time Susanne was sure she heard a sound. "I'm sorry, but I better get off the phone. It sounds like the girls might be coming in. I'll let you know if anything more happens."

Meagan and Brianna came in through the laundry room. That meant neither one had been in the house during her conversation, so all was well.

Unfortunately, it didn't stay well. A few minutes later, the phone rang. Meagan picked it up.

"Hello?" She listened for a moment and then put her hand over the phone, frowning at her mother. "Mom, it's DSHS, and they want to talk to you. You aren't wanting to get another foster kid, are you?"

"No, why?"

"You aren't trying to send Brianna to a foster home? You wouldn't do that, would you?" Meagan gazed at her mother, her eyes huge.

"No, honey, I'm not. Please don't worry. We'll talk later. Just give me the phone now, okay?" She shooed her daughter up to her room. Right before Meagan disappeared, Brianna stepped into view before turning to follow Meagan. Her wide eyes and stiff stance told Susanne she'd have more to deal with before this day was over.

"Hello, this is Susanne Carson."

"Mrs. Carson, this is Trudy Sorensen with DSHS. How are you?" the polite voice said.

Susanne knew most of the caseworkers but didn't recognize this woman's name. "I'm fine, Mrs. Sorensen. What can I do for you?"

"Ms. Sorensen, if you please. I'm calling in regard to a complaint filed against you and your husband."

"A complaint!" Susanne plopped down hard into a kitchen chair.

"Mr. Arthur Warren came in and filed a formal complaint. He claims you're keeping his niece against his wishes. He filled out all the necessary forms. I'll need to come by to see both you and Mr. Carson. It would be helpful if you could meet with me later this afternoon to expedite this matter," the brisk, impersonal voice continued.

"What?" Susanne sputtered. "You need to check the facts before making any rash decisions. Brianna is my husband's daughter, and we have every right to her." She tried to keep the frustration out of her voice, knowing it wasn't going to help her case with this woman.

"I am not in the habit of making rash decisions. I'm simply doing my job. We may need to remove Brianna to a temporary foster home until this has been resolved."

"I'd appreciate talking to Mrs. Trenton, please."

"I am the supervisor now. Mrs. Trenton recently retired. I'll be at your home in two hours, and I'd appreciate if your husband could be present. I'd like to wrap this up today, if possible. Will that work for you?" The resolute voice on the other end of the line was businesslike, leaving no room for disagreement.

"I suppose, but this is a terrible mistake. You'll understand after you meet us and hear what we have to say." Susanne no longer cared whether the woman knew she was angry or not.

"We'll see. Good day, Mrs. Carson."

Susanne hung up the phone with shaking hands. She realized caseworkers had to keep an emotional distance from their clients and children, but this woman sounded as though she'd already made up her mind. David needed to know. She snatched up the phone and dialed, praying the guys didn't have any loud power tools running.

David's voice answered after two rings. "Susanne, is something wrong?"

David must have worried Arthur Warren had reappeared. She almost wished he had. It would be easier dealing with him than this new threat.

"I can't believe what happened. A new supervisor from DSHS called, and she'll be here in two hours."

"Slow down. Two hours? Why?"

"Arthur Warren filed a formal complaint against us for keeping Brianna, and this woman mentioned the possibility of moving Brianna to a foster home till this gets resolved."

"She can't do that! I'm Brianna's father. I don't care what her uncle says. He can't change that no matter how many complaints he files."

"Just come home now, okay? She's coming whether we like it or not. I asked to talk to Mrs. Trenton, but Ms. Sorensen said she retired and that she's the new supervisor. She was quite insistent."

"I'm on my way. I'll be there in thirty minutes. Don't worry. We'll figure this out. I have the letter from Brianna's mother saying I'm her dad. That has to count for something."

The phone clicked off. Susanne was thankful David would be there to help handle this crisis. She listened at the foot of the stairs, grateful the girls hadn't come down. She'd check on them later, but first she'd call her mother. She could use the moral support right now.

Susanne was glad Steven's friend had invited him to spend the night. It was enough trying to keep the two girls out of the room while they dealt with this newest crisis. Steven would have been nearly impossible.

Promptly on time, a dark, four-door sedan pulled into their drive. A small woman, who appeared to be in her late fifties, stepped out of the car and rang the bell. David opened the door, with Susanne right behind him. The woman wore a business suit, her salt and pepper hair pulled into a bun. Not a hair was out of place, and no sign of a smile marred her somber features.

"Mr. Carson, Mrs. Carson, I'm Ms. Sorensen. How do you do?" She extended a pale hand and gave each one a firm but quick squeeze, as though their touch was unpleasant in some way. "Let's get right to this, shall we?"

"Certainly. The sooner it's over, the better." David's voice held an edge. "Please, come in and have a seat." He led the woman into the living room.

She chose one of the upright chairs near the end of the coffee table.

Susanne watched with fascination as the woman's hands moved with birdlike quickness, snapping open her briefcase and removing a small sheaf of papers. She adjusted her wire-rimmed glasses and peered at the papers.

After several moments of silence, David cleared his throat. "Excuse me, Ms. Sorensen. Could you explain what this is about?"

"I explained to your wife on the phone. A Mr. Arthur Warren filed a complaint with our office. He states he is the legal guardian and only living relative of his niece Brianna Warren. He claims you're keeping her longer than agreed and that you refused to return Brianna to his custody. You didn't allow Mr. Warren to talk to the girl when he called, and he wasn't allowed to see her when he stopped by here a few days ago."

"When Mr. Warren called, he'd been drinking, and we didn't feel it was wise to let Brianna speak to him. She wasn't home when he came here a few days ago, also with liquor on his breath. It's not our intention to keep him from seeing his niece, but we don't believe it's best for her to live with him."

"That will be for the court to decide." She returned her attention to the papers she held.

"You mentioned you have some type of formal complaint filed by Mr. Warren. May I have a copy of that, please?"

She raised her eyes. "Certainly. I intended to give you a copy, Mr. Carson." She drew another set of papers from the bottom of her black briefcase and handed them over.

Susanne sat on the couch and leaned against David's shoulder, reading the document along with him. His frown deepened, and he shook his head.

"I'm sorry. This is *not* correct. This states Mr. Warren dropped Brianna off with instructions he would return for her. That was not the case. He dropped Brianna at our door without a word. He didn't take the time to speak to my wife at all."

"You're welcome to put that in your statement. However, the point remains that Mr. Warren is Brianna's uncle, and you are not a documented relative. Legally, the girl belongs with her family." She sat back in her chair, her hands lying quietly in her lap, but her tapping toe conveyed her irritation.

"Not a relative? I'm her father! Did Mr. Warren provide documentation?" David stared at the woman, and Susanne felt her own anger rise. "Look at this letter as well as her birth certificate. This will prove what I'm talking about." He dropped the two documents onto the table.

Susanne was thankful for his presence and more rational approach. If it were up to her, she'd be saying things she might later regret.

The supervisor picked up the papers. Interminable minutes ticked by. She seemed to be trying to memorize each document, shifting back and forth between the two.

"Well?" David asked.

"Yes. Mr. Warren alleges his sister was dying of cancer when she wrote this letter and not thinking clearly. Her doctor can testify to her mental condition. Mr. Warren also made some other, ah . . . allegations that are best saved for court. But suffice it to say that he believes you may not be the girl's father."

David glowered at the woman. She stared back at him without flinching. He shook his head, rubbed his hand over his jaw, and gestured at the papers. "Did you even look at the birth certificate? Do you see my name is listed as her middle name?"

"Yes, but your name is not given as her father. And her middle name is spelled *Carsen*, with an *e*, not *Carson*, with an *o*. Simply put, it means nothing in a courtroom. I'm sorry," she said without a hint of emotion.

"Did you meet Mr. Warren?" Susanne asked.

"Yes, I did," she replied. Her face seemed carefully bland.

"When he arrived here, he stank of alcohol, and it was obvious that his only interest in Brianna was monetary."

"I found Mr. Warren to be quite presentable. I questioned him about his ability to care for Brianna. He assured me he recently married, and his wife is anxious to care for the girl. They are living in a small rental, and I'll be visiting their home before the girl is placed there permanently."

David crossed his arms and leaned back. "I'm Brianna's father, and I'll take whatever blood tests are required to prove it. Mr. Warren's claims are not accurate, and I don't intend to sit by and let him take my daughter."

"I believe Mr. Warren's claims are in order. I find it odd you refused to allow him to see his niece or return her to his care when he requested, Mrs. Carson." Her small eyes, magnified behind the lenses of her glasses, stared at Susanne.

"I can't believe this." Susanne's voice started to rise.

She felt David slip his hand over hers, giving a warning squeeze, and she lowered her voice. "You haven't heard a word we've said. That man showed no indication he cared about Brianna. The wife you mentioned yelled at him from the truck when he didn't bring Brianna with him. The only thing she wanted was money from the state. When I refused to give Brianna to him, he threatened me."

"Did he threaten to harm you physically or assault you in any way?"

"Well, no. He just said I'd better watch myself, but in an ugly tone, and I took it as a threat."

"I'm sorry, but you have no proof he meant that as a threat, and I can't take it into consideration. So far nothing you've told me has been substantiated." She stuffed the papers into her briefcase.

"Brianna is afraid of that man. She told Susanne that he's mean when he drinks. I think she should have some say in where she lives. She did just turn fourteen."

"In the state of Washington, minors can't decide where they live. The state or the court will decide what's best for her." She stood to her feet.

David pushed up from his place on the couch, towering above the diminutive woman. "I'll be contacting an attorney immediately. I'm not letting my daughter leave my home without a fight."

"That's your privilege. You'll be hearing from the court. Good day." She strode to the door and left without another word, closing the door behind her with a decisive click.

Susanne stared after the disappearing car. Didn't the woman have any emotions? And where in the world was her brain, falling for the lines Brianna's uncle had given her?

"Oh, honey, what're we going to do?" Susanne moaned. She

turned away from the window and dropped down on the couch. "That woman is completely unfeeling. She doesn't care what's best for Brianna. The only thing she cares about is following the letter of the law and making sure whoever *she* believes is the legal guardian gets Brianna."

David settled beside her and squeezed her hand. "Yeah, it was weird. Like she already had her mind made up before she met us."

"I don't get it. Why wasn't she willing to listen? We've been foster parents several times in the past few years and have an excellent record. Does she have something against us?" Susanne asked.

"I can't imagine what. We've never met her. I think she's a cold woman who made up her mind before she came and had no intention of changing it, regardless of what we said. But it's strange she'd take up for someone like Brianna's uncle."

"Can't we go over her head? It scares me to think we could lose Brianna after all we've been through this summer."

David picked up the papers and scanned them one more time. "We're taking Brianna to a doctor tomorrow and getting a blood test. I'm proving I'm her father. Any judge who has a brain and sees us together will be able to figure it out without a blood test, but I'm not taking any chances." He threw the papers on the coffee table, scattering them across its surface and onto the floor.

Susanne knew exactly how he felt. She could break something right now. How could a supervisor in that woman's occupation not care about the welfare of a child? It didn't make sense.

Chapter Thirty

"DAVID, I NEED TO CHECK ON the girls. They've been in Meagan's bedroom all evening, and I haven't heard a sound in a couple of hours. I don't think I could eat anything, but it's getting late, and I'll fix something for them and you, if you want it."

"Nothing for me. It would choke me, but go ahead and see about the girls." David got up and stood at the window, staring out into the gathering darkness.

Susanne headed across the living room, through the dining room, and stopped at the foot of the stairs. "Meagan?" she called, running up the stairs to the girl's room. "Meagan, honey, are you girls hungry?" She tapped on the door, then pushed it open to find Meagan sitting on her bed, alone.

"Where's Brianna? Did she go to her room?"

Meagan turned dull eyes toward Susanne. "No, Mom. Brianna's gone."

"What do you mean, gone?" Susanne asked, a sick feeling rising in her throat.

"She ran away. She knew you were going to give her to her uncle, so she ran away."

Susanne whirled to the door. "David, come up here!"

His feet pounded up the stairs. "What's wrong?"

"Meagan says Brianna ran away."

He stopped short in the doorway, his eyes wide with disbelief. "Ran away! Where is she? Why didn't you come tell us she left?"

A tear trickled down Meagan's pale cheek. "Because before that lady from the state came, Brianna heard Mom on the phone saying she was sending her away with her uncle. She didn't want to go. She's afraid of him. Mom said she didn't want Brianna to know about it ahead of time, because it would upset her. So she told me, and I helped her get out of the house." Sobs began to choke Meagan's voice.

"Meagan, if we're going to find her, we need your help. You have to calm down and answer our questions. Do you understand?" David asked.

"Yes, Dad." Her voice shook. "But why did you want to send Brianna away with that man?"

He bent over the bed, his face coming close to Meagan's. "We don't want to send her away, Meagan. You need to tell us where she is. We need to start looking for her. It's dark outside, and she could get lost or someone could pick her up if she's on the road."

Susanne waved him back. "Meagan, listen. Brianna didn't hear my whole conversation, and she misunderstood. I was telling Grandma that Brianna's uncle was trying to get her back, but I didn't want any of you kids to worry about it. Your dad and I want to keep Brianna."

"Oh, Mom, I wish I'd known!" Meagan's voice rose to a wail.

Susanne put her arms around the distressed girl, holding her in a fierce hug. "We'll find Brianna, honey. Do you have any idea where she might be?"

"No, honest I don't. I helped her put some clothes in her old suitcase, and she took a blanket, in case it got cold. She didn't want to try to carry a pillow too, but I made her take a flashlight 'cause she's afraid of the dark."

Susanne held her daughter and rocked her, shaking her head at David.

"She doesn't know anything else, David. We need to call Mother and start looking. I can't imagine where she's gone. If she went down the road, Ms. Sorensen would have seen her on the way down the hill and called us by now. A teenager with a suitcase would be hard to miss, and it's a long walk to town."

"She could've gone up the road toward your mother's." David

picked up the phone and began dialing, then hit speakerphone as Susanne poked her head out of Meagan's room.

"Claire, it's David. Have you seen Brianna?"

"No. Was she coming over here?"

David's shoulders slumped. "No, she's missing. Meagan said she ran away. Brianna overheard Susanne talking to you about her uncle and assumed we wanted her to live with him. She panicked."

"Is there any possibility she'd try walking to town?"

"We don't think so. Brianna's smart enough to know people would spot her if she did. Could you come over and help us look? We're worried."

"Should I check around my house first in case she came here to hide? I doubt she'd go far. She's afraid of the dark, you know."

"Good idea. That might be best. We'll do the same here, then we'll fan out into the woods and trails. Come over as soon as you're done and bring your flashlight." David hung up and turned to his daughter. "Meagan, Mom will be back in a few minutes." He motioned to Susanne, pulling her out of Meagan's room and shutting the door.

"Your mother had a good point. She doesn't think Brianna will go far tonight. She could be hiding, waiting till daylight and hoping to get a ride with someone. I doubt she's planned anything. More than likely, she bolted without thinking it through. I want to start checking around our place, but I'd like you to stay here with Meagan. Would you do that?"

"But why? Meagan is fine in the house by herself, and I need to help you look. Brianna could be hurt or scared, and we need to find her quickly. It'll go so much faster if I'm helping."

He put his arms around her and looked into her eyes. "Right now Meagan is scared, confused, and hurting. She thinks it's her fault Brianna is missing. She needs you, and I need to be the one looking for Brianna."

Susanne gazed up into the warm brown eyes above her and nodded. "Okay. But when Meagan is settled, I'm coming out to join you. Meagan will probably want to come, too. Do you think I should call the sheriff's department?"

"Not yet. I think she'll be nearby. If we don't find her soon, we'll call. Your mother should be here in a few minutes, and maybe the three of you can start looking together." He lowered his arms from her shoulders and ran down the stairs to get a flashlight out of the closet.

Susanne went to Meagan's room. She started to open the door but hesitated, hearing Meagan's voice. Was she talking to herself? David had been right in urging her to stay. Her hand released the knob, and she listened.

"Please, God, don't let Brianna die. It's my fault she ran away, so please don't punish her. I'm so worried. What if she gets hit by a car or some bad person picks her up on the road?"

Susanne heard a hiccup and a short sob and reached for the knob again.

"God, if you have to take somebody, please take me instead. I'm ready to go to heaven, and I don't think Brianna is. She doesn't know you yet, Jesus, and I don't want her to miss going to heaven."

Susanne froze, unable to move as the prayer continued.

"I've had a father and a mother all my life. Brianna needs a family. She's so sad and mixed up, and she misses her mama so much."

The muffled voice got quieter, and Susanne peeked through the barely cracked door. Her daughter lay stretched out on her bed, gripping her big teddy bear in her arms and struggling to keep her eyes open.

"Please, God, let her come home so I can have a sister again. I promise I'll tell her about You if You'll give me another chance."

Meagan's eyes closed, and her arms around the teddy relaxed.

Susanne stood for a moment, watching her precious daughter, and her eyes filled with tears. Not for the world would she wake her now. Rest would help calm Meagan's overtired emotions. Susanne tiptoed down the hallway and slipped into her room.

So much had happened in the last few days. Her mind and emotions reeled. She'd barely gotten used to the idea of Brianna becoming a permanent part of their family, when it appeared she would be ripped away from them instead. Now, due to her own careless conversation on the phone with her mother, Brianna had decided to run. They hadn't given her any reason to believe they'd protect her. Brianna believed she was in danger and Meagan was the only person she could trust.

Susanne lay huddled on her bed in the softly lit room, staring at the ceiling and searching for answers. *What a sorry excuse for a parent I am. All this time, I thought I was capable of running my own life and taking care of my family. I didn't think I needed God and didn't want Him interfering in my life. Meagan wants God to spare Brianna's life and take hers instead. She's the only unselfish one in this family. Steven is too little to count, but David and I certainly aren't.*

David bought a Bible for Brianna and started spending time with her after work. They were forming a bond. Sure, Susanne had agreed to let Brianna stay, but she never let the girl into her heart. *I turned Brianna away the day she arrived as surely as if I slammed the door in her face. What's wrong with me? Am I really a cold, unfeeling person? Have I been putting on an act all these years?*

Susanne knew she hadn't done a good job taking care of much lately. Especially not since Brianna had appeared. The past couple of months, her whole life had shifted. Nothing remained the same. She didn't have much faith in the strength of her marriage or her ability to control her world. It didn't feel like any place was safe or secure any more.

Or was there? What did their pastor say once? David repeated it often. Our security could only be found in one place. Kim had tried to tell her that too, the day of the fair. "You'll never know true fulfillment or peace, until you've relinquished control of your life to the Lord." The words hung there as though Kim were standing in the room repeating them. *Is that the key I've been missing all these years? Is there really peace in giving control of my life to the Lord?*

Susanne laughed softly, the irony of what she'd asked sinking in. Could she trust God to take care of her? Was there someone she knew who could do a better job? Jeena had tried, but Susanne knew where that would lead. She'd be in no better shape—and probably worse—if Jeena had her way.

What about David? She'd always trusted him in the past. Now she realized he was fallible too. He wasn't perfect and had never claimed to be, but he loved her and the kids. She'd been angry so long, she'd forgotten that fact. He would be the first to tell her not to place her entire trust in him.

Who does that leave? Myself?

The past few days had shown her how ludicrous that was. She finally admitted she needed help. She wouldn't make any deals with God about giving her life to Him if He kept Brianna safe. No, this needed to be a personal decision, birthed from a pure motive. She swung her feet over the side of the bed and slipped to her knees, feeling a bit self-conscious but wanting to do this right.

"Oh, God, this isn't easy for me. I began to open my heart to You years ago, but it ended there. I've never let You into my life, and I haven't wanted You in control. I'm changing that now. I'm sorry for being selfish and stubborn. Would You please change me and take control of my life? And please, please help us find Brianna. And if there's some way You can help us save her from her uncle, that would be wonderful, too. Thank You, Jesus. Amen."

She stayed on her knees a few minutes more, soaking in the warm peace enveloping her spirit. Panic at being out of control no longer bound her. The fear evaporated. Could it be that easy? *All these years, I've needed to let go and let God be in control to have this feeling of peace? If I'd listened to David years ago instead of fighting him over church and God, our marriage could have been so much better.*

She got off her knees and realized this was the first moment of her new life. Looking back was worthless—it was time to look forward. But the most important thing right now was to find Brianna.

David spent thirty minutes in a state of frustration and growing agitation. Fear set in. He checked the barn, going up the ladder to the loft and shining his light around from the landing at the top. All the stalls down below were empty. There was no sign of Brianna in the building that housed the well, pump, and pressure tank. He'd walked through the woods just beyond their pasture, calling her name. Had she headed down the road? She could have ducked behind a clump of trees any time a vehicle approached.

He'd wasted too much time searching their property. He should've called the police as soon as they'd discovered her missing. He'd been so certain Brianna wouldn't have left their property due to her fear of the dark. Where would she head, and to whom would she run? He knew she felt no one in her life loved her or cared but Meagan and Steven.

He stepped back through the open doors of the big, dark barn and sank down onto a bale of straw, groaning in shame. He was Brianna's father, and he hadn't tried to love her. He called himself a Christian, but he sure hadn't acted it these past two months. No wonder Susanne had so little interest in Christianity—he wasn't much of an example. How could she or the kids respect him as a husband or a father?

He sat in the darkened barn, knowing that only God could bring them through this trouble. He'd made a mess of everything from the day Brianna came to their door. His marriage had suffered, he'd lost the respect of his wife, and his relationship with his kids had become distant until the past couple of weeks when he'd made a small effort.

"God, I'm not sure how we got to this point, but I know You are the only one who can make sense of it. Show me what to do and how to find Brianna. I need to know if it's time to call the police or if You want me to keep looking. Please, give me some kind of sign." He bowed his head, his face in his hands. Never had he felt so helpless or seen how much he depended on God.

"Meow."

David raised his head. He hadn't seen any sign of Smoke or her half-grown kittens when he'd been in the barn earlier. Brianna loved the kittens. Was it possible she'd hidden somewhere with them? He heard it again and shone his flashlight beam around the barn, trying to locate the cat.

"Smoke? Come on, kitty, kitty. Talk to me again. Where are you, girl?" He continued to look, praying the animal would show herself.

He heard a scampering overhead and directed his light up the ladder to the loft. The light glinted off a pair of green eyes. Smoke peered over the edge. Had she climbed the ladder? And where were her kittens? Another pair of eyes appeared beside her as one of the kittens answered her cry.

"Smoke, good girl! Is Brianna up there with you?" He hurried to the base of the ladder. David had checked this area once before, but in his rush to find Brianna, he hadn't gone into the back corner behind the largest stack of hay.

He reached the top and sneezed. A light breeze came through the loft from the open door, swirling the dust and loose bits of hay around his feet. He called Brianna's name, keeping his voice soft. He didn't want to startle her if she'd hidden behind the hay.

David jumped as the beam from his flashlight unexpectedly illuminated a darting figure, another of Smoke's kittens. Hopefully, they were all up here because of Brianna. He could imagine the girl wanting company while hiding in the darkness of the barn.

He walked across the rough boards of the loft floor, his footsteps muffled by the loose hay. When he approached the end of the large stack, he slowed his pace. A feeling of dread assailed him. What if he rounded the corner and found it empty? No, he'd prayed. He needed to trust God. Maybe God had sent Smoke when he asked for a sign.

He stepped around the hay and shone the light into the darkest area of the loft. Cocooned in a deep pile of hay lay a sleeping Brianna. She had a blanket drawn around her and her suitcase handle held loosely in her fist. David's breath left him. He sat on a bale of hay nearby, watching the tear-stained face of his daughter. How precious she was. Why hadn't he realized that before? God had given another child into his care. His child.

If he woke Brianna now, she'd most likely be groggy and difficult to help to the bottom of the ladder. She looked comfortable enough, and no danger threatened her here. But he couldn't leave her alone through the night, and he hated to wake her.

He went back to the ladder, descended rapidly, and jogged up the path to the house. Light bobbed on the path coming down to the barn—Susanne and Claire were outside, flashlights in hand.

"Did you find her?" Susanne asked.

"Yes. She's in the loft, in the corner behind the hay, asleep. I missed that area the first time I went up and just now thought about checking it again. Smoke came to the top of the ladder and started to cry. I'd asked God to give me a sign and show me what to do, and seconds later Smoke appeared." He felt humbled and grateful at the way God had worked.

"David, that's wonderful!" Claire burst out, reaching to hug Susanne.

"Why didn't you bring her to the house?" Susanne asked.

"She's asleep. The light on her face didn't wake her, and she slept through my calling her name. She must be exhausted. If I wake her, it'll be difficult getting a sleepy girl down that ladder."

"Do you want us to help?" Susanne asked.

"I have a better idea. I was thinking about getting another couple of blankets and a pillow and sleeping up there beside her. I don't want to move her, but I can't leave her alone all night, either. I think the best plan is to stay till she wakes up. When she does, I can tell her she's safe."

David watched Susanne's face, illuminated by the floodlight outside the back door. He knew she'd been worried about Brianna but wasn't sure how she'd take this suggestion.

Susanne nodded. "Good idea. You can get a decent night's sleep if you spread out plenty of hay and put a blanket or two over it, and Brianna will certainly be safer with you there. Let's grab what you need, and I'll help you take it down."

Claire had been listening, a small smile playing around the edges of her mouth.

"Mom, would you mind staying with Meagan? She's sleeping in her room right now, but if she wakes up, she needs to know Brianna is okay. Before we go to bed, I'll tell her so she doesn't wake in the middle of the night and worry."

"Sure. I'll go up and make sure she's all right." Claire patted Susanne's arm and hurried off, leaving David and Susanne to find the items they needed for David's temporary bed.

Chapter Thirty-One

EARLY THE NEXT MORNING, DAVID WOKE. Beams of sunlight shining through the loft door created a golden haze as the shafts hit the bits of dust stirred by the shifting of their bodies in the night. It took him a moment to remember where he was. His mind slowly cleared, and he flipped from his back to his side, lifting up on his elbow to search the loft. He relaxed. The quiet form of his daughter lay curled in her blankets a few feet away, one of the kittens tucked against her side. The cat opened his eyes, stretched, and sat up, then settled back down, beginning his morning bath.

David lay down and held still, thankful for the time alone. He wanted a few minutes to thank God for the answers He'd provided last night. His life had been so hectic the past couple of months that he'd often dashed off prayers to God on the fly without taking time to listen. Changes needed to take place, not only in his relationship with the Lord, but also in his family. He'd allowed his job to take top priority and knew that had to change. Hopefully, he'd be able to show Susanne how much he valued and loved her, and he could continue to make up for his neglect to all of his children.

An hour later, Brianna stirred. Her eyes opened slowly, and she looked around the barn, confusion clouding her face. David sat up and spoke in a quiet tone, hoping to soothe her fear.

"It's okay, Brianna. You're in the barn loft."

She clutched the edge of the blanket and pulled it under her chin. "Why am I here?"

"You came to the barn last night after you overheard Susanne talking to Claire. Do you remember?" He reached out to touch her, but she drew back and started to scramble to her feet. She grabbed the handle of her suitcase. The kitten jumped out of the way, darting behind a bale of hay, its tail standing straight up like a miniature flagpole.

"It's all right. No one's going to hurt you." David hoped his composed voice would reach through her panic. "Your uncle isn't coming here, and we're not going to let him take you. There's no need to be afraid."

"But I heard Susanne tell her mother he's coming to get me." She continued to grope for her things, her face closing like the door of a prison cell slamming shut.

"Brianna, listen to me, honey. You misunderstood because you didn't hear the entire conversation. Susanne meant that your uncle might try to come here, but she didn't want to worry you in case it didn't happen. We're going to keep you safe, and you're not going to live with that man."

She slowly released her hold on the handle of her suitcase. "Then where am I going to live?"

He drew his breath in sharply. *What she must have gone through last night.* "You're going to live with us, Brianna. Forever. We don't want you to go anywhere. We want you to stay with us."

He hoped she understood he meant it and would trust him and not try to run again. Somehow, he needed to convince her that their decision was firm.

"Do you understand what I said? We want you to live with us and make this your home. You won't ever have to leave unless you want to." It dawned on him that she had a choice. She might be so hurt and disillusioned by his and Susanne's behavior that she no longer wanted to remain. His heart contracted at the thought, and he realized how much it mattered to him that she decided to stay.

Brianna's hands clenched into fists. "How about Susanne? What does she want? She doesn't like me, even if she has tried to be nice. I know she wishes she could've found another place for me to live, and I figure she's probably happy my uncle wants me back."

"I want you to stay too Brianna." Susanne slipped out from behind the large stack of hay. Her husky voice choked with tears. "I am so, so sorry, honey, that I ever made you feel like I didn't want you. I've done a lot of thinking the past few days and a lot of praying over the past few hours." She shot a quick look at David before continuing. "I've been so wrong in how I've treated you, and I hope you can forgive me."

Brianna hesitated a moment, a worried frown creasing her face. "But you don't like me. You didn't want me here because I'm not your daughter. I heard you talking one time."

"I know you did, and I feel terrible. Meagan and Steven are the only ones in the family who made you feel welcome. But this is your home from now on."

"You don't hate me anymore?" She crossed her arms over her chest, gripping her elbows until her knuckles turned white.

Susanne gave a small gasp, her face turning white. "You thought I hated you?"

"Don't you?"

"No. I've never hated you. I was mixed up and not thinking straight, and I said things I didn't mean. I've been fighting with myself ever since you came, knowing I wasn't treating you right. I do care about you, and I hope you'll give me the chance to start loving you." She reached her arms toward the girl.

Brianna gave a little cry, breaking into sobs and running to Susanne's open arms. The two stood holding each other for several minutes, while Susanne gently rocked the girl in her embrace. Susanne stroked Brianna's hair, its dark strands softened by the filtered sunlight coming through the knotholes in the barn wall.

David remained silent, listening to the muffled sobs of his daughter and not wanting to disrupt what he sensed God was doing. He believed a bond was forming between Susanne and Brianna that wouldn't be broken. He knew his wife well enough to know that once she took Brianna into her heart, it would take an act of God Himself to change it.

What did Susanne mean when she mentioned praying over the past few hours? God often performed miracles, and David knew he was witnessing one right now. But he was afraid to hope Susanne could be softening toward the Lord.

Brianna pulled back from Susanne's arms, her tear-stained face turned up. "Are you really sure? You won't change your mind?"

"I'm sure. And from what I heard your dad say, he's sure too. We both want you, and that isn't going to change. I'd like to ask you a question, if you don't mind."

"Sure."

"Grandfather whispered something in your ear one night that made you smile, and then when he left, he reminded you of it. Would you mind telling us what he said?"

Brianna's head went down, but a smile flickered across her lips. "He told me I was his family, and I'd always have a home. He made me promise I'd call him if I couldn't stay here, and he'd keep me."

"That sounds like something Grandfather would do," David said.

"You don't have to worry about that anymore. You're home now." Susanne stepped back a little and brushed the hair out of Brianna's eyes. "Come on, honey. Let's head to the house and show Meagan you're okay. She's been worried sick since you left last night. She's convinced it's her fault. Besides, we have a lot of work to do today to make sure you stay a member of our -family."

David watched as the two smiled at each other, then turned toward him. "That's right," he agreed. "We're heading to the doctor's office for blood tests to prove you're my daughter. And when that's finished, we want to see about getting your last name changed to Carson to make it legal. That is, if you think that's something you might want us to do?" he quickly amended, not at all sure what Brianna might think of this idea and shooting a glance at Susanne. David realized he'd spoken without thinking and hadn't discussed it with his wife. He hoped he hadn't put his foot in it again and given Susanne another reason to be upset.

He felt profound relief when Susanne nodded her head.

"My thoughts exactly, David." Approval shone from her eyes. "I thought the same thing and planned on talking to you about it later."

"You mean my last name will be the same as Meagan's and Steven's? I'll really be a part of your family?" Brianna choked. "I'll never have to go to a foster home or have kids tease me again about not having a dad?" She turned her head from one to the other.

"Yes," they both chorused at once, then smiled through their tears.

"We both want you to stay," David said. "I want to make sure you have my last name so everyone knows you belong in our family and your uncle can never bother you again."

Brianna's joy faded, replaced with a somber expression. "I'd forgotten about him," she whispered. "Will the judge make me live with him?"

Susanne put her arm around Brianna's quivering shoulders, giving her a small squeeze. "Not if we can help it. Besides, we're all praying, and it's going to turn out all right, I'm sure of it." She smiled at David.

He felt his mouth fall open. He could barely contain his curiosity, but now was not the time to question Susanne. Time enough for that later. Right now, a child's future hung in the balance, so they'd better start saving it.

The day ended up being busy, but that wasn't a surprise to either parent. David scheduled an appointment at their local clinic to have blood drawn and sent to a lab for DNA paternity testing. He also made an appointment with a local attorney who specialized in family law. They felt it only fair that Brianna accompany them to the attorney. At fourteen, she was old enough to be involved and deserved to understand what might be coming.

Susanne hadn't had a chance to talk to David privately, but she could tell he was fighting to keep quiet and give her a chance to explain what had happened. He had to be eaten up with curiosity about the comments she'd dropped at the barn, and she felt a bit sorry for not having time to let him know. The discussion wasn't something she wanted to rush, though. He'd waited years to hear about her decision.

Hopefully, they'd have time when the kids were in bed that night, if nothing came along to interfere as it had last night. She was ready for peace to reign in their home again, but with these new developments, she had a feeling it could be a while.

The kids piled in the car, and they all headed for Claire's house. Normally, Steven and Meagan would be thrilled at spending the day with their grandmother, but this time, they were both disgruntled.

"It's not fair, Mom. We want to know what's going on. Why are you only taking Brianna to town?" Meagan's normally happy face was scrunched in a frown.

"We told you all you need to know for now. We're going to talk to a man about Brianna being able to stay with us. She doesn't want to live with her uncle. If she wants to share more with you after we get back, that's up to her."

"We want to go too!" Steven begged.

"That's enough. You're going to your grandmother's house, and we expect you to behave. No more whining." David's frown didn't have the normal effect this time. Both kids sulked the short distance to Claire's.

They pulled up in front of her home as she stepped out the front door and onto the lawn. The kids didn't jump out of the car with their usual alacrity, and Claire looked at Susanne, her eyebrows raised.

Susanne pushed open the door and stepped out of the car, moving over by her mother. "They aren't happy with us. They want details about who we're going to see and why we'll be gone all afternoon. We gave them the basics, but it's up to Brianna after this. Her life's being impacted, and we want to treat her feelings with respect."

Claire's smile was warm. "That's wise. Brianna needs to feel in control of something in her life, even something so small as how much to tell Steven and Meagan." She walked to the car and opened the back door, then reached in to give Brianna a hug. "Keep your chin up, Granddaughter," she said, getting a huge hug in response.

She shut the door firmly and turned to her other two grandchildren moping by the front door. "Come on, you two. Let's go bake cookies and watch a movie!"

Susanne climbed into the car and smiled at the sound of whooping kids disappearing into the house. She thanked God for her mother. Someday soon, she'd need to explain her recent decision. Claire had never been averse to Christianity; she simply followed the lead her father and Susanne had set and had never fully investigated a life of faith. Susanne believed that given the right opportunity, her mother's heart would embrace the truth.

She leaned over her shoulder to the teenager in the backseat.

"Are you scared of needles, Brianna?"

Brianna turned from looking out the window. "Not really. Grandma gave herself shots, and sometimes I helped when her hands were shaky. She had diabetes, and besides her pills, she needed a shot every day."

"I'm glad you aren't afraid. The blood test is to prove David's your dad. We didn't want to talk about it in front of Steven or Meagan, and it'll be your decision how much you share when we get home."

"I don't mind telling them. Especially Meagan. She's been so nice to me since I got here."

Susanne smiled. "Yes, she has. Meagan really loves you."

"I know. I love her too."

David glanced in the mirror. "After we're done at the doctor's, we'll be going to the attorney's office. If you have any questions while we're there, we want you to ask, okay?"

Brianna nodded. "Okay."

The doctor visit went swiftly and relatively pain free, although David was a bigger baby about the blood being drawn than Brianna. The nurse took Brianna's blood first and complimented her on how little it seemed to bother her.

When David's turn came, he flinched when the needle slid into his arm. "Your daughter is braver than you are, Mr. Carson." She smiled at the girl standing nearby, not seeing the look Brianna shot David and Susanne.

"Yes, she certainly is," David said, pride evident in his voice.

"She used to help give her grandmother shots for her diabetes," Susanne explained. "That's why she does so much better than her dad." She grinned at Brianna.

Brianna's face lit up as though she'd been given a gift. What a small thing their words were, but what joy they conveyed. Susanne reached out to give the girl's shoulder a quick squeeze, then ushered her two patients out the door.

David stopped before leaving the room. "How long does it take to get the results for paternity DNA testing?"

The nurse looked startled, glancing from David to Brianna and back again. "That's why you're having blood drawn? I noticed the DNA testing, but I didn't realize it was for paternity authentication. Who in their right mind could look at the two of you and not know she's your daughter?"

"We need to prove it to a judge. It's a long story," he hedged.

"Of course. It normally takes about ten days for a simple paternity test. That includes the shipping time and notification by certified mail as soon as the results are finalized."

David thanked her and left the room. It was time to see what help the family practice attorney might give.

Chapter Thirty-Two

A HALF-HOUR LATER, THEY WERE ushered into the office of Jay R. Thorne, family practice attorney-at-law. He offered them a seat, shook hands, and urged them to call him Jay.

"I'm a country boy at heart, and I don't stand on formalities," his hearty voice rang out, and he winked at Brianna.

Susanne sank into her chair and took the opportunity to look around. Neither this man nor his office was pretentious. Jay dressed in slacks and a short-sleeve shirt, and she noted he didn't wear a tie. The top shirt button stood open, giving a casual appearance to his already relaxed air. His sandy hair appeared rumpled, as though his fingers were drawn to it on a regular basis. Other than the unbuttoned collar, he looked neat and clean-cut, matching the feel of his office. Books lined one entire wall from floor to ceiling, and she observed a few classics mixed in with the legal tomes. *A lover of the classics in the form of a country boy. Quite an unlikely combination.*

Her attention was diverted from the beautiful print of a fly fisherman standing in a stream by Jay's voice. "So what can I help you with, Mr. and Mrs. Carson? And Miss Carson?"

"Well, you see, that's the problem. She is Miss Carson, but she isn't," David said. At the attorney's look of confusion, he hastened to add. "I think I'd better start from the beginning, but first, you need to see what we're up against." He dropped the envelope containing the legal complaint onto the attorney's desk. "If you'd take a few minutes to review that, we'll explain our side when you've finished."

Several minutes passed while Jay examined the papers. He didn't rush, and Susanne felt thankful he was thorough. But part of her wanted to scream at him to hurry—they were dealing with a child's life here, and he needed to set it right. She knew it wasn't logical, but logic had no place in her feelings. She'd finally opened her heart to Brianna, and her maternal instincts were operating at full force. Susanne was focused on one thing and one thing only—how to beat Brianna's uncle. She hated giving the man the dignity of that title. He didn't deserve to be the girl's uncle.

Jay placed the documents on his desk, then laced his fingers behind his head and leaned back in his chair, his attention directed at David. "I assume since you're here that there's more to the story than is told in this complaint against you."

Susanne noticed it was a statement, not a question, and relaxed. She hadn't realized that for the past five minutes she'd been gripping the arms of her chair and tapping her foot against the rug. It seemed, however, that this man wasn't going to pre-judge them based solely on the testimony he'd read.

"You assume correctly. I'll try to include all the details. If anything's not clear, please feel free to interrupt."

David spent the next ten minutes explaining how Brianna came to be in their care and the pertinent facts up until the time the DSHS supervisor visited their home.

Jay listened attentively, jotting down occasional notes. When David finished, the attorney rubbed his chin. "Hmm."

They waited in silence, giving him time to think, while the minutes ticked off on the grandfather clock sitting in the far corner of his office. "You say you had blood drawn and sent to a lab?" He moved to the most recent event first.

"Yes. They assured me the results would be mailed in no more than ten days."

"I see this form is signed by a Ms. Sorensen. Is that the same person who came to your home?" He continued getting clarification on the details for several minutes, then set his pen down and focused on Brianna. He smiled at the girl, who sat unmoving in her seat.

"Well, young lady, we've yet to hear anything from you. How do you feel about this? Do you want to live with your uncle or with your dad and stepmom?"

Susanne felt a small thrill go through her at Jay's words. Of course, she'd be Brianna's stepmom. Hopefully, someday the girl would let her into her life enough to think of her as a mom—step or otherwise.

Brianna smiled shyly, responding to the kindness in the man's face. "I don't want to live with my uncle, sir. I want to live with"— she hesitated and looked at David and Susanne—"I want to live with my dad," she said in a rush, her face turning pink.

Jay didn't seem to notice her hesitation and moved on with his gentle questioning. "Is there any particular reason you don't want to live with your uncle?"

"He drinks, and he was mean to my mother." She retreated into her chair and turned her head away from his gaze.

"Can you tell me how he was mean to your mother?"

She shook her head firmly, still not meeting his eyes. "I can't tell you any more than that."

Susanne wondered once again what Brianna was hiding. Was she making the story up, or was she afraid to tell the truth?

"That's all right, Brianna. You don't have to say any more right now. But you need to understand a judge might ask you the same question. If he does, you'll be under oath to tell the truth and it's important you do. Do you understand that?" His voice was kind, but firm.

"Yes." She looked up from where her hands were clasped in her lap. "If a judge asks me to tell him the truth, I have to do it," she repeated.

Jay nodded, then turned to David and Susanne. "It's too late this afternoon, but I'll make a phone call to DSHS first thing in the morning and see if this case is on a judge's docket. A custody hearing might already be scheduled, but if not, I'll make sure one is as soon as possible after the DNA results come in. I'll also let Ms. Sorensen know I'm representing your family, and she is absolutely not to remove Brianna from your care until the hearing takes place."

"That would take a lot of stress off, but she won't be happy to hear it," David said.

"I'm sure she hopes to find a judge who'll give her permission to remove Brianna without a hearing. She's apparently too new to realize it, but that's not going to happen. I know the two judges in this county most apt to hear this type of case, and they won't sign their name to an order like that without personally reviewing the details.

"I think Ms. Sorensen will be shocked when she appears before either of them. They're both family men, and one has a granddaughter about your age, Brianna. I doubt they'll be happy the DSHS supervisor is trying to put you in the custody of a person like Mr. Warren." His frown deepened, and he ran his fingers through his hair again, causing it to stand on end and giving him the comical look of a little boy.

Susanne hid her smile and sank deeper in her chair, relieved at what Jay had shared.

"I don't want you to worry anymore. I think the judge will wait to see the results of the blood test before he makes a decision. That is, if he's too blind to see you look exactly like your dad," he finished with a grin.

Brianna's hands loosened their grip on each other, and she sat up with a smile. "Thank you, Mr. Thorne."

He let the formal use of his last name go and thanked her in return, assuring them he'd be in touch in the morning.

David shook his hand. "We so appreciate your willingness to help."

"I have a daughter myself, Mr. Carson. And from the description you gave me of this Warren character, there is no way in . . . well—let's just say, there's no way I'd ever allow her to be in the custody of that man." He glanced at Brianna, reached out to ruffle her hair, and saw them to the door.

"David?" Susanne touched her husband's shoulder as they lay side by side in their bed. "Do you want me to switch on the air conditioner? It's muggy tonight."

"Yeah. Thanks."

She slipped her legs over the edge of the mattress and flipped the switch on the window unit positioned to blow across their bed. Summer evenings normally cooled down a bit at their two-thousand-foot elevation, but today had been a scorcher, and the heat hadn't completely dissipated.

She lay down, and David reached out, drawing her head to rest on his shoulder. Susanne snuggled against him and wrapped her arm across his chest. "I've really missed you, you know that?"

"I've missed you too. I was wondering if I could tell you something that I've been struggling with," David said.

"Of course." Her heart beat faster, not sure what might be coming.

"I think I've figured out one of the reasons why I've been so stubborn about hanging onto Brianna."

"Whatever the reason was, I'm thankful for it now."

He was quiet for a moment, then continued in a soft voice. "You know the story Grandfather told about Little Raven questioning his grandfather about the orphans?"

She nodded, then realized he might appreciate an answer.

"Yes, I remember." She waited for David to continue, sensing he might be having a difficult time, but the silence was gentle this time. What a blessed relief from the heaviness and stress of the past few weeks.

David stroked her hair, then pushed himself up on his elbow and looked into her eyes in the dim light. "I'd heard that story more than once while growing up, and I couldn't get it out of my head. I kept seeing Brianna through the eyes of Little Raven— thrown away, abandoned at the white children's orphanage. Something in me rose up in protest. Even before I acknowledged her as my daughter, I knew I couldn't throw her away. I wanted to be true to my ancestry, however small a part it might play in my life today."

Susanne lay still for a moment, thinking over what she'd heard. "I had a feeling that story impacted you at the time he told it. But I'm not clear on something. You didn't seem to be interested in Brianna or want to spend time with her. If you didn't want to throw her away, as you call it, then why didn't you put out more effort?"

He frowned and gave his head a slight shake. "I guess the main reason, at least at the beginning, was because I saw how upset it made you. Fear of getting involved, in case we didn't end up keeping her, played a part, as well. My relationship with you outweighed a potential one with a daughter I didn't know existed before this summer. Only later did my heart get involved with Brianna, and I couldn't turn back."

Susanne reached up to give him a gentle kiss. "I understand, and I'm glad you told me."

He smiled. "Thanks, honey. I appreciate you, very much. May I ask you a question?"

"Sure."

"I'm not sure what's happened, but whatever it is, I'm

thankful. You seem different somehow."

"I am." Her voice softened to barely above a whisper.

"Do you want to talk about it?"

She looked into her husband's eyes, holding his gaze for a moment, then slid her fingers down his arm and gently pulled him down beside her. "Yes. Last night, when we couldn't find Brianna, I overheard Meagan praying. The words she said didn't impact me as much as the selflessness she showed in her prayer. That little girl of ours asked God to take her to heaven instead of Brianna because she was worried Brianna wasn't ready to die."

David's arm tightened around her. "That sounds like Meagan."

"I know. She fell asleep right after she finished praying, and I returned to our room. I felt like my entire world had caved in around me. First, when Brianna came, I found out about your past, and I had no control over my circumstances. Right when we'd begun to have a measure of peace in our family and I was beginning to get used to the idea of her staying, her uncle showed up and tried to take her. After the DSHS supervisor left that night, I felt like we were going to lose her. Then we found out Brianna overheard me talking to my mother and decided to run away. She truly believed we might give her to her uncle." Susanne trembled as she thought of the ramifications and felt David pull her a little closer.

"That wasn't your fault."

"But that isn't the point. I knew I needed help outside myself, that I couldn't control anything happening around me."

David drew a deep breath and gently released it. "I understand what you're saying. You told me about your grandpa and his influence on your life when we first met. I guess that affected you more than you realized."

"It did. When I was growing up and he lived with us, he

encouraged me to think for myself. He didn't respect people who he believed used God and church as a crutch. He drummed it into me that I needed to be responsible for myself, and as a result, I've felt the need to stay in control. I thought I was doing a fair job of it. I didn't want anyone telling me what to do or how to do it, not even God." She needed to explain, maybe more for her own sake than his. The cleansing process had begun with her spiritual transformation and talking with David helped affirm her decision.

"I think that's hard for all of us at some point or other. Giving control to God, not knowing what He might ask of us can be a scary thing." He propped himself up on his elbow. "I'm so sorry for what I put you through by not being honest years ago. Part of this could've been avoided. Even though Brianna still would've come, you'd have been better prepared if you'd known the truth. I hope you can believe me and forgive me someday."

"I have, David. I realized the other night that I was still holding onto hurt and it wasn't right. I've made so many mistakes myself that I have no right to judge. I do forgive you, and I hope you'll forgive me too."

His face was almost comical as he gaped at her. "Whew. Guess I didn't expect to hear that. Of course I forgive you. But I need you to know I hate that I lied to you. Being afraid that I'd lose you then almost made me lose you now. I'd give anything to go back and do it over."

"I believe that. I really do. I want to let it go and move on."

He leaned over and gave her a gentle kiss. "I love you so much, and I'm proud of you."

He lay down, and she nestled into his shoulder, giving him another small hug. "I had a tough time getting to this point. Jeena was pulling me the other direction, trying to convince me to leave you and start a new life."

David stiffened and opened his mouth, but she slipped her

hand over his lips. "Don't worry. It wasn't even a consideration. After hearing some of the things she said, I realized she wasn't a true friend."

"I always wondered what you saw in her. She seems nice enough on the surface, but she's shallow and selfish if you look very deep."

"Jeena has a lot of good qualities . . . she's loyal to a fault and generous, but she wants to promote her own agenda. I don't need someone else telling me what to do. I've made enough of a mess by myself. I told her I wouldn't be seeing her again, and I have no desire to. I do feel sorry for her, though."

"Why?"

"Her life is filled with material things, but she doesn't have many friends. Even with all her possessions, she's not happy."

"You've been friends for several years. That must've been a hard decision."

"Yeah, but I think I was ready to move on. She'd been pushing me the last few times we were together. Whether out of jealousy because I'm married and have a family or because she does care in her own misguided way, I'm not sure. But it was time to let go."

"I'm glad, honey. I apologize for the times I've put pressure on you, but I never trusted her. I should've had faith in your judgment. I'm sure my pushing didn't help."

"Yeah, I might have made the decision sooner, but I knew you wanted me to."

They lay there for a few minutes, both caught in their own memories and regrets. As she snuggled beside David, she noticed the full moon shining in their window. The peace in the room enfolded her.

"I have one more thing I want to tell you." She reached up to run her fingers across his cheek and gave him a quick kiss. "After I went to my room last night and thought through the past two months, I made a decision." She felt his body grow still. "I haven't done a great job running my own life, and I needed to turn it over to someone who could do it better."

"And who would that be?" he asked quietly, but she felt the tension in the arm holding her.

"Jesus. I turned my life over to Jesus last night, and I've never been happier. I can't begin to tell you the peace I've had since making that decision."

She thought for a moment that her six-foot-two husband was going to cry as he took in what she'd said. Instead, he whooped and wrapped both arms around her, giving her a bear hug that almost threw them both off the bed.

"Not so loud!" She laughed and struggled to loosen his grip. "You'll wake the kids, and you're going to suffocate me if you keep squeezing so hard." She patted his face before pulling back a few inches.

"You have no idea what this means to me!" David loosened his grip, his face radiating a glow of its own.

"I think I do. I tried thinking about what it would've been like if I'd been the one who loved the Lord and actively served Him all these years and you'd been stubborn and proud. I'm not so sure I'd have been as committed to our marriage as you. I know it couldn't have been easy when I tried to shut you down all the time."

"No, but not because I wanted to be right and prove you wrong. It was because I love you so much, and I couldn't stand the thought of missing eternity with you. You are the love of my life, and more than anything, I want us to be one." He stroked her hair.

She nestled against his side, feeling his tenderness in every motion of his hand.

"Is it all right if I ask you something? I'm almost afraid to, but it's going to keep bothering me if I don't." She pulled away, sat up, and wrapped her arms around her knees.

"Of course. Anything. What is it?"

"You remember when we went to the fair and the Slater family arrived?"

"Yes."

"I saw you watching Kim and Phil, but it looked like you were watching Kim. Has there been a time when you were attracted to her or regretted that you married me?"

"No way!" He sat up. "I've never regretted marrying you for a second. I wasn't watching Kim. I was thinking about something they had that I wished we had."

She sat motionless, her head cocked to one side.

"Phil and Kim love each other the same as we do, but it's deeper than that. They also both love the Lord, and He's the center of their marriage. I wished we had the kind of closeness I've always seen in their marriage. Does that make sense?" He took her hands, pulling her toward him again.

She didn't resist but scooted over beside him. "Yes, it makes sense. It wouldn't have if you'd tried to explain it that day, so I'm glad I waited to ask. I love you, and I'm so glad you never gave up on me." She reached up to give him a hug and a promising kiss before nestling down beside him once more.

Chapter Thirty-Three

THE NEXT MORNING, DAVID STAYED HOME from work, anticipating the call from their attorney. Jay called at eleven, and David spent a few minutes talking.

David stretched and yawned after he hung up, taking his time before pulling out the chair across from Susanne at the kitchen table. A smile played around the edges of his mouth.

"Give, David. What did Jay say? You look pretty happy, so it mustn't have be too bad."

"Yeah, it wasn't too bad." He grinned, teasing for another minute. He ducked as she reached across the table to swat his arm. "Jay informed Ms. Sorensen this morning that he'd been retained as our attorney. He told her he's requesting a custody hearing and will be filing a petition to keep Brianna in our care until the hearing."

He leaned back in his chair, and Susanne could tell he clearly enjoyed the thought of Ms. Sorensen's discomfort.

"Good. What did she say? Did Jay tell her that you and Brianna took blood tests and you intend to prove you're her father?"

"You bet. It was one of the first things he told her. He asked at the courthouse about Ms. Sorensen. It's rather odd. She has a good reputation with the other caseworkers, for the most part. She's brusque at times and tends to abide by the book, but in the short time she's been here, she done all right."

"That surprises me. From the way she treated us, you'd think people wouldn't care for her."

"Yeah. He did say that one person hinted at trouble at her last job but refused to give him any details." He shrugged, then took a big swallow of the hot coffee and spluttered. "Ouch!"

Susanne patted his hand, then sighed. "I suppose she's doing her job."

He snorted and shook his head. "Her job is to protect the children in her care. If she steps outside of those boundaries, then she needs to be dealt with. I have no sympathy for someone who puts her career ahead of the safety and welfare of children."

"What happens next?"

"Jay told Ms. Sorensen to get a court date set by noon or he'd get in touch with a judge and see to it himself. She apparently took him seriously because she called him a few minutes ago."

"All right. Do we have a hearing?"

"Yep. In front of Judge Travis next Tuesday at eleven o'clock. He's an older gentleman, according to Jay. You remember him mentioning a judge with a granddaughter about Brianna's age?"

"Yes. Is that who we got?"

"Uh-huh."

"That's wonderful! We need to tell the kids. Let's head outside and find them." She pushed her chair away from the table and reached for his hand. "Thank You, Lord," she whispered as David took her hand and they headed out the door. "Thank You for answering my prayers, even when I didn't deserve it."

David talked to Brianna while Susanne took Steven and Meagan aside. "I'm sorry kids, but you won't be allowed to go."

"Ah, Mom, no fair. You don't let us do anything fun," Steven said.

Meagan kicked her foot against the gravel on the path. "I want to go with Brianna, Mom. She needs us there."

"I understand how you feel, but we don't know what Brianna's uncle might say or do, and we don't think you should be there. But your dad and I have an idea, and it needs to be a secret for a while." Susanne leaned close and whispered her plan.

"Oh, can we?" Meagan squealed, then clapped her hand over her mouth. She lowered her voice, glancing over at Brianna. "That is so cool!"

Brianna stood with her back to them, listening to what David was explaining, and didn't appear to notice.

"Whew, sorry, Mom. I almost blew it." Meagan's face was almost comical, and Susanne stifled a laugh.

"We need to be careful if we want to keep this a surprise until after the hearing. It may take a little while for us to put it all together. Steven, you have to promise not to say anything to Brianna. Can you do that?" Susanne asked the beaming boy.

"Yeah, I promise, Mom. I won't say anything. This is so neat!" He danced from one foot to the other.

Susanne gave them both a quick hug and shooed them off to play, then joined David and Brianna.

"I want to make sure you know what's going to happen, Brianna," David said. "Judge Travis probably won't make a decision that first day. It's a preliminary hearing. Jay said he doesn't even need to be there unless we want him to because the judge will simply review the complaint and Jay's response, and maybe ask a question or two."

Brianna bit her lip, then glanced up. "Do I have to talk to my uncle?"

"No, you don't, and we'll make sure he doesn't bother you."

"Good. That's my only question." She looked across the lawn to where Meagan and Steven played kickball.

"Go ahead, Brianna. That's all we needed."

She raced down the slight slope to the area where the kids played, her laughter floating back. David shook his head. "Have you noticed she's starting to come out of her shell? We've rarely ever heard her laugh, but it seems to be coming more easily now. Maybe we'll get to meet the real Brianna when this is over."

Susanne brushed the moisture from her eyes. "I truly hope so. She deserves some happiness in her life, and this family is going to see that she gets it."

That evening, David decided they all needed a distraction. He took the family to a movie and stopped for a snack on the way home. The kids drooped in the backseat on the drive home, and the silence that lay between Susanne and him resonated with peace. He felt blessed in the wife and children the Lord had given him.

He pulled the car to a stop, shut off the motor, and prepared to unload the sleepy kids, when he saw a movement in the trees not far from the house.

"Stay here, Susanne, and don't let the kids out of the car."

"What's wrong?" Susanne rubbed her eyes and yawned.

"Probably nothing. I thought something moved beside a tree when my headlights turned off. I want to check before we go in the house."

"All right. But be careful."

He slipped out of the car and walked toward the trees. If only he had his flashlight. It would be difficult to see anything on this moonless night.

"Is someone there?" He stopped to listen.

The sound of crickets chirping in the brush and the bellow of the frogs at the pond were all that broke the hush of the evening. He searched for a few more minutes, then returned to the car.

"What was it?"

"I didn't find anything. It may have been a deer, but they don't normally come this close to the house. Let's get the kids in. I'll check again after they're in bed. No sense scaring them."

Thirty minutes later, they'd tucked in the kids and met at the front door.

"Stay here while I look around." David took his flashlight and scoured the area around the house. Pine needles covered the ground, making it impossible to find any tracks.

Susanne opened the door, poking her head outside. "Anything?"

"No. The ground is too hard. The pine needles keep footprints from showing. It may have been my imagination. We'll make sure everything is locked tight tonight, just to be safe."

"Good idea. I don't ever think to check the windows, especially in the summer when it's nice to have them open."

They made the rounds of the house and headed to bed when they'd satisfied themselves all was secure.

"I'm probably a little jumpy after the episode with Brianna's uncle, and then Ms. Sorensen coming," David said as he settled beside Susanne and reached over to switch off the lamp.

"I'm glad we took the kids to the movie. It was a nice change, and they all seemed to enjoy it." Susanne patted her pillow and snuggled deeper into the bed.

"Yeah. Me too. We'd better get to sleep. Night, hon."

They were drifting off to sleep when a scream sounded from upstairs. "Help! David, Susanne! Come quick!"

"Is that Brianna?" Susanne jumped out of bed.

David bolted for the door. "Yes, hurry!"

They flew up the stairs and toward her room, passing Meagan's and Steven's rooms on the way. Both kids peeked out of their doors, and Susanne stopped long enough to gather them close. "Stay with me until we find out what's wrong."

David switched on Brianna's light to find her buried under the sheet. "What happened?"

"Somebody looked in my window." She emerged from under her sheet, her chin quivering.

"Did you see who it was?" David rushed to the large slider,

one of two in the house that opened onto a deck and outer stairs leading to the ground. "Did you hear someone come up the steps?"

"No. I was almost asleep, but I got thirsty. I sat up to get my water and glanced at the window. I couldn't see very well because it's so dark. But a face pressed against the glass, and I think it might have been my uncle, but I'm not sure." Her body shook, and she wrapped the sheet tight around her, tears trickling down her cheeks.

Susanne left Steven and Meagan and sat on the bed, taking the sobbing girl into her arms. "It's okay. Don't worry. We locked the house, including all the windows. No one can hurt you."

David looked from one young, scared face to the next before he spoke. "I'm going outside to look around. Whoever it is can't have gone far. Meagan, Steven, you two stay in here with your mother and Brianna. I don't want anyone going downstairs until I get back."

He took the stairs two at a time, grabbed his flashlight off a table, and bolted out the door. It had to be Brianna's uncle. They'd never been bothered in all their years of living here, and he doubted a random passerby would peer in their windows— especially one upstairs. That must be what he'd seen earlier. Why hadn't he stayed out longer, searched harder?

The ground at the base of the outer steps had been disturbed. He could see a spot where a boot heel had struck the ground. Brianna's scream must have sent the man flying down the steps before he'd jumped and hit the ground running.

The area between the house and the pond abounded with areas to hide, including a rock wall holding large flowering bushes and trees that encompassed a park-like setting. He headed to the pond and shone his light along the bank, probing the shadows. The bullfrogs ceased their bellowing, making loud plunking sounds as they jumped into the pond. A rustling in the cattails and splash of water told him he'd disturbed the small family of ducks living there.

"Nothing," he muttered.

He circled the house three times, widening the area with each sweep and checking every spot he could think of where a man might hide. He came up empty. Whoever it was had to be long gone.

He stepped into the house and shut the front door behind him.

"David, is that you?"

"Yes."

Susanne came to the top of the stairs. "I've got the kids settled. Brianna moved in with Meagan for tonight, and Steven is sleeping on the floor in our room. None of them wanted to be alone."

"No problem. I didn't find much, but there's evidence of someone being here. I found a heel print at the bottom of the steps leading to Brianna's deck."

Susanne paused with her hand still on the rail. "Her uncle?"

"I'd bet on it. I'm going to call the sheriff's department. At least it'll be on record that someone was here. We can't prove his identity since Brianna didn't get a good look at his face."

"What do you think he wanted?"

David placed the flashlight on the desk nearby pulled off his boots. "I don't know. He may have arrived before we got back from the movie. He might have hoped to break in, but we got home before he had the chance. Why he hung around is anyone's guess."

"Do you think he'd be stupid enough to try to take her right out of her bedroom? Could he have watched other nights to see which room she's in?" Susanne covered her mouth with her hand and sank down onto a step.

"It's possible. I'm thankful we had her outer door locked." He secured the front door and tested the handle, then walked through the room, checking each window for the second time.

"I don't know if I'll be able to sleep tonight."

"We need to pray over our family." He headed for the kitchen. "I'm calling the sheriff. Would you make sure all the rest of the windows are locked?"

Thirty minutes later, David met a deputy at the door and filled him in. The deputy took the report and scouted around the house, starting with the boot print at the base of the steps.

David followed him but kept out of the way, watching as the deputy shone his spotlight from the steps out to the brush, encompassing a fifty-foot circle. The melancholy sound of coyotes yipping out in the field made the hair stand up on the back of his neck. The crickets and frogs had ceased their singing, and the darkness seemed to intensify as the two men prowled through the brush. No further sign of the intruder materialized. The men returned to the house and checked the print once more.

"I think you're right. Looks like he took off in a hurry to make that much of a print in this hard ground. Must've hit hard and fast and probably kept going." The deputy got up from his crouched position but kept his light trained on the indentation in the dirt.

"Brianna screamed pretty loudly, and it must've spooked him. He may have thought we were asleep and didn't expect to be spotted." David continued to cast his light around the area, hoping to find another clue they'd missed.

"We'll keep a car in your area tonight, patrolling this road. I doubt he'll be back, but we'll keep our eyes open. Too bad your girl didn't get a good look at his face."

"Yeah." David leaned against the outer doorjam, as weariness set in. "I appreciate the patrol."

"We'll send an officer tomorrow to check over the area, but I don't think we'll find much." The deputy pulled open the door of the patrol car. "That's it for now. We'll call you in the morning if anything new comes up. Good night."

"Good night, and thanks again." David stepped into the house, locked the door, and headed to their bedroom where Susanne waited.

"I checked on the girls again, and they're sleeping," she whispered. She sat up in bed, a large stack of pillows at her back.

David stepped over the still form of his son sprawled on the floor. "He's out."

Susanne peeked over the edge at Steven and smiled. "Yeah, didn't take him long. Everything okay?"

"Yes. There'll be a car patrolling our road tonight, so I think we can sleep without worrying too much."

"I'm not sure about not worrying, but I'll try." Susanne yawned. "I don't know if I'll be able to sleep." She tossed the extra pillows on the floor and fell back on the bed.

"I hear you. Mind if I pray?" He still wasn't used to this new wife the Lord had given him.

"Sure."

He slipped into bed and she rested her head on his shoulder. His prayer was brief, and he heard a soft *amen* at the end.

"I love you, Susanne. God is good, no matter what else happens. I know He's watching out for our family, and we'll get through this together." He gave her a kiss and turned out the light.

He probably wouldn't sleep, but that was okay. He'd lie here and count his blessings until it was time to get up.

Chapter Thirty-Four

SUSANNE WOKE AT SEVEN THIRTY SATURDAY morning, amazed she'd slept all night. She glanced outside to see David patrolling a section of fence some distance from the house and she guessed he hadn't slept much. In the past, she'd be uptight after a night like that, but not today. After David had prayed, her fear had lifted, and she'd felt a gentle peace envelop her. She must have gone to sleep within minutes.

"Hey, Mom, did they catch the bad guy?" Steven came bounding down the stairs and into the kitchen before she finished preparing breakfast.

Susanne poured grape juice and handed Steven a glass. "Not yet."

He took a big gulp and wiped his mouth with the back of his hand. "How come you didn't wake me up when the sheriff came? I wanted to see his car."

"You were tired and needed to sleep. Besides, the deputy didn't have time. He was busy." She ripped a paper towel off the roll and pushed it into his hand. "Use this to wipe your face next time, okay, bud?"

"What was the deputy doing? Trying to find the bad guy who looked in Brianna's window?"

"Yes."

"How come he didn't find him?" He set down his glass and went to the refrigerator, pulling out a piece of pie.

"Whoa, there. No pie for breakfast."

"Why not? I'm a growing boy, and I need pie." Steven gave her an impish grin, almost making her give in.

She laughed and put the pie away. "You'll grow just fine with a normal breakfast. Go find your sisters and Dad, and we'll eat."

"Okay." He left the room, giggling and skipping on his way out the door.

The sheriff's department called at nine with nothing to report. It'd been a quiet night, and they'd spotted no one on the roads. They filed their report and promised to keep an eye on the area. They were sending a man to see if they could lift any prints from the window but doubted they'd have much luck.

The two girls were quiet and stayed close to the house all morning. Neither seemed inclined to talk about the incident, but David and Susanne agreed it shouldn't be ignored or fear would mushroom.

Right before lunch, Susanne sank into the rocker in the living room and smiled at both of the girls. "Dad said the sheriff is still keeping an eye on our house. I don't think we need to worry about Brianna's uncle coming back tonight. We're glad you're staying close to the house, but we don't want you to be afraid."

"That man really scared Brianna, Mom." Meagan sat close beside Brianna on the couch.

"I know. He scared all of us. We don't want anything to happen to Brianna or any of you. But we believe God is taking care of our family." Susanne stopped rocking and reached out to pat Brianna's knee.

"I've never heard you say anything like that before," Meagan said.

"I know. It's kind of new to me, but I believe it. Why don't we make this a fun day? We can invite Grandma over and play games. I'll even make another pie so Steven has plenty for lunch. How does that sound?"

"Super! Thanks, Mom." Meagan's smile made the effort worthwhile.

They would be fine. Susanne had to believe that. It felt strange depending on God, but deep inside, she knew He would care for their family.

Sunday morning arrived—the first Sunday Susanne could remember looking forward to church. She had an added reason for excitement this morning. She'd asked her mother to go with them, and Claire had accepted with little protest.

Before church, Susanne told the kids about her decision. She knew Meagan would be thrilled and Steven would take it with a shrug. At his age, he hadn't been aware of his mother's struggle. She felt uncertain about Brianna but hoped the girl might come to faith in Christ someday.

She gathered them together on the king-sized bed and told them about the change in her life. As she expected, Steven appeared only a little interested, then scooted out of the room to play.

Meagan bounced on the bed, her expressive face showing her joy. "Mom, that is so awesome! That's why you said that yesterday, about God taking care of us. I've been praying for you." She reached over to give her mother a hug.

"I know, honey, and I'm glad."

Susanne glanced at Brianna, who sat silent on the bed. "Did you have a question, Brianna?"

"I remember you telling me after I first came that you were mad at God, but you didn't really explain why. Was it because I came? Are you still mad at Him?" Brianna sat fiddling with the corner of the bedspread.

"No. Mostly I didn't trust God to take care of my life because I thought I could do better. A few days ago, I realized I was wrong. I told Him I don't want to be in charge because He can do a lot better job." She reached out to stroke the girl's hair.

"Do you still blame me for Meagan's accident?"

"Oh, honey, no. I'm so sorry. With everything that's been going on, I forgot to talk to you about that. The night I put my life into God's hands, He showed me what a mess I'd made of everything. I haven't done a great job taking care of myself or my family. Meagan's accident wasn't your fault but mine."

Brianna's head shot up, and her hands dropped in her lap. "Yours? But I threw my jacket. You weren't even in the pasture when Glory bucked."

"You're right. But I didn't care enough to teach you the things you needed to know, or to be down there when Meagan worked with you. I left your safety up to Meagan. I'm the adult, and it was my responsibility, not hers. If I'd spent time working with you, it wouldn't have happened."

"So you aren't mad at me?"

Susanne reached out and wrapped her arms around Brianna's shoulders. "No, and I never should've been. I was mostly mad at myself and didn't know it. Will you forgive me?"

Brianna slipped her arms around Susanne's waist, giving her a long hug. "Uh-huh."

"I'm glad you came. God needs to be in charge of our family. David has always known, but I didn't agree. I understand now that God really does love us and it's okay to trust Him."

Brianna nodded and moved out of Susanne's embrace. "I think I'd like to do what you did, if that's okay. I'd like to ask God to take care of my life."

"Of course it's okay! In fact, it's wonderful."

Meagan began bouncing on the bed again. "We can pray right now, can't we, Mom?"

"Of course." Susanne led Brianna in a prayer, giving her another long hug when she finished.

"Now you're my sister for real," Meagan exclaimed, "and we'll go to heaven and be together forever!"

The two girls left the room, their arms around each other's waists, and Susanne thanked God for the miracle that had just taken place.

The deputy sheriff called again. They'd canvassed the homes in their area, but no one had reported any break-ins or problems. One person heading home about the time the intruder disappeared reported seeing an old pickup traveling with its lights out not far from the Carsons' driveway.

The police weren't dropping the case but felt they'd come to somewhat of a dead-end. With no witnesses placing Arthur Warren at the scene, they could do little. They planned on questioning the man but doubted that would yield results.

David called Jay on Monday morning. "Jay, it's David Carson."

"Good to hear from you. What's up?"

"Someone tried to break in to Brianna's room the other night."

"Did you call the police?" His relaxed attitude gave way to that of an attentive attorney.

"We called the sheriff, and they sent a deputy right out. They didn't find much. The prints on the glass were badly smudged."

"Did Brianna see the person?"

"It was too dark to be sure. If the man hadn't pressed his face against the glass, she wouldn't have spotted him. She screamed, and he ran across the deck and down the stairs. By the time we checked on her and I went outside, he'd had time to get off the property."

"You think it was her uncle."

"We do, but we can't prove it. He may have been checking out our home, figuring he'd grab her if he loses the custody battle. He could disappear, and we might never find her again."

"That's possible." Jay hesitated, and David could hear what sounded like a pencil tapping the desk. "Is the sheriff's department watching your house?"

"Yes. They took it seriously. There's so much on the news about kids getting taken from their beds."

"I'll put in a call to a deputy I know and urge them to stay on it, at least until after the hearing."

"Thanks. Can we use this in the hearing? Let the judge know we think it was Brianna's uncle?"

"Without getting a positive ID, it's not admissible. There's no other evidence?"

"A neighbor saw an old pickup traveling with its lights out not far from our driveway that night. He dismissed it as a teenager driving without lights as a prank. It wasn't until the sheriff questioned him that he thought about it at all."

"And your wife said Arthur Warren came to your home in an older pickup?"

"Yes. But again, no one can substantiate it's the same one."

Jay heaved a sigh. "No help there then. I'll talk to my deputy friend and make sure your home gets a steady patrol. We'll decide if we need to do more after the hearing."

"I'm glad it's tomorrow. We hate the waiting and want this over."

"I don't blame you. I'll stop by the courthouse tomorrow. I'm seeing a client at the same time you're in court, so I can check on how the hearing is going. But like I said before, this should only be a preliminary hearing and nothing more. We'll talk over our options before the next one is scheduled."

David hung up the phone and went in search of Susanne. It would help set her mind at ease knowing Jay would be there when needed.

Chapter Thirty-Five

TUESDAY DAWNED BRIGHT AND CLEAR. It would've been a wonderful day to stay home and work in the garden, but they had more pressing business. Susanne had tried to lie still last night and not wake David, but dire thoughts about the hearing kept assaulting her.

David got up earlier than normal for work. She dragged herself out of bed, her body feeling drained.

"I'm kind of worried about the hearing. What if the judge doesn't see through that man?"

"From the way you described him, I don't think anyone could help but see through him." David gulped down his breakfast and kept an eye on the clock.

"But Ms. Sorensen said he looked fine when he came to her office. He might be able to pull off a decent appearance in court. Can we tell the judge what happened the other night?"

"I don't think so. Remember what Jay said. We don't have any proof. It's not like we filed charges since Brianna didn't see his face clearly."

"If the judge forces Brianna to live with her uncle, even for a short time, I'm afraid she'll try to run again. Not that I'd blame her." Susanne couldn't eat. She fixed a cup of tea and sat at the table.

"I doubt that'll happen. The paternity tests should be back soon, and we'll have proof."

"But the judge might think he needs to be fair. She's been living with us, and Arthur Warren is her uncle. He might make her go with her uncle until the tests come back."

"Let's not try to figure it out now. We've prayed about it, and we need to keep praying. God will take care of this." He pushed his chair away from the table.

"I'm trying. But this faith stuff is new to me. It's hard not to worry." She set her cup down and folded her hands, hoping to still the shaking.

"A part of me is worried too, but a bigger part knows God is in control. We have to trust Him, honey." David reached over and gave her a kiss. "I'm sorry, but I need to go. If I don't leave, I won't finish a few details on the job before I meet you at the courthouse."

"I know. Thanks for listening, and I'm sorry for worrying." She stood and followed him outside to his truck.

"Don't be sorry. I'm thankful you're willing to pray about things now. Try to have a good morning, okay?" He shut his truck door and pulled out of the driveway.

Susanne hurried through her chores, anxious to get the housework finished and hoping the time would pass quickly. The sooner this day was over, the happier she'd be.

David would meet them at the courthouse a little before eleven. Claire would come over to stay with Steven and Meagan.

Steven had managed to keep their secret from Brianna without dropping a hint. How much longer he'd be able to do so, Susanne couldn't tell. She hoped this would be over soon, and life could return to normal.

The girls were in Brianna's room, picking what Brianna would wear to court. Meagan still struggled with not being able to go, since she felt responsible to take care of her new big sister.

At ten o'clock, Claire tapped at the front door and stepped in. "Good morning! Anyone home?"

"I'm in the kitchen, Mom, trying to relax for a few minutes. Want a cup of coffee?"

Claire sat on one of the kitchen chairs. "No thanks, I'm fine. I don't think coffee would do me much good. I'm already a bundle of nerves. How are you holding up?"

"All right, but I'm still worried. Jay assured us this judge is a decent man, but there are always unknowns. I didn't sleep well, and I'm guessing that neither did David or Brianna. I know Meagan's prayed about it, and she's probably doing better than all of us. She seems to have a profound faith that this will be fine."

"Meagan has a lot of her mother's stubbornness . . . and her big heart." Claire reached out to pat Susanne's hand. "And since you mentioned prayer, I enjoyed your church service last Sunday. I should've started attending long ago but never got around to it. I was always busy or tired, and since you didn't mind one way or the other, it didn't seem important."

"I'd love it if you come with us every week. I'm sorry I've never asked you. To be honest, I didn't care myself. I made some decisions about my commitment to God recently, and that's changing. Sometime when we're not under pressure, I'd like to tell you about it."

"I'd love that whenever you can make time. But right now, you'd better throw on your lipstick and tell the kids you're leaving. The last thing you want to do is keep the judge waiting." Claire looked at the clock on the kitchen wall and rose from her chair. "It takes fifteen minutes to get there, and you wanted to meet David early, so you'd better scoot."

"Oh, man, I didn't realize it was so late." Susanne stood. "I'll get Brianna. Could you check on Steven? He was behind the house working on the jumps for his bike," she called before she hurried up the stairs.

Two months ago, I resented Brianna. Now it's all I can do to keep from choking the man who's trying to take her. Lord, You'll have to help me. I can't forgive that man right now, but I'm willing to try, if that's what You want.

A few minutes later, Susanne and Brianna pulled into the small parking lot adjacent to the West District Court. Susanne scanned the area and was relieved to see David already waiting beside his pickup. He looked as nervous as she felt, and she didn't know whether to be comforted or worried.

When David stepped beside her, Susanne whispered, "Have you seen Ms. Sorensen or Brianna's uncle?" She hoped Brianna might not hear, but the girl glanced around and Susanne rebuked herself for not being more careful.

"No, but it's possible they got here ahead of us. We're only fifteen minutes early. We'd better let the clerk know we're here." David gave Brianna a quick hug and offered them both a reassuring smile, then ushered them toward the courthouse steps.

Susanne's eyes stared at the steps, but her mind focused on the drama that lay ahead.

"Oops! I didn't see you." She grabbed the arms of the person who barely missed knocking her down the stairs.

"Susanne?"

"Jeena! What're you doing here?"

"Nothing. Look, I have to go." Jeena started down the steps.

Susanne reached out to grab her wrist. "You've been crying. What's wrong?" The woman who always had her image so together looked like she'd fallen apart. Her puffy eyes, normally perfect makeup now smudged from tears, and her rumpled clothing gave the appearance of a distraught mind.

"Just legal business." Jeena stepped back, but Susanne wasn't ready to let go.

"Wait a minute, please? We're in a hurry, too, but I'd like to tell you something."

Jeena shrugged.

Susanne released her wrist, and Jeena dropped her arm and brushed her hand across her eyes. "I wanted to apologize for being so short with you," Susanne said. "I shouldn't have shut you out of my life. A few days ago, I gave my life to the Lord. I hope you'll forgive me, and I'd like to talk to you about my decision."

Some of Jeena's old bravado returned, and her eyes took on a cynical glint. "I'll pass. I've had enough religion. Besides, you were right. We don't need to hang out with each other. Have a good life!" She nodded sharply to Susanne's family, then turned to go, then she whirled around to face David, her mouth twisted. "You finally got your way. You must be proud." She gave a snort of laughter, then marched down the steps to the parking area.

David reached out, touching Susanne on the shoulder. "Honey, you okay?"

She shook her head and stared after Jeena. "Yeah, I guess. I didn't expect that. I hope you didn't mind me taking the time to talk to her, but I want her to know where I stand. I wish she'd listened."

"I'm glad you did. Maybe the Lord can use the problem she's having to soften her heart."

"Yeah. I hate the way this turned out—she *was* my friend."

"I know."

"I wish I hadn't cut her off the last time we spoke. She's extreme in some ways, but she's also loyal and caring. I thought she had her life together, but now I realize I'm the one who's blessed."

"I've been too angry to pray for her, but I'll change that." He glanced at his watch, then caught her hand and reached for Brianna. "Hey, we'd better hurry. We only have a few minutes until our case is heard."

David talked to the clerk and got directions to the courtroom. They spotted the doors a short way down the hall and walked that direction, almost reaching their destination before a voice sounded off to their right.

"Brianna! Come here and give your uncle a hug." Arthur Warren's tall, thin form rose from the nearby bench. He stepped toward the girl.

Brianna drew back. "You said I wouldn't have to talk to him."

David had yet to meet this man, but he didn't take the time to look. "You don't have to talk to him, and you certainly will not give him a hug." He stepped between them.

"Mr. Carson, I see you have Brianna with you." The low, firm voice of Ms. Sorensen hit Susanne's ears. She walked the short distance from the bench to the waiting family, her heels clicking on the slate floor. The black leather briefcase that swung at her side matched her modest skirt and jacket. A topaz broach pinned to the neck of her cream-colored blouse helped soften her austere appearance.

"I don't think it would hurt to let Mr. Warren talk to his niece." The woman maneuvered her way between David and Brianna and leaned over the girl. "You should be polite to your uncle, young lady."

David forced himself between Ms. Sorensen and the girl. "Brianna is in my care, and she doesn't have to speak to Mr. Warren. You're not in a position to contradict our decision. Now excuse us. We don't want to keep the judge waiting."

The woman folded her arms across her chest and gave an amused smile. "We'll see what kind of position I'm in after this hearing."

Susanne couldn't have been prouder of her husband. She smirked, then sobered quickly. It might be satisfying to put the woman in her place, but they hadn't won the custody hearing yet.

They might need to soften their approach for Brianna's sake, on the chance things didn't go well in front of the judge.

Chapter Thirty-Six

DAVID, SUSANNE, AND BRIANNA ENTERED THE courtroom. Two massive wooden doors swung inward from the hall where they'd entered, and a smaller wooden door stood closed behind the desk on the platform. They stood at the rear of the room for a moment, trying to get their bearings. The room was small, not over twenty feet wide and forty feet long, with two narrow rows of wooden benches located in the center and an aisle in between.

A few people sat scattered across the seats near the back. David and Susanne made their way to the front and slid onto a wooden bench in the first row, Brianna between them.

Susanne took a moment to study her surroundings. The courthouse was almost a century old if she remembered her history, its age reflected in the size and decor. Dark oak appeared to line much of the room, probably sawn in one of the old mills that populated the area. Natural light streamed in through two double-paned windows on each side of the room.

"All rise," the bailiff's monotone rang out as the judge entered the room. "The Honorable Judge Gerald Travis presiding."

Large, ornate chandeliers hung from the dark wood of the ceiling, casting a soft glow over the room. They illuminated the massive platform at the front, a short distance from where the black-robed judge appeared.

He took his seat behind the desk, which seemed to tower above the rest of the furniture in the room. Intricate carving covered its front, similar to the scrollwork on the massive columns in each corner of the room.

"You may be seated," the bailiff intoned.

Judge Travis took a moment to arrange his robes. He placed a pair of glasses on his nose, then reached out for the papers handed to him by the bailiff, who stood off to one side.

Susanne certainly hoped Jay had been correct in his assessment of this man as he didn't appear as she'd envisioned. She'd pictured a smaller, white-haired, elderly gentleman, a bit stooped in the shoulders, with a kindly smile on his face; not this sixty-ish man with salt-and-pepper hair, square jaw, and intense, slate-colored eyes, who sat before them. He was large—she would guess well over 250 pounds—but didn't give the appearance of being fat.

He read through a stack of papers on his desk, a scowl darkening his craggy face. "I see this is a custody hearing with a complaint filed by Mr. Arthur Warren. Is Mr. Warren present in the courtroom today?" He looked over the top of his glasses, peering down at the still room.

"Yes, sir, Your Honor. I'm Mr. Arthur Warren," the man in question spoke up. "And I brought my wife with me. She's the one that will care for Brianna."

Susanne hadn't noticed Arthur had brought his wife. The short, rather plump woman sat ramrod straight in the seat beside Arthur, her prim mouth pursed in a tight line, her hair pulled into a severe bun at the nape of her thick neck. Susanne took a moment to size Arthur up, hoping for the slightly unkempt look he'd presented at her home.

The man standing next to his seat across the aisle caused Susanne's heart to drop. She felt as though she'd stepped off a curb and the ground had rushed up to meet her, sending a jolt through her body.

She could hardly believe this was the man who'd confronted her at her home, spewing threats and smelling of stale beer. He was neatly dressed in a new navy suit and sporting recently trimmed hair; his previously bewhiskered face shone clean-shaven; and his shoes were polished to a high sheen.

Had Ms. Sorensen taken him in hand? No. Susanne remembered the woman had mentioned his appearance as being neat when he came to her office. Susanne gripped the edges of the bench in an effort to still her shaking hands. Only God knew what the results of this day would be.

"You may take your seat, Mr. Warren," the judge directed.

"Ms. Sorensen, I see you're present as well." The judge gazed at the diminutive woman, who rose from her seat and stood at attention.

"Yes, Your Honor," she said in a brisk voice.

"And who are you here to represent, Ms. Sorensen?"

"Brianna *Warren*, your honor," she said in a smug tone.

"Thank you." He gave a curt nod. "You may sit down."

His penetrating eyes seemed to take the measure of the two adults sitting side by side on the bench in the front row. "Mr. and Mrs. Carson, I presume?"

David and Susanne both stood. "Yes, Your Honor. I'm David Carson, and this is my wife, Susanne, and my daughter, Brianna." He reached out his hand to the girl, who stood shyly.

Susanne watched in amazement. The judge's face altered before her eyes. Gone was the harsh, sharp look. Off came the glasses and the frown. In its place, a beaming smile was directed at the girl who stood before him.

"How do you do, young lady?"

No longer did Susanne doubt their attorney's word, for here sat a man who most certainly cared about children.

He leaned forward and laced his fingers together on top of his files. "Are you Brianna?"

She nodded, then must have realized she needed to reply. "Yes, Your Honor, I'm Brianna, and I guess I'm all right, sir."

Susanne hoped the judge heard the quiet response. She didn't want to antagonize him.

"Thank you, young lady. You may sit down, all of you." He gestured toward David and Susanne. "I don't take this type of case lightly when the life and welfare of a minor are involved. These are serious allegations Mr. Warren has brought against you, Mr. and Mrs. Carson. This is not a typical court case where each party needs representation, but rather a simple hearing, where each party may explain the facts as you see them.

"I've read the papers before me, but I'd like to hear from both of you before we go any further. Mr. Warren, since you're the one who filed the complaint, let's hear from you first. Please come up, take a seat, and let the bailiff swear you in."

He motioned to the man, who confidently strode to the front of the room, then hesitated as he glanced from the judge to the bailiff before stopping before the judge's desk.

Judge Travis nodded to the seat on his left and waited till Mr. Warren was seated and sworn in.

"We're setting aside the normal formalities of the court this morning. I already know your names, and I don't need to hear them again. I'm going to ask you to present whatever you'd like me to hear; then I'll ask any questions as I see fit. Do you understand, Mr. Warren?" He steepled his fingers and tapped the tip of his nose, peering at the man.

The man straightened as the judge's stern eyes rested on him. "Yes, Your Honor, that sounds fine."

"Please proceed with whatever you'd care to tell the court, Mr. Warren."

"Well, sir, it's this way. I left my little niece here"—he pointed his thin hand at Brianna, who sank back in her chair—"at these folks' house and asked them to take her in for a short time until I could get a good job and a place to live." He smiled ingratiatingly at the judge.

"I was a bachelor, and I figured a girl needed a mother to care for her. I didn't have a wife at the time. A few weeks ago, I married Mavis." He tipped his head toward the woman sitting below. "She's prepared to love and care for the girl just like she was her own mother."

The judge glanced at the woman sitting in the galley and nodded. "Go on."

"My poor sister died a while back, and there was no one to care for Brianna." His eyes took on a sorrowful, shadowed look, and he again cast his eyes toward Brianna.

"Mr. Warren, please keep your attention up here," the judge snapped, and his frown deepened.

"Yes, sir. I dropped my niece off at these folks' house and told them I'd get her soon as I could. I kept my word and came back. But that woman"—he pointed a quivering finger at Susanne—"she ordered me off the place. She told me Brianna couldn't come with me, and she threatened me if I didn't leave. I went to my truck and headed home, then called DSHS and filed a complaint with Ms. Sorensen here." He smiled at the caseworker. "And I thank you for your help, ma'am."

Judge Travis's eyes narrowed, and his voice dropped in warning. "Mr. Warren, please direct your comments to me."

"Oh, yes, sir. As I was saying, my sister put the girl in my care when she was dying, and I feel terrible I wasn't able to give her a home straight through. I know I should've kept her and not dropped her at the Carsons', but now I want to make it right." His chin jutted in the air, and he crossed his arms.

"These folks, they don't have a right to the girl. They aren't related. My sister loved me and trusted me. She wanted me to have Brianna, and I've regretted leaving her there from the moment I left the driveway."

"Is that all, Mr. Warren?" the judge prompted.

"Just one more thing, Your Honor?" He leaned toward the judge and dropped his voice.

"Go ahead."

"I don't like to speak ill of the dead, you understand, but my sister, well, she got around, you know? She claimed Mr. Carson was Brianna's father because he had more money than the rest." His eyes lit with a malicious light, making Susanne want to turn her gaze away. Her body felt frozen, and she continued to stare as she listened to this little man weave his lies.

"Anything more?" the judge asked.

"No, sir, that'll be all." He smiled.

Judge Travis motioned toward the seat Arthur had vacated in the gallery. "You may step down."

Arthur gripped the arms of the wooden chair and stared at the judge. "Don't you have any questions?"

"Not at this time. I'll hear both parties before I question you, Mr. Warren. Now please step down." The judge's cold voice brooked no argument.

Susanne watched as he scrambled from his perch and sauntered over to take his seat between Ms. Sorensen and his wife.

Ms. Sorensen's narrowed eyes went from the judge to the man beside her. Susanne could imagine the woman's mind racing ahead, congratulating herself on the choice she'd made in championing this man.

"Mr. or Mrs. Carson, which one of you would like to speak?" The judge's tone was still stern but no longer harsh. He peered over the top of his glasses at the small family sitting before him.

"We decided I would, Your Honor, since I was home the day Mr. Warren came." Susanne rose from her seat and made her way to the front.

She slipped into the chair. After she was sworn in, Judge Travis instructed her to begin, with a gentler look than any thus far except when directed at Brianna.

Susanne said a silent prayer then took a deep breath. "About two months ago on my birthday, Brianna arrived at our home. I had no idea at the time that God gave me a precious birthday gift, but I do now." She smiled at Brianna, whose face relaxed.

She tried to still her racing heart and turned her eyes to the judge. "Contrary to what Mr. Warren claims, he did not come to the door. He dropped Brianna off in our driveway in his old pickup and left while she rang the bell. I found her on our step with her suitcase. When I asked how I could help her, she informed me she was my husband's daughter and her mother had recently died. Her mother had instructed Brianna's uncle to bring her to live with us before she passed away, as she believed David to be Brianna's father."

Judge Travis leaned back in his chair, raising his eyebrows at this declaration. "And how would you know what Brianna's mother had told her brother, Mrs. Carson, or what she believed to be true if, as you say, she was deceased?"

Susanne looked the judge directly in the eyes. "Brianna brought a letter with her, Your Honor, written by her mother and addressed to my husband. It stated she did not wish her brother to have custody of Brianna." She gestured toward David and nodded. "We brought the letter with us if you'd care to see it."

"I certainly would. I'd also like to know why this information wasn't mentioned in Ms. Sorensen's report, but we'll get to that later." The look he gave Ms. Sorensen had her shifting in her seat. "Please go on, Mrs. Carson," the judge urged.

"Thank you, Your Honor. Brianna lived with us for nearly two months with no word from her uncle. My husband called DSHS to see if any relatives had come forward to claim her, and none had. When he explained his possible relationship to Brianna, they told him to take care of it himself. Apparently, they had a heavy case load and felt if David was Brianna's father, they didn't need to be involved."

Susanne watched Judge Travis shoot an irritated look at Ms. Sorensen. The woman glanced down at her hands clasped in her lap, but Susanne noted her face had paled a degree.

"Go on."

"We purchased clothing for Brianna. She had very little to wear. We were trying to keep our options open, but we both believed David was her father, based on the letter and her strong physical resemblance to David. It wasn't until Mr. Warren came forward with his complaint that we decided to take action and requested a DNA paternity test. We should have the results in a few days."

"Yes, I read that in Mr. Thorne's report. Although I, too, have little doubt of the findings based on the striking resemblance between your husband and Brianna. Is that all, Mrs. Carson?"

"No, Your Honor. I'd like to add one more thing." She took a deep breath.

He stretched his long arm across the desk, reaching for a pencil and tapping it against the surface. "Take your time."

"I need to be completely honest with you about why we were trying to keep our options open. I had a hard time committing to keeping Brianna." She drew back at the frown that crossed the big man's face.

"I was fighting, sir, fighting myself and fighting God. I love kids. In fact, we've been foster parents off and on for years." Susanne saw the judge glance at one of the papers on his desk, then nod.

"I didn't have anything against Brianna, but I resented the circumstances surrounding her birth and arrival at our home. I'd always had a choice before—a choice to take kids or not. But this time it was out of my control." She ducked her head for a moment, then raised her eyes to his. "I guess I've always had a bit of a problem with not wanting someone else to be in control of my life."

Judge Travis gave a small chuckle, then quickly straightened his features. "I doubt you're the only one with that problem, Mrs. Carson."

"Yes, sir. But it caused serious problems in our family. Our daughter Meagan took a spill from her horse a few weeks ago, which resulted in a concussion and hospitalization. I was trying to find someone to blame for my problems, and it only made things worse. A few days ago, Mr. Warren came to our door, demanding we return Brianna to his care. The comments made by his wife in my hearing"—she glanced at Mavis—"made it clear they hoped to get money from the state. When I refused to give Brianna to him and asked him to leave our property, he threatened me, then stated he'd get Brianna one way or another, and left."

The judge swung his eyes over to Ms. Sorensen and back again to Susanne. "Did you report this threat to the authorities?"

"Not to the police, Your Honor, as it wasn't a specific threat, but he was angry and said I'd better watch myself. In hindsight we realize we should've reported it, so it would've been a matter of record. My husband did report it to Ms. Sorensen, but she didn't think worth worrying about."

Susanne noted the stormy look in the judge's eyes.

"When all of this happened, Brianna ran away."

"If the girl ran away from their home while under their care, Your Honor," Ms. Sorensen broke the stillness, "you need to ask what prompted that action."

"Please be quiet, Ms. Sorensen. I'll ask the questions." His bushy brows lowered over fierce eyes that turned their full force on the supervisor, then returned to Susanne. "Please continue, Mrs. Carson."

Susanne noted the narrowed eyes of the caseworker, then looked at Brianna. "She didn't run because she didn't want to stay with us but due to fear that we'd send her to her uncle's to live. She's afraid of him, sir. You'll have to ask her why because she won't tell us."

The courtroom grew still as the judge appeared to digest this information. He nodded and glanced at Brianna, a solemn expression creasing his face.

"While David was looking for her, I overheard my daughter praying. She asked God to save Brianna and take her to heaven instead. Meagan felt it was her fault Brianna left because she helped Brianna sneak out of the house."

The bushy eyebrows raised over the gray eyes, a gentle light appearing to soften the stern expression. "How old is your other daughter, Mrs. Carson?"

Susanne didn't miss the use of the word *other*, and her hope mounted at the kind look on the man's face.

She leaned forward, clasping her hands in front of her. "She's eleven, sir, and very unhappy we didn't feel she was old enough to be here today. She's protective of her big sister." She smiled at the memory. "After hearing that prayer, I broke. I realized how selfish I'd been and asked God to forgive me for not loving Brianna. After David found her asleep in our barn, I asked her to forgive me, too. Since then, I've realized I love her and want her as a permanent part of our family."

She took a deep breath, held it, then slowly let it out. "I might get in trouble for telling you this, sir, but something happened at our house a few nights ago. I was told it couldn't have any bearing on this case, but would it be all right if I tell you and let you decide for yourself?"

Ms. Sorensen stood. "I object, Your Honor. If Mrs. Carson has been advised it doesn't have any bearing, it shouldn't be mentioned. Besides, I haven't been made aware of anything else that happened. In fact, the girl running away wasn't even brought to my attention."

Judge Travis swiveled and pinned the woman with a glare. "This is not a formal hearing, and I will listen to any testimony I see fit. Sit down, Ms. Sorensen. You'll hear the statement at the same time I do." He kept his eyes locked on her as she sank into her seat, then turned his attention to Susanne. "Go ahead, Mrs. Carson."

Susanne let her eyes drift over the room for a moment before answering. The tension in the courtroom was palpable. David sat straight in his chair, his face drawn, and Brianna gripped his arm. Even Arthur Warren sat frozen in his seat, and the prim woman next to him appeared to have shrunk several inches into her seat.

Susanne nodded and tried to smile, then drew a small breath. "Friday evening, David and I took the kids to a movie and dinner. When we got home, David thought he saw something in the trees near our house. He checked and didn't find anything, so we got the kids in the house and into bed. We were starting to fall asleep when Brianna screamed. She'd seen a man's face pressed up against the glass of the door that leads out onto a deck off her room." She glanced at David. He leaned forward in his seat and gave her an encouraging smile.

"I stayed in the house with the kids, and David searched the grounds. We found a boot print where the man jumped off the bottom step, so it wasn't Brianna's imagination." She wiped her damp palms on her slacks.

"Did you report this?" The judge leaned over his desk, his brows furrowed.

"Yes. The sheriff's department came up that evening but didn't find anything."

Judge Travis looked out over the courtroom, then back at

Susanne. "And Brianna didn't recognize the face?"

She hesitated a moment and cast a quick look at Arthur Warren. "She thought it might've been her uncle, but it was dark, and she couldn't be sure. It frightened her so badly she didn't get a good look."

He tapped his fingers against the desk, beating a light tattoo. "I imagine it would. It would frighten an adult to have a man peering in their window at night, much less a fourteen-year-old girl."

"A neighbor told the sheriff's department that he saw an older pickup not far from our driveway, traveling with its lights off about the time the person left. He couldn't give any more information than that." She twisted in her seat and looked up at the judge. "That's all, Your Honor."

"Thank you, Mrs. Carson. You may step down." He waited a moment until Susanne crossed the small open space between his desk and the bench where her family sat, then turned to the bench across the aisle. "Mr. Warren, what type of vehicle do you drive?"

"Your Honor, that doesn't seem pertinent." Ms. Sorensen's hand tapped on the table in front of her.

He held up his hand, barely giving her a glance. "Answer the question, Mr. Warren."

The man shrank in his chair, his skin a pasty white. "I . . . it's a pickup, Your Honor."

"What year?"

He ran his fingers through his hair. "It's a '77. But I wasn't at their place. I was down at the tavern that night. You can ask anyone there."

The judge gave a small snort. "I may do that, Mr. Warren." He glanced at the occupants of the courtroom before continuing. "I planned to ask Ms. Sorensen and Mr. Warren a few more questions, but I think I'll go another direction. Brianna, could you come up and sit beside me?" He motioned to the girl, giving her a grandfatherly smile.

Brianna looked at David, a question in her eyes. David patted her hand. "You do whatever the judge asks you to do, Brianna. Remember, we talked about this?"

She turned fearful eyes toward his face. "Yes."

"It's important you tell the judge the truth. Will you do that?"

Her lips quivered, but she nodded and stepped toward the front of the room.

The judge leaned across his desk toward the girl, then motioned to the chair to his left. "Sit down, Brianna. I want to make sure you understand that when I ask a question, you'll answer me honestly. Can you do that?"

She nodded once again.

"You have to answer out loud, Brianna. The court recorder needs to write your answers down, and it's hard to write a nod."

He smiled when she started to nod again, then caught herself. "Oh, yes, sir. I can do that."

"Good. Now then, I want you to think about this question carefully. Would you rather live with Mr. and Mrs. Carson or with Mr. Warren?"

"I beg your pardon, Your Honor, but I must object!" Ms. Sorensen's stern voice spoke again from the front of the room. "In the state of Washington, a minor is not allowed a choice."

Judge Travis leaned over the top of the desk, and his size seemed to increase. He reached his long arm out and shook his finger in her direction. It looked to Susanne as though he could almost touch the woman's face.

"Ms. Sorensen, this is my courtroom, and I will ask whatever I please. The state of Washington isn't deciding this case. I am. If you continue to interrupt, I'll have the bailiff remove you. Is that clear?" His voice vibrated across the short distance to the woman sitting forward in her chair.

Her voice softened, and she straightened the collar of her blouse. "Yes, Your Honor, I simply thought—"

"That's the problem—you didn't think! Now be quiet and let me talk to this young lady." As suddenly as the storm began, it passed. He turned a calm face toward Brianna, who sat open mouthed in her chair, staring from the judge to Ms. Sorensen and back again.

"Don't be concerned, Brianna. I'm not going to shout at you. I don't shout at young ladies, especially nice, polite ones like you." He encouraged her with a twinkle in his eyes. "You go ahead and answer my question. Who would you like to live with?"

Brianna hesitated only a split second before she replied in a clear voice. "My dad."

"Fine. Now I have another question for you, and remember, I want an honest answer." He waited a moment before continuing. "Are you afraid of Mr. Warren, Brianna?"

She hesitated a little longer this time, then nodded. "Yes, sir."

"Can you tell me why?"

"He drinks."

His eyes narrowed, and he seemed to make an effort to keep his face from twisting into a frown. "Did he do anything that frightened you when he drank?"

"Your Honor!" sputtered Ms. Sorensen, beginning to rise from her chair.

"Bailiff!" The judge beckoned to the silent man standing against the wall.

Her shoulders slumped, and her face paled. "I'm sorry, Your Honor. It won't happen again."

He glared at the woman. "You're right, it won't. Sit down and be quiet."

Ms. Sorensen sank into her chair.

"Go ahead and answer, Brianna," he said quietly.

Brianna hung her head.

Susanne held her breath, almost afraid she'd scare the girl if she breathed. The judge's demeanor had changed to one of a gentle friend. She glanced at David to see his hands clenched into fists and his narrowed eyes staring at Arthur Warren, who glowered at Brianna, his face twisted into a scowl.

Judge Travis cleared his throat and tried again. "There's nothing for you to be afraid of. Now then, did Mr. Warren do something bad when he drank?"

Brianna pulled her eyes away from her uncle and turned to the judge. "Yes. Mama and I lived with him for a while before she died. He could be nice when he was sober, and he acted like he cared about Mama. He even took us places and told Mama he'd take care of me when she died. But when he got drunk, he turned mean. A lot of times, I'd hear him cussing at her, and she'd be crying. More than once, she sent me to my room and made me lock the door. I think he hurt her, but she always told me later that she was okay." Brianna's voice shook, her face reflecting the pain of the memory.

The judge kept his voice low, his tone soft. "Is that all, Brianna? How about after your mama died. What happened then?"

"Do I have to tell?" she whispered.

"Yes, Brianna, it's important that you tell me the truth."

Brianna glanced toward her uncle. Susanne turned her gaze the same direction in time to see the man glaring at Brianna with hate in his eyes so strong Susanne thought it would scorch her. He leaned forward, his hands twisting his hat, and his mouth turned down in a snarl.

The judge glanced at Brianna's face, then followed her gaze. His expression hardened when he saw the man struggle to smooth out the lines that contorted his face.

"Brianna." The judge spoke sharply to the stricken girl. "Brianna, I want you to look at me and nowhere else in this room while we're talking, do you understand?" He allowed her nod to suffice. The sharp tone of his voice fell away. "Now tell me what else happened. Can you do that?"

"I guess. My uncle got really drunk a couple of times. One time he slapped me, hard. I cried, and he grabbed me around my neck and hit my head on the wall. The other time, he started chasing me, screaming and cussing. He only hit me once before I got away from him and hid." She started to cry, and Susanne started up out of her seat.

The judge held up his hand toward Susanne, shaking his head. "I need you to finish, Brianna. You're almost done. Is that all?"

"No, sir," she said, her voice barely audible. "He told me if I ever told anybody that he'd hit me, he'd kill me, and I believed him. He said he had killed somebody before, and it wouldn't bother him to kill me too." She finished with a shudder, dropping her face into her hands and crying in earnest.

"Mrs. Carson," the judge said in a gentle voice, "why don't you come up now and get your daughter."

He turned to Ms. Sorensen sitting in stunned silence. "Ms. Sorensen, I'm initiating an inquiry. I'm not happy with your involvement in this fiasco or with your lack of judgment. I'll be speaking to the state supervisor in charge of this county, and I'm sure you'll be hearing from him." He dismissed her protest with a curt gesture.

"Bailiff, call an officer to take this man into custody until an investigation is started." He motioned toward the shrinking man whose face flamed red, then paled. The bailiff swiveled on his heel and strode to the back door, shoving it open and speaking to someone outside the courtroom.

Judge Travis turned his attention to the small family sitting quietly before him. "Mr. and Mrs. Carson, this case is dismissed, and you're free to take your daughter home."

The woman Arthur had presented as his wife rose and turned as though to flee from the room. "I had nothing to do with any murder. I'm not even married to him. You can't take me with him." Her rising voice filled the room and escalated with each word. "And don't think I'll be waiting around for you when you get out of jail, Arthur. You promised me money, and there isn't going to be any. I'm leaving." She spewed out the words before scrambling to the end of the wooden benches in an effort to escape.

The judge banged his gavel. "Bailiff, remove that woman."

The bailiff grabbed Mavis by the arm, all but dragging her the rest of the way to the door. An officer arrived at the front of the room and handcuffed Arthur Warren, leading the protesting man down the aisle.

Warren passed Brianna and her family and shot a malignant glare at them. "You're welcome to the little brat. I hope she's as much trouble to you as she was to me. All she ever did was blubber. She brought me more misery than she was worth."

After the scene quieted, the judge spoke to Brianna. "Young lady, I appreciate your honesty and trust. Rest assured. Your uncle won't be troubling you again. You've been blessed with nice parents. You see that you obey them and be a good girl, you hear?"

Brianna's wide smile transformed her normally solemn face. "Yes, sir. I will."

The judge stood and gathered his robes, then strode from the room before the bailiff had a chance to ask the people seated in the galley to rise.

Susanne and David reached for a weeping Brianna, enclosing her in a hug they hoped would reach through to her heart and help her begin a new journey that would last a lifetime.

Chapter Thirty-Seven

THE NEXT WEEK FLEW BY FOR Susanne, but Steven and Meagan thought the time would never arrive when they could present their surprise to Brianna. Susanne decided a bit of a distraction might be in order and took Brianna aside to share her idea.

"Brianna, I've been planning something and want to see what you think." She'd waited until Steven and Meagan were out of sight in another room before speaking.

"Sure." Brianna lowered her voice.

Susanne drew her over to a window overlooking the pasture, and the girl sank into a nearby chair. "I know Meagan wanted to teach you to ride, but what do you think about surprising her instead?"

Brianna raised a finger to her mouth and nibbled on a nail. "Oohhh, I'm not sure. I feel pretty good around the horses now, but I've never ridden one." Her face puckered in a small frown, and her hair swished as she shook her head.

Susanne leaned against the windowsill and smiled at the girl. "I'd help you and if you got scared, you could stop. But I know you can do it."

"How would we keep it from Meagan, and how about Steven? I'm afraid he'd feel left out if we only do something for Meagan."

"Good point. It wouldn't be hard to get Meagan out of the way. Carrie can invite her over for the night and clue Ashley to be busy today. We'll see if Steven can spend the night with his friend Brian." She narrowed her eyes and tapped her fingertips against the glass. "Now we have to think of a surprise for Steven."

Brianna's eyes lit up from the brilliance of her smile. "I have an idea! Maybe we could borrow a bike, and I could ride with him."

Susanne clapped her hands. "Even better, we'll buy you a bike! We should've done that a long time ago."

"Cool! I'd like to have a bike if it's not too expensive."

Susanne waved her hand. "Not to worry. Tell you what. You head on out with the kids, and I'll call Carrie's mom. We'll get this moving and see if we can pull it off in the next few days."

Brianna jumped from her seat and headed for the door, then turned. "Thanks, Susanne. You're the best." She blushed and ducked her head before bolting out the door.

Susanne smiled. *Life is good.* Now to see what they could do on yet another surprise. Being a part of it all brought such joy. She revised her earlier thought. *God is good.*

Susanne and Brianna took the two kids down the hill and dropped them off mid-morning, then made two stops—the first at a bike shop, where they picked up a new bike for Brianna, then the Side Saddle Shop for a pair of boots.

When the clerk disappeared into the back room to find the right size, Brianna swiveled in her chair toward Susanne. "But what if I stay scared?"

"That's a chance I'm willing to take, honey. I think once you're up on Bones you'll change your mind, and I'm betting you'll end up loving riding. It isn't safe riding in tennis shoes. Boot heels don't allow your foot to slip through the stirrup. I'll feel better with you in boots."

"But you already spent so much on a bike. Meagan and Steven aren't getting anything."

Susanne reached out and tweaked Brianna's nose, a smile softening her face. "You're worth it. I don't want to go through a scare with you like we had with Meagan. One daughter injured this summer is enough. Besides, they get a new sister and someone to ride with, so they'll be thrilled." She marveled at how easy that came out, and even more astonished that she meant it.

Brianna's face pinkened, and she ducked her head. "Thanks."

Susanne touched the girl's shoulder, then placed her fingers under Brianna's chin and raised her smiling face to meet her own. "I love you. I hope you'll be able to believe that one of these days."

Tears sprang to the teenager's eyes, and a quiet joy shone through. "I'm glad," she whispered.

Susanne believed the trust would continue to build, and one day Brianna would feel the same.

An hour later, with new boots laced and clothed in comfortable jeans, the co-conspirators stood next to a sleepy Bones tied to the hitching rail.

"Does he ever buck? I mean like Glory did when she dumped Meagan?" Brianna stopped short of the horse and didn't move to pet Bones.

Brianna must be reliving the scene of Meagan's accident, but the picture of Bones trying to get his lazy hind-end off the ground enough to produce a buck almost brought a chuckle. "No, he's never bucked since we've owned him, not even when he was skinny. Now he's fat and lazy, and all he wants to do is eat and sleep. He'll hardly notice you up there."

Brianna stood motionless, seeming reluctant to move closer now that the time had come to climb up what must seem an insurmountable height. "He's so big."

"I have an idea. I'm still new at this, but how about we ask God to help you get over your fear? It's okay to ask questions, but you don't want fear telling you what to do."

Brianna turned troubled eyes her way. "Okay, if you pray."

"Dear Father, I'm not very good at praying, but Brianna needs Your help. Please calm her fear and help her have a good time. Thank You, Lord. Amen." She raised her head and smiled into the deep brown eyes so much like David's, eyes she truly loved looking into now, and ones she longed to see shine with joy rather than fear.

"You'll love it once you're up on his back," Susanne said. "I remember the first time I rode a horse. I wasn't as scared as you, but I had to learn too."

A startled look crossed the girl's face. "You did?"

Susanne smiled. Did Brianna think she'd been born on horseback? "My parents didn't have horses, and the first time I rode was at my aunt's house. I rode behind her when I was younger than Steven. I loved it, but it did seem like a long way to the ground."

"Did you ever fall off?" Brianna asked with a frown.

"Yes, I did." She watched as Brianna took a half-step from the horse at this rather surprising revelation. "But it didn't hurt. I kind of slid off his back and landed on my bottom. My aunt told me I had to get right back on again or I'd be afraid the next time. It wasn't near as scary because I found out it hadn't really hurt."

Brianna absorbed this information and determination filled her face. "I guess I can try it. If you were younger than Steven when you fell off, I shouldn't be a baby."

"Step over here and stand facing your horse's head. Put your right hand on the horn of the saddle and your left hand up on the horse's neck and get a good handful of his mane. I'm going to help you this first time and give you a leg up."

Susanne watched with satisfaction as Brianna concentrated on following her directions and not flinching when Bones shifted his weight. Brianna gripped the saddle horn with both hands, and Susanne gave her a boost.

"I did it!" Brianna cried. "I'm sitting on Bones!"

Susanne laughed at the girl's beaming face. "Yes, you did it. Here, I'll show you how to hold the reins properly. Don't worry. I'll lead him." She moved forward to demonstrate what she wanted

Brianna to do.

A few minutes later, Susanne took the horse's lead rope and urged him forward at a slow walk. He'd almost fallen asleep and was in no hurry to move, so she asked Brianna to squeeze him with her legs and cluck. Bones responded and moved out.

Brianna's eyes lit up, and her shy smile grew to a grin. "He did what I asked!"

They made a few circles in the safety of the metal round pen. Brianna started to relax and loosened her grip on the horn, sitting naturally and holding the reins. She might have a chance of becoming a decent rider if her interest became personal rather than only a desire to please Meagan.

Not wanting to overdo the first ride, Susanne brought Bones to a stop after a few more circles. Brianna's fear had been real, and Susanne didn't want to push her too hard.

"I'll show you how to dismount now."

"When do I get to ride again?"

Susanne laughed, thrilled with the response. "How about tomorrow morning before we pick up the kids? We'll take you out of the round pen and try trotting if you think you're up to it."

"That would be great! This is a lot more fun than I thought."

Susanne couldn't be happier. Meagan would get her riding partner, and Brianna had discovered that with determination and God's help she could conquer her fear and find something new to love. Tomorrow would be a good day. A very good day, indeed.

Brianna and Susanne wanted to spring their surprise as soon as the kids came home the next day, so they got up early and practiced for more than an hour. True to her word, Brianna asked Bones to trot, and grinned around the entire circle, holding onto the horn and bouncing all over the saddle. God had completely removed the fear, and in its place had come joy.

They ended the lesson with a hug from Susanne. "I'm so proud of you! I can't believe you got on Bones for the first time yesterday. Meagan will be shocked. Let's tell her that we're giving you your first riding lesson this afternoon."

Brianna giggled. "Super! I can't wait to see her face when I get on by myself."

Susanne didn't think she'd ever tire of that giggle. It came more frequently now and was such a blessing.

On the way home after picking up Meagan and Steven, Brianna commented, "Would you help me with Bones today, Meagan? I might be ready to get on him if you and Susanne help me."

Meagan squealed, bouncing in her seat and clapping her hands. "That's awesome! Of course I'll help. How about you, Mom?"

Susanne kept a carefully neutral face. "Sure. We have time this afternoon if Brianna thinks she's ready."

"Ah gee, how 'bout me? You guys always do stuff with the horses, and I get left out," Steven pouted.

"Tell you what. How about when the girls are done, I find something fun for you to do with Brianna? I'll bet if we try hard enough we can come up with something." She smiled at him in the rearview mirror and shot a quick glance at Brianna.

"Okay, I guess. But what I want most is to have her ride bikes with me, and she doesn't have a bike. Maybe we can play a video game or something." He bit his lip and frowned.

"It'll work out. When we get home, everybody change into your old clothes and head to the barn."

Minutes later, two eager girls and one not-so-eager boy bailed out of the car and headed inside the house. The temperature had cooled the past few days, and the feeling of an early fall sparkled in the air.

Susanne poked her head in the front door. "Come on, Meagan and Steven. Let's head down and throw the horses some hay to make sure they stay around while Brianna finishes changing."

Moments later, Meagan spotted Brianna starting down the path toward the barn. "Hurry up. I caught Bones, and we're ready to start," Meagan called, too excited to notice what Brianna was wearing.

"You don't have to be afraid of him," Meagan instructed as Brianna came close. "He won't hurt you. Mom and I already saddled him, and I'll show you how to get on."

Brianna hid a smile as she watched Meagan give a demonstration on properly mounting her horse.

"We'll need to adjust the stirrups since her legs are a bit longer than yours, Meagan." Susanne lengthened the stirrups a notch, then turned to Brianna. "Okay, young lady, let's show her what you can do."

Brianna moved forward and reached up to the horse's neck and the saddle horn, put her left foot into the stirrup and swung her other leg over the saddle, settling into the seat.

"Brianna—you didn't need any help! And you're wearing riding boots." Meagan's eyes widened as she stared up at the smiling girl in the saddle.

"Are you surprised, Meagan?" Brianna asked, a hint of pride showing in her voice.

"You aren't even holding the horn, and I thought you were afraid of him!"

A huge grin covered Brianna's face. "Your mom helped me while you were gone. I had two riding lessons, and I love it!"

"Wow! That's awesome."

"Want me to show you what else I learned?"

"Sure!"

Susanne stood back and watched as Brianna put Bones through his paces in the round pen. She'd give them a little while longer together before she shifted the attention to Steven.

"Mom, Mom!" Steven's high-pitched voice rang out from the doorway of the barn a few minutes later. "You'll never believe what I found. Somebody left a brand-new bike in one of the stalls!"

Susanne groaned and slapped her hand against her forehead, then glanced at Brianna, who stared with a blank look. They both broke into laughter that continued until both Steven and Meagan protested.

"Hey. What's so funny, and what's Steven talking about?" Meagan asked.

"Come on, Brianna. I guess you'd better dismount now that Steven has discovered your surprise. Leave it to him to figure it out ahead of time." Susanne shook her head and continued to chuckle as she reached for Bones' reins.

Brianna swung down from the horse almost as though she'd been riding all summer, and Meagan beamed with pride.

Steven did the little dancing jig he often fell into when excited. "What's going on, huh, guys? Whose bike is that?" His voice hit a higher note, and he tugged on his mother's free hand.

"Calm down and come here. Let Brianna tie up Bones, and we'll explain," Susanne said.

A few minutes later, Brianna headed into the barn. Susanne caught Steven's arm as he tried to dash past. "Hold it, young man. Let Brianna do this alone."

Brianna came out riding the bike, wearing a sheepish expression. "I'm sorry we didn't hide it better, Steven, so we could've surprised you."

"Huh? But whose is it?"

Susanne and Brianna broke into another laugh. "It's mine. Your mom bought it for me yesterday so I can ride with both you and Meagan."

Astonishment flitted over the boy's face then a wide grin took its place. "Way cool! Can we go for a ride now, Mom? Please?"

Susanne tried to catch her breath and wiped the moisture from her eyes. "Sure, Steven. Meagan and I will unsaddle Bones and turn him out while the two of you ride your bikes."

Steven whooped and ran for his bike with Brianna trailing along.

Meagan watched them go with a satisfied smile. "Isn't it cool to see Brianna so happy?"

"Yes, honey, it certainly is." The laughter had died, and a sense of wonder took its place. "Very cool, indeed."

Susanne stood for a minute longer, reveling in the feeling and thanking God for all He'd brought to pass that summer. She could definitely get used to having a second daughter and she planned to enjoy every minute of the years Brianna still had in their home.

It hadn't been easy, but somehow Steven had kept their secret for a few more days. They stopped by Claire's, and she followed them to the county seat with a mystified Brianna and two excited younger children in tow. The three adults stepped out of their cars in front of the courthouse and stood waiting, staring at each car that passed.

"When's he going to get here, Dad?" Steven stood on his tiptoes and tried to peer over the passing traffic.

"Ohh, he's here!" Meagan let out a squeal and grabbed Brianna in a hug.

"Who's here? What's going on?" Brianna stared from one excited family member to another, a slight frown pulling at the corners of her mouth.

"Grandfather!" Meagan and Steven whooped together and

raced for the car pulling in at the curb.

A soft glow transformed Brianna's serious face. She hung back while her two younger siblings swarmed the man stepping out of his car.

Grandfather drew them both into a hug, then straightened his tall, lean form and turned to the quiet girl with a grin. "Brianna? Come here, honey, and let me give you a hug."

Susanne's feelings were a far cry from the first time Grandfather had met Brianna. Pride and joy warred for domination as she watched her new daughter embrace the older man.

"Well, Granddaughter, it looks like I didn't need to keep my promise to take you home to live with me. I'm happy you've found a family at last." He stroked his long fingers down the length of her dark wavy hair, then placed a knuckle under her chin and tilted it up. "Are you happy?"

"Yes, Grandfather." The words were a mere whisper, but they slammed into Susanne's heart with the force of a prize-winning punch.

"Claire, it's good to see you again." The silver-haired man nodded at the beaming woman standing beside Susanne, then turned to the kids. "Let's go take care of business, shall we?" He waited for David to steer them toward the doors at the top of the flight of concrete steps.

The Carson family entered the courtroom with Judge Travis officiating, mysterious smiles adorning their faces and a mystified Brianna following along. David ushered his family to the same bench they'd chosen at their last visit.

Susanne waited for the middle-aged bailiff to lift his booming voice, knowing what was coming, her heart full of thanks that no fear preceded them this time.

"All rise, the Honorable Judge Gerald Travis presiding." A

small smile played around the edges of the bailiff's mouth. He shot a wink at Susanne's two youngest children and nodded at her husband.

The family rose to their feet. Judge Travis once again took his place behind the massive oak desk on the platform. Brianna's eyes darted from David's face to the judge's and back again.

What a difference in the man who sat behind his desk, adjusting his robes before raising his smiling face to look over their family. "So you're back in my courtroom again, hey? And I see you brought the rest of the family today." He too, winked at her children, causing a chuckle to escape from her husband. "Before we move on with the most important event of the day, I thought you might appreciate an update on Arthur Warren."

Susanne gratefully noted the absence of the word *uncle* in connection with Brianna.

"He's being held on a charge of child abuse based on the testimony given in this court. The authorities are questioning the woman whom he claimed as his wife concerning the other matter mentioned that day." He glanced at Steven and Meagan as he skirted the mention of a possible murder. "I believe he'll be going to jail, and you won't be bothered by him again."

"Thank you, Your Honor." Brianna let out an audible breath and gave him a grateful smile.

He nodded and turned his attention to David. "There's also the matter of Ms. Sorensen. Her supervisor put her on immediate suspension, per my suggestion, pending a full investigation. It seems she's been a busy lady since taking her new post under a year ago."

"Busy with the kids in her care?" David asked.

"Much more than that. Taking bribes. We believe she did so at her last job, as well, but never got caught."

"Bribes? Why would anyone bribe her?" Susanne sat up

straight, her attention fixed on the judge.

He steepled his fingers and tapped his thumb on his chin. "Look at your situation. Let's say Mr. Warren was wealthy but might not be a fit parent for Brianna. He could pay Ms. Sorensen to overlook certain items on his background check and see that he obtained custody."

David snorted and shook his head. "I doubt Mr. Warren had any money. Why would she help him if she didn't get paid?"

Judge Travis emitted a small grunt of agreement. "That's what the district attorney wanted to know, so he started digging. It seems Ms. Sorensen had a personal vendetta against your wife."

"What? We'd never met the woman." David's voice registered shock.

The judge nodded. "But you met a niece of hers a couple of years ago. A young girl about Steven's age by the name of Rae Anne. Do you remember?"

"Yes, quite well. What does she have to do with our case?" Susanne asked.

Judge Travis heaved a deep sigh. "It was a sad situation. You were the intake family when she was taken out of her home due to suspected abuse. From what I understand, you obtained information from the little girl while she was in your care. That led to the arrest of Ms. Sorensen's sister. When Ms. Sorensen transferred to this county, she tried to find a way to get even."

David slapped his hand across his knee and leaned forward. "So Arthur Warren presented the perfect opportunity."

"Exactly. The DA has her up on charges of case tampering and accepting bribes. She won't be interfering with children's lives anytime soon."

"I must say I'm shocked. I had no idea helping Rae Anne would cause so much trouble," Susanne said.

"It's over now. Let's move along to today's business." Judge

Travis beckoned to Brianna. "Come stand up here beside me for a minute." He patted the surface of his desk and smiled.

She came to the front of the desk and stood on tiptoe, trying to see the judge.

He raised a beefy hand and pointed to the space to his right. "I want you to come up on the platform behind the desk and stand next to me." He waited until the girl stood beside him. "This isn't another custody hearing, I hope?" His genial voice rumbled, his question directed at Brianna.

She shook her head, then remembered her instructions from before. "No, Your Honor, at least, I don't think it is."

He gestured to the other six who silently waited in the front row. "I want the rest of you people to stand down there in front of my desk." He beckoned to Steven, who'd stopped a moment to swing the short gate they came through on their way to the front. "Snap to it now, and no dawdling."

"Do you know why you're here, young lady?" The judge asked in a mock serious voice, leaning sideways over the massive expanse of the desk.

"No, sir. I mean, no one told me. I think Steven and Meagan know, but I don't." Her voice quivered a little. The judge immediately lost his grin and patted Brianna's hand.

"I'm going to ask you a question, and it's important you give me an honest answer. You'll do that, won't you?"

"Yes, sir."

"These people want to legally adopt you. Your dad doesn't need to, as the paternity test came back positive that you *are* his daughter." He waited a moment, and his gaze rested on the upturned face beside him. "Your stepmom wants to become your real mom, and it seems as though Steven and Meagan have petitioned the court to become your full brother and sister. And I understand your grandmother Claire came along and your grandfather made a bit of a drive to be included, as well."

He grinned at the two younger children bouncing on tiptoe in front of his desk and smiled at the stunned girl. "Your dad could've changed your last name to match the rest of the family after he proved he was your dad. But your family loves you and want to show you how much by doing a formal adoption. I have one question for you. Do *you* want to adopt *them*?"

"Oh, yes, sir," she whispered.

"How about you hug your new family, then. I'm granting the petition for adoption." His gavel banged on the desk once again.

Brianna flew around the end of the desk and into the waiting arms of her exuberant family, forever home at last.

Note from the Author

This was my first novel after the Lord spoke to me through a visiting special speaker at church (Rev. George Watkins) that he felt the Lord directing me to start writing. He didn't get any direction on what I should write, but he felt it needed to be published. I started by writing an autobiography concerning my life since getting married and many of the ways the Lord had met me, but I had no plans to publish it—it was more for my family should they ever be interested. Then I moved on to writing short stories based on true events and selling several to magazines. It surprised me how quickly they sold, but I didn't feel that was the end goal. I wasn't sure what to tackle after that, until a friend suggested I consider writing Christian fiction in novel form.

I balked at that suggestion, as I didn't feel I had a creative brain cell in my head. However, she urged me to think about an event or life experience that was real that I could change into fiction. After thinking and praying, the nucleus of a story came into being, based on a true event in the lives of my husband and children. When our daughter Marnee was about fourteen years old and our son around eleven or twelve, we received a very surprising letter.

A young woman by the name of Tricia wrote to say she believed my husband was her biological father who she'd never met. She had recently turned eighteen and asked a family friend who had been a detective, if he'd help her find her dad. We received a letter when Allen was at work, and I asked him to go for a drive after he got home, as I didn't want our two children to overhear our discussion. I was shocked and disbelieving but needed to know the truth.

At that time, I was a strong Christian, and Allen wasn't really sold out to the Lord, although he'd accepted Jesus not long before we married. He'd drifted to a certain degree at that point, but he wasn't antagonistic as Susanne was portrayed in the story. We also had taken in foster children over the years, and even had a sixteen-year-old girl living with us at the time who returned with us from Alaska with her parents' reluctant permission, do to a number of family issues. We lived out in the country in a two-story home on 30 acres very similar (including the pond and large pasture) to the one portrayed in this book.

Allen was as surprised as I was by the letter, but after much discussion, and seeing that Tricia wasn't asking for support or anything other than to meet us, we decided to check out her story. Allen had a similar experience as David's, although we weren't engaged or even dating yet when the incident happened. He wasn't a Christian at the time at all and had never attended church or had much experience with Christianity. He was a partier and drank, as well as enjoyed hanging out at an old, country grocery store that housed a pool room. A girl who he believed was seventeen, hung out there as well, and had been spending time trying to get to know him. One evening, he'd had a few beers, and she asked for a ride home. One thing led to another before he dropped her off, and Tricia was conceived.

She went to his home months later and told Allen's mom she was pregnant and who she believed the father was. His mom didn't believe her, as Allen didn't have that kind of reputation at all, but her middle son did. She thought it was possible it could have been the brother but asked around and was told the girl was promiscuous. It turned out (years later) that we found that wasn't the case prior to the event with Allen, but his mom brushed it off and only barely mentioned it to Allen...and not until after the girl and her mom had moved out of state.

He said something about it to me when we were engaged but

told me it hadn't gone all the way and there was no medical way the baby could be his. He explained why and I believed him. It wasn't until Tricia came forward and I talked to my doctor that I discovered it had gone far enough for her to have gotten pregnant. We were both shocked but that, and the pictures she sent of herself in grade school that bore a family resemblance, convinced us it could be possible she was his daughter.

We met her a couple of weeks later at a restaurant half-way between our home and hers, about a two-hour drive away. Her mom was willing to take a paternity test, and that, coupled with the fact Tricia wasn't asking us for anything, how much she looked like Allen, and the assurance her mom had never been with anyone else and knew Allen was the father, made us believe it must be the case. Also, Tricia had been told all her life that her dad didn't care and didn't want anything to do with her. She needed a dad. She also looked a lot like one of the other guys from high school who had bragged he'd been with her mom, but we decided that didn't matter. This girl needed a dad, and the other guy had died in a car accident a few years before and wasn't a good role model. We accepted her and moved forward.

She didn't live with us or put any claims on us at all. We didn't do a paternity test, and that was fine. It took Allen a few years (like David's struggle) to feel like she was his daughter, but that eventually came with time and getting acquainted. I did have a few of the same struggles Susanne did, but not to the same degree. I didn't feel the intense feelings of betrayal, but I did struggle with the fact my husband had been with someone else, and I'd saved myself for my husband...and he hadn't been completely honest with me about the incident that happened. We did work through that, and because I have a huge heart for children, I was able to accept Tricia without reservations, setting my personal struggles aside.

She eventually married and had three children. She's a wonderful mom, and I had the privilege of leading her to the Lord. God has taken us on quite a journey, and this book has reached and blessed more people on a deep level than any other I've written. I believe that *The Other Daughter* (which I originally titled *Yesterday's Child* prior to publication), was the book the Lord wanted me to write and to have published.

My publishing journey had the hand of God all over it. From the time I finished writing this book (which only took five to six weeks to crank out the first draft) until the time it landed a contract with Kregel Publishing, to my obtaining an agent, was less than a year. It was fast-tracked and released a little over a year later and went into a second printing.

The Other Daughter has a sequel—*Finding Jeena*—the story of Susanne's friend and why she was crying when she stumbled down the court-house steps and her journey to emotional healing and freedom. I hope to someday have the time to write a third book in this set about Joy, and young woman we meet in *Finding Jeena*. However, my writing career took off shortly after writing that second book, and most of my books since have been historical romance, along with a set of six horse novels for middle-grade girls (Horses and Friends) as well as a book that became a made-for-TV movie, Runaway Romance, a contemporary romance. I have another book under option, Finding Love in Bridal Veil, Oregon, that will be filming sometime in 2019 as a contemporary rather than a historical, as historical movies aren't doing well on TV or the big screen at this time.

If you've enjoyed this book, I hope you'll drop me a note at miraleef@gmail.com and let me know if it ministered to you in any way, as well as post a review on Amazon, Goodreads, BarnesandNoble.com, and Facebook. You can also find/follow me at these sites:

My blog/website/newsletter sign up: www.miraleeferrell.com
Facebook—my author group: http://bit.ly/2reGsvZ
Twitter: www.twitter.com/miraleeferrell
Instagram: Miralee Ferrell Author (MiraleeFerrell_Author)

9 781943 959648